THE CHIEF OF PUBS

NEAL GRAHAM

SILVERSMITH
PRESS

Published by Silversmith Press–Houston, Texas
www.silversmithpress.com

ISBN 978-1-967386-19-2 (Softcover Book)
ISBN 978-1-967386-20-8 (eBook)

CONTENTS

CHAPTER 1

OPEN JAWS

I was destined for Cape Town with my brother Harry, a retribution, I suppose, for the troubles I unintentionally brought to Cooper Wine and Spirits, our five-generation family enterprise, which he'd have people believe I brought close to bankruptcy. All I did was raise some capital in return for a public offering of 39%, still leaving the family with a controlling interest. The stock offer flew high, but forces of gravity overcame it, sending it crashing into the ground. I became the one to blame for our embarrassing reversal of fortune. If I could have walked away from Cooper without giving Harry one more reason to question my ability or loyalty to my family, I would have gladly done it. Instead, I accepted his truce to take over the position of our East Coast distribution manager. Harry even convinced our CEO and Father I was the man responsible for our inventory shrinkage, rather than our light-fingered minimum wage help. I had no choice in my relocation to New York and would have preferred to put some distance between me and Wall Street in the aftermath of my unpleasant stock market venture.

Whenever I spent time with Harry, he would mention our stock meltdown and link it to me. He didn't want to hear what I might have to say about stock jockey gamblers who believed they were investors, but who were, in fact, looking for fast money and quick to abandon a game they were losing. No matter what I thought though, the bottom line was I had to move our eastern distribution office to the westside dock area into a converted warehouse, formerly housing ocean shipping containers. It was light-years from the shiny midtown towers we were used to. My new strategy was to pay our New York employees better and give our northeast salesmen more incentives. By holding biweekly staff meetings, I hammered home the theme that if the Cooper Company improved its fortunes, success would be all of ours as well. That must have been the right message because I moved 26% more wine and spirits in just one year. That's also why it came as a surprise after improving our East Coast numbers, the home office was reorganized without me. Instead of rewarding or acknowledging my successes, Harry gave me the board's decision (really the decision of Father who held 51% of Cooper's shares) to take me out of New York altogether. Rather than give me credit for my accomplishments, he was treating me as if I should be quarantined. Worse, he was trying radical measures, cutting me out as skillfully as a surgeon might slice off some flesh, mistakenly believing he'd excised the whole cancer and cured the ailing patient.

Harry's rationale was that our lease had expired, and it was more cost effective to piggyback on a former competitor's distribution network, rather than continue with our own. Rather than move me to the St. Louis home office with the same responsibilities I was accustomed to handling, Harry bought me a one-way ticket to South Africa, banishment. My mission—should I choose to accept it—was to broker a partnership with the owner of a vineyard and wine bottling operation in South Africa.

The trouble was, I didn't know the country, and it didn't make sense to take on operations halfway around the world. Neither had it made sense that the investors in Cooper had suddenly let fear overtake them, causing them to take their bets off the table for alcohol-related businesses of any kind. Just as investors had earlier run away from cigarette manufacturers, fear of litigation against those of us who made the booze caused backers to leave. The investors' herdlike stampede away from our stock offering didn't make any sense to me, and neither did Cooper's reaction to it. Our stock value was down to a quarter of what it was in the opening IPO days, and the board was determined to cut costs. Despite my protest, we ended up ditching some of our well-run and profitable regional operations we should have kept. Compounding that error, now my brother was sending me out to expand, not just offshore, but to South Africa! If he thought East Coast distribution was difficult, how did he think we could function on the other side of the world? Maybe the real issue for Harry wasn't shipping our product to a bigger market, so much as shipping me where I wouldn't bother him. If he sent me far enough away, I would pose no challenge to the complete control he hoped to command as CEO once Father finally retired. In the meantime, the best scenario for Harry would be for me to fail in my assignment so he could be justified in ridding himself of me altogether.

During the ninety days I was given to close our lower 12th Avenue office, an increasing gloominess overtook me. During the workday I was far too busy to think of anything but my deadlines. At night I couldn't sleep. Had we gone public to fulfill my father's dream to build our line to international standards? Or to yield to Harry's ambition to expand operations into Europe? If I had successfully campaigned against big expansion, I would have killed the whole misbegotten IPO before it even got to the planning stage. But instead of working to abort Cooper's overly ambitious expansion, I aided and abetted it, buying a half-dozen small European distilleries, as well as Werner-Nichols Wines. The retreat of our no longer optimistic investors left us without sufficient operating capital to update our new obligations.

We had no choice but to jettison our new acquisitions, except for Werner-Nichols Wines out of Germany. It was not our strongest holding, but one which Harry persuaded Father would serve us well in the lower cost South African wine market. Harry had convinced him that the collapse of our foray into Europe was caused by revenue projections I had developed to market the IPO! My own brother accused me of misrepresentation, successfully diverting responsibility from himself, and initiating enough doubt in the home office that I found myself with no choice. I accepted his challenge to "rationalize" our Werner-Nichols holdings by leaving the States and secure the balance of their operations in Cape Town.

It was bothering me to be scapegoated by Harry for his failed ambitions in Europe. The losses of the IPO shareholders troubled my sleep. On more than one occasion, I awakened in the dark, feeling like a disoriented, fearful child, not an executive who had simply been overwhelmed by market forces.

Nevertheless, I did my best to retain a positive demeanor and to accept Harry's explanation that my mission to South Africa was an opportunity. I wasn't sure what he expected me to accomplish there, nor why our flight was booked with an open jaw stop in London—nor why Harry was accompanying me, which made me feel not like his brother, but as his chattel.

The lights were off in the plane, and I dozed off for a bit of welcome sleep. Later, I returned from the bathroom, Harry was in the seat next to mine and began briefing me on his plans to overhaul the Cooper Company from the ground up. Then he headed toward the back of the plane, shifting his attention to a blonde flight attendant. I returned to sleep.

I was disoriented when I awakened, not realizing at first, I was in flight. Looking through the window at the black sky didn't help orient me, but the airline map posted on the movie screens did, displaying our position a couple of hundred miles east of Nova Scotia. It occurred to me with startling clarity that we were situated seven miles above the spot where the Titanic had struck the iceberg and sank. Some passengers had a fighting chance, I thought, those who got off the ship and into lifeboats. Now, as air passengers, our only lifeboats were plastic life preservers, as if that would do any good if our jet dropped into the cold water. Once I was clearly awake, I realized I wasn't in immediate danger, that the plane wasn't about to fall from the sky. That left me with my true waking concern, the one about being separated, not only from my company and St. Louis, but from my country, all in service of what might prove a fool's errand.

Harry was back, shouting an order at me as if he were a career Navy officer. He had stayed in the Coast Guard long enough to get a mermaid tattoo on his arm, and to realize his life's work would be at Cooper.

"It's late, Harry," I said, pushing him away from me, refusing to comply with his order, whatever it was.

"No problem, Leon baby, I'll be back."

When I reopened my eyes, the blonde stewardess was trying to get my attention. She turned on the reading light and sat across the aisle from me. Her almost white hair could have been that of an older woman, but looking more closely, I could see that she was pretty and young.

"Your brother's told me so much about you, Leon," she said in a not-quite-British accent. She turned on the overhead light to better show Harry's face. "The family resemblance between you two is astonishing, though I must tell you, Harry, your younger brother is a handsomer because his nose isn't broken like yours. Now, why did you bring me to him?"

"Would you believe he pushed me down the stairs when we were little because I borrowed a toy robot of his? Leon fights dirty."

"He also dresses better than you do, Harry," she observed, looking first at his warmup suit. She took the cuff of my silk shirt between her fingers, then looked directly into my eyes and smiled. "My name's Alicia Nichols." She shook my hand in a businesslike way I didn't expect, assuming she must have been instructed to keep a professional distance from the passengers.

"My brother is Ted Nichols, the object of Harry's desires. If you want to know about me, I'll say that once I loved to travel, especially to remote islands with mild climates and pleasant beaches. But as a flight attendant, stopovers are too brief to enjoy. And yourself?" She placed her arm on top of mine in an encouraging manner.

If Harry weren't there listening and ready to interrupt, I would have given her a similar short story of my life, but instead simply gave her my card with my new job description. "COOPER WINE AND SPIRITS, the finest since 1846. Leon Cooper, Import/Export Manager, Europe & Africa," she read.

"Do you plan to sell liquor to the natives? Harry, have you told him about the lions that roam the streets at night just outside Cape Town?"

"No problem. Leon's no fool. He'll be careful."

Alicia winked at me, making it all a joke between us and on Harry. I appreciated her wit.

"If you want to know about South Africa in general, and my brother's wine business in particular, Chandra Kassie will be help you while you lay over in London. Then on your trip to Johannesburg, which is also my flight, I'd love to hear what you gentlemen did in London to amuse yourselves. In the meantime, I must begin preparing breakfast if I don't want to get sacked! It's been quite a pleasure."

Now that Alicia Nichols was gone, Harry moved by me into the seat where he belonged.

"So, this is why I'm not flying direct, but open jaws

via London, so I could meet Ted Nichols' sister? I don't get it."

"The main thing you'll need to know is that when you meet Mr. Nichols, he fancies himself an international businessman, rather than a regional player. We're not going to turn you loose with Ted until you know everything about him that we know and can bring back a good deal for Cooper."

"Then who's Kassie?" I asked.

"Him? He may look like a dothead Indian, but he's a hundred percent South Africa. I think you'll get on with him. These South Africans do business differently from Americans, especially from riverboat gamblers like yourself, Leon. Take my advice: he might not be as patient with your friction-free economy theories as I am."

"I've had more than enough nonsense from you today, especially with your secret plans! Don't condemn what you don't understand!"

"I understand you better than you think, Leon. You thought the business climate was so good, so friction-free that we could not only raise quick stock market money and take on debt based on it. God, we were crazy to go along with you and get ourselves in over our heads! For your own good, don't be giving these South Africans your friction-free American advice. They probably don't believe in blue skies forever like you do. Remember that, and maybe you won't blow it this time."

We arrived in London early morning, and I had fourteen hours until my flight to South Africa. All I wanted to do was get away from Harry and find a hotel where I could get a few hours of uninterrupted sleep, so I bought a day's lodging through a hotel agent at the airport.

"I wouldn't stay there if I were you, Leon," Harry shouted, having waited to offer his advice until I was climbing into the hotel shuttle bus. "They have hookers in those fleabag hotels!" I instinctively retreated off the bus.

"Where do you think you're going?" he asked once I was back at the curb with him.

"If I don't get a couple of hours sleep soon, I'm going to crash."

"Too late now to be worrying about yourself, you've already crashed and burned! The good news is you're hurt, but you're not quite dead. We're giving you a second chance. Most people aren't as lucky as you."

I didn't care for his scolding attitude and didn't like to feel at his mercy. "Harry, I've had enough! Once I get over there, I'll be sure to send you progress reports. Now quit following me!"

He was studying me carefully, his arm hooked around mine, attaching himself like a barnacle. "I wish I could turn you loose, but you need my help. You're technical but I'm better with people, which is nothing but sales—right? You'll find Ted Nichols won't be an easy sell. He's made good money and could easily retire, but he has no one in the family to take over after him, although Alicia would love to replace him. She's much younger than him, a change-of-life baby, I understand. Did I tell you he fancies himself a sophisticated international businessman, rather than just a local wine merchant? You know all about vanity and pride. Just appeal to his, and you'll get along fine."

"Very interesting, but where are you taking me now?" I asked.

It would have been satisfying to shake myself free of my brother, but not until I could pry more information from him about precisely what the Cooper Company expected from my mission to South Africa, beyond the broad directive to establish a working relationship with the Werner-Nichols vintners in the wine country outside Cape Town.

We headed to downtown London to the gargantuan Harrod's department store, which had just opened for the day. Harry was in a buying mood and quickly charged his business card with several hundred British pounds worth of canned delicacies—caviar, preserves, quail's eggs, pheasant—all on after-Christmas sale.

"Never too early for holidays," he explained. I need to buy my Christmas gifts when the price is right." He handed me one of the sacks of his booty.

In the men's department, he put on a heavy tweed sport coat. "This jacket would be okay for the fens and the bogs where it's always damp, but heavy woolens are no damn good for where you're headed, Leon. What do you think a businessman should wear in South Africa?"

Harry retreated to the changing room and returned in charcoal slacks and a cashmere sports jacket. He was accompanied by an Indian man in a coffee-colored suit, who was folding over his cuffs to the right length, as a tailor would.

"How about a genuine Saville Row suit?" Harry continued, pointing to the suit the Indian I took for a tailor was himself wearing. See how the English like to shape their suits more than we do in America? Leon, meet Mr. Chandra Kassie," he said, placing our right hands together. Chandra had a gentle grip, quite unlike the American go-getter's firm handshake. "He's an old hand at brewing beer, but I'm sure you'll find him helpful in teaching you about the South African way of making wine. For now, let's rely on him to guide us to clothing of lighter weight and lighter color for you as well."

"It depends on where one must travel," Kassie said, with a slight bow. "In the vineyards, a broad hat would serve best. In the winery or the brewery, working man's clothes. But in your brother's role as a white man making a deal, perhaps a nice suit would be most suitable."

To my eyes, the tan suit complimented Kassie's dark skin, as did his gold watch on one wrist and bracelet on the other. He was well turned out, careful to make a good impression.

"Clothes make the man, though not in your case, Chandra," Harry laughed, again making me uncomfortable with his thoughtless words. "So, Leon, take my advice, or take Kassie's, but if you represent Cooper, you'd better dress the part. Here, this one should be your size," he said and handed me a tan suit, which he insisted I try on. "Excellent!" he said after one look.

Once I removed the suit, Kassie took it to the clerk, a man a bit browner than Kassie, and charged it to Harry's company card. It didn't matter that I didn't need a suit and certainly didn't want it, but its purchase was meant either as a peace offering or as a sign to Kassie that Harry was the man in charge.

"A lot of Indians living here in the UK?" Harry asked Kassie once we were out of the clerk's hearing range.

"No, sir, that bloke's Sri Lankan, whereas my forebears come from Bombay."

"Same difference," Harry persisted.

"To the contrary, Mr. Cooper, there is a big difference between a Hindu such as myself, and a Tamil such as the chap at the cash register. He is a Moslem, the same as most Pakistanis, as well as the Sikhs in India."

"I thought the sheiks—you know, the Arabs on the camels—wear burnooses on their heads and the long robes." I couldn't tell whether Harry was serious or trying to be funny. Evidently neither could Kassie, who looked at me, then at Harry, as if trying to gauge whether I understood his religious distinctions any better than my brother did.

"I don't judge a man by his clothes anyway," Harry continued. "That's why I like dealing with you Indians as much as the Jews, because you know how to do business! But I'm going to leave you two and use the rest of today to see the lions in Piccadilly Circus! Keep my brother out of trouble, will you?" he said, threw me the bag with my suit in it, which I'd have to get hemmed in Cape Town, then disappeared into the crowd of shoppers.

When Harry left, I felt relieved yet strangely disoriented. I didn't appreciate being abandoned in the middle of a confusing three-continent open jaws journey. It was obvious that was part of Harry's master plan, passing me from his supervision over to Kassie's.

"I am honored to serve as your guide for the remainder of today," Mr. Kassie said with a bow, outside Harrod's. "Men like us have a commercial bent with a view toward today. But don't you believe we must strive to temper our acquisitive nature with a long term, historical view of how men behave?"

It was a leading question, one I didn't understand nor

trust, believing he was simply trying to impress me with his smart observations. I realized though my first impressions were often dead wrong, so I took the path of least resistance, and I decided to trust and accompany him into a tall, black Austin cab he hailed.

"Do you think your brother favors khaki because it was the color of the British forces occupying South Africa, or other warm colonies such as India? Perhaps he believes it's a powerful color for a suit to conquer Mr. Nichols," he remarked once we were underway. Before I could respond, the cab stopped, and he jumped out and came to open my door, assisting me to the curb as if I were a matron.

"Mr. Cooper, as long as we have the time before our flight, may I show you two episodes of the same story, examples of man at his most creative, then man at his most acquisitive?"

He was talking in riddles, but since we were in front of the British Museum, I guessed he wanted to pique my curiosity and draw me inside with him. I really didn't know where else to go for the remainder of the day, so I accompanied him.

In the museum we entered a room of paintings of 19th century French women, their bodies softer and fleshier than the health club toned girls I'd known. He turned me by the shoulders, so I was standing squarely before a flat wall of stone carvings.

"This masterpiece was removed from the Parthenon. It's a frieze of men in battle, fighting with the assistance of their patron gods."

"Are you showing me this to kill time?"

"No, sir, to show you the booty the English Lord North

took from the Athens 150 years ago. He was justified in removing these treasures to this safe mausoleum."

"Don't you think it's a bit late now, Mr. Kassie, seeing that here we are 150 years later?"

"To the contrary, Mr. Cooper. The museum could now return all these pieces to the Greeks and the account would be settled. Likewise, in South Africa, we have many accounts that still need to be settled with former masters such as yourself.

"I hope you're not confusing us Americans with your former masters, because we come as friends."

"Friends bringing welcome American dollars. But wherever you travel, you cannot help but bring your old self. My concern is that you proceed cautiously."

"I don't know you, and I'd be surprised if my brother really does either, yet you'd have me believe you're personally concerned about me! If you've been listening to my brother—"

"Yes, sir, I'm an excellent listener. He also spoke to me of the great deeds your dollars will bring. I told him a man's deeds can sometimes be greater than the man. Don't you agree?"

I couldn't tell whether he was criticizing Harry or myself, or just trying to amuse me with platitudes, but in any event, I didn't want any more of his attention, not right then.

"You've got to quit following me!" I said as we were leaving the museum. He hailed a cab for us.

"Sorry, your brother wanted me to lead, not follow you, at least until we've returned to earth, and our wheels have touched ground in South Africa. May I buy us coffee to clear our heads?"

I could have declined and walked away, but I went along with him to the Windsor Cafeteria. I took a table by the window and could see him on the sidewalk doing a routine of stretching exercises. After that, he ate an English breakfast of eggs, sausage, bacon, rolls, and more. I didn't eat with him and could have excused myself, but instead Kassie took me to an American movie about an independent bookstore owner driven out by a big chain store and a businessman with whom she fell in love via the internet who will not only bankroll her, but ends up marrying her, *You've Got Mail.*

"Didn't that remind you of the life your brother tells me you're leaving behind?" Kassie asked me on our way back to the airport.

"Not exactly."

"If you didn't see yourself in the movie, perhaps you saw people you'd rather forget, or perhaps those you are attempting to escape?"

It was Kassie I couldn't escape. It was hard for me to tell how much he had heard from my brother, and how much was blind conjecture, disguised as leading questions. Once we were in the airport terminal waiting for our flight, I was saying as little as possible to him.

"We have more in common than you believe," he said, once we were in flight. "We all must deal with disappointments in our lives."

I resolved to yield Kassie nothing, so I simply stared at him. This time, it was his turn to explain himself.

"We're both beer makers," Kassie continued.

"Is that your arrangement with my brother, as a beer consultant?" I asked.

"A beer maker brews with grain," Kassie added. "A

wine maker uses fruit. A farmer on a tractor cuts barley for the beer maker. On the other hand, the wine man must grow and harvest his grapes with far more careful timing and skill."

He continued in generalities, not answering my question about the deal I know he struck with my brother to escort me to Cape Town. Once he finally understood I had nothing to share with him, he could quit poking his nose into my life.

"We beer makers don't have to graft, fertilize, prune, water and crush grapes at their peak," he continued. "We practice our art on grain, harvested and shipped to us by ordinary farmers, not the pampered fruit the vintners cultivate. Our customers aren't prima donnas, and neither should we be. I'm confident I could run a better business with Cooper Inc. than Mr. Nichols could manage without my help."

"Why do you say that?"

"Because Mr. Nichols is from generations of vintners. Vintners understand grapes. Brewers like myself and Cooper understand barley, sorghum, and hops. That's why we must work together if we are to show Mr. Nichols your value to him."

"Thanks for the tip, but I'm not too concerned, so long as I can speak to him directly in English, Chandra."

"Quite likely, sir, he will prefer dealing with you, a white man, rather than with an Indian such as myself. But I would suggest that if you and your brother truly want to buy a winery with your dollars, you must calculate its true cost."

"I'll worry about that later."

"That's what my son Rajesh would say," Kassie said,

then showed me a photograph of a dour young Indian man on a beach blanket. He was pulling close to him an Indian girl with a lovely body and exotic features. "Here you can see him with his fiancé Sunitha. What do you perceive by looking at this image of them?" Again, he thrust the picture in front of me.

The choice was mine, to offer him no opinion, or else to throw back at him the same sort of blind conjecture which he'd been using to draw me into telling me about my own life. "Your son Rajesh looks outmatched by this girl with the fine form and face."

"Interesting. What else do you see in this snapshot?"

He probably didn't care to hear that critical opinion of mine, any more than I cared for his analysis of my character. But I wasn't done. "You must have been the one who snapped this picture and are showing it to me because you had doubts about them. They're not a matched pair. I can't imagine what kind of babies they'd produce."

"An excellent insight, Mr. Cooper!" he thundered. "Just what I've been wondering myself, as I've been thrashing through London the last couple of days. I've come to realize I can tell Raj all the secrets of brewing, but regarding choosing a friend or a woman, he's on his own. Unless, of course, when you meet him, you care to give him a younger man's opinion about women. You must understand that an older man like me must increasingly rely on the memory of his life, which may not seem relevant to his son's situation today."

He seemed to be honestly telling me why he was having trouble speaking to his son, and reaching out to me, who knew neither of them, to act as a go-between. I needed to know if that was Kassie's plan. "An expensive air ticket to London for a vacation, just to get away from your business and your son for a few days, Chandra?"

"Did you think I came this distance for a little escape? I don't have such resources at my disposal. I came as a guest of your brother. We were to speak of my role in any wine operations you plan to launch. What a pity he had to leave so abruptly with you in his place. Leon, if I may call you that, I sense that you have great doubt about this journey. Excuse me."

Kassie then arose and left, and like my brother's sudden disappearance in Harrod's, this seemed arranged in advance. His seat wasn't empty but a minute before the towheaded stewardess took it.

"Alicia Nichols, in case you forgot," she said, pulling on the lapels of her pastel green blouse, which complemented her fair complexion and emerald earrings. She shook my hand in the businesslike way I remembered from the night before.

"You're out of your uniform. Are you traveling as an ordinary passenger?"

"Not exactly, I'm returning home on a three-day holiday. My brother would never forgive me if I don't at least make an appearance at their party tomorrow, though I am still lacking an escort. And forgive me if I've bored you by showing you the threadbare tapestry of my life, holes and all."

"Wasn't I a good listener?" I asked. "If I came across like a cold fish—"

"I'm used to cold fish, if only because my English forebears have passed down the art of the stiff upper lip. However, as a white South African, I've learned the value of making friends and assisting them."

"Friends talking to friends, a grapevine—Harry talking to you and you to me. Then there's Chandra, whose seat you've taken and who will pass on what he's been able to extract from me. But, Alicia, what I can't figure is where your brother Ted Nichols figures into this grapevine."

"I'm glad you asked. As much as my brother respects their business skills, he's not one to socialize with the coolies."

"Coolies?"

"The ones who were originally shipped over to work the cane fields, which is why he'll still call the Indians coolies, for how hard they used to work. They've come a long way and learned to become great shopkeepers, which is why my brother respects Chandra Kassie so much."

"I still don't understand the connection between you, Kassie, and him."

"You are a detail man. I'd love to tell you more, but not now. Let's simply say to casually entertain a man is not the same as taking him overnight under one's roof."

I wasn't sure whether the confusion she was creating in my mind was intentional or accidental. Was she bashing or praising Kassie? Was she was praising me? Was her attention to me part of Harry's plan to explain to me the rules of etiquette in South Africa. I was sensing that her country was like a human a game park with high fences where the humans live close enough together to size up each other's strengths and weaknesses and stake out their territories. Chandra reappeared, taking the nearest seat to me, which was one row forward.

"Chandra," Alicia called to him, reaching over the seat to tap his head, pointing through the window, "we thought you bailed out of the emergency door. Is there anything more awe-inspiring than that country below, the sand dunes of Kalahari?"

"Sorry, this high up I can't see that well, Miss Nichols," Kassie said.

"That's okay," she said and pointed below. I could make out some undulations in the sand 30,000 feet below me. "This is Bushman country. They have pointy ears and peppercorn hair and can't read and write, but it doesn't matter because they've trained themselves to remember everything that ever happened to them, going back centuries. That's why they're such great story tellers. I'm always excited when I'm approaching home. Aren't you, Chandra?"

"They're extinct, Miss. Nichols. They were replaced by the white men."

"But, Chandra, how can you account for all those Cape coloureds with the same pointy ears and the peppercorn hair? You take a mule and a horse, and you get a donkey. You can take the Bushman out of the bundu, but you can't take the bundu out of the Bushman. Mr. Cooper understands."

This seemed like a family feud where I was an outsider who didn't know any of the contenders, much less what they were disputing. I thought I'd try distraction, asking her a simple question. "The bundu?"

"You know, the veld, the bush, the wilderness. As I was saying, you can see Bushmen-type faces all through Cape Town or Joburg. Before the white men came, they were hunting antelope in the veld and painting pictures in caves. But now we're the Rainbow Nation, because we're all colors blending together. Aren't we, Chandra?"

But Chandra had put on his headset and didn't answer.

"I've only meant to entertain," she said to me, "but I'm afraid I've bored you with our folkways. Now I shall leave you to your own devices."

Once she had left me, Kassie moved beside me. He was counting two colors of banknotes. "Trying to figure out how much money you have left to make it until the end of the week?" I cajoled.

"No," he said, putting his money in his passport and opening up his plastic folder of snapshots. He was looking at a picture of the same girl he showed me before, sitting between a smoking incense urn and a statue of Buddha.

"Nice robe she's wearing."

"A Hindu robe, a sari. Sunitha's far more traditional than Raj. She can lead him in a better direction than I've been taking. God help us all, Leon."

I knew nothing more about Hindus than I did the Bushmen, didn't care about his family, and needed to focus on the Cape Town South Africans if I was ever to successfully do business with them. I couldn't let myself be distracted by problems that didn't involve me. Soon we were descending, and I was anxious to be freed from the plane and begin my challenging journey.

CHAPTER 2

CHATEAU DRAKENSTEIN

Cape Town. It was ground zero, where I'd have to over-come the blame for the misfortune I brought to Cooper by achieving as much success as possible. Outside, the air was hot and humid. I was in the customs line for foreigners, while Kassie and Alicia quickly passed through the one for South Africans. I was surprised to see how many of the white South Africans were dual citizens, carrying second passports from other countries, especially the UK and Holland. Apparently, they were keeping one foot in Europe, with the other foot in South Africa. Maybe they knew something I didn't, planning for a quick escape. But there was no turning back, not before determining this country's potential for Cooper, Inc., and hopefully reclaiming my credibility.

I was heading for a black minivan when Kassie grabbed my luggage from the driver and pulled me away. The black driver argued with Kassie over me, his fare. A couple of the driver's friends appeared from nowhere, and now three black men were shouting at Kassie in a language unlike any I ever heard. It was getting ugly when Alicia produced some cash, handed it to a black man in a chauffeur's uniform, who in turn gave it to the van driver. The peace offering seemed to work. They took the money and left without further complaint.

"We refuse to let those bandits take you," Alicia said.

"You know them?" I asked.

"We'd never let anyone we know travel with that lot."

"You must understand they're different from you and me," Kassie added, putting my and Alicia's luggage into the trunk of a waiting Chateau Drakenstein Mercedes, and insisted I join them. "They're quite fierce, sir. When they have a spat, they will often shoot at one another, rather than resolve it. Afterwards, they drop back into the township, much as their ancestors dropped back into the jungle after a headhunting raid."

Kassie seemed to distrust the black drivers as much as Alicia did. There was a pecking order: blacks on the bottom, whites on the top, Indians in the middle. Or maybe that was the old order, and now the blacks sat on the top. At any rate, I felt uneasy hearing their easy explanations to me of the social order, since I had no way of knowing where I might fit in, nor what they really thought of me as an American.

Alicia was sitting in the back with me, Kassie in the front. "Many of those black taxi drivers are convicts, sir," our black chauffeur said. "Some of those vans don't have proper brakes. You must be cautious, lest they mistake you for a tourist."

"Thanks to whomever sent you, but—"

"Call me Tembo. Mr. Nichols dispatched me with a message of greeting. He will be honored to receive you, sir."

On the open highway we were hitting 220 kilometers an hour. Alicia noticed my accelerated breathing. "We travel too fast here, whether or not we have a reason," she whispered, while taking my hand for a moment. Kassie turned to us with an approving smile. "Tembo, you're terrifying our Yankee friend. You must slow down."

In a quarter hour we left the highway for a narrow road. At a stop light, vendors walked between the cars with toys, coat hanger sculptures, food, and open hands. "Stop that hawker with the grapes, Tembo," Alicia said and handed him a bill. "Chandra, go help him."

They returned with a five-kilo crate, which she inspected. "In season, Mr. Nichols enjoys grapes by the bunch," Kassie explained to me, then dispatched Tembo for more fruit, this time a bag of oranges. "He likes to sample the grapes ordinary farmers produce, though the common table grape bears little resemblance to a fine wine grape. He feels one needs to know the market, even when there's no competition. I've learned a great deal from my association with the Chateau."

An hour later, we turned into the Chateau estate, and traveled down a road lined with lush trees. "I've never seen trees like that, bushy at the top, their trunks so stout."

"Perhaps you've looked at them in America without truly seeing them," Kassie admonished. "They're camphors, and they grow in California and Florida. There aren't many things that we have that you don't. Like many things South African, they were transplanted, in this case from China."

"Chandra," Alicia said, "you have a wealth of facts at your fingertips. Do you read to give yourself an edge, or for the good of mankind, once you become a guru?"

"Facts merely lead us to knowledge. Knowledge is only one step towards wisdom."

"Do you collect this extra knowledge because you already know everything about the beer business? Or are you striving to become cleverer than your future daughter-in-law Sunitha?"

"What's burning?" I asked. Beyond the vineyard I saw a smoky fire.

"Chandra, perhaps you can show him what's smoking, while Tembo and I search for our lord and master," Alicia suggested.

Following her plan for a tour, Chandra took me to the smoky vineyard, where we watched black workers harvest the grapes, collecting them in plastic baskets. The men were singing a chorus, and the women sang a response. Each worker filled then dumped his basket into a V-shaped grape trailer which was close to the smoky fire.

"I don't know why they're doing this now," Kassie observed. "Usually, they burn the deadwood after they've picked the crop and moved it indoors for the crushing. I wonder if Mr. Nichols knows about this burning. Where is their supervisor?"

"What difference does it make?" I asked.

"Firstly, the grapes must be brought in at their autumn peak, namely right now. Secondly, the smoke might affect the flavor of the grapes. Thirdly, this sort of worker must learn to follow a set schedule if he or she is ever to learn how to do a productive day's work. You'll learn our ways though, once you work with us."

Us? Who did he mean? I didn't know why he was sympathizing so much with the absent boss and so little with these workers, who seem to be doing a hard job just fine.

"I don't get it," I said.

"Get what, sir? Are you lacking something?"

Kassie swatted the back of his neck. Bugs weren't biting him. I could see he was being pelted every few seconds with tiny grapes the size of pebbles, but I couldn't see who was launching them at him. He knew he was being hit but was taking it with self-control, resisting the temptation to look backwards, and still gave me his attention.

"I mean, if it's true, as Alicia was telling me, that your people were brought over on boats from Delhi a few hundred years ago by Europeans to work the cane plantations—"

"It was true, but for many Indians of a different class than myself, sir. Regarding my own family, none of my relatives was ever an indentured servant. I can trace my lineage back for one thousand years, fifty generations, and throughout that time we have been independent traders and merchants, never common laborers such as this lot of workers."

"I mean, if the Indians could change from field workers into prosperous and respected citizens, why don't you think these blacks could?"

"Leon, that is because we Indians remain close to one another so that we neither expect, depend upon, nor miss anyone's respect. We are not black, sir, though we may appear that way in your eyes. I must remind you our ancient Sanskrit was the mother language upon which all you Europeans fashioned yours."

He just put me in my place as a Yank who wasn't

even sure of the names of my four great-grandparents, much less able to trace my family history back further than my great-great-grandfather Winston Cooper who founded the company. Already I could see how each little group in this country staked out its claim and defended its territory. I'd barely gotten off the plane, and already each wanted me to immediately join up with his forces. I supposed I had to pick the strongest one, if I planned to return home with something to show for my drastic relocation.

From behind a tractor someone emerged with a black cloth draped over his head and shoulders, held on by a round embroidered hat. This fellow had a handful of pebble-sized grapes and must have been the one pestering Kassie. He picked up a bowl of white food that looked like rice farina, formed it into little balls and began pitching these at Kassie. The pickers had put down their baskets of grapes and were sitting on the ground eating yellow meal from bowls with their fingers, watching the spectacle and laughing.

"Please, not here, Hassan," Kassie implored his tormentor, having taken him away from the workers to speak to him alone.

"Hassan, do all you Moslems feed on them rice balls?" yelled a tiny man with features odd to my eyes. My first impression of this black field worker, because of his wrinkled and loose skin, was that he was very old, too old for heavy labor. Perhaps his hide looked like leather from years in the sun, and I could see points on his ears, like the Bushmen Alicia admired.

"This is couscous, Desmond, a wheat," the man with the brimless pillbox hat and black head kerchief explained. "We like to eat our soft rice, instead of that squishy yellow corn mealie-meal you eat with your fingers."

"So, Mr. Larabie Hassan," one of the women workers retorted. "Why don't you aim them rice bullets into Mr. Kassie's mouth instead of his neck if you want him to convert him to eat your Moslem food." She was young, her head shaved, her features pleasing.

"Moslem! Hassan, will you tell Lucy that I'm not some Moslem Tamil from Sri Lanka?" Kassie said without looking at her, making the same distinction he had made so emphatically in Harrod's to my brother.

Hassan smiled at me. "Ah, you must be the American Mr. Kassie promised to bring to us. Welcome to South Africa! You like it here?"

"Never mind that, Hassan," Chandra interrupted. "Please make this crew of yours know Hindus would rather die than convert to another faith, especially the Arab one. No offense intended."

Hassan looked at me again, embarrassed. *"Masepa d'katz,* Lucy," Hassan said, then impatiently pulled her from the ground back to her feet.

"You must get a wife soon, Hassan, so not to bother a good girl like me," she said, wagging her finger in his face.

"Mesoenoe kanjok!"

In response, she slapped Hassan on the back of the head, then ran away in the direction of the winery buildings, laughing. "Get your American to the big house, Mr. Kassie," Hassan said, kicked off his shoes and chased the fleeing woman with fast barefoot strides. "It's not dark," Hassan shouted, quickly closing the gap between him and the black worker, "not time to quit yet, Lucy!"

"They must be wondering where you are," Kassie said as we watched Hassan bring Lucy back to work. The other workers returned to picking grapes after quickly finishing their mealie-meal. "Hassan, that rascal, told that girl she was a pretty thing. He'll tell them anything to win their favor, though he only understands his own kind."

"What kind is that?" I queried.

"A tough lot. This is a step up for him, being supervisor at the Chateau. He knows little about wines but does know how to keep a crew in line."

"Then why would Mr. Nichols keep him here?"

"He's quite clever, actually. He comes from Belhar township, where the Moslems clamor very loudly against drugs and gangs. That's what we mean by welcome to the New South Africa. You'll see."

The main house was a white masonry building with elaborate Dutch-style scalloped gables. A high-arched entry led into a courtyard where flames lept from gas-fed torches on high steel poles. Tembo was one of several waiters serving guests eating there.

"I see you're busy on the evening shift now, Tembo," Chandra said.

"Care for some braii, Mr. Kassie?" Tembo asked, handing a sausage on a stick toward Chandra who took a couple of steps backward.

"My family waits for me. I must go before they worry about my whereabouts."

"Is that why you never stay for these parties, sir, or because you don't eat meat?"

"Exactly, Tembo, but I take comfort knowing you're here serving my special guest Mr. Cooper and will tell me all about these guests tomorrow."

A man in a draped cream-colored shirt with diamond cuff links, linen pants and a thick gold watch passed through the arches, drawing the attention of several men who intercepted him and formed a semicircle to talk to him. Most of the guests, married couples over fifty years old, seemed to know one another, while the younger unattached people cruised the courtyard, sizing up one another. A young woman with tight curls walked past me, turned around then passed closer to me. I helped myself to a miniature sandwich, and she stood next to me, just staring.

"Have we met before?" I asked, looking down at her bare feet, instead of at her face.

"Certainly not," she said, touching my shoe with her pearl-gray painted toes. "Are you terribly patient?"

"Excuse me, but should I know you?" I asked her.

"I am your host's niece, Nicole," she said, pointing to the man with the sparkling cufflinks. "If you're curious, I'm moving to the UK to study art. If you want to know more about him, ask your girlfriend."

"Who?"

"Whoo whoo-hoots the owl! Are you flying blind, Mr. Cooper? Alicia Nichols, of course!" This strange girl turned my question back on myself, shoving me closer towards the pool, showing surprising strength for a small girl, pushing until I began to lose my balance. I couldn't let her topple me or fall in and make a fool of myself in front of the party. She wouldn't stop and soon I had no choice but to send her flying with a hard push.

35

"Don't mind her. She's a vixen, Leon!" Behind me in the pool Alicia called out. She was facing towards the late afternoon sun, eyes closed, doing backstrokes.

"My cousin Alicia wants your attention, Mr. Smart Owl. You fly blind as a bat, but she flies a metal bird, always rushing for a schedule, except for layovers."

"And you, Nicole, are flying low, dropping guano on our heads." the man with the sparklers in French cuffs intervened.

"That's not nice, Uncle Ted." He was Ted Nichols, the man I had come so far to meet.

"Too bad it's necessary for me to remind you that you're not behaving yourself, young lady."

"But Mr. Cooper looked so out of place, I wanted to make him feel at home."

"Didn't your parents tell you this was an adult party?"

"Don't mistake me for a child, Uncle Ted."

"Then don't act like one."

"But what about her!" she said, pointing to Alicia. "Everyone else is dressed, but she doesn't even have on clothes!"

"My apologies, Leon," Ted said to me alone. "This is precisely why I'm a man alone, wanting to avoid bold children. As your American MacArthur said, I shall return, though I don't think he could hold a candle to our General Montgomery."

The rude Nicole was trying to get away from him, but he had a strong grip on her arm, leading her where he intended. He signaled to her mother and father, I presumed. He had a straw boater hat and she a wide-brimmed sun hat and together made a stylish couple.

"You're looking at Colin and Amanda Nichols, that

lovely child's parents," Ted explained. But Ted didn't explain why Nicole called Alicia her cousin, rather than her aunt, if both Amanda and Alicia were Ted's sisters. I hadn't been at the party half an hour, and I was having trouble understanding how the two Nichols were related.

"If you hurry," Ted suggested, "Alicia can introduce you before they must evacuate that brat, Nicole."

Alicia had lifted herself halfway out of the pool and was resting on her arms on the pool's edge. Her bathing suit was skimpy, and standing above her, there was plenty of her figure to admire. "Like what you've seen of us so far, Leon?" she asked, fully aware she had captured my attention. She lifted her head and smiled.

"I'll tell you a little more about our family, if that would help. In the meantime, why don't you pull my brother-in-law Colin into a corner, your corner, so you can at least tell him your purpose here. Afterwards, if you need to know a little more about me, I place myself at your service."

Alicia wrapped herself in a towel, hurried to the house, and looked back with a friendly wave. Ted successfully ejected Nicole and her family, but now Ted was about to move on from me, after I had come so far to meet him, that left me wondering why I was brought to his party. I hadn't traveled this far just to eat his hors d'oeuvres. I needed to find out what he required and make a deal with him.

"My brother Henry sends his best," I said, shaking Ted Nichols' hand.

"His best? Are you referring to yourself?"

I didn't know how to answer him. Did he think I was boasting, or was he testing my composure? "Perhaps when I left New York, when I was in better shape. I've been traveling two whole days and hardly slept at all, but instead of tired I feel strong."

"Good for you. Only the strong will prevail, the difference between dodos and eagles."

"I know, Mr. Nichols."

"Do you? But I misspoke, Leonard."

"Actually, my name is Leon."

"Close, but still off target. When I spoke of dodos, I meant pigeons, which I see thriving everywhere when I travel to Europe. I may fly like an eagle, but on the ground, we cautiously step around guano, and I'm surrounded with fat pigeons! And what migratory bird might you be?"

"Like yourself, Mr. Nichols, an eagle who never flies in formation, and certainly never with pigeons, turkeys and other heavy birds. I know just how you feel."

"Has the Cooper organization sent you on a clandestine mission, or do you care to share with me what you've seen that interests you the most about us?"

I wasn't sure of the direction he was leading me. He could have been talking about independence and power, intending to give me his true opinion about himself and the world. Or he could have been presenting me with the illusion of candor to win my confidence.

"I hear you South Africans make the most of adversity," I said, trying to match Ted Nichols' transparency.

"Absolutely. We can overcome almost any obstacle. What in particular?"

"I haven't been here long enough to know for sure, but it seemed half the South Africans coming through customs had two passports, one for here and one for somewhere else. They must have quick reflexes to live with one foot on the pier and the other on the boat."

"If that's how you feel about us, what really brings you here to temporarily join us? Have you simply lost your way, Leon, or are we your true destination?"

"Anyone can see what a wonderful business you've built in this magnificent setting. Some would think your Chateau is paradise."

"My friend, what's the real purpose of your journey, to see paradise or to do business with me?"

"Business, as you know, Mr. Nichols."

"Interesting. Two problems, however. Chateau Drakenstein isn't simply a business. It's my life, as well as home to ten generations of the Nichols family. We've been making wine here since the 18th century."

Colin had been listening to Ted Nichols from a dozen feet away. "Excuse me, I'm back," he announced, "because there was no need for both of us to miss this wonderful party to take our daughter home."

"Colin is our auditor and responsible for our books, in case you haven't met him, Leon. I wasn't sure he'd take to the isolation here after his tenure at Standard Bank on Adderley Street."

"To the contrary, Ted, wine flows through the veins of all us Coetzees. The Nichols family may have been vintners in South Africa since the 18th century, but the Coetzees go back to the 17th."

"That's why we English had to show you how to graft and improve your poor stock." Ted laughed heartily as we were taking another round of drinks.

"We Dutchmen were always the farmers, and you Limeys, the sailors and soldiers. If you hadn't outnumbered and outgunned us, I wouldn't be working for you today, Ted."

"That can be rearranged," he said with another laugh.

A comment with a bitter edge that a laugh could not quite erase. The Nichols against the Coetzee families, the English versus the Dutch, yet they've intermarried. Maybe the issue was one of personality differences rather than of family origins. In any event, Colin backed away a couple of paces, leaving me to continue with his in-law Ted.

"As I was saying, Leon, this soil is under my fingernails, and the Chateau is my lifeblood. How could I quote another man a price for my life?"

Nichols seemed to be raising his flag on a high pole. Did he want me to salute it? He was either very devoted to his work, or else would have me believe because this lovely place was almost beyond price, I should make him an offer beyond reason. He wasn't going to be an easy man to deal with, but I was determined not to return home without a viable partnership. My battered credibility was at stake.

Alicia had slipped behind me, in the same manner that Colin had come up behind Ted. I wondered how much of her brother's boasting she'd heard. He gave her a kiss on her forehead, stepped back, and smiled with pride. She had changed into a flowing white dress and wore a heavy gold necklace with an aquamarine pendant, matching her eyes. I looked at them together and saw her eyes also matched his, although he was a good twenty-five years older than his sister. Colin had a grim look on his face, not pleased to have lost Ted's attention first to me, then to her.

"What are you fretting about this evening, Colin?" she whispered to him, now that Ted was distracted by an admiring female guest, "that Ted believes we come from the original line of grape growers, after Adam and Eve?"

"With Alicia's special privileges she speaks freely," Colin said.

"Special on what account?" Alicia asked suspiciously.

"I mean the privileges of your career, not of your special relationship with him, our boss. It must be fun to fly all over creation, not staying cooped up in an office as I do."

"Well, he wouldn't have placed you in your office without good reason. You Coetzees always did make outstanding auditors and solicitors."

"No need to flatter me, Alicia. We all know that before I arrived Mr. Van Dyke was doing an adequate job running the office, and that I wouldn't be working for the Chateau if I hadn't married into the family. Not that I couldn't do just fine on my own in Cape Town. I could always leave the area, maybe even relocate to Johannesburg."

"You know better, that fresh innocents like yourself are always the very first killed in the cities. Here we are in paradise, and you're tempted to leave us. Please, Colin, no more whinging before our guest. We've traveled from the other side of the world, and we're tired," she said, leading me by the arm away from Colin toward her brother.

"The musicians are running behind schedule," Ted said, looking at his watch, then at the five-piece band warming up on the other side of the pool. "If you have no more questions—if that's all for now, I'll leave you in Alicia's capable hands.

I worried I hadn't made the best impression on Ted Nichols. I hoped he hadn't seen me as a stranger wanting something of him, rather than as a potential trusted friend. I also wondered what Alica thought of me. Why was she standing there staring at me as Nicole had done earlier?

I wanted to retire, but I had no idea where I'd be staying. Alicia, on the other hand, seemed to have plenty of energy left for the party.

"Your blacks are just like ours, so musical. Listen to the lead saxophone blast out that tune. That's what I truly love about you Yanks, your black songs." She was tapping out the beat on my chest, singing the lyrics, *"Blue skies smiling at me. Nothing but blue skies is what I see."*

She was looking to see if I had a song on my lips and I obliged her, not only singing along, but pulling her towards me so we could dance together. *"Bluebirds singing their song. Nothing but bluebirds all day long."*

She continued our round. *"Never saw the sun shining so bright. Never saw things going so right."*

She laughed, grasping me tightly. It would have been easier to say nothing, but I needed to set her straight. "It was written by Irving Berlin, a Jewish man, not a black. I hate to prove you wrong."

"No, you Yanks believe you can stride the world in twenty league boots and walk over anyone who gets in the way."

"He can walk over me anytime," a new woman said. This one was in her mid-30s, wearing a dramatic dress with a long slit down the side. Her hair was very black, drawn in a long ponytail, contrasting with her pale skin.

"Dee DeVilliers, meet Leon Cooper," Alicia introduced us.

"Delighted," Alicia's friend said. "So glad you're with us. I hope you'll be staying for a while, Leon."

"Why's that, Dee?"

"She's here for no other reason than to give you the opportunity to meet Frederick DeVilliers, who couldn't be here. He's always looking for new opportunities, if that's what you've brought with you from America."

"I've already seen two," I said taking each of their hands, which I kissed one after the other. I was being charming, never an easy task for someone naturally reserved like me.

Alicia took me away from Dee after she wrote out on a cocktail napkin the number of her brother Frederick DeVilliers, the banker, and led me towards an oval table set in the lounge just off the pool. Ted had changed into a shiny black jacket, not a tuxedo, but more formal than what the guests were wearing. He circled the table as guests filtered in from adjoining rooms, the garden, and the pool, intercepting them, helping ladies into their chairs, leaning over men's shoulders with jokes that made them guffaw, being an all-around excellent host. Assisting Ted in bringing the guests to their seats was Tembo, with a big smile I took as honest, not servile. Two female servants in aprons and head scarfs shuttled trays from the kitchen to commence the dinner.

When everyone was seated, Ted signaled Alicia and me to sit beside him. I moved to take my place, but she was standing in front of the chair intended for me. She was whispering to him, but I couldn't help but hear their conversation.

"What sweet temptations you've provided this evening," she said, "but I don't dare taste them if I want to pass weigh-in."

"The plane won't leave the ground if you put on an extra pound or two?"

"You never did take my line of work seriously."

"You do confuse me, dear. If you're not happy making endless circles about the world, perhaps you should come back down to earth."

"Perhaps if you had something better to offer than what I have."

"What to offer you? If it was only that simple."

"It is, if you're willing to offer me a suitable, well-paid position."

"You know as well as I we're not looking to hire even the most experienced management now," he said with a worried look on his face. Then he pulled Alicia away from the table to his game room. I followed, not willing to be left behind.

"Certainly not at the salary which you would like me to pay you," he continued as we were walking. "Too bad it always comes back to money between us, Alicia, as if I were the source."

"I'm not asking you for any favors, but I do wonder why you're treating Colin like a son, rather than a cousin in-law."

"There's no place for sentiment in business, young lady. Would you agree with that in principle, Leon?"

"You can appreciate I'd have to know more before—" I hedged.

"Before what?" Ted persisted.

"Don't put him on the spot," Alicia said.

"You're looking for a well-paid position, Alicia? You know I can't afford to play favorites. Colin's very competent with our accounts and very happy in his office."

"To the contrary. You barely tolerate each other. He just told me—"

"I reward merit and never listen to rumors. We were talking about you, who's never seemed happy except when you're traveling anywhere else but South Africa. As the Americans crooned during the war, '*How ya' gonna keep 'em down on the farm after they've seen Paree?*' Since you were a little girl, you haven't demonstrated much patience, which one needs in abundance to make wine, Alicia. In the meantime, why don't you show our guest some of our history? Starting now. Cheers, Leon."

Ted returned to his guests, but Alicia made no attempt to return to her place at the table. She shook her head, saying nothing. I thought she would have introduced me to Ted with less drama. This argument between them wasn't going to help me get near to him, especially if he suspected I was taking sides with her. They seemed close to one another, which was probably the reason he could afford to be oddly irritated at her demand to give her access to the inner circle at the Chateau.

Rejoining the table, Alicia and I kept the conversation light, especially with Ted, after their thinly masked dispute. Ted kissed her cheek after the first course, a reconciliation.

"I know what you were thinking," she said to me after dessert, "that he interferes too much."

"He acts as if he knows what's best for you, probably because he's old enough to be your father."

"That's a terrible accusation!" she said, bringing me through a roundabout detour of rooms where there were hardly any guests. We stopped at her car. "I dare say he refuses to act his age because he likes the young girls far too much. I needn't return from the other side of the world for him to tell me I know nothing about grapes, even though I was weaned on grape juice from our vines."

"He didn't seem to favor any lady over the other tonight, not even the youngest and sweetest ones."

"Only because my brother has the good sense to keep his trollops out of sight, never allowing them near these parties. Unlike myself, he has no trouble finding companionship."

There was no need for a beautiful woman like Alicia to be lonely, but come to think of it, by covering so much territory and never stopping long enough to see any place in depth, how could she have been making friends other than her crewmates? I wondered if she'd taken an interest in me, simply because she was looking for a friend. Or did Ted assign her as my escort in order to keep an eye on me?

"More importantly, how do you feel about my brother—your partner-to-be, or not-to-be?"

She was probing too close for my comfort. It was time to turn the conversation back to her. "Apparently he's not ready to put your abilities to work, not yet."

"Let's forget about Ted for now. About tomorrow, which I have free, I was hoping you could take me somewhere."

"Should I take you to one of those pretty places Ted says we shouldn't miss?" I teased her.

"Let's not let him plan my layovers, which are short enough. It's awkward enough that when I come to the Chateau, he believes he can control me like a little girl!"

"Sorry."

"I enjoyed the party. Thanks for bringing me, but now, if you don't mind, I should be checking into my hotel."

"Never mind about that. I had Chandra cancel your reservation. We've booked you instead into a place I know you'll enjoy far more."

"I'd like to see it first before I make a change."

"It's too dark to see much tonight, but don't worry. We'll wake up tomorrow to a fine day, and I'll show you a lovely village inhabited by the white tribe, unless you don't trust the new sleeping arrangements we've made for you."

CHAPTER 3

WHITE TRIBE VILLAGE

I awakened in a wide bed of dark carved wood with a fine embroidered cotton spread, quickly got up and threw open drapes covering a floor to ceiling glass door. Bells pealed from across a cobblestone road, the belfry set in the spire of a building with a Dutch-style entrance, embellished with fluting and a clamshell at the very peak. I was dressed but for my bare feet, when Alicia let herself in after a single knock.

"I was going to wake you up an hour earlier for services," Alicia said, "but I decided against it." She then walked to the glass door connecting my porch to the town outside. Where she stood, the intense light shone behind her, illuminating her hair.

"Like what you see?" she asked, then led me outside the Bergkloof Inn where she and Chandra had booked me. She walked me through the garden to the parallel wing of the old H-shaped house.

"Did Ted assign you as my guide to keep an eye on me, or what?"

"What kind of hosts would that make the Nichols family? You think because I'm related to him, he can tell me where to stay when I'm home for a few days? It was my idea to bring you here to Bergkloof village, Leon,

49

a special place I thought I'd share with you. I've been coming here as long as I can remember. Sometimes I forget that Peter and Jan, our hosts, aren't family. Peter is a LeRoux, and his family and the Nichols family go back centuries together."

"That's just what your brother said about the Nichols and Coetzee families. As a newcomer, then should I be worried that you measure people by how many generations back you can trace their family trees?"

"No need to worry. You're among friends," she said. She led me to a public room, smiling at the half-dozen people eating breakfast around the twenty-foot-long trestle table. They were served by a slender lady with salt-and-pepper hair who wore a dark blue apron with the same monogram matching the guests' napkins.

"We see you found your room key," this tall lady remarked. "I trust you settled in last night without stopping at our reception desk."

"We took two keys for two separate rooms," Alicia said pointedly. "Sorry, it was so late, but I didn't want to awaken you."

"So, who have you brought us today?" our hostess asked, referring to me. She placed the tray of pastries in the middle of the table and seated us.

"He's Leon Cooper, a dear friend of mine from America," Alicia introduced me, holding my hand possessively.

"Here on business or pleasure?"

"Both, I hope."

"Did she know you previously, or did you find each other on the plane? I'm Janice LeRoux, by the way. But if you call me anything but Jan, I shall be insulted. Jan is a common man's name here in South Africa, but that works for me because I try to be my own woman. No doubt you've noticed Alicia does as well. Now that you're here, what do you think of us?"

I wished she hadn't put me on the spot, as I had been many times yesterday at the Chateau. These white South Africans were anxious to know what the outside world thinks of them, now that they'd lost their long battle for control.

"Your country's blessed with brilliant sunlight. I feel like a bat who's flown out of a cave into the blinding light. I'm coming from New York where the skies stay gray for months at a time," I said looking out the window, rather than at her.

"But do you like what you see in our South African sun?" Jan LeRoux asked.

"Excuse me," I redirected, pointing beyond a couple of German tourists in cork sandals and heavy socks, "but isn't that our friend Kassie?"

"He's too early," Alicia said. "He shouldn't be here yet."

"He's wearing a track in your lawn," I said. "Why don't I get him now?"

"I'm sure Mr. Kassie prefers to remain where he is for now," Jan said. "Lovely to meet you. Excuse me, but I must return to my crew in the galley."

Alicia followed her into the kitchen, and myself behind her. "So, where's your kitchen help this morning?" Alicia asked. "Leon, meet Peter LeRoux, Jan's galley slave for the day."

"That's because there's no staff here this Sunday morning," Peter replied. "Obviously, not after their Saturday night toot. Welcome to the new South Africa."

Peter LeRoux was working with a spatula in each hand,

turning over small potato pancakes with one hand, and an omelet with the other. His thick hair curled below his white chef's cap. He was a slender man with large skeptical eyes, a precisely cut Van Dyke beard and round wire-rimmed glasses. He turned to see his wife, who placed her finger over his mouth before he could say anything. "Our friend Alicia must have misheard. I told her you were my love slave, not my galley slave."

"Never mind their slave talk, Leon," Alicia said. "Ever since I was little, when I was alone and very quiet, I could hear the slaves talking to me."

"Careful, or Mr. Cooper might think you daft, talking with the spirits," Peter said, rushing past us to set the hot food on platters Jan had set out for him.

"Very pretty," I said, "This is a breakfast like a dinner."

"Our best imitation of a full English breakfast," Alicia said.

She seated me at the head of their huge table. Someone had opened the door behind me, and the curtains adorning it blew onto the table. I got up to close it when I heard Kassie call me from outside.

"Mr. Cooper, this way!" He was twenty yards away, hidden by a stand of odd trees. I stepped outside to learn what he wanted. He had two cups of coffee and gave me one.

"Where did you get that?" I asked as we sat down at the patio table, hidden from the view of those eating in the house.

"We Indians have shops everywhere, Mr. Cooper, even in this white tribe village."

"This is a very strange place to me, these trees for instance."

"They're jackalberry and camelthorn trees, which don't belong here in the Cape, but north in the bushveld. They've been transplanted to the strange soil of the southern Cape, as have my people. The colorful vines are bougainvillea, which I understand are also in America, and should be familiar, unless you're too busy with business to sniff the rosebuds when they bloom."

Alicia had come up to Kassie and was standing behind him. "Leon, you must return before your meal goes cold. Chandra, do you understand?"

"No problem, ma'am. I'll return later when the paying guests have filled their stomachs. I'll be in the drostdy, which you would call the town clerk building. Look for me there when you need me."

"But they must be closed this Sunday morning!" I said.

"Sundays mean nothing to me because, with all respect, I am not part of Christian Sundays, no more than I am part of the breakfasts you fair Europeans prefer to eat without me."

"You know it's not like that, Chandra, not at all," Alicia called to him as he vanished into the trees and away from us.

"Don't listen to Chandra. He knows the LeRouxs are pious Christians and love all God's children."

Alicia led me back into the Bergkloof Inn, which was her home away from home, she explained, where she spent many years. I had to wonder if when she slept there now as an adult, she dreamed about hearing the ghosts of slaves, or believed they still lived there. And could she believe I'd better appreciate her lodgekeeper friends by offering her assurance they love God's children? This love, however, didn't seem to extend to Kassie.

Once inside, I imagined hearing voices, the same black slave voices Alicia confided she'd been hearing—now in the kitchen—additional slave voices! But what I saw in the kitchen was a tall black woman in an apron like Jan LeRoux'. There was also a black man in a cook's cap like what Peter had worn. I myself was spooked enough to begin imaging the dead servants' voices, while at the same time watching their descendants at work. Jan insisted I leave the kitchen and take the chair at the head of the table, just as I had at Ted Nichols' dinner party. I was flanked by her and Alicia and had apparently become the object of their full attention.

"Welcome to Bergkloof. It must seem very different here than in American villages," Peter said, leaning to shake my hand, though we'd already done that.

"Berg probably means a town, but a *kloof*?" I asked.

"A kloof is a neck, a bit of land holding the rest of the earth together," Peter explained, using a fork and knife and a plate on each end to illustrate a narrow mountain pass for me. "Remember last night when you were driving over the mountain pass between us and Chateau Drakenstein? That was a kloof."

"And a drostdy?"

"That's what we call the place we keep the deeds and such, our village hall."

"And I call it a miracle that it survived the disaster so well," Jan added.

"She means the earthquake," Alicia said.

"The earth shook," Peter continued, "opened up, and swallowed two dozen of our neighbors, rest their souls."

"But keep in mind," Jan said, "the worshippers in church that morning were spared, every one of them. The Lord worked in strange ways, destroying almost every building, except the church."

"Mr. Cooper," Peter said, "our people were praying in church that Sunday of the earthquake, half a century ago, and we'd be there this morning if we could find more reliable help."

"Deadly weather tends to make people suddenly religious," I said.

"Alicia, are you going to tell us where you found Mr. Cooper?" Jan asked again. "On the plane, or somewhere beforehand? Not that it's my business at all."

My mission was to see Ted Nichols, not his sister Alicia nor her friends, and since I had no further business in this town, I planned to check out of the Inn after breakfast and pass through the Kloof to the other side of the Drakenstein Mountains and to Cape Town.

Peter moved his chair to my end of the table and sat between Alicia and me. "Alicia, you always come back to Bergkloof, yet it's always seemed too slow for your liking. Perhaps that's because the choice in young men here is too limited."

Jan glared at him, then at Alicia. Could her problem be that she disapproved of Alicia's poor marriage prospects, or perhaps of her constant travel? The LeRouxs seemed quite satisfied with themselves, yet frustration seemed close to the surface, whether at their hired help or at Alicia. It was time to change the subject. I pointed to the ring on Jan's finger.

"This is a lovely ring," I said, taking Jan's hand. "May I take a closer look? Two carats anyway, nice color."

"Three point five, actually, and blue-white," Peter corrected me.

"Quite valuable, if someone were to buy this in the States."

"We once prospered here in South Africa, but no more. In fact, she shouldn't even be wearing this ring anymore," Peter whispered, "If we weren't blessed to be living in one of the remaining safe havens, though with this new boldness of the blacks—"

"They seem bold now that they're taking back what they thought always belonged to them, rather than to us whites," Alicia said.

"Leon, you must understand," Peter said, "everyone in the new South Africa's whinging because the rand used to be worth more than a dollar, and now it's deteriorated, worth just pennies on the dollar."

"How can you begin to know our troubles, Alicia, since you alight here so seldom these days?" Jan asked.

"Because the more things change, the more they remain the same," Alicia answered with a composed smile. "Come on, Leon, I've got some things to show you. Let's leave them be."

"Show him what?" Jan asked as we left the table.

"Bergkloof, of course, as it's been restored to its almost former glory."

"Almost?" Peter questioned.

"First the cataclysm of the earthquake, then the disaster of the new government," Jan said.

"Don't let her give you the wrongheaded idea that we long for the old days, Mr. Cooper. In a day or two when our dear but misinformed Alicia is done showing you the sights, please remember where to find us."

Alicia took me to the cobblestone main street. It seemed they over restored the village, made it too perfect, more like they hired toy makers rather than carpenters. That is, except for a cluster of abandoned grain silos and shacks set back, but not quite out of sight, grass grown high all around them. She knew all the buildings, and pointed out the former parsonage, the former wagon house, the former blacksmith, and the old schoolhouse. She named former residents of the houses that had been converted to lodges and restaurants. By the time we passed the Bergkloof Dutch Reform Church, she looked at her watch.

"I didn't realize the time. If we go any further, I'll have to talk to everyone coming out of church. I hope you understand," she said and looped back to the Inn, then to an outbuilding serving as a garage. She got her car, a white BMW that seemed new.

"Of course, I understand why you wouldn't want to introduce me to the church people." I said, talking to her through her rolled-down window, "but I don't understand why you seem to regard this village as your home if you grew up on the other side of the mountains in the Chateau."

"Exactly where I must go. I'm running late. Ted's expecting me."

"Fine, let me ride with you. I'd love to take up where we left off last night at the party."

"Is that what you'd love the most?" she taunted me with an odd smile.

"No, I'd love to talk business with the boss, since my time is also limited."

"Exactly, and so is Ted's. That's why I will never

speak business with him on a Sunday. That's his well-earned day of rest, his favorite time for fishing on his fast boat, and why I've come to Bergkloof for so many years on Sundays, to stay out of his way, as you may also want to do."

"Unless, for some reason, you're trying to get away from him on this side of the mountains."

"That's a strange thing to say to someone you don't really know yet. What exactly are you suggesting?" she said, at first looking at me sternly, then sweetly. She leaned through the window, surprising me with a kiss on the cheek. "Perhaps we can remedy your ignorance sometime, but not now. In the meantime, I'm sure Chandra will be able to take you wherever you need to go. He's waiting for you over there, in the drostdy," she said pointing down the cobbled street we had just toured.

"Don't expect me to sit idle for very long."

"I don't expect anything, but I do hope you can forget about your business project long enough to enjoy yourself with Chandra."

"Then what?"

"Then me, later."

Then me, later. I wish I knew what she was suggesting. A promise? But of what? She'd been a good hostess, working hard to keep me interested in her, but why was she bothering with me if she was going to get on a plane in a day or two? Was she suggesting a one-night stand? If that was her intention, why would she have taken me to this tiny village of churchgoers who seem to know her well? Was she trying to be helpful, tempering her brother's bad moods for me? She was a beautiful woman, probably used to men's admiration without needing mine. I enjoyed her attention, but I couldn't understand her connection with Ted in the Chateau, any more than I could figure her connection with the LeRouxs there in Bergkloof. If she was so interested in escorting me since we left the plane, why she was so quick to bring me, then dump me here in the White Tribe Village? Unless that was part of the plan, to keep me there in her museum. Or was this really a zoo where she could show me off as an interesting new creature?

I went to the drostdy because I promised Kassie I'd meet him there. Looking through the front windows, I saw no sign of him or anybody inside, only big pieces of furniture. After a few minutes of circling the building, I heard music. A knock on the front door brought no answer. The back door was closed, but not locked, so I let myself inside. I heard a scratchy recording of a soprano singing *Ave Maria*, which I followed to its source, a century-old gramophone in a room of old gramophones and newer phonographs. The front rooms housed a spinet, sideboard, hutch, alcove-sized clock, crystal chandelier, love seat, dining set, and living room suite. I heard heavy repeated blows like a sledgehammer's. I followed the pounding toward its source, the basement, where stairs led to a landing. I sensed someone waiting there for me.

"Hello, I'm up here!" I called so as not to be mistaken for a burglar and startle a guard, if that's who he was.

Hassan arrived, smiling. "I knew you'd be visiting me here at my second job. Why you may ask. Did Alica tell you I was ambitious? I'm splitting wood for the fireplace in the servant's bedroom. I sleep there when I cannot get to town in time for bed. It's cold at night, but the village don't want to heat this place to keep me comfortable, even though they pay me little to guard this treasure from the bad people."

He was splitting firewood with a maul, taking apart crates with Arabic writing. I smelled something pungent, earthy. Hassan read the curiosity in my face.

"Stinkwood," Hassan informed me. "Split open a log, and it smells bitter to your nose. The big stinkwood trees were saved for all that furniture you saw above upstairs. Strange how wood so stinky can be made into pretty furniture for our masters by artisans like from my family."

"It must smell even worse when you burn it at night."

"Me, I can't smell as good as I once did, not since my nose was broke."

"That's too bad."

"That was in a fight I did not start. He smashed my nose with a stick, but I whacked him with a stone. That's how we settle things in the townships. I was only twelve, but even the older boys respected me as a warrior."

"What did the other boy want? What happened to him?"

"I was going to the store for groceries with money in my pocket." Hassan was smiling again, showing white teeth. "He was barefoot and wanted my money. I made sure he'd never go after my shoes or my money. I was a hero, like David of your Bible."

Why was he looking at me so closely after revealing his story? Perhaps he had told me more than he intended. Was he wondering whether a dozen years after the implied killing, would I then pass his boastful story to the police? Self-defense or murder, it sounded like he'd used his victory to his advantage. Nevertheless, it was helpful for me to know what I was confronting in South Africa. In this country if you could be killed or get away with murder if you're the quicker, more aggressive one, I would have to be careful not to stray far unaccompanied by strong guides and avoid unnecessary battles. There was no need to challenge him, especially here on his own territory, but just the same, he had some explaining to do, starting with Kassie.

"I wasn't expecting to see you in here, especially on a Sunday," I said. He led me upstairs before I descended further into the basement. "If you don't mind my asking, what are you doing here?"

"Afrikaners, except for farmers, they don't care to work on a Sunday. They need somebody to watch their properties, but they hate to leave the black man, who they will never trust. The coloureds, like myself, they must trust a bit more, because we fix the trucks, run the presses, stitch the clothes, work the machines in the factories. We always be the artisans, and the whites the bosses. The Afrikaner's still the boss here in Bergkloof. I'm here to stop any bad man who sneak through the door like you did."

He seemed agitated, now that he told me not only of a killing, but how he fit in the pecking order of the races. To make his point, he pounded the entryway table harder and harder until the visitors' log crashed to the floor. He retrieved it, then cocked his head to one side, evidently hearing something I couldn't. He signaled me to be quiet as we stepped outside. I took my eyes off him, and he disappeared, so I returned inside. In a couple of minutes, I heard a lawnmower, then saw Hassan riding it close enough to the house for him to see me through the window, and he waved to me.

I felt a hand on my shoulder and spun around to see Chandra Kassie behind me. "Just the man I've been looking for," I said calmly as I could, though my heart was racing.

"Maybe this will calm you down," Kassie said and placed a disc on another of the music machines. *Mammy, This is Sammy from Alabamee!* "An American tune, you must recognize, Leon. He's Alan Jolson, one of your first American sound movie entertainers. He painted his face black, did he not? Why would a white man do that, so people in the theater would laugh at him, or because they didn't want to hire actors with real black faces?"

"That was a long time ago."

"No, you Americans still entertain us and probably the rest of the world with your movies. You influence us more than you know. I envy you your freedom to laugh at the black man."

These South Africans, whether they were brown or white or black, always seem to want to talk about race, as if they can never be sure about their own position. They tried hard to gauge where I stand, as if my opinion represented America. They'd been isolated a long time and now seemed to be grasping for information from the Western world. It was time for me to change the subject.

"You and Hassan seem to be world apart in music. He likes the timeless classical, you the American pop from early in the century."

"Then he was playing a recording for you, which one?"

"Not for me, for himself, *Ave Maria*."

"What a shame! He was entrusted to maintain these antique machines, not to play with them. Thank you for telling me."

"No, that wasn't my intention!"

I never intended to involve myself in their disputes, especially if I didn't know what they're about. I didn't know what I'd said to cause Kassie to move outside in a hurry to get to Hassan, who in turn stopped his mower to speak with him. I could hear them exchange louder and louder words I couldn't quite decipher.

"Chandra, someone sent you here to spy on me," Hassan started, once the three of us were together inside. "I know Sunitha always trusted me, but your boy Raj, was it him who found out why I'm here in this pretty town? Is he afraid he's missing out on this easy money? Would your son work hard as me keeping the Afrikaners' grass mowed low and their phonographs running nice?"

"They don't ask you to fix anything," Chandra Kassie said, "and they don't want you playing those old wax cylinders, which wear so fast. My record was more modern and won't wear out so fast, while yours—"

"My tune was in the Catholic language," Hassan said. "I speak Allah's language. You speak the coolie language, but the tune you play was English, which don't belong to me or to you. Mr. Kassie, you can't be telling me the English language is any better to us than the one Afrikaners speak."

Hassan had served up a whole cauldron of his resentment. Kassie, on the other hand, didn't seem so bitter.

Maybe he was just better at not showing it. More likely, as a Hindu, he was used to looking for more peaceful solutions and would not allow anger to overtake him. I was wondering if Hassan was talking for all South African low-paid workers who weren't white, for Arabs, or just for himself. I was concerned this pervasive suspicious attitude could become a problem for me in dealing with resentful employees like him. I was there as a businessman, to build on opportunity, not to involve myself in their rivalries. In the meantime, I wouldn't sample the nasty brew Hassan was offering, and led him to a more positive subject.

"I don't understand why you're hanging around here today, Chandra," I said, "to keep an eye on me or on your associate Hassan?"

"As we breathe the same air, Mr. Cooper, I hope we can become friends, or if not friends, at least associates doing good business together."

I didn't mean to insult him, nor could I believe he meant to put me on the spot. I had that coming, but now I needed to make it right between us if I was ever to rely on Chandra Kassie to help bring me closer to Nichols.

"And, sir, in case you are wondering," Kassie said, "I trust Hassan as much as I do my son Raj, who counts him his best friend. But I do not know why he needs our family as friends when he makes so many friends in the shebeens during the evenings."

"What's the difference, Mr. Kassie?" Hassan asked. "You brew beer, and my friends drink beer, even if they don't care for your recipe. So, Mr. Cooper, let me take you sometime to my other friends."

"No, you must keep Mr. Cooper away from those ruffians."

"Mr. Cooper, I am told in your country you brew beer. In America are you afraid to go to the shebeens where you sell your beer?"

"We distill spirits," I said. "I know nothing about beer, no more than I do about your saloons."

"See, Mr. Kassie, you're a fish out of water," Hassan said.

"I would be honored to show you the best places for swimming in South Africa, sir."

I had no idea where this young Arab guard wanted to take me, but I was not interested. It made no sense why Kassie had made it a point to introduce me to Hassan again, since he seemed to disapprove of him so much. Neither did I understand what Hassan could know about the beer business, nor why he was questioning how Kassie, a master brewer, ran his brewery. If they were bickering in a long-standing dispute, I was not interested in getting in the middle.

"Thanks, but no need to bother, Mr. Hassan," I said. "You gentlemen have showed me plenty already."

"No, I must show you more than this white village," Kassie said.

"But last night didn't you take the American to Mr. Nichols' party to eat his papaya and melon and passion fruits from a crystal tub? Did you also eat cheese, little cakes, and wine from Europe?" Hassan stood and walked across the polished honey-colored drodsty floor, then circled Kassie sitting in the overstuffed chair. He looked at him from all sides, then square in his eyes. "Did you want to leave Mr. Cooper at the master's party? Or was it Mr. Nichols who made you stay away from his smart friends? Mr. Kassie, you have more education than plenty of them. "

"A man who takes money from his boss has no right to criticize. Mr. Cooper came halfway round the world to do business with him. If you have nothing better to say about Mr. Nichols, you ought to stop working at the Chateau."

"Sorry, I'm not half as educated as Mr. Kassie," Hassan said. "And Mr. Cooper must have more school than you. So, I must listen to Mr. Cooper—and what he thinks of me."

"Well, if nothing else, you seem ambitious, keeping two jobs."

"I'm ambitious to stop being poor very soon. What else, please?"

"We noticed how well you got on with the black grape pickers, but you seem to get along even better by yourself here at this museum."

"Here there's no one to bother me!" Hassan said, retreating to a back room full of wooden filing cabinets. "Except the ghosts!"

"The pretty ghost village of Bergkloof," Kassie whispered.

"It you mean Alicia, she was talking about ghosts too," I said.

Alicia, Hassan, and now Kassie were all mentioning ghosts. They were only visitors here, but it seemed that right there the gloom of the drostdy building was affecting them, making them think of departed souls from their gloomy past. Maybe I didn't understand South Africans of any race, how on one hand they desperately wanted to forget their past, yet on the other, allowed it to haunt them.

"The slave ghosts," Kassie explained. "You stayed in the old slave house last night."

"And I sleep in the house of the bandits," Hassan called to us from the other room.

Kassie rolled his eyes, obviously not approving, though not responding any further. He waved to me to follow him, while he headed for the door. "I wish we could stay longer," Kassie said, "but my family—"

Before we reached the gate, Hassan rushed out of the drostdy with a file of papers and a map. "Never use your family for an excuse to be coward, Mr. Kassie. I use mine as a reason to be a brave man. These are the sad records of my Hassan family!" he shouted, placing receipts before my face with the Hassan name on them.

"Now what's troubling you, Larabie?" Kassie asked, placing his hand on Hassan's shoulder.

"My trouble? These papers tell how my family lost their land! This drostdy where they keep deeds for all the territory tell my story. The Hassans used to be farmers and worked their own land. Because we had no deeds in those days, it was easy for Afrikaner men making up new deeds to take our homes away from us! They steal from the coloured man to make Bergkloof village!"

To make his point, he took deeds with Dutch names on them from folders, laid them on the grass, and held them down with his foot. Now Kassie seemed nervous, looking up and down the street, as if afraid someone might overhear.

"Hassan, this is very bad, breaking into the records.

You are a crazy man today. You must bring those official papers back, before it's too late. We must leave you now," Kassie said, pushing me along until I was walking at his brisk pace, not quite a run that might attract attention to us.

CHAPTER 4

RAJ

After leaving Hassan railing about his dispossessed relatives, I gladly accepted Kassie's offer to tour the bigger wineries, including the Morgenhof estate with its fragrant herb garden. The Neil Ellis operation had been upgrading its vineyards with new Cabernet Sauvignon grapes, and the Neethingshof winery included its showplace mansion where we ate in their Palm Terrace restaurant, surrounded with antiques. My tour guide drove his dozen-year-old Mercedes and took great pride in showing me the extensive varieties of protea and fynbos plants. He showed me a bird unique to the Cape— the cape sugarbird with a tail twice as long as its body, and with a thin hummingbird's straw-like beak. But my thoughts returned to Ted Nichols, the dominant creature in this territory, the strongest of raptors, the unchallenged eagle, watching from a high vantage point, never seen by his quarry until the moment he strikes. My guide Chandra Kassie was more a placid ground-feeding dove, Although I was beginning to appreciate his local knowledge, I might have better enjoyed his companionship under different circumstances. But I was there on mandate to bring home a trophy for Cooper.

Later, we dined in a restaurant near his house in the

Athlone Indian quarter, staying several hours visiting with his friends. Strangely, most of the Indian men seemed to leave their wives and families at home, spending their evenings away from their families. Kassie kept introducing me as a big deal international businessman, no matter how many times I asked him to help me keep a low profile. I wished he'd quit it.

"You've shown me most everything," I said as Kassie dropped me at the lodge in Bergkloof.

"Just the things any tourist should see. There is so much more I must show you tomorrow when our work-day begins."

That night I was overtaken with a dream. I'd changed forms so that I could speak with the generations of slaves I'd displaced there in the Inn, in my room. If only I could have understood their language and communicated with them. These ghosts had shovels, ropes, and saws, and appeared ready to begin work. One was on my bed, poking my feet, rousing me from my sleep to join him, awakening me. It was the first hint of dawn, and when I turned on the light, I saw Kassie sitting on my bed.

"You must come with me," he whispered, "before the workers arrive."

"I can't, Chandra. Today I must take care of my personal business."

"Yes, sir. Yesterday you tasted wine like a tourist. This morning though we must commence business."

"You really shouldn't be in my suitcase!" I said as he handed me my clothes.

"You must know I am your friend and am only trying to help, sir."

This was my chance to shake myself loose of him, but that could have been a mistake. So far, in this crazy country I found I could rely on no one else more than him. If nothing else, he assisted me as a driver and a translator.

"It's a good thing I didn't mistake you for a burglar," I acquiesced.

"And a good thing you come from America to show us your way to do business."

"No, I have nothing to show you. I only deal with principals, and since you have no direct connection with Mr. Nichols—"

"Very sorry, sir. I see I must now tell Rajesh I disturbed you too early this morning, that you prefer to go back to sleep instead of letting me introduce you to businesspeople more important than myself."

"Now don't get the idea that I don't consider you important."

"Between friends like us, no need to explain, no problem. I go now, sir."

"I wish you'd call me Leon," I said, holding him from leaving me.

"Anything else, Leon, sir?"

"You must have gotten up at 4 A.M. to pick me up—"

"Sorry, but I commenced at 3:30 A.M."

"Then I'd be some kind of fool to ignore you."

"What kind, Leon, sir?

"Never mind! I'm simply Leon to you! Let's just go, Chandra!"

"The Cape Flats was no good for growing crops, the Europeans found, no better than the Karoo," Kassie explained as we drove toward Cape Town. He pointed

71

out the white sand on either side of the road, where at the top of one of the mounds I saw family groups scavenging. "Four hundred years ago the Dutch wanted to use the Cape for stocking ships with meat, vegetables and water, and weren't too keen to colonize it with many people. Now we have so many mouths to feed, some of these blacks live off these garbage dumps, which they also use for disposing of bodies."

I couldn't tell whether he was apologizing to me for his country or was simply unsure of where he as an Indian stood in it. He was probably telling me more than I needed to know to do business with them. Another few minutes and we were passing long stretches of a shantytown.

"More babies, more squatters every day," he further explained. "As soon as the bulldozers knock them down, they build new ones. The poor must live somewhere, I suppose. In America, I understand you put them up in flats and pay for their heat, food and electricity."

He was looking at me for my response, trying to gauge my sympathy for the poor. Across the highway a young woman, an old man, as well as a dog the size of a hyena were crossing in the high-speed traffic. Thud! I looked for a clue of what happened.

"We've got to turn around! Someone's been hit!"

"I'm hoping it was the dog," Kassie said with a nervous glance in his mirror. "These squatters shouldn't build their shacks on both sides of the road and so restlessly cross to their friends on the other side. They have no sense, and not only have skins darker than mine, but wear dark colors, even in the middle of the night. We are a poor country. A shame, isn't it?"

A poor country where a body flying off the roadway gets left where it landed or tossed in the dump! A country where those with property and money desperately try to keep what they have. Harry must have been crazy thinking he could make money here. Had he sent me to pick up assets on the cheap in this depressed land of the walking dead, or was he punishing me for taking the Cooper Company to the brink?

"Poverty anywhere can break the strongest spirit," I said from my American perspective. "I think you've made an unfair comparison. If we took our poor to live in your country, they would certainly make your poor envious."

"Unfair, most unfair—I agree, Leon! Already we have many poor guests, uninvited slipping across the frontier."

"I was not suggesting dumping our own American poor—"

"These refugees come from all over Africa—Uganda, Congo, Nigeria—because they think we are better off here in South Africa. They don't understand if there are not enough jobs for our people, there aren't enough for them too."

A universal law, big fish swallowing little fish. But I hadn't come here to observe their feeding chain, nor to figure out problems, maybe practical business problems. Yet these people each wanted me to hear their side of a big sad story, although I couldn't see how would affect my assignment.

"I understand how hunger can drive a man to be a criminal," Kassie continued. "There are too many hungry people in these black townships. That's the reason why my headquarters is in a good Indian district, near the restaurant where I took you last night, Leon, where neighbors all work hard and look out for one another."

The industrial district of Athlone had mostly unpaved streets. Kassie slowed to follow the horse cart ahead. It was filled with plastic, wood, a sheet of rusted steel and electrical wire. He shouted to the horse driver to go elsewhere.

"This scrounger fancies wire," Kassie said as we passed. "The smart ones know how to cut our power circuits and to hack it off the poles. The wire thieves shut down the plant once and left us in the dark for two days."

"Why don't the police—"

"These vultures fly away fast from police. See that watchtower? In apartheid days there was a policeman around the clock to stop the riots. Now the police don't bother coming here much."

"That's funny, I see in one direction the signs say *Section*, in the other, *Block*."

"Not funny, sir. The police have lost their maps and forgotten the directions to Athlone. They have trouble finding their way to us when we call for help."

We passed shops for manufacturing sauce, mattresses, candy, dinner plates, doors, and for welding, tires, exhaust and transmission repair. None had more than a dozen workers, with many of them working outside on the street. The buildings had boarded up windows, uncollected trash, rusted signs, cracked masonry. Soon the industrial buildings began to look better repaired, more prosperous, after which we approached little houses with neat, fenced yards and paved roads.

"The Indian district, my home," Kassie informed me.

Taking up the space of a dozen of these homes, stood a collection of commercial buildings surrounded by a masonry wall, topped with steel spikes and a Gazelle Beer sign with bullet holes. Chandra Kassie paused directly in front of the barred front office window and tooted his horn, waited for his man to switch open the electric gate. Inside, a couple of trucks pulled up to a loading dock, taking on cases of beer. Kassie talked to the drivers, looked at their invoices, and repeatedly shook his head, not pleased at what he saw.

"Meet my son Rajesh, who knows more than anyone else."

Rajesh resembled him, though his skin was close to the color of a brown paper bag, while Kassie's was more like coffee without cream. The younger Kassie bore an intense expression, his face in a permanent squint.

"I just go by the recipe book, whereas father has written the book."

"No, Raj, not my own manual, but wisdom borrowed from thousands of years of brew masters."

They were looking at each other with mutual admiration. But once Raj left us in the office, Kassie's expression changed and looked as grim as it had been while he was by the trucks looking at invoices. I needed to find out what was bothering him.

"You do a brisk business here," I observed.

He wasn't looking at me, but past me onto the brewery floor, where Raj was now ladling out little samples of brew from the vats. He stopped at one vat where he took several samples. There was a problem that Chandra had sensed just by watching his son from twenty yards away where we were separated from him by glass.

"Leon, I assure you anyone who knows quality beer buys Gazelle."

"Quality. That's how we built our Cooper brand," I agreed. "Anyone who knows whiskey buys Cooper. Quality brought us steady business. I understand."

"No, Leon, sir, many people buy your Cooper spirits, but it is different for my Gazelle. My beer is superior to the big Lion and Castle brands, but their names sell far better than mine."

"Brand loyalty can carry you or kill you, depending on how you're positioned in your market. It is hard to pull people away from familiar brands. That's why in our home market in America with people drinking less spirits, we've added wine to our line, though as distributors, not as growers."

"Then the Coopers would like the South Africa wine trade enough to buy the business from Ted Nichols?" Kassie queried.

I wondered how much Harry had briefed Kassie on my game plan for South Africa. We were intending to assert ourselves as active managing partners in Ted Nichols' portion of their operations. I suspected Kassie was too willing to share what he knew or what he suspected of my goals with Alicia, as well as share his intel with Hassan, whose true role I still didn't comprehend.

"I can't blame you, Leon," Chandra continued, "wanting to buy a good existing winery. The secrets of wine grapes are too difficult for restless men like us. Wine men are more like nursemaids. You must breed good grapes carefully as a racehorse. Champion wine grapes are very delicate and take sick too easy."

"I know, for our spirits we need good corn, rye, or barley. In your beer business you need decent hops."

"No, not the same, Leon, because the grape you must pick exactly the right day, one hand at a time. To make your whiskey or my beer, a tractor can harvest crops standing in the field. But you can't pick wine grapes so fast. You and I don't have patience for playing around with grapes and wine. Your liquor business is much like my beer business. I can show you everything you need to know about beer in South Africa. You said New York City was too cold when you left, that you prefer our sun."

"If I were looking for more sunshine, I didn't have to travel halfway around the world to find it."

"You wouldn't have to look for sun if you were a member of the British empire because the empire owned it. The sun never set on the British empire, they once said. In those times when an English civil servant died far away in a colony like South Africa or India, what was there to do for his burial? If he was important enough, they returned him to England. To keep the body nice for the funeral, they would throw the bloke in a barrel of whiskey, and he'd sail long months port to port. Meantime the dead man's spirit would seep out of his body, through the whisky and into the wood barrel. That's the reason they call whiskey spirits."

I didn't know whether Chandra believed this fable. If he was simply trying to divert me, it was not working. Meanwhile, Rajesh brought a couple of jars from the brewery floor for us to sample. Chandra made a sour face at what he tasted, accidentally dropped one of the jars on the floor, then quickly walked to the vat with me following.

Raj responded to his father's problem by calling over a tall Indian woman with imposing eyes, wide-set and large, nicely balanced by her full mouth. Her dun complexion called for dark eyes, but hers were green. I remembered this woman from the snapshot of Raj and her on the beach. Rajesh gave his fiancé another ladle to taste the sample from the batch. She winced, confirming it had gone wrong.

Raj rushed to several workers, reprimanding them, which drew more workers into an escalating dispute that was making me uncomfortable. A small man climbed a ladder up the offending vat, leaning far down into the top inspection hole. His body disappeared but for his legs, kept from falling by a bigger man holding him by the ankles.

"Aren't you concerned that he might slip in and drown?" I asked.

"That man Mafumo is the one responsible," Chandra whispered. "If he was to land in this ruined batch, then we could see if beer preserves a black man so good as spirits. Perhaps I should find an oaken barrel the right size and preserve him long enough to ship him back to his homeland."

Nasty talk. There was no love between him and his black employees, not a friction-free workplace were management and labor work together. Maybe I was expected too much, hoping to apply advanced business management techniques there. The reality each group was vying for control at the other's expense.

"Isn't South Africa his homeland as much as yours?"

"Yes, we're suddenly all brothers and sisters in the new South Africa. Officially we don't have homelands anymore. It almost makes me long for the apartheid days where at least we knew where we belonged. We Indians were primarily shopkeepers and kept to ourselves and could hold our employees accountable for their actions without their insolence."

Chandra was about to say more, but instead he walked out of the office. I hadn't asked for him to be my tour guide of this old brewery in the middle of the Indian quarter, but I didn't care to be left behind in the escalating fight, which neither father nor son seemed able to reduce. The lesson I was seeing unfold was that it wasn't good enough to simply show workers how to run the machinery.

When we came to his car, Kassie rushed to my door in order to hold it open for me.

He had parked the car across the road under a tree, and from there he could watch the plant entrance where more shouting workers were gathering. His hands were tightening and releasing on the steering wheel.

"These big Benz cars seem to be the only ones which improve with age," I said.

"Actually, this was the smallest of Mr. Nichols' fleet, which is why he signed it over to me as part of our arrangement.

"Quite safe, just the same."

"Safe for us, perhaps, but not for that mangy dog or dog's master that crossed our path earlier this morning," Kassie laughed. "I sometimes prefer to take my tea break without the tea and instead gather my thoughts sitting in my car at a distance from all that sort of noise," he said with an angry gesture at the Gazelle brewery.

"From me you can learn everything you need to know about producing beer, the secrets passed down through the ages, beginning with the god Indira, who first gave beer to man. In exchange, from you I hope to learn strong business magic, commencing now, even before we become full partners." The shouting grew louder, workers pushing and some throwing punches. "Leon, they say you know how squeeze blood from the fruit of the turnip and turn it into money."

He probably got that notion from Harry, ever the salesman. Did he see the American way of running a business as a collection of magic tricks, or was he flattering me? In the meantime, the employees seemed to be squaring off for a grand battle. It appeared the situation was growing critical.

"Chandra, I don't know what Ted's told you I can accomplish, but if you're looking for a recipe for turnip soup, I'm afraid you're going to have to cook it up yourself." I couldn't help but laugh at the thought of involving myself in such a chaotic mess.

"Do we amuse you?"

"To the contrary, Chandra. What I see concerns me, but I have no answer for you. You may think I can teach you magic tricks, but what you need right now is courage. If you want my advice, you ought to get out of this car and engage them before this gets much uglier."

"Absolutely," he agreed. "We must get to the source of the problem."

He scooted around the car to open the door for me, no doubt assuming that I would walk back through the gate with him. Was he expecting me to do a trick that would pacify his enraged workforce? Rather than confront the men outside, we kept a safe distance from them, and I followed him to the source of the problem, the bad batch inside the vat.

"*Masepa d'katz!*" Raj called sternly to Mafumo, who was back on the ladder and lowering a stainless-steel jug attached to a rope into the beer.

"*Oriking!*" Mafumo called back, laughing.

"*Kiripoep. Mafumo!*" Raj persisted.

"Are you speaking Afrikaans?" I asked Chandra, who shook his head no. "Hindu?"

"Zulu," Chandra whispered. "These two are from up north, from Durban, not the southern Cape. They think of themselves as Zulu warriors. When my ancestors lived there, they would rob us blind with every chance they got." He took a few steps away where he could speak more freely. "It's a timing error. Mafumo didn't follow our procedure. He was assigned to scrub vats six and seven, and since we now have two contaminated flat-tasting batches, he obviously did not clean them well."

Meanwhile, Mafumo lowered his bucket of beer to Raj and scrambled down.

"*Hunba gathla!*" Raj shouted and threw the bucket of the spoiled sample down the nearest floor drain.

"My son tells the fool Mafumo 'enjoy your journey,'" Chandra explained to me, "because he's done working here at the Gazelle company. Now you see why we cannot afford to keep these climbing monkeys."

Sunitha's been charting data. Raj looked over her shoulder at her clipboard, ignoring the angry workers arguing and trading blows in front of the building. She took a brass cup hanging from her waist and filled it with a sample, which he tasted, and backed away from the commotion.

"No question about it—off taste, Sunitha, a total loss," Raj said, which she recorded. "Perhaps my father forgot the rule of thumb."

Sunitha studied me carefully. I was making a conscious effort not to reveal my frustration with this building confrontation, then looked to the elder Kassie. We then moved toward the front door and saw two men wrestling with a crowd cheering them on.

"Mr. Kassie," Sunitha said, "I don't think Mr. Cooper understands Raj. Perhaps you can explain."

"The brewer's rule of thumb," Chandra said. He closed his eyes, to concentrate and block out the distracting fighting. "Centuries ago, the brewer used to put his thumb in the wort to tell if consistency just right for adding yeast. Timing's very important. It appears that someone failed to add yeast soon enough."

"Raj, it may be best you take your tea break now," Sunitha said, backing away from the open door with me, now with both Kassies following.

With her white lab coat and her clip board, Sunitha appeared to be the competent technician. Chandra, with Raj at his side, talked to the workers seeking to argue their grievances. Quite agitated, they were pushing hard enough to knock each other down. I couldn't understand their languages, and hadn't brought a bag of negotiating tricks, so I followed Sunitha back to the office.

"Locking the barn door after the horse escaped?" I asked her as she locked the door behind us.

"Mr. Cooper, has Raj's father shown you we are very

modern? We do not use horses for power anymore, but modern machines. Sometimes I wish we didn't need manpower," she said, looking through the window at the plant floor below. "If only our people worked as well as our machines. Thanks to our investor, we've been able to purchase new stainless-steel vats, which should give us better control of our product."

"Your investor, who might that be?"

An innocent question, but maybe too direct for her liking. She looked me over. Who knew what she was thinking about me?

"Any other questions, Mr. Cooper?" she asked. Here I was, barricaded with a woman who smelled sweet as spring flowers.

Meanwhile, I saw Chandra struggling to talk sense to his angry employees. He was standing in the bed of a truck addressing two groups of workers, the pacifying Indians and their loyal allies, as well as the angry Zulus and the friends of the fired worker, Mafumo. The workers took sides based on skin color, an old story in South Africa. But from what the Kassies had previously told me, the conflict within Gazelle had gotten worse since they let go of ten percent of their people. The remaining ones seemed more like hungry dogs fighting for table scraps than like reasonable employees who could ever learn how to work friction-free.

"Chandra's quite a man," I said to her. "He was teaching me about Indira's gift of beer before that mob got his attention."

"Excuse me, Mr. Cooper, but rather than Indira, he must have been thinking of Ra. Ra was a god to the Egyptians, not to the Indians, the one who they believed gave man beer, which was red in color. Mr. Kassie is a wonderful teacher, but like Rajesh and your pretty friend Alicia, and like yourself, sir, you should listen to him carefully, perhaps discounting a few such details."

I wasn't sure whether she was praising Chandra, so much as criticizing her fiancé, Rajesh. Nor was I sure why she was talking so freely to me, someone she hardly knew. I heard breaking glass—bottles being hurled at the barred windows! Then I saw the martyr Mafumo himself, with help from a couple of his Zulu and Xhosa allies, smashing full bottles of Gazelle Beer onto the floor. That is, until confronted by some loyal coloured and Indian workers, who took up plastic shipping flats, using them as shields to push the rebels out of the building. Half a dozen workers were wielding a steel I-beam, repurposed as a battering ram to smash in a bolted door! I could see this group of Indians were Chandra's allies. With no time for explaining their plan, they escorted Sunitha and me outside, to the opposite end of the lot where he had been trying to calm the workers agitated about Mafumo's sacking. Our Indian escorts took us to the equipment repair shop. It was detached from the main plant, marked DANGER HIGHLY FLAMMABLE.

Rajesh threw open the door and pulled Sunitha inside. I was followed by a couple of the loyal workers. "The danger is very great inside here because of these," one of the loyalists said, pointing to a barrel of solvent and several five-gallon cans of fuel.

"Certainly no place for a lady," Rajesh said to me. "That's why I urged Sunitha to leave with the other women employees."

"It is written man has seeds of a woman; woman has seeds of a man," she added with a weird composure. "That is why I don't care to strike out on my own at the present time, unlike the other women working here who are on their way to their homes." She directed her intense green eyes at me once again, rather than at him. I tried to figure out whether she was pledging her loyalty to Rajesh, or simply saying events had gone too far for her to abandon the plant now.

Suddenly the Indian shift manager burst into our retreat, his shirt torn. He clasped his hands together, gave me a little bow, pointed through the barred window to the fighting outside, where Chandra like a fearless general, walked the battle line, reasoning with both sides to return to their stations. "It's a bit hectic, Mr. Kassie," a man with a security guard patch on his sleeve said to Raj. "You should take the American and Miss Bala away from here, now that the animals are rattling our cage!"

"There goes Baas Rajesh!" someone yelled from the irritable crowd, trying to intercept us, until he was fought back by a loyal manager. The aggrieved workers were focused on Rajesh, yelling at him. Aggressively, they tried to move toward him and away from Chandra's crowd, believing they'd found a new listener for their complaints, but in the process blocking an escape path the security guard seemed unable to effectively clear. When Sunitha stepped in front of us though, they respectfully stepped aside. Incredibly, we were now able to walk through them as if through parting waters.

We now quickly locked ourselves in a Gazelle delivery truck, Raj at the wheel. It was impossible for him to see over the stacked beer cases in the cargo box the crowd forming behind the truck. "I have no other choice," he said, and began to repeatedly toot his horn, then eased backwards, looking in his side mirrors only. "Did you hear those thumps? I did not run over bodies, did I?" he asked, assigning me to look backwards through the passenger side window as we were making our escape. As we passed Chandra, he shouted for the three of us to leave without him. He chose to stay and reason with his agitated workers. It was a choice I wasn't about to share with him.

We were about a quarter mile outside the Gazelle plant gates when we began hearing pounding on the roof! Then I could see an unexpected passenger hanging down outside my window, an iron bar in hand

"We must stop to let him down," I said.

"To the contrary, sir! He cannot mean us well, so he must suffer the consequences," Raj said. He began weaving violently from one side of the road to the other, then alternately braked and accelerated. In the process I heard a final shout from the falling worker, along with the breaking glass of several cases of beer, simultaneously thrown off the truck. Then once again he drove for another mile, when he finally stopped.

"I see no damage," he said, and aside from some lost product, there was none.

"No harm, no foul," I concurred nonchalantly. That violent clash between the workers and management had done plenty of damage to my opinion of Kassie's old plant. I decided that not only was it functionally obsolete, but that in its present location with its present work force, it had to be scrapped.

"Now you can take me back where I came from."

"To Bergkloof? Or to America?" he teased me, but I was in no mood for quips.

"And what about Sunitha?"

"I am guessing you two know each other well enough to work that out.

"And my father?"

"Good question," I said, providing no answer.

"But I have to make deliveries."

"Well, they'll just have to wait until after you get me to the Inter-Continental Hotel."

CHAPTER 5

INTER-CONTINENTAL HOTEL

I considered staying at the Bergkloof Inn to be closer to the Chateau, but decided my time would be far more productive spent in Cape Town. At city center was the Inter-Continental Hotel, a showcase smoked glass and steel tower that wouldn't have looked out of place in Los Angeles. Cape Town sits precariously close to a harbor nearly as dangerous as the broad ocean, in which a late nineteenth century storm, for example, sank all the ships anchored there. Subsequently, the old harbor had been engineered into submission by dredging, filling and dyking, so now piers, roads, and stores stand stood on land reclaimed from the Atlantic, a direct challenge to the forces of nature. The view from my hotel was dominated by Table Mountain, which in prehistoric times had been entirely under the ocean. I'd been getting emails from the home office that I was booked for only the first week there, after which I was to find a less costly flat to rent, asserting that I'd been overspending my expense account. My brother and I both knew about the KWV Afrikaner-dominated cartel in South Africa, which was almost as dominant in the wine business as DeBeers was in the international diamond business, controlling nearly 90% of the wineries in South Africa. If they expected me to build the independent Drakenstein label into a powerhouse competing with the consortium, they ought not to have griped about petty expenses! They knew my assignment, though not impossible, was certainly no lark and that it was essential for me to operate out of a good address if I was to keep up appearances and have maximum clout. From this hotel it was a short ride to the business leaders whom I had to get to know. To survive against KWV, I needed to find the right allies in one or two suitable food or beverage producers.

Unlike doing business in the States, these businesspeople didn't hide behind secretaries assigned to run interference from callers. They were quite willing to give their cell phone numbers, answer them day or night, and didn't mind making appointments with me. I was a curiosity, and they enjoyed hearing about a Yankee's travels in South Africa. Another pattern I saw was their complaining about how their currency was worth less every day compared to our dollars. Yet they didn't seem to be looking for my American dollar solutions in the form of any joint venture. There was plenty of talk from these captains of South African industry with no action, just like Ted Nichols so far.

For weeks now I had several meetings workdays with these sociable but noncommittal talkers. Under less frustrating circumstances, I might have enjoyed Cape Town from my room on the 25th floor. From this vantage point in the early mornings, I watched sidewalks and streets filling with workers from the townships, who would empty out of downtown by evening after work.

After finishing my day's roster of appointments, I did my best to put business out of my mind. Instead, I'd imagine how the Cape used to be before the Brits, the Dutch, or even the Bushmen or Zulus, millions of years earlier when the ancient sea had retreated from Table Mountain and the mammoth sea beasts were learning to walk on land. I imagined myself as one of the sea creatures who had to learn to adapt to new conditions.

Late one afternoon when I returned to my room, Tembo was waiting for me, watching my TV! As soon as I entered, Tembo raised his feet and removed his chauffeur's hat. He was watching a tribe dancing, accompanied by village musicians, playing instruments ranging from a drum small enough to be held in one hand, as well as one nearly as tall as a man. The singers were divided into high and low men's voices and high and low women's, each section trading choruses. Dancers were moving to this music in a frenzy. Young and nubile women as well as older and women with heavy flopping breasts, were all dancing with inspired lightness.

"These are my people, Zulus," he tried to explain. "When we are not pressed to war, we have much music in our hearts."

"I wish I could dance like that," I said, getting into my briefs. "Your music is the source of American music. It came from hard work on the plantation, the blues. But I doubt you've come here to entertain me with music, Tembo."

"Sir?" he asked innocently.

"This is a long way from the Chateau, and it must be after hours for you. Should I assume Mr. Nichols is paying you overtime to look after my welfare this evening?"

"Your welfare? Good news for you, I hope, sir. But if you think I came here to spy on you, I must leave now."

Whether honesty or hostility, I couldn't tell his intention. He smiled at me, handed me an envelope, then looked at me carefully as I sat at the desk to read the faxed message he's come to deliver:

FROM: HAROLD COOPER, SENIOR VICE PRESIDENT
TO: L. COOPER, INTERNATIONAL MARKETING DIRECTOR
RE: YOUR EMPLOYMENT CONTRACT

The board of directors has just completed its second quarter review of your progress report in South Africa. Original deadline for dispatch of first draft of joint venture/buyout contract past due. No contingency plan anticipated for open-ended extension of your marketing assignment.

Regarding establishing an alliance with other than the target business you have been pursuing, not much enthusiasm on the part of the board.

Regarding continuation of your employment with Cooper Spirits in developing offshore market alliances, to be decided. That, however, should not preclude obtaining for the Company an action plan for development of a Werner-Nichols partnership package prior to our next quarterly board meeting.

Sincerely, Harry

P.S. To date I've done all I can to assist you. As you can appreciate there's no place for sentiment in business.

Sincerely? Rather than sincerely assisting me on this difficult mission, I suspected my brother simply wanted me out of the organization, seeing me as a liability, and still doing his best to let me take the heat for the failed stock venture. Our key people, inside and outside the family, bought their options on shares at only $5 average price, so the family and the other directors didn't lose any more than phantom profits. It wasn't my fault that Harry was foolish enough to exercise his options, then hang onto his stock too long before our company was delisted. Nor that he overextended himself based on his phantom profits and had to sell his two-million-dollar Victorian brick house on the Mississippi. Now from eight thousand miles away, he was evidently trying to punish me. For my part, I'd foolishly yielded to authority on behalf of the company! Just a few weeks ago when he launched me on this fool's mission, I was international marketing director, and now I could be demoted to sales manager. Or maybe the real reason Harry had been so slow to release funds to South Africa had less to do with Cooper's banking problems than with his intention to cut me off to make me look bad and thereby give him an excuse to replace me with someone less of a threat to him.

When we were strictly a family business, we Coopers had for generations managed to cooperate among ourselves and thrived. That was until a dozen years ago when Mother finally walked out on our CEO, accusing him of loving the business more than her. I would have been visiting her more often than just holidays if it wasn't for her cocky new husband who never cared for me or Harry. I never chose to live with Father to appease him. Until I found the right woman, I just wanted to remain in my apartment in the house that great-grandfather Hiram Cooper built after he gave up his barrel-making trade for spirits-making. I complied with Father's wishes to reside very close to him so that Harry and I could more efficiently coordinate our family's management of Cooper Spirits!

Now I was seeing things in a different light. In earlier years I'd given my unwavering loyalty to Father and the company, to the point of keeping my distance from my own mother after she left him. For what? I came to realize now that Father had come to believe Harry cared for the company more than I did. I had to conclude Harry was trying to eliminate me as his competition, which would leave him in line to take over when Father was out of the picture. If Harry thought because the financing went sour he'd found an airtight excuse to squeeze me out, he underestimated me!

Tembo was still in my room. I should have ejected him for breaking into my room when I first had the chance. He was annoying me, handing me my shirt, pants and shoes. I was an American, not some refined Englishman demanding the services of a butler! The sooner I got him out of the room, the better. But what was Tembo up to now, holding the door open with his foot, refusing to leave?

"Excuse me, sir, but do you think it's a good idea for people to read that?" he asked, pointing back to the Harry's message which I had left on the bureau.

"What part of my letter did you find the most interesting?"

He seemed about to answer, but stopped himself, and shook his finger at me.

"Since I know you believe I am spying on you, do you wish to execute me now?"

He was good at sidestepping embarrassing questions, but I wasn't going to let him wriggle away from me so easily.

"Not you, Tembo, but the one who put you up to trailing me."

He returned with the letter, which he folded and tucked into my breast pocket. In the elevator, he looked at his reflections in the gold-tinted mirrors, removed his hat and ran a comb through his hair. In the lobby we saw a couple at the concierge's desk, wearing matching khaki safari pants and jackets. They were booking an extensive tour including the savannah, the Karoo desert, and mountain ranges. Because we shouldn't have been eavesdropping on the tourists, I pulled him away.

"If you did not have important business to achieve, Mr. Cooper, I could show you the great animals where the grass grows high after the rains. You could use me as your personal guide."

We passed through the revolving front door, where the chief doorman stood watch. He was dressed in a long green coat, quite heavy for the warm climate, and decorated with rows of medals and ribbons. Seeing Tembo, he dispatched a boy to retrieve his car. The Chateau Mercedes arrived, but before Tembo explained where we were going, Alicia walked up to me. She was rolling a flight attendant's bag, the same blue as her uniform. A bellman took the suitcase from her and rolled it into the hotel.

"Could you be as hungry as I am?" Alicia asked, ignoring the coincidence of our intersection. "If so, there's a nice restaurant just this side of the park where they serve fish on wooden platters in iron skillets instead of on plates."

She addressed Tembo, quickly sending him away; I had been handed off once again! I was learning not to resist the wisdom of my handlers and planned to benefit from their association. Without further discussion, we set out for the restaurant she had in mind.

"You're braver than me, Alicia, walking downtown after the sun has set. See those two men?" I said, turning to a couple of men half block away who had been following us.

"Don't look any more, or they'll sense your fear. Hurry!"

We reversed direction, and they reversed as well, so I grabbed her hand and together we ran from them, hindered by Alicia's built-up heels. Once we ducked through the hotel's revolving door, they were gone. Back to square one, it was a close escape from an ambush on the street. Or had we just run from shadows, imagining enemies who didn't exist and letting fear get the better of us? I didn't care to ask her how to identify and avoid my enemies, not wishing to spoil the dinner we were about to enjoy.

She chose a table in the most visible part of the lounge, allowing us to easily watch the lobby. I had just opened a bottle of wine, when a woman in a blue uniform like hers passed. Alicia called her over, inviting her to join us.

"Your wine, Chateau Drakenstein, I see," this flight attendant noticed, smiling at Alicia.

Alicia turned her attention to her friend's clam-sized gold cross, which contrasted dramatically against her chestnut brown skin. Napu was beautiful, tall and lithe, with a graceful neck and perfectly round head with small balanced features.

"Are you interested because you like my jewelry or because you are a fellow Christian, Alicia?" Napu responded to the compliment, but Alicia moved on.

"Napu, don't you sometimes wish you could stay at home?"

"If I lived in a castle like yours, certainly," Napu said.

"You're welcome to visit during business hours when I'm at the Chateau, Napu. You can ask one of the staff to see if I'm available."

"I have not toured the wineries. Those Afrikaner winemakers don't like my people to tour their premises and sample their wares. Old habits die hard in South Africa."

"I do wish management would allow us to wear a bold Crusader's cross like yours." Alicia shifted again, avoiding any further talk about who controlled the wine or the country.

"You still haven't told me why you like this chain. Are a Christian like myself?" Napu pressed.

"Oh, excuse me, Napu," Alicia pivoted, "this is Mr. Leon Cooper, a close friend of mine. He's a lonely tourist I am trying to entertain." Alicia took my arm, put her face next to mine and mugged for her friend.

"Is he up for that pleasant assignment?" Napu asked. She was looking for my response to Alicia's quip, when a man in a loose-fitting African suit approached her.

Napu pushed back her chair to greet this friend of

hers, who stooped to be eye level with her. They spoke privately, too low to overhear and they soon excused themselves and left hand-in-hand.

Watching them exit, Alicia whispered to me. "Beauty and tall genes; some of them make great runners and can fly across the veld for hours without fatigue, unlike you and me." That compliment led me to look her over more carefully. It was easy to see how Nebu attracted men.

"You're right, Alicia, she's lovely. He's a lucky man."

"For tonight anyway. A warm berth can seem very inviting to a tired mate," she said with a mischievous smile towards me.

"Clarify, please. A berth as in a bed? A mate as in a friend?"

"Don't worry, Leon, I'm quite direct. I mean this hotel is where the airline puts us up for layovers. But sometimes in the room that's been reserved for us, we have women sleeping shoulder to shoulder. If I had an alternative, I would not be in the same room with so many thrashing, restless women."

"Is that why Napu left with that gentleman? Because he has more spacious quarters?"

"I can't speak for her, or for you as a businessman on the road. However, I can imagine your loneliness. I'm here as a friend who owes you a favor for saving me from thugs on the street."

She and Tembo both concerned about my loneliness—quite a coincidence! Placing her hand on mine, she leaned over and kissed my cheek, but her attention didn't stay with me. She focused on a man standing by the marble fountain, a briefcase at his feet. He checked his watch, as if waiting for an appointment. I knew she wanted to rush over to him, but I wasn't about to release her. She did the next best thing, leading me by the hand to him. His suit had a fitted Italian cut, his eyes and his mouth had radiating lines, as if he'd spent most of his life in the weather. It felt strange being introduced to him, each of us wondering, no doubt, whether the other was Alicia's boyfriend. I was not pleased with the clandestine way she arranged for Tembo to pass me to her, and now, evidently, I was in the middle of yet another handoff, to this man with the undisclosed appointment.

He preferred that the three of us sit on lobby chairs, which he regrouped into a tight circle. I was guessing he had a business proposal, and I couldn't afford to ignore any business prospect. He seemed nervous, his soft tan leather briefcase between his feet, like a courier guarding a shipment of jewels.

"Otto Kruger, is that an Afrikaner or a German name?" I asked to make conversation, since he was making no attempt to engage with me.

"Like the game park, Kruger Game Park."

"Like Paul Kruger," Alicia added, "the Boer president of this country, a stern ruler. You're looking at his great-great grandson. He's too modest."

"President Kruger was so stern and unyielding he even drove some of his own people, Afrikaner whites, to emigrate north to Kenya, where they homesteaded on the White Highlands next to the Kenyan Brits. Wonderful horse country up there. Of course, the settlers were resented by the displaced Mau Maus, who organized to become guerillas. Those whites had spear-throwers to contend with then, while these days we have our urban gangsters shooting machine guns in the streets, like what you have in Chicago."

Did this man actually believe Chicago in the mid-90s was the same as it was in the 30s during Prohibition? The direct descendant of one of the most famous politicians in South Africa, this man hadn't too accurate a notion of the outside world. He seemed to prefer the old regime before the Rainbow Nation—another member of the white tribe in search of a secure homeland, one where they might be free to ride their horses from prosperous farm to prosperous farm, with no fences, no government, and no Mau Maus anywhere.

"What's your trade, Mr. Kruger, sales?"

"My pleasure!" He opened his salesman's sample case and pulled out a brochure promoting a soft drink bottling plant. He watched me carefully as I looked through it. "Oasis Spring Water, Ltd."

"The sort of thing you Coopers make back in America—beverages," Alicia interjected. Was she really comparing making whiskey to bottling soda pop? For someone who grew up next to the wine business, she apparently failed to understand the art and science of distilling liquor!

"You're making some extraordinary claims for your product," I said, holding up one of his brochures to him, which featured a bottle of Power O drink, humanized into a cartoon figure with arms and legs. "Should I believe if someone drinks your soda he'll be energized to jump far and high and accomplish extraordinary things?"

"I think it's better they drink Otto's soft drink than your hard liquor," Alicia added.

Just what I would have expected to hear from her, a child of the Chateau. These wine-and-cheese types always think their wine's healthier than whiskey or gin.

"How can you say that?" I asked, with nothing to lose, my mind having dismissed his drink as of no interest to Cooper. "Your product would appear to contain little more than water, flavoring, sugar, with a little shot of carbonation."

"Not carbonation, but oxygenation. We add oxygen, the fuel for life. Add oxygen to our blood and we're supercharged. Power O is a unique health drink Alicia asked me to show you."

"Excuse me, but it's well past my bedtime," she whispered. "I mean this feels like 4 A.M. to me. If only I could get accustomed to this jet lag."

I looked at Alicia, but I couldn't get her attention. She covered a wide yawn with her Hong Kong newspaper. Jet lag was her excuse to make an abrupt exit and leave me alone with him. So, without any mention of where she and I might meet next, she left, brushing her hand across my shoulder as she passed.

"It's revolutionary because it boosts the oxygen in our body," Kruger persisted, undeterred by Alicia's departure. "This product makes up for the depleted oxygen in the air we breathe—depleted by all the engines of these automobiles and factories. Nothing grows or heals without sufficient oxygen. Without oxygen, there's no life. Do you realize in Pittsburg on a bad day when the sky is black with soot, people have less than twelve percent oxygen to breathe, which is why they're suffocating without realizing it?"

I had to believe his great-great-grandfather Kruger

was running this country with better discernment than he evidently had. Did he really believe he was winning me over, that he was impressing me with his knowledge of America, talking of Chicago in the 20s and Pittsburgh in the 40s like it was today! But he was talking business, so I made the effort not to judge his proposal on its slim merits.

"At Cooper Spirits we pay particular attention to our water source. How do you treat yours?"

"It's excellent mineral water as it is."

"I mean how do you filter it?" I asked.

"There's no need of it, ours is so pure."

"I respectfully must disagree, Mr. Kruger. Unfiltered water is always full of bacteria, including giardia cysts, flukes, nematodes, parasites, ringworm and hookworm, not to mention chlorine, acetone, heavy metals—a deadly chemical cocktail. High quality filtered water, free of contamination, is essential to any beverage partner we could consider."

"It's the same water I've been drinking all my life, and it hasn't killed me yet!" he responded, holding himself as some sort of example, "I'm living proof!"

"Proof of what?" I couldn't help but chuckle aloud. I feared I'd insulted him, but thankfully he laughed with me, then shifted the topic.

"We'd have to be blind not to see how attractive a woman Alicia is, wouldn't we?" he suggested for no good reason. "She makes it hard for friends like us to get to know her, doesn't she?"

"While she's on the ground she must play hard, making up for lost time."

"Friendship and business, aren't they the same thing,

Mr. Cooper? Didn't your guide Mr. Rockefeller once say that a friendship founded on business is a good deal better than a business founded on friendship. What do you think?"

Again, he's fixed on the 20s! First, with the gangsters and their tommy guns, now with John Rockefeller ruling his empire from his headquarters in New York. I suppose they both followed self-serving principles of ironfisted rule, just with different management styles. I was tired of listening to him, and I was ready to walk away, yet I didn't care to make unnecessary enemies. I listened to him, a persistent salesman, trying again to convince me of the wonders of his oxygen-injected sugar water.

"Otto—may I call you that, now that we're friends—I just don't think the Cooper line is compatible with your soft drink.

"Then why did Alicia tell me you needed me for a partner?"

"Perhaps you misheard and that it was you, not me, she needs for a partner! If I were you, I'd find that pretty lady right now!"

He was laughing with me again but evidently was taking my advice about leaving and stood up, closing up his presentation briefcase. He shook my hand and walked away toward the elevator. If he'd finished his business with me, where could he be headed, except to meet up with Alicia? I called after him to wish him luck.

My day had been frustrating. I had meetings with owners and managers in the elusive search for a reasonable prospect, then capped it off with Tembo in my room. I had received Harry's notice of demotion, then I was passed off to Alica, then passed again to her Afrikaner friend Kruger, who apparently wanted to hitch a ride on Cooper's good name. Where did that leave me? Returning to my room for the second time that evening, I repeatedly tried to get the plastic card to admit me. Like many things that day, this didn't make sense, being locked out of my own room! I gave the steel door a kick.

"Leon, don't frustrate yourself," I heard whispered from inside.

"If this is some kind of a joke, you'd better—"

"I'm letting you in right now," Alicia said. She quickly pulled me into my room.

She was wearing my robe, the belt hanging loose, revealing her bare body underneath. Her hair was unpinned and hanging free. Again, she had a plan and was trying to fit me into it. This was a fine irony, my wishing Kruger good luck with Alicia, though apparently, I was the object of her desire.

"I don't want you to have the wrong idea," she started.

"The wrong idea, what would that be?" I asked.

"That I'm a sailor in port, looking for a good time. I'm not one of those quick and easy flight attendants, living for the moment. Forgive me if I've taken you by surprise, but I am not here on my own free will."

"It sounds like you have a problem."

"I sensed from the first how perceptive you are," she said

Immediately she flicked on the television, and what came up was the porn channel Tembo had evidently been watching. "Actually, I could use your advice, Leon."

"My advice, really? You turned Kruger loose on me, rather than stay long enough for me to give it—"

"If I've been negligent, I am full of apologies."

She'd missed the point entirely. I wasn't asking for favors, just trying to figure out what was bothering her. The phone rang, and she rushed across the room, as if expecting it, and answered it on the first ring. She hooked her leg over the desk, stretching like a dancer warming up. Her robe fell away, revealing herself completely to me.

"No, Napu, I'm not busy. Why are you whispering? Is he finally asleep...? Don't worry about me tonight... No, I don't believe Mr. Cooper would mind... Not a problem... I don't care much for hotel rooms anyway, no reason for you to rush..."

She hung up the phone and shifted her weight until she was standing on her left foot and extended her right leg onto the desk. She bent over, touched her head to her knees, leaving nothing to my imagination. She glanced backwards at me in the mirror, enjoying my attention, which she must have taken for male admiration.

"Now I'm confused. I thought Napu went off with her boyfriend to get away from your crowded bunk room."

"If that were the case, if she didn't commandeer the room, would I be here with you now?"

"Alicia, I'm thrilled to have you here. There's no need to explain, not that it would make sense to me."

"You're too kind," she responded quietly.

She had more to show me of herself, pirouettes a full turn to the right, then to the left. She took a bow, fishing again for my approval. Her signals were clear, but I wondered whether I was irresistible to her, or whether she'd come to me for a bigger reason than a place to sleep. Whatever her motivations, she slid into my bed and waited there for me. I slipped beside her, where she lay facing away from me.

"You fell asleep," she said after some time. "I must bore you terribly."

"Hardly boredom, Alicia."

"Hardly?" she asked. "Where would you like me to start?"

It was never my plan to make love to her. I'd been trying to keep a low profile, to keep my stars and stripes folded and not displayed, certainly not to play the industrialist power broker. I then put those reservations out of my mind to concentrate on Alicia herself, who turned out to be a responsive lover. After our initial intersection, she propped herself up on the headboard and turned on the lamp.

"Let me assure you, I don't make a habit of visiting men unexpectedly in their rooms. But for you, I made an exception."

"No need to explain."

"You must understand I'm here not for me, but on account of Napu."

"Alicia, I have no interest in anybody but you."

"Hold on a second. Let me tell you something about Napu. She's of Nilotic stock. Her people are from Kenya, Maasai herders. They are tall and have extraordinary running and jumping ability. The way she proudly carries herself, I see in her a kind of bush nobility, that she could be a chieftain's daughter. One must admire her for rising so far above her origins. We'd be blind not to appreciate her beauty, which I know firsthand she works quite hard to maintain, especially to relax her wooly hair. As a friend, I appreciate the challenges she must face," Alicia elaborated. "But the smoke from her curling iron and the rancid smell from her hair solution makes the room smell quite unpleasant, like Hades! I try to do unto others, etcetera, but don't you agree there is a limit to the sacrifices one is willing to make? I once asked her why she always wants to bunk with me, instead of one of the other black flight attendants. She said she needs to live in close quarters with a white person to understand us, and that I'm the most tolerant white person she knows. Nevertheless, I've reached my limit, Leon, which is why I'm appealing to your sense of fair play and ask you to give me sanctuary. For the sake of peace in the new South Africa, should I really have allowed Napu to eject me from the room, knowing that in my absence she'd be with that man who whisked her away, a virtual stranger who couldn't know her a hundredth part as well as I know you?"

I didn't know how to answer her. Was Alicia trying to convince me, along with herself, that she was colorblind? I didn't care. These South Africans, whatever their background, all seemed to be jockeying for position in the last horse race that was started the day the New South Africa was declared. I'd just as soon have been watching her little drama from a distance. Nevertheless, she convinced me to let her stay with me.

Standing before the mirror bare from the waist up, she brushed her teeth, then checked in the mirror to confirm again whether I was watching. The phone rang and she grabbed it, then handed it to me.

"Hello, Mr. Cooper, are you busy? This is Sunitha.

Are you keeping well? I do not mean to bother you, but I'm calling from the lobby, and we must see you immediately!"

"Leon, if Napu's on the phone, I won't tell her I'm with you, if you won't tell!" Alicia said into my free ear, sitting beside me on the bed, despite my signals to be quiet.

I put my hand over the receiver, hoping Alicia hadn't inadvertently broadcast our encounter, unless it was part of her plan to scare Sunitha away by allowing her to hear the voice of a woman guest in my room. For all of Alicia's charm and sophistication, I got the uneasy feeling this too had been planned.

"Mr. Cooper, I do not mean to interrupt your evening, but please prepare to receive us directly."

"Sorry, but you should stay where you are for now. Bye," I said, then quickly disconnected.

"If that was Napu, I should have spoken with her."

"No, it was Sunitha and somebody else."

"Already you found a new girlfriend?" she teased. "That was quick."

"Not to worry. I think you're more than enough, Alicia," I assured her, kissing her once more.

"I hear you've been traveling with Sunitha during business hours. She's smart, certainly one of the prettiest Indians I've known, a friend of mine."

I was confused by words of faint praise for Sunitha, like her compliments of Napu. Was it her way to see flaws in other attractive women? Or was her pattern to make friends across race lines, then retreat to the Caucasian side as a critical observer? Should I have been concerned how quickly she befriended me, and that soon she'd return to the white tribe village with bad reports about me of the American tribe?

"Even if I'm your intimate friend, Alicia, I'd better be careful what I reveal to you."

"You've revealed enough to satisfy... my curiosity."

She kissed me, then began helping me dress. Another valet, and just a few hours after Tembo's similar assistance! There was no hiding from these unexpected helpers! But in Alicia's case, she was using it as an excuse to tease me, hindering my progress until I gently pushed her aside.

"Well, if you're in such a rush to move on to the next lady, you can zip me up and send me on my way."

"Women who wear zippers shouldn't live alone," I contended.

A hard rap on the door startled me, making me catch her silky skin in the zipper. She stifled a scream.

"We need you now, Mr. Cooper. Hurry!" I heard Hassan through the locked door.

Opening the door to them, Hassan's face was resolute as a Bedouin warrior's. Sunitha looked at me, reading my response.

"By the look on your face, Larabie, whoever's out there isn't your friend," Alicia said.

"I fight for the Chateau with all my blood. Do you know what I mean?"

"I know you like the back of my hand," Alicia said, "but no, I don't know why you've arrived so suddenly, except to scare Mr. Cooper."

"That's not our purpose," Sunitha said.

"Well, what is your purpose?" Alicia asked, giving Hassan a surprising, familiar squeeze of his hand.

"Don't you think I have the right to know anything affecting the Chateau and you?"

"Of course," Sunitha agreed, "which is why I promise to let you know afterward, once we know. Let's go, Mr. Cooper."

"I have no idea what you're into this time," Alicia said to Hassan, looking away from him with a guilty smile.

"Excuse me now," I said, walking Alicia out of my room and down the corridor. "Alicia, I apologize for their unexpected intrusion, but rest assured, I'm not about to leave you alone."

"Don't worry about me," she said. "I've got some accounting homework this evening, which I can do in the lobby. I need to know my figures well enough to worry Colin that I'm smart enough to replace him. You, Leon, I'll figure out later," she said and gave me a long kiss before continuing to the elevator. Without more apologies and without asking her where she planned to stay for the evening, I slipped her my duplicate key card assuring her a place to sleep if she planned to wait up for me later in the evening.

CHAPTER 6
MARAVILLE

"Hassan, why did you bring Sunitha with you if you intended all along to leave her behind with Miss Nichols in the hotel?" I asked as we were driving away from Cape Town.

"I find, Mr. Cooper, if you leave a woman to wait too long, she leaves you for another man. How long do you think she care to stay in the lobby waiting for you, Mr. Cooper? I help you out by bringing Sunitha with me to keep your woman Alicia company. Besides, I thought you was more likely to let me in your room in case you got tired of white meat and want to try dark!" He was blunt and obnoxious and had a lot of nerve to previously barge into my room. I had considered throwing him out, until he convinced me that he would have never interrupted me if it weren't for a very important reason, to introduce me to one of the most powerful men in Cape Town, the one he insisted I meet if I planned to expand Chateau's business into the townships.

I suspected he meant to lure me from my hotel room on some pretext before I commenced an entangling alliance with Alicia, the sister of the Chateau's boss, but was unable to get there in time. But how would he have known our intentions, and who would he be trying to protect? Her from me, or me from her? I found it strange that Tembo, Hassan, Rajesh, Chandra and Sunitha—all Chateau employees—kept such close track of me while their boss seemed to evade me.

"I'm with you now, Hassan, only because you promised not to take me more than half an hour away and for no more than an hour. Where are we?" I asked.

We turned off the highway, passed cranes for loading ships on the waterfront, then drove away from the bay onto the main street of Woodstock. As we waited for a red light, two kids ran towards the car from behind. The third one held something like a hatchet and came at us from the front! Hassan quickly cut the wheel hard left and accelerated toward the last kid, bouncing him off the fender and onto the pavement! A rock shattered the rear window as we escaped these predators!

"They hurt my car because I don't have no protection, only you. Right now, I get my tough boys. Next time we catch street gangsters, we make them pay."

"I don't care if they're gangsters or street kids, count me out!" I insisted as we raced down main street. "I don't want any part of your fight. If you're looking for one, let me out now!"

He concentrated his attention on the rear-view mirror, not on what I was saying, then suddenly stopped at a grocery store. The whole storefront was open to the street, and on the sidewalk were a couple of men at a table with a red and white checkered tablecloth, playing dominoes and smoking pipes.

They seemed glad to see Hassan and followed us to the inside the store. Hassan disappeared to the back room and brought one of the storekeepers, an older man in a white robe with a white beard. Joining them by the counter were a couple of men buying snacks and several younger men whose aquiline noses were identical to the older man's. One of the customers, a workman with grease on his shirt, carefully looked at Hassan's sharp soccer outfit.

"A football player, he looks good to the girls on or off the field. If I wasn't a married man, I'd ask you to spare me a nice one with big bosoms and all her teeth."

"Larabie, do the women like a PAGAD man like you to become a better warrior than you used to be?" asked the workman with the dried wallboard mud on his pants.

"I don't know what you're talking about," Hassan said with a withering glare.

"About the gangsters. You punishing them good?" the workman persisted.

The patriarch of the storekeepers stepped up to the customer questioning Hassan. "It is past our time to close, so you must go home now." The old man then escorted him to the door and locked it behind them.

"We have a flat upstairs over the store and dare not leave it," explained one of the storekeeper's sons, blood splattered ominously on his butcher's apron. "That way if the gangster devils from CORE try to strike again, with Allah's blessing, we're on hand to punish them, whether or not you boys from PAGAD arrive next time to help us."

If I had any doubts about what Hassan was doing when he wasn't on the Chateau's grounds whipping the employees into shape, it was now obvious. He didn't just have friends in PAGAD, but he was an active PAGAD organizer himself. But why? To assist in a religious jihad? As a vigilante in the townships to fight only the thieves, killers, and drug dealers who happened to be black? Or working hard to convince not only the Moslems, but all Cape Town they're fighting a just cause, rather than a self-serving turf war?

"What's CORE anyway, your enemy?" I asked Hassan.

"Not my enemy, but enemy to all poor people with no one to protect them. The CORE boys been raiding them all along, and which we going to crush once and for all!" he said, raised both hands and in turn slapped the hands of his sons.

"CORE's big men still gangsters," said the brother with grape stains on his shirt, "no matter how they try fooling the people that they retired from their gang,"

"But they wasn't fooling Ahmed a couple of days ago," said the patriarch, "when one of them CORE gangsters under their boss man Ozeer was holding up a halal butcher shop."

"What's halal?" I asked. "And I still don't know what CORE means."

"My friend Ebrahim and his sons here and their families only eat the holy halal food because they grow up better Moslems than me," Hassan said. "CORE's no more than a fake name the gangsters call themself for the newspaper, Community Outreach Forum. Before I trust a CORE gangster, I will believe the hyena can lose the spots on his yellow hide!"

"And what about Ozeer?" I asked.

"You have been in our country for some time now, Mr. Cooper," Ebrahim, said to me, stroking his white beard, "and still your friend Larabie Hassan tells you nothing of Ozeer? How could he forget to tell you and that black friend of his how Ozeer and his CORE gang-sters been raiding us here in Woodstock over the past weeks?"

"An enemy may be worse than a friend, but at least he never gives you advice," the older son with the red splattered apron and the rugby jersey replied.

"Ahmad, if I did not know better, I worry right now you forget what I do for you, ever since PAGAD call me to help protect you," Hassan said, poking the brother in the chest. "But if you don't think I'm your friend, better tell me now!"

Rather than answer, Ahmad retreated with his father Ebrahim to another corner of the store, leaving me with the younger brother. Before shaking my hand, he washed his hands, which remained stained blood red afterwards.

"We know you have come to Woodstock to visit your man, Tembo. The people do not understand why you and your rich boss Mr. Nichols place Tembo in the Maraville flats, from which we clean out the CORE gangsters only last spring. We think Tembo's too dan-gerous to leave there, even though you think he safe because he have a black skin. We think you wrong to leave him in danger there. It don't matter to us if Tembo a kaffir like the CORE men, he still your friend, Hassan, and still work for the big man, Mr. Nichols. Don't you worry if they capture him, maybe they think they learn all the secrets of the big wine company, that they make you pay big to get him back? We don't drink alcohol, we don't sell the drugs, and we don't want any more raids in Woodstock."

It was a hard message the young shopkeeper just

delivered, judging by the sweat on his forehead. The father then handed the telephone to his older son and said, "He will call ahead to Maraville to let them know you are on the way. Larabie, you should also leave the American behind and keep him away from us and our troubles, unless you wish them to grow bigger. My wife a good cook, and we take the American home with us tonight, if he like!"

Maybe the father was offering me good advice that Hassan, the PAGAD protector and enforcer, who took me to the townships where he almost killed a thief, was a dangerous man to follow. Even his friends seemed to know he attracted trouble like we had this evening when were ambushed in our car. Now he wanted to lead me to a place his friends were urging him to avoid, especially with me.

"I don't need to go any further tonight," I said to Hassan, once we left the store. "I agree with Ebrahim, I could do you no good in Maraville. You can bring me home now."

Hassan began to laugh. "Easy for him, giving advice. A man who prays four times a day, much better man than you or me. He come from old family of strong holy men, mullahs. In ancient times there was even a caliph, he claims. That is why father Ebrahim has no use for what please a man. That's why he don't want you to see Maraville, because he thinks everyone who live there a prostitute or drink too much. He don't realize we clean up the place nice after the CORE gangsters push on us too hard, but we can never stop pushing them back. If I believed they would come back for trouble at Maraville, Mr. Nichols would never rent a flat there for Tembo. He makes sure our friends there stay happy, and our enemies stay scared. Ebrahim can't make a man like you or me better than we want to be, right?"

That rogue Hassan was again comparing himself to me. Perhaps we were more similar than I cared to admit, and he was more honest than I had reason to believe, or perhaps I had failings I could not see. He seemed to be telling me what he thought I wanted to hear, working to make me his friend, giving me excuses for escorting me to dangerous neighborhoods where he felt above the danger. In any event, I changed my mind about returning to the hotel. I needed to talk to Tembo, if that's where Hassan was taking me.

Off the commercial street, we were now in residential Woodstock. Narrow whitewashed houses with tile roofs stood very close to the streets with groups of young men prowling them. The streets were so narrow Hassan had to drive onto the sidewalk to let another car pass. Dogs were traveling in packs. I heard loud dance music with a thunderous bass before we turned the corner, emanating from an apartment block, the Maraville complex. It was six stories high, and half a city block long, surrounded by a concrete wall, topped by razor wire. Hassan pulled the car to the gate, called ahead to one of the flats, looking nervously behind him. He changed plans and backed onto the street, raced through the narrow streets, then stopped a couple of blocks away from Maraville. Then we waited.

"What did you see? Something scary?" I asked.

"Not sure, but I think it was Sollie and a couple of his boys cruising."

"Do you look for trouble, Hassan, or does it just find you? Let's go home."

"Woodstock is my home, where I was born. We never run from them. Maraville still belongs to us!"

We drove again through Woodstock through serpentine streets. We circled the compound several times before Hassan felt it safe to enter. He spoke into the intercom by the gate, and the steel gate slid back to let us enter. Once inside, we parked under a light close to the front entrance. Now I heard the beat of many drums, reverberating between the building and the compound's perimeter walls. We had taken only a few steps from the car when a glass bottle exploded behind him, then another landed between us. There was laughter from the flats above. On one of the porches a couple was dancing, on another, men were singing, bottles in hand. Directly above us stood three women, one very light, another very dark, and one in-between. The first wore a low-cut sheath; the dark one, a halter top; and the third, a very tight and transparent blouse, and she was the one leaning over the railing and laughing.

"Look out below! Am I too late?" said the light-colored woman in the red sheath.

"Katie Ann, why you home early? Slow night in the shebeens?" Hassan shouted, pointing to the woman in the skimpy blouse. "You aim for me, or you aim for my friend? I should come up and spank you hard, girl!"

The women laughed. "Don't expect to lay your hands on us for nothing, Larabie Hassan! We knew you was on the way and want to make sure you don't pass us by. Bring your American friend up so we can show him something."

"Nothing I haven't seen before. Not interested!" I shouted in my own defense.

"Katie Ann's a funny girl," Hassan said to me, "the prettiest woman ever to live here at Maraville. Used to be dark and dirty, now this place nice and clean. Still, Tembo better be careful leaving her here with all these hungry men like you and me."

Again, someone was comparing himself with me and trying to bring me down to his own level. Perhaps I had too good an opinion of myself, or one too critical of him. I wished I could cut him loose. I now heard loud arguing, echoing from one of the flats. From another, there wafted sweet-smelling weed smoke; yet from another, hip-hop music from America! If they were listening to our music, then I hoped they would like things American enough to allow me safe passage.

We walked up a concrete stairway, open to the weather, from which I could see the ship cranes on the wharf and the lights of Cape Town. When we passed some young men on the stairs, one quickly threw something into a paper bag, while another stuffed a wad of cash in his pocket.

"Asief, you best be more careful." Hassan chided, slapping the shoulder of the one taking the money. "Just because this is Maraville don't mean you can get away with murder."

"No one got hurt that bad since last year," said the one with the bag. "This is a good place for us boys to meet now."

"We don't think so," Hassan said. "Good thing I see you in the hallway before the police come. If you don't pay rent, you don't belong here."

The three of them studied him with a combination of anger, respect, and apology. None of us spoke. I heard an African percussion echoing the same fast beat as my heart, and then a woman's hard accelerating panting, the sound which was making the three men laugh and slap hands, including Hassan's.

"Larabie wants us to stay here at Maraville because the landlord's Ighaam," said the young man now holding the wad of cash in his pocket. "You want us to pay the money for a flat here, because it really goes to PAGAD, where you get your cut."

"A cut—that would be great for me!" Hassan shouted. "Now I know why I must still work so hard for so little, Asief, because you have neglected to tell Ighaam Arendse that he owes me a cut! Mr. Arendse must be forgetting about me, leaving me a poor hard-working man. Now could you help me find him and remind him to pay me a wage so I can afford a wife!"

The men looked at one another, laughing again. Another joke in which I didn't care to be involved, any more than I did in Hassan's disputes. I backed away, drawn by curiosity to the heavy breathing of a woman. Nearby, there was a door fully open with iron bars separating me from them. By the light of a candle, I could see her white legs wrapped around him, his dark back undulating in synch with her.

From behind I was pulled by my collar away from the burglar bars and shoved against the wall. I shook myself free, infuriated to see it was Hassan's hands on me.

"I've had it with you, Hassan! I've seen more than enough! Take me back downtown right now!"

"Not now," he whispered, "but soon. We must wait until that girl finish this round, then we can say hello. She knows important people you need to know if you want to do business with people like me who can travel where no one else you know dares go."

"I don't know where you and the Kassies get the idea I want to have anything to do with Gazelle or any beer, for that matter," I hissed back.

"Because you come here for the money, and you make more money with poor people drinking beer than the few who afford to drink Chateau wine."

Hassan was a rough and dangerous character, someone I was reluctant to trust, yet unquestionably he knew this territory. On one hand I was demanding he take me back to my posh hotel. On the other, I had to agree that I couldn't afford to dismiss this huge market, unlike Chateau's market, especially since I hadn't gained traction in negotiations with Ted Nichols for a joint venture with their winery. It left me in a compromised position—waiting for Hassan's friends to finish their lovemaking! The woman's moans and cries seemed to build, and I was uneasy being where I don't belong, while Hassan continued mugging grins and obscene gestures synchronized to their mating noises.

"I think she's done giving it to him," Hassan said once they went quiet and extinguished their candle. "Let's wait to see our man Tembo after he gets off her... You think they wipe themselves clean by now?"

Hassan let me pass first through their barred door, then closed it behind us with the clunk of a prison door. Immediately the room lights came on, revealing the master of the house, Tembo. He led me to the best chair in the flat, the easy chair of honor in the living room, from which I had a direct view into the darkened bedroom. In the spillover light I saw his lover, slipping into her skimpy pastel blouse. Crossing the threshold toward us, I saw that she was one of the women who had dropped the bottles on us! How could she have gotten from the porch to her position underneath Tembo so fast? And why? For recreation or for money? It was none of my business.

"You look like you never saw me before," she said. "Do I look so different when you were looking up at me than face-to-face?"

I believe she was enjoying my confusion, as well as the attention of men in general. She leaned first over Hassan to me, giving me the opportunity to see her brown nipples as she shook my hand.

"I'm Katie Ann Arendse," she introduced herself to me.

"Arendse?" I asked, "Any relation to the landlord of this compound, the Arendse that Hassan wants me to meet?"

"Larabie, did Mr. Arendse give you permission to talk about him to Mr. Cooper?" Tembo asked.

"If you must know, Mr. Cooper," Katie Ann said, "I am Ighaam's cousin, and I help him out when he is short-handed."

I couldn't sort out the truth from half-truths from outright lies anymore! Was everyone in this compound a hustler of some kind? Was Maraville really a fortress for their mutual protection? What kind of work would this woman be doing for her cousin Ighaam, who seemed to scare Tembo and whom I had yet to meet? And what was the intention of these two new visitors who had just shown up, the woman in the red sheath and her companion with the halter top?

"Are you here for the shebeen queen," Hassan asked them, "or is one of you ladies looking to entertain Mr. Cooper?"

"Larabie," Katie Ann said to her friends, "if you insult us anymore, we be of no service to you when you need some!"

"I do not speak to Katie Ann, who is a lady, but to you two. Are you visiting because it has been a slow night, or because you wish to keep Mr. Cooper and me company?"

"We are in no rush," the woman in the red sheath said, wedging herself in with me on my easy chair, stroking my leg.

"Just because you have blonde hair does not mean that Mr. Cooper has time for you!" Tembo said harshly to the white-skinned woman. "He comes here for business with me, not with you!"

"A rude kaffir, isn't he?" she mumbled so I could hear, but not Tembo.

People like her on the Cape were mostly descended from European sailors and lonely for women. Four-hundred years later, on the surface they could act colorblind, but it didn't take much for them to show their race differences and stake out their territory. This white woman in red smiled, leaned back in the easy chair, and waved Tembo closer. In an instant she coiled her legs and launched him across the room into Hassen with a two-legged shove, apparently petty revenge taken on Tembo for his insult. Katie Ann and the blue-black woman in the halter top guffawed as Tembo picked himself up from the floor. The white woman left her chair and pressed herself against me.

"Don't believe that son-of-a-whore Hassan," she whispered. "No need to be ashamed if you care to take me out to dinner. I'm Felicia. Remember my name, Leon, Mr. Friction-Free man!"

I didn't mind if this lady of the night called me by my first name without knowing me, but as the friction-free man? She must have heard that from Hassan, or perhaps Raj. My business reputation had preceded me, with the help of my brother, no doubt. He had never made the effort to understand what friction-free commerce means, yet his rumors managed to label me a practitioner of voodoo business theory, even to these prostitutes!

We left Tembo's flat in search of Ighaam Arendse. Climbing the stairs, I tripped on something soft, a rat!

"He can't hurt you no more," Hassan said.

"Forget this! I'm calling it a night!"

"I am ashamed for you to see the way these people live like animals!" Tembo shouted.

"Don't complain, Tembo," Hassan replied. "They don't have running water or a doctor or shoes or enough to eat in your black homeland in Lesotho. Don't forget where you come from, or how to stay away from that starvation!"

"You are right. Maraville is far better," Tembo said. He picked up trash strewn about a garbage pail and slammed the lid down upon it. "We're very sorry we forgot to do a proper clean-up before you arrive."

"Now I take you to the nicest spot in Maraville, Mr. Arendse's penthouse," Hassan said. He was blocking my way back downstairs in case I changed my mind and wanted to escape. Being close to Hassan, I imagined I was touching a lightning rod in a storm. He attracted danger, potentially lethal. I didn't want to be there with him.

"You still don't understand. Count me out."

"Okay, one hundred percent, but first we go to the penthouse. Mr. Arendse would be very angry if I forget to say hello this evening. I'm his man on the street. He gets news about the Gazelle plant from me, understand?"

Was he telling me he had to report to this gang boss in his bunker? Pieces of the Gazelle puzzle were coming together. Ted intended to work with the Kassies, assuming he'd already bought into their beer label. Evidently Hassan was Ted's point man in this project to break into the lucrative township beer market. But why was Hassan now reporting to the gang boss about the Gazelle workers' strike? Did Ighaam get rakeoffs from the shebeens in his territory?

We climbed to the fifth floor of Maraville. Built on the roof was a masonry single-story structure. Its tile roof was similar in appearance to the neighboring houses. Completing the illusion of a freestanding home on its own plot were a lawn statue of a classic nude and wooden recliners on a carpet of manmade turf. A few couples were dancing to American band music from the World War II era.

Hassan faced me, turning his back towards the men. "They don't know you yet, so not a good idea to look at them too hard."

"Why? They think I'm the law coming after them?"

"The police?" he laughed. "There aren't many of

them in the new South Africa, not in our neighborhoods. That's why we take care of our own. Let me
introduce you, before they take you for someone who
don't belong at this party."

Hassan turned to them. "Mr. Cooper here's a friend of
Mr. Nichols. I want you to meet Mr. Moegamat Mongrel
and Mr. Mikah Booley. These gentlemen Mr. Arendse
trust with his life. Any trouble tonight, boys?"

"You the one with the troubles," Booley said. He had
a tattoo of a warship on his forearm. "We have no
troubles up here, but down on the street, the bad boys
make us trouble."

"Yes, Hassan was telling me how your group fights
them all the time," I said.

"Our group?" questioned Mongrel. "If he told you of
the Ighaam Boys, Hassan digs his own hole."

"Not to worry, everyone knows about PAGAD already."
Hassan reassured.

Mongrel had a dense, oily beard of red hair and a
stocky body. Orange freckles covered his face, neck and
arms. He deliberately dropped the ash of his cigarette
on Hassan. Booley and Mongrel laughed at Hassan's
attempt to put out the live ash by beating it with
his cap. A gray-haired man appeared, about sixty and
dressed in different shades of white. The two men stood
stiffened, as if coming to attention.

"You need me to do something, baas?" Booley asked
attentively.

The man pointed to the far side of the roof, where
the party was continuing in earnest, then looked at
his watch. "Time for them to go home. See to it these
people leave now."

"Mr. Ighaam Arendse, Mr. Leon Cooper," Hassan introduced me to this man giving the orders. I noticed he was carrying a green camouflage bag.

Mongrel and Booley broke up the party, escorting straggling guests out as instructed. The boss stared and circled me, inspecting front and back. He shook my hand, then draped his arms over our shoulders escorted Hassan and me to a quiet corner of his roof domain.

"Nice view from here," I said, as we looked toward the sea from the penthouse, his center of operations.

"On a clear day you can see a fishing boat fifty kilometers away, to the curve of the earth," Ighaam Arendse said. "We have pleasant breezes on even the hottest summer evenings. Big winds move from Devil's Peaks. See?" Behind us was a mountain wall rising above Woodstock.

The winds stay calm now," Tembo added. "They pass between those two peaks, horns of the devil, zoom through Maraville to Table Bay then to open sea. In winter, if you walk on the Foreshore, which the Europeans stole from the sea by filling it, the winds race fast enough to knock over a man who don't have his feet on the ground."

"Tembo, you sound very wise. Mr. Nichols should be as impressed with you as I am. But tell me, Hassan, why you bring Tembo to me tonight?"

"We need him for the black districts in Lotus River and Bel Har where we're not ready to fight with CORE."

"Tembo," Ighaam Arendse said, "we're neighbors in this building, ever since Mr. Nichols installed you in the flat so you could be nearby when PAGAD needs you."

"Thank you for your confidence, Mr. Arendse," Tembo said.

"I also understand you've become close with my niece Katie Ann. But I don't think it would be such a good idea to bring her into your bed again. Not ever."

"It was her idea, sir, not mine, I promise you. But I do as you wish," Tembo said tersely. "Now if you'll excuse me, I am returning to my bed alone, you will be happy to know," he said and left us.

"Mr. Cooper, you and Hassan came too late for the party, unfortunately," the boss said. We were alone except for Mongrel and Booley. "So, what business have you?"

"Mr. Arendse," Hassan said. "You know from Mr. Nichols about the fighting at the Gazelle plant. Tomorrow, I tell you who makes the trouble. Tonight, we just come for a quick hello and goodnight from Mr. Cooper."

Arendse signaled Hassan to be quiet. He removed a pair of military night vision binoculars from his case and inspected the streets below. He handed them to me, and I saw three young men and the stream of passersby stopping to speak with them and make handoffs.

"I wish I could see what they're trading. Not many streetlights work because the boys shoot them out. They're amateurs, waiting for police to sweep them off the street," Ighaam remarked. "These small-time crooks come into our neighborhood and trade! They think we don't know. We will keep our eyes on them until we can sweep them off our streets."

I didn't dare ask him what was being traded by his opponents on the street, any more than I'd ask him what his partisans were trading in the stairwells of compound he controlled. I wondered whether PAGAD's talk about stopping the black gangsters' drug trade was really intended at eliminating competition for the same market!

"I've never seen anything like these heavy field glasses."

"Never? Were you never in the American army? This is genuine U.S. Army surplus for finding your enemy in the dark. I like American goods, though they can be too dear for us in South Africa. That is why Ted Nichols and me want to trade with an American like yourself, Mr. Cooper."

"I was wondering what you had in mind," I said. "Is that all you want?"

"It's not what I want, Mr. Cooper, because I'm nobody, just a friend of Hassan's. It should only matter what Hassan's and your boss Mr. Nichols want, now that you've become his consultant. First, you must help replace the Indians still running the Gazelle brewery with South Africans."

What did he think of me, I wondered. Was I being more fool than savior, an accomplice to push the Kassies out of their lifetime business? I understood why Ted Nichols would want to get into beer, a larger market than his upper end wines. But why would he want to bring in Ighaam with Hassan as his man on the street, unless for the same reason they'd installed Tembo, for access to townships and neighborhoods they could never crack by themselves?

"I don't know if I can be of help to you, Mr. Arendse."

"Of course, you don't. Not yet. Not until you see we are your best hope. We can do a good business together friction-free, American way." He handed me the bin-oculars again. "Do you see Mongrel standing by that little Morris with the fat tires? He's waiting to take you home."

"I have someone waiting for me. I already have a ride with Hassan."

"Hassan? I'd like to keep him here to learn how much damage the troublemakers did to the Gazelle plant, and what can be done to fix it. But, if you need him more than I do tonight, let him carry you to the nice place you came from. Go away before Maraville swallows you, but don't forget to visit us again here in the eagle's nest."

It seemed less like an eagle's nest, more vulture's nest. I was glad to leave this dangerous place before someone had the opportunity to pick my bones clean. I had no plans to return anytime soon.

CHAPTER 7

SUNITHA

Mafumo, the man who had contaminated the Kassies' beer, was on a ladder. With a rope he was taking a sample from the batch when he lost his balance, slipped and fell into it. Though he had no way to pull himself up the high walls, he managed to stay afloat for a day and a night. When the Ozeer gang heard their man Mafumo was in the vat, they rescued him, alive against all odds, and brought him to the care and safety of their shebeen.

It was early Sunday evening, and I had dozed off into a dream of Mafumo. When I came back to reality, Chandra was standing before me in my room in the Inter-Continental. He was staring at me without speaking, just as he had that morning at the Bergkloof Inn. Over the last few months, I'd laid the groundwork for a South African presence for Cooper, though my progress had been slower than the home office would have preferred.

"Mr. Cooper, you're having a nightmare! Wake up!" Chandra said, shaking me. "You are smiling so perhaps it wasn't a nightmare, but a pleasant dream about Alicia?"

"Alicia?" I echoed him, half-awake but clearing my head. "What are you doing here, Chandra? Why are you people always breaking in my room?"

"Leon, I am an honest man. You may check my pockets."

"I'm not calling you a thief, but tell me why you're here unannounced?"

"Because I'm your guide, and so I must stay close to you. Your workday is over, and now you have time to go visiting."

"I'm afraid not. No thanks."

"Does our country frighten you after dark?" Chandra laughed, speaking the truth precisely. "I would not take you away from your comfortable quarters if I did not have a problem to solve in my family. I need your help, please."

"Help with Rajesh?"

"Rajesh, yes. Nighttime he now lives at the plant, defending it with his friends. It is in the dark that Ozeer's gangsters prefer to vex him."

The Kassies have been at a low-grade war for so long, fear had become a way of life for them. I let him know he was right, that evenings I preferred not to stray too far from home base. Did he wish me to confess that I was braver than I was, that I had no intention to allow fear to overcome me, that I could travel through their urban war zone with no cares? The truth was to be effective I could never let their battles become mine.

"You people are full of strange requests. Remember a few months ago when Hassan and Sunitha barged in on me unannounced? That night I let him take me to Maraville? Do you have any better reason than they did why I should go with you tonight?"

"Yes, to help me with Sunitha. She's a fine girl. In the old days, elders such as myself would have gladly chosen her for Raj, but now young people marry for love, whatever that means. Rajesh does not realize the spirit of love that once existed between them has flown away. With all the troubles at Gazelle I truly believe my son has grown too crazy for loving. That is why I ask you to take the time to see what she truly needs, now that my son occupies himself against nighttime attacks against the plant, and even our home."

"You said it was Ozeer harassing him, but I've never even seen him and don't really see what I can do to help you."

"For tonight, you forget about Ozeer. He has been a danger to anyone doing business without his permission in the townships he controls. Rajesh doesn't listen to me that he can never come to a good end fighting such a man, especially with just his few allies. Instead, I am asking you to help me with Sunitha who I regard like a daughter, and for who there is much hope with your help, sir."

Had Chandra not been indispensable in orienting me to this strange world, I never would have gone with him at night to Valhalla Park to intervene in family troubles. Our destination was a house with a fence of rusty spikes set on a masonry wall. The patterned ceramic tiled porch floor had many black spaces, like missing teeth.

"If we had only made plans in advance, I could have arranged a fine Indian dinner."

Sunitha was struggling with the heavy steel door until Chandra assisted her, and we could enter. The last time I saw her outside of work, she invited herself into the room where I was with Hassan. Between her and the Kassies and Tembo and Hassan, I felt like a ball tossed about in a perplexing game that only they seemed to understand, with Ted Nichols and Ighaam Arendse as the referees!

"It smells very sweet here," I remarked as she took my jacket, then loosened my tie.

"What do you think of my new rented quarters?"

"It's too early to tell."

"Sunitha," Chandra said, "you know I do not approve of your move here. I don't think you should be here alone."

"Where else can I go? Aunt Giri and I are not speaking, and I had to leave her house."

"That is not for me to decide. I promised to let her know that you're safe," Chandra said.

Sunitha led me into the dining room, but Chandra didn't follow any further than the entry. Without further explanation, he left us alone and actually drove off without telling me when I could expect his return. I felt like I'd been abandoned on a life raft on the high seas!

Again, anxiety intruded. I had to make the best of this chance to meet Sunitha in her own environment. She picked out some leaves from a brass bowl, held them so I could smell them, then chewed them one by one.

"This is what you must have first noticed," she said. "Most people find these pan leaves pleasing to the nose."

"You snack on those leaves often?"

"I find the leaves soaked in rose water help digestion, as tonight when I grew concerned that you and Chandra might change your minds and decide not to visit, Mr. Cooper."

"Please call me Leon."

"Leon then."

It was strange that Chandra went to all this trouble

to bring me here and leave me alone with Sunitha. Was it a setup? I tried not to show my hand but was again feeling manipulated. She took me to the front room lit by a couple of candles and offered me a heavy wooden chair with a straight back and high arms. I faced an odd bronze figure, nearly life-size, a bizarre representation of a man split into several poses, seated cross-legged with extra arms, palms forward, and shiny eyes, polished smooth. For some reason, I imagined a third black stone eye, set within the bronze head. I felt energy coming through his eyes and energy that passed from my eyes back into his! I stared at this cast god until Sunitha very quietly returned, startling me.

"You must have a great deal on your mind," she said, kneeling and placing a calming hand on my arm. "You might wish to share your concerns, if you decide it's in your best interests to trust me."

"I must admit ever since I've arrived in your country, my mind has been uneasy."

"We are all uneasy here in South Africa. Let me show you," she said.

To make her point, Sunitha took me out of the house and onto the front porch. She poked a broom into a hole in the front wall, knocking out some loose stucco, then pulled off the plywood replacing the glassless window above it. With a cautious sweep of her eyes up and down the street, she stepped from her vulnerable porch to the gate, and locked us inside behind the burglar bars, then dead bolted the warped inner door, similar to the way the tenants at Maraville did to secure their flats.

"Yes, I quite agree," I concurred, "though you, no doubt, have greater reason."

"You are studying me very hard for a reason," she said knowingly.

Sunitha looked at me with curiosity. She had apparently taken care to prepare herself for this evening. She wore a transparent dark lace shawl on her head, which matched her saffron sari, and a golden comb in her hair. Gold pins secured a gold ribbon intertwined with jade beads that complemented her green eyes.

"The butterfly breaks from the cocoon. Today you're a golden girl. You look quite different from your workday. Quite interesting."

"I'm nothing special," she demurred, looking away, "This traditional Indian chignon style must seem peculiar to you."

"You've surrounded yourself with so much mystery, and I'm looking for some answers."

"Enlightenment is posing questions. It is only after we pass from this life that we can approach the source of all answers."

"Then our life here on earth doesn't matter as much as the one afterwards? Forgive me if I don't understand what this bronze Buddha means, although I must admit, I am now feeling his energy."

"Not Buddha, but Brahma, the central power and the life force of the universe into which Buddha wished to merge. The Buddha was a man, a great student of the Brahma before us, an enlightened man who worked through all his life on earth to lift the veil of delusion so that his spirit could meet the Brahma."

"Then is that why you've placed your masterpiece in such a prominent place in your home? To guide you safely to the next world?"

"This Brahma belongs to my Aunt Giri Bala, and she insisted I bring it to protect me from my folly!" Sunitha spoke with a fierceness I had never seen before. "My Aunt has much faith in Brahma. On the other hand, Rajesh has always hoped I would worship the Vishnu that he feels so strongly resides in his karma."

"And what does Vishnu do?"

"He walks with long strides across this earth. He is so big and destructive he walks over little creatures, including men, and crushes them to death. You must understand believing in Vishnu is very unlike your cold Western beliefs. He is passionate and often assumes the shape of a man's lingam."

She felt at ease, the way she placed her hand on my arm. She was always one to speak her mind in the workplace, never one to win favor by holding back problems needing to be addressed. I appreciated this straightforward style in a country full of mirages and deceptions. I doubted she would speak with such familiarity with a man she didn't trust. Sunitha was a beauty with a gentle heart. She'd won me over in part, I suppose, because her Indian bearing seemed exotic and charming to my western eyes. She poured us a first-class Chateau Drakenstein Pinotage wine, the estate's specialty.

"Raj gets along well with Aunt Giri. She's like the mother he lost, and I suppose he's like the son she never had."

"That sounds like a good arrangement for Chandra as well, for the three of you." I raised my glass. "To an international friendship! Too bad Raj isn't here to join you."

"I must confess, Leon, I don't think about Rajesh outside the office."

"That's good, separating home from work," I agreed. "You don't understand. I have no further interest in Rajesh. If only my aunt felt the same way! I wonder whether Auntie cares more for him as the son she never had than for myself. Rajesh told her he wants me to uphold the tradition of a submissive wife, since Aunt Giri upholds many traditions she feels I've abandoned. I have learned much from her, but we have little in common except our blood. You see, she has not forgotten her connection to the wealthy landowners on her side of the family in India. She is from the old school and does not approve of my modern ways."

Sunitha was moody. She was speaking boldly and assertively, now that she was away from the brewery. She complained I didn't pay attention as she recited differences with her aunt, whom I'd never met! She was eager to hear my opinion, then had little patience to hear from me, unless I completely agreed with her. Maybe I was reading too much into her hot and cold behavior. Rather than at me, she was looking out the window distracted by the fireworks exploding down the street. She stepped away and I moved the curtains back for a better look, but she pulled me back.

"Please, you must remain inside with me."

"Are you worried about my safety?"

"I am not saying you need to worry, but you are not used to our customs, and that requires more caution than you probably used where you came from. If you walk where you shouldn't at night your pale skin might make an easy target. Please forgive me for inviting you to this danger zone. I assure you I am here not intentionally, but due to circumstances."

She was speaking of her reduced circumstances, since she'd been ejected from her aunt's home. An Indian woman living by herself in this war zone—if not terrified, she wasn't paying attention! Because I too had been cut off from my home, I understood her loneliness. In the States I made a point of not socializing with the employees after office hours. Here the rules were different. My relationships with Tembo, Hassan, and Alicia didn't have neat borders, no more than did my relationship with Sunitha, whom I found quite attractive. But I had to be sensible and remember how little we had in common.

"I assure you, it's not necessary to explain your home life to me, Sunitha."

"As a businessman, do you wish I didn't have to report to you at work?"

"Not at all. I regard you as a friend."

"I'm pleased our association is more than business!"

She drew herself close to me. She was a classically symmetric beauty, with white teeth, full lips, and a graceful neck.

"I have something sweet for you, Leon," she said, going to the kitchen.

When I opened the window, I heard a volley of gunshots, no more than a few blocks away. These were not fireworks, not a children's game, but an armed battle! If Chandra figured this neighborhood was safe for Sunitha, it was safe for me. Or maybe he realized it wasn't safe and hoped I'd somehow rescue her! Had I known I'd need some tough guy escort, I wouldn't have allowed myself to be stranded with a woman in this fragile outpost. But unlike her, I had the option to leave. I also held a return ticket that would take me out of this country once I'd completed my mission retraining Ted Nichols' crew to run an expanded, more profitable business.

With another explosion the lights went out. Sunitha signaled me to follow her to the kitchen, closed the doors to the front room, then lit a candle.

"We mustn't let them know we're here," Sunitha whispered, keeping the front room dark. I agreed that the back of the flat would be safer.

She entertained me by candlelight in this bunker, taking a bowl of prepared dough from the refrigerator. She molded tiny pancakes, fried them in a pan, then served them melted in butter.

"These loochis cakes are best served hot off the fire," she said.

"That's how I feel, under fire," I laughed, eating the sweet treat.

"I've grown up under fire, Leon, living in my aunt's house. She has never judged the Kassies badly for their brewery business, simply because they are men. However, she has judged me harshly since I began working there, not believing it's proper work for a respectable Indian woman. Over the last few years, she deluded herself, believing Raj would marry me and rescue me from Gazelle."

Sunitha wasn't simply an ambitious working woman, content with her life in a traditional Indian home run by her widowed aunt. She never had any intention of marrying Rajesh. From what Chandra told me, she was ejected from her Aunt Giri's home for defying her wishes that she lead a more conventional life than an assistant manager of a brewery. But primarily because she had backed away from marriage to Rajesh. Yet it seemed an extreme measure to exile herself to Valhalla Park to avoid family acquaintances who might criticize and condemn her, unless she hadn't enough money to pay rent in a better neighborhood. I heard more gunshots that seemed closer than before.

A shot hit a lamp on the porch, shattering its glass. I dropped to the floor, pulling Sunitha down with me. She looked nonplussed as I crawled across the kitchen to avoid becoming a target if we were being watched. She intercepted me.

"Please don't be afraid. Tonight, we are here together," she said.

I followed her downstairs where she lit a votive candle beside the bed, then quickly placed a plywood board over the sole basement window.

"Had Hassan told me of all these distractions, I would not have chosen to live in these quarters, although it costs me nothing to stay here. Few of the houses have basements, only the ones belonging to the gangsters such as this one, which Hassan believed would be more secure for me."

"Hassan's told me nothing of this arrangement! Why has he led you here and abandoned you?"

"He has my interests in mind. We are like his family, and he visits every day directly after I return from Gazelle while it is still light. Before dark falls there is usually little mischief, but tonight is worse than usual. I would not want to alarm him that this house of his friend's was in danger. Valhalla has been calm until recently."

"What friend? What about your danger?"

She did not respond, turning her back to me. She lit

another candle, revealing a ceramic statue of a man cross-legged, his joined hands folded low in his lap, similar to the bronze Brahma upstairs.

"Let me help you," I said, helping her lift the wooden god off the stool where he sat.

"Then is this man the Buddha?" I asked, lowering him to the floor. She shook her head yes. "So does that make you a Buddhist or a Hindu?"

"There's more light on this side of the room," she said, bringing the stool beside the bed where she was sitting. "If you want to know what I am, I can explain. The difference between a Christian, such as yourself, and me is perspective. Until very recently, you Christians would torment people who believed the earth was not the center of the universe. We Hindus have always seen a bigger picture of an infinitely large universe which will endure forever. But all creation must pass through cycles of four billion earth years. Each cycle begins with Vishnu lying asleep on a thousand-headed cobra. But I see in your smile my belief seems quite fantastic."

Upstairs, I was paying more attention to the gun-shots than to an explanation of her beliefs. But down here with the shots muffled by the concrete walls, my interest in spiritual matters was focused.

"Perhaps I'm grinning because you amuse me, or else because I have a gallows' humor, or maybe because you are tickling my feet."

"Shall I stop?" she asked, lifted her fingers, pausing the massage she started. "I feel a great deal of tension within you, Leon, passing through your feet. You are a man presenting a brave face to the world, though under-neath your calm exterior you have a great deal of anger or passion. It's too early for me to fully comprehend you. If I amuse you, perhaps it is because you do not believe I can feel your spirit travel through your limbs."

"But I still don't know if you worship Brahma, Vishnu, or Buddha. Are these all Hindu gods?"

"It's no use," she said, "In the short time we are allowed, I cannot put the pictures in my mind into words to share with you."

I'd been presumptuous to ask her to explain her faith to me. I hadn't been in a church since our Uncle Timothy died, and my brother and I were expected to attend his elaborate funeral and reception. I wished I knew how to pray. Unlike her, I believed I could call someone to get me out of this place. I felt a responsibility to Sunitha to bring her to safety. As I touched my cell phone for Chandra or a cab or anyone to come for us, she brought my stool closer so that she could take my feet to manipulate my toes.

"I sense you are uneasy and wish to leave," she said. "If you can't find Chandra, you can call one of your drivers to take you safely away from my danger and myself. Be careful not to make the wrong decision."

For an uncomfortable minute I was immobilized and didn't move. She seized the moment and pushed me gently onto the bed, extended my legs and propped up my torso with pillows. She seated herself beside me, held my right hand and looked intently into my eyes.

"I want you to know I come here in friendship, nothing more," I explained.

"No apologies necessary. You needn't stay longer, unless you care to know more about the energy traveling through you."

"I'm listening," I responded.

"No, right now you're too distracted by fear to listen well. I feel negative energy passing through your hand into mine. Would you prefer I release you?"

I paused, considering. This delay encouraged her. With her free hand she continued examining me, moving to the toes on my left foot, one by one.

"I feel, Leon Cooper, you are very literal-minded, yet you would also like to follow your dreams. For some time now, before South Africa, you've convinced yourself you can sleep soundly without dreams. That is because you have willed yourself to forget them very quickly after you awaken. While conscious, you let fear overcome your dreams, fear of failing, not meeting your brother's challenge."

I realized I'd been entangled within an invisible web of gossip, which seemed to cling to me no matter where I went. She must have heard these details of my life from Raj and Chandra, who gathered their news from Ted Nichols and Alicia, and who in turn had received their biased reports from the ultimate source, my brother. Or else she was throwing out to me indisputable yet universal cliches, using them to encourage me to talk about myself.

"My appearance may be misleading you," I said, not caring to reveal too much more about myself.

"Once again, Leon, you are free to leave," she said. She released her grip on me, then stood up and tugged at me until I stood before her. "Or you may wish to let me help you tap into your source."

This was the second time she'd suggested we part company. I didn't believe she'd be so ready to eject me if I hadn't hurt her feelings. Did she really want to get rid of me? I couldn't tell for sure. She turned away from me, opening the door of this bedroom, and stood between it and the Buddha, waiting for my decision.

"Return to my source—like I'm the Nile River and you're an explorer, looking for my headwaters?" I asked.

"No, I see you as you really see yourself, a soul who does not know where to rest. Is that why you seem uncomfortable here with me?"

"Sunitha, with all due respect, this isn't appropriate between us. I come from the other side of the world. I've been away from home long enough to feel lonely for a woman from time to time."

For as long as I'd known her, I hadn't detected any hint of pride or arrogance. Maybe she was trying to reverse the roles between us, leading me to forget that at work she would still have to report to me, regarding Gazelle business.

"Although you are not happy, you are smiling." she said. She sat down by me on the bed. "The Man-lion and the Dwarf battle within you."

We lingered in conversation, and she answered my questions about her faith—Vishnu, Shiva, and more. She was knowledgeable—and beautiful—and seemed in earnest to probe my soul.

I heard more gunshots, the closest ones so far. Her hands locked on mine, an instinctive reaction. Rather than show my fear, I accepted her invitation to stay and pulled her toward me on the bed. She tasted very sweet. At first, I thought it was the petals sweetened in rosewater she'd placed on her tongue, followed by the pancakes she fried. They were kisses unlike any I had experienced in a long time.

I really didn't belong in her house, any more than she belonged in this neighborhood; a double mistake that I found myself stranded with her. I had to set matters straight with her.

"Sunitha, there's one thing you must know about me: don't think because I come from America, and I know how to handle employees and money for the Cooper Company, that I am well off."

"I care little for this life's material rewards, Leon."

"Let's forget about business for now. What I'm trying to say is I prefer not to operate under false pretenses."

"Operate as a doctor would with a sharp knife?"

"Look, Sunitha, I don't know how you see me, but I may not be as I appear!"

"I see you as you may become in the journey past this life."

She was looking at me again with a detached smile I couldn't read, then placed a quick kiss on one ear. Then she handed me the cell phone which I still hadn't used to call for my ride out of her neighborhood.

"I have a lot of work to do for you, but you might not be ready right now."

I didn't understand.

She lifted the window board to listen outside. "The gangsters may have settled their differences or else run out of ammunition. I sense you are restraining your-self from fleeing the danger of this district. But this puzzles me. Why does Hassan call you the Chief of the Shebeens?"

I wasn't there as a missionary, but more as a

mercenary on an ambitious expansion assignment for which I didn't volunteer. I had no need to explain Cooper's master plan to her, not yet, but I couldn't leave before learning whether she really knew as much about me as she'd have me believe.

"In case you haven't guessed, I'm not here to save the world, just to reorganize you people to work more efficiently."

"It will be good for Mr. Nichols and the Kassies, and even Hassan, that you share your knowledge with them. They are lucky to have a fine American manager. I do worry about the moral price we will pay to build a first-world business machine."

My brother and my father would avoid bringing management into discussions with employees about policy, yet that was what I was doing with Sunitha. I noticed though instead of honoring the confidence I'd placed in her, she used it to make an indirect complaint against American-style business.

"I'm here to teach you how to build a better rat trap, unless you prefer that I return home with my plans and let the rats continue multiplying, attacking and eating your rations until you starve."

"I'm more interested in learning more about you, Leon, than you've already shared with me." She took my hands in hers and positioned herself in the bed, sitting crossed-legged, similar to her god.

Since coming to South Africa, I had probably revealed more to her than was prudent. If she wanted to analyze me, to meditate with me, or to call up dead souls in a seance of some kind, throwing caution to the wind I decided I'd be her subject!

"You've led me to believe your company is running you through the ringer and that you're doing penance to them for losing money. You have a great deal to prove to them. You are a soldier shipped to a land not of your choosing and that you must return with a medal, or else die."

"It's not as desperate as all that," I disagreed.

"But we are speaking truthfully, aren't we? I can stop if you wish," she paused. "You are proud and sensitive and expect loyalty from those close to you. On the other hand, it is difficult because you see as betrayals what others would take as slights. Nor do you suffer well the company of fools, though you must often do business with them and hide your displeasure. Right now, you are not too pleased with me. First, although you try to be democratic, you see me as a woman from a lower caste. Secondly, you think because our distance from one another is so great, I am bothersome."

"No, to the contrary, you give me much to think about."

"Let's set aside thinking for now and move to the realm of feeling. If you have not remained on my bed because you trust me, speak up now." Another pause to allowed me to reconsider the next step with her. "So, Leon, we may have had enough of truthful words, so perhaps you care now to quench too much revealing light. I am here for you."

Without any more questions I got up and snuffed out one of the candles. There had already been more than enough words between us.

Our coming together felt very different, far more relaxed and slower than I could have imagined. I had to wonder how she learned this way of making love. Afterwards we lay on our backs for some time and soon I drifted off to sleep. I dreamed I was eating breakfast in New York in my apartment with Elise, the one I was set to marry. I lost her over my business fiasco. Her hair and skin were fair, like Alicia's, perhaps one reason I was so susceptible to Alicia that night in my room in the Inter-Continental. In my dream my fiancé let her long hair fall loose onto the shoulders of the Chinese silk robe I gave her for her twenty-second birthday. I was still riding high and successful. We were on our balcony overlooking Central Park, watching the people below jogging, skating and walking in the park. But I awakened and immediately recalled it was all gone. The apartment, Elise, and money. Instead, there was a beautiful Indian girl propped on her elbow gazing at me. For a moment I couldn't remember her name, nor could I recall why I was underground with her.

"You are like a fish who has jumped out of the water," she spoke gently.

"Well, I didn't know what you wanted—Sunitha," I said, grateful to have remembered.

To please you, naturally," she laughed.

"You seem to know a great deal."

She was kind and well-meaning and I took her at her word. This time when we made love, I couldn't help feeling that I was being measured and tested. But unlike any other woman I'd known, Sunitha wasn't evaluating me for any form of competition. Her motives were pure, I would come to learn.

CAPE OF GOOD HOPE

CHAPTER 8

GENTLEMEN'S AGREEMENT

No matter what time of day I might have an appointment with Ted Nichols, he's late. I believe he makes me wait to push me to better respect his position as the representative of the majority shareholders. We'd signed a cooperative agreement, which required me to work as a consultant in setting up several new taverns. Many of them were in townships where I was not comfortable working, some far more dangerous than Woodstock. Bottom line, we still hadn't come to final terms on a master plan for Cooper's continuing role in the expansion we were planning to financially back.

Meanwhile, the home office was impatient for me to begin breaking ground on a new Gazelle brewery to replace the Kassies' antiquated, damaged one. Harry knew we couldn't go ahead until we had the final documents presented, not only by Ted, but by his board in Germany, then by our board in St. Lewis. I was afraid he'd pull the plug on the entire project if I didn't come back with results soon.

To entertain me during my hour-long wait for his boss, Tembo brought me to the most impressive room of the Chateau, the one with the thirty-foot, three-story vaulted ceiling, the dining room where Alicia had brought me as one of Ted Nichols' seventy dinner guests. I remembered seeing remarkable paintings on the walls: an exquisite landscape, an eight-foot-high oil painting in a heavy gold leaf frame, and more. But all the artwork was gone now.

In the place of those dozen paintings, there was only one now, that of a young woman in her garden, wearing only gold bangles and a luminous pendant on a gold chain, her breasts tilted upward. She was sitting naked at a glass table, her bare hips and thighs magnified.

"This lady," I casually asked, "is she a friend of Mr. Nichols?"

"She's Mrs. LeRoux, more than a friend. She always liked to sit in the shade to avoid blistering her fair skin."

LeRoux? Could she be related to Alicia's friend in Bergkloof, Janice LeRoux? I wished the lady in the garden were turned full-face and not in heavy shadow to have a better idea of her identity. She was rendered with the same squarish jaw as the mistress of the Bergkloof Inn. I couldn't help comparing this naked lady to the elusive lady LeRoux Tembo seemed to know so well. I compared her with Alicia, the woman I'd been doing my best to leave behind. I was trying to understand my real motives for consenting to this exile to the white tribe village. Was it to try to put my missteps behind me, including the loss of my ex-fiancé? Where did that leave me, but still dwelling on a woman on the other side of the world? I wished to excise her entirely out of my mind, since Sunitha had managed to capture and astound me, as a lover with a generous and powerful spirit.

From the moment I landed in South Africa, it seemed essential for success to build allies of those who would

offer themselves into my service. I might have otherwise felt I was taking advantage of Hassan and Raj and
even Sunitha, if they hadn't each actively sought me out
in the first place. I had to put Alicia in the same category, though I was having a hard time knowing what
she really wanted from me. Their battles and alliances
were unclear, but in South Africa I couldn't escape their
conflicts. I realized whatever their motivations, I would
do well to rely on their goodwill.

Suddenly, the lights went dead, leaving us in darkness. When the lights came on, Ted Nichols was standing between us and the painting of the woman. He was
wearing a khaki jacket with large exterior snap pockets
and seemed a man with an undisputable advantage over
me, a hunter-killer.

"Sorry for the inconvenience," Nichols apologized,
"must have bumped the light switch. A question,
Tembo. Fifteen years ago, when Mrs. LeRoux was posing in my garden, were you watching her?"

"Of course not, Mr. Nichols" came his reply. "I understood when she draped her bathing suit on the lowest
limb of the cherry tree, I should move no closer. I'm
always careful to avoid going where I am not wanted."

"Leon, now you see why I chose Tembo for my personal guard, not simply because he notices everything
important to me, but because he is loyal."

"Thank you, sir," Tembo said.

"Now why don't you make yourself useful by leaving
us, and when he arrives keep watch on Hassan? He's
overdue. I'll let you know when I'm ready to receive
him." He turned to me when we were alone. "So, Leon,
what do you think of this artwork?"

"Nice color scheme."

"A scheme, yes, a painter's plan to make this woman interesting to all men so they can imagine how they all would enjoy possessing her."

"I mean the purple color scheme, starting with the amethyst around her neck, the purple pansy in her hair."

"No, a pansy would suggest that she was weak-willed," Ted interrupted, "which would not fit her fierce character at all. Those are asters, also in the background."

"And purple lilacs in the tree behind her," I added.

"Actually, not a tree. It's a bush which grows bigger than the azalea bush by her feet."

"And the amethyst? Was that real or the painter's invention as well?"

"A beautiful stone she thought had great value, though in reality it had little. Mrs. LeRoux treated it as a diamond though, wearing it when entertaining my friends. Not many knew that even a flawless amethyst will never have any serious value. But she and her pretty stone are gone. Only this painting of her remains. I suppose there's a lesson in this, the sentimental amateur and the appraiser disagreeing irreconcilably over its value. Just as a wife and husband can disagree on the value of their marriage.

"You must realize, Leon, I don't regard you as just any man. I rarely share my personal affairs with business associates, but in your case, I'm willing to trust you because I understand you've been seriously disappointed in an affair of the heart. Still, I doubt either of us would have the time or inclination to attend a lonely-hearts club."

"If you're worried I'll tell your secrets, then please tell me no more, Ted."

"We are business partners. I know you would not compromise my trust, no more than I would ever embarrass you. That is why I will try to make you even more productive as a minority advisor for the duration of your stay in my country. I'll be introducing you to your key players and, if you wish, to the right women."

Jan Le Roux still meant something personal to him, though in all our background information about him I didn't recall even seeing her name. Similarly, I wondered how much the Werner-Nichols researchers out of Bonn uncovered about Elise leaving me in New York, or whether they assumed I was sent to South Africa primarily because I had lost so much money for Cooper. Strangely, Ted warned me not to gossip about him, but for his part, he couldn't know these unpleasant events in my life, except by listening to gossip. I hadn't told anyone here the details about my lost girlfriend and my bankruptcy. Had Harry betrayed my confidences again?

"Look, I don't know the connection between you and this lovely sunbather, any more than I know why all those wonderful paintings I saw before are gone, replaced by color scheme nudes. It's none of my business, Ted."

"Really? Nevertheless, come with me to Bergkloof to sort out this matter of the value of these paintings, especially this one. You're a bit of a collector, so your opinion might help my cause."

"I don't believe my opinion would carry much weight. Before I came here, I lived in a small apartment little space for artwork of any kind. I had reduced my collection substantially, parting with..."

"Honestly?" Ted interrupted. "You Americans are

quick to speak boldly, if not entirely honestly. Let me tell you why I chose you to assist me in evaluating those paintings. I know you personally parted with a distorted Bacon painting of the low lives in London, and of a hyper-real David Hockney, one of his skinny-dipping boyfriends. As far as I'm concerned that makes you something of an expert in collecting art."

I knew nothing about what I was seeing, and he knew it, but maybe that didn't matter to him. Was he planning to pass me off as an expert or appraiser? Maybe he was looking for someone who appeared knowledgeable to convince Jan that the replacement nudes now on the wall had more value than they did.

"Thank you for the vote of confidence, but I fail to see the connection."

"We wouldn't have to mention that you had to sell these pieces because you lost your home and your lady friend and your credibility with Cooper. I know because I did my homework, but I won't hold this against you. As far as I'm concerned, if someone doesn't make mistakes, he isn't improving and innovating. That applies in business, as well as in life. I'm not asking for your art collector's credentials. I just want you to speak to Jan as if you were a bit more substantial and a bit more knowledgeable than you might be. Don't worry, you're more likely to impress her more easily than you can impress me."

"Ted, I can't believe that you've brought me here to settle some old scores. I may have purchased a few valuable paintings, but I must decline to represent myself as having any sort of expertise. In good conscience, I must decline your offer to participate."

Ted didn't look at me, but beyond. As he turned away,

a hand clamped my mouth shut! I began prying the attacker's hands off me, hoping it wouldn't be necessary to immobilize him with a kick to his shin. Another pair of hands helped me, Tembo's. Once freed, I saw it was Hassan who set upon me, grabbing me as he had in Maraville, simply to silence me and with no real malice intended. Now he was laughing at me as I provided the inspiration for his horseplay.

"Mr. Nichols don't worry about Mr. Cooper's conscience! Welcome to South Africa, where the Indian Ocean and the Atlantic Ocean meet. Here we are natural people living like fish in the sea, where big fish swallow the little fish."

"Hassan, weren't your people on your father's side traders who came in caravans to South Africa?" Ted asked him, a strange and embarrassing question coming from a discreet man like Ted.

"Slave caravans, slave traders speaking Swahili," Tembo added.

"Hassan," I asked, "were you taking up where Ighaam's Boys left off, or was that simply your way of greeting me?"

"The devil works his mischief in you, Larabie," Tembo concurred.

"The devil? If I were you, I wouldn't be trying to pass myself off for a Christian."

"To the contrary, if any of my key players are misbehaving, I need to know as soon as possible," Ted said. "If Hassan or any of his friends haven't been treating you well, I need to know."

"I suppose the fault's partially mine for letting Tembo bring me to Maraville," I said.

"And what did you see there? Did Tembo show you his flat?" Ted asked me cautiously.

"Not only Tembo's flat, but I was introduced to Hassan's and Ighaam's associates."

"Yes, Hassan introduced him to the important businessmen roosting at the top of Maraville," Tembo said.

"And, Mr. Nichols, Tembo can tell you about the whores, as well as the outlaws," Hassan suggested with a conspiratorial smile at Tembo.

"I trust Hassan wasn't wasting your time introducing you to common streetwalkers," Ted said sharply.

"Actually, they introduced themselves to us," I said, "by raining bottles upon us from their balcony, after I unsuccessfully tried ignoring them."

Tembo headed out of the room, but Hassan rushed to the door, intercepted him and led him back to Ted. "Tembo, that whore friend of yours Katie Ann Arendse, can't you see she's a waste of time?"

Hassan evidently was putting Tembo in the spotlight to divert attention from himself. Tembo looked trapped, with no desire to explain himself.

"You mean the woman who visits her uncle Igham Arendse?" Tembo asked evasively. "I've been keeping a very good watch on the big boss of the streets, sir, ever since you moved me to my flat."

"I mean Katie Ann Arendse, on top of who Tembo roosts from time to time!" Hassan said. "Was that the purpose for placing him in Maraville, Mr. Ted?"

Ted looked hard at Hassan, not at all pleased. "I give my people a fair amount of latitude. They know I will tolerate no illegal sort of business, such as prostitution. Tembo, I'm disappointed in you."

"But, sir, as you ordered, I never give her money," Tembo said. "She likes me and does not need it. She is a businesswoman with beer customers in two or three shebeens."

"Another a shebeen queen? Don't you know by now they're nothing but trouble?" Ted Nichols asked.

"She does not lead the shebeen life. She lives away from Valhalla Park and Lotus River. She manages a few of Ighaam's shebeens there and in Maraville near the flat you are leasing for me. She is my neighbor. We have grown fond of each other, and she tells me many useful things you need to know about Ighaam's Boys."

"That sounds reasonable, but I caution you against speaking too freely to any woman while you lay your head on a pillow. This Katie Ann may prove helpful to Mr. Cooper though," Ted said.

"That's just what I thought," Hassan said. "That's why I introduced him to some of Katie Ann's friends, including the one with the pale skin. Didn't you find her pretty, Mr. Cooper?"

I was beginning to wonder whether Ted really trusted Hassan, or if I ought to trust him to lead me through any new districts. Hassan either had his foot in his mouth, or else he was working hard to place both Tembo and me in a bad light, so he'd look better by comparison.

"I wouldn't answer that, Leon, if I were you." Turning to Hassan, Ted added, "It's best to judge visiting strangers, like yourself, gently."

"Yes, sir, treat Mr. Cooper as one of our own," Tembo said. "That comes from the Christian Bible, the book of Matthew."

Rajesh arrived with his shoes in hand and slid over the buffed parquet floor in his stocking feet.

"No, Mr. Nichols knows as well as I he is quoting from the Jewish Old Testament, the book of Leviticus," Rajesh said with a bow to Hassan, then to me.

"Jesus Christ, Raj, your people never eat beef, no more than mine will eat a pig. What do you know about those Bibles?" Hassan laughed at his observation.

"My father reads about you Christians to know you better," Raj said, looking at me cautiously for my response.

"Or you might learn more from the Zulu," Tembo said.

"Learn what? What weeds your witch doctor mixes to cure you when you are sick, Tembo?" Hassan asked, picking up a handful of nuts from a bowl as he made his way out of the room.

"Not so fast, Larabie, as one who has broken every rule in the holy books and the law books—" Ted began to ask.

"The law, what does that have to do with me?" Hassan grinned at Ted, then walked over to me. "Mr. Cooper, this is South Africa, where the laws mean very little, and in the townships mean nothing at all. You Christians outnumber me here, so unless you want to hear something from my Koran, I should go now."

Hassan made his way to the door, leaving our meeting, which had evidently grown uncomfortable for him. Ted signaled Tembo with a motion of his head, who responded by rushing to Hassan and bringing him back to us.

"Tembo says you came here to eat," Hassan said, looking at his watch. "I didn't realize how hungry I am. Can you believe I forgot to eat today?"

"How convenient," Ted said.

"No, sir, it's not convenient for me to find a grocery store open between here and Stellenbosch. But carry on without me, and I'll come back later."

"It's convenient that you're hungry, Larabie," said Ted. "I like to work with hungry men like you and Rajesh."

"Yes, sir," Raj said, "You get more work out of a man who's a little hungry than one who stuffs his belly all the time."

"You Indian shopkeepers will never go hungry," Hassan said, "so long as you own all the food stores!"

"And you Arab flesh traders will never starve, so long as you control the black market trade on the street!" Raj said.

They had soundly insulted each other, leaving each quiet and sullen. Ted intervened by taking them to a nearby public room with bar with stools and half dozen round tables. I followed him.

"Our tasting room, Leon," Ted Nichols explained as a waiter brought us one bottle of Gazelle beer with three glasses to sample it. "It's still a little bit off, I believe," he grimaced, then looked to Raj.

"That's because we lost some of our best brewers in the walkout. Timing is everything in making a good beer. Those of us remaining don't have the time to check our batches as carefully as we should. I'm very sorry if we have failed to please you."

Ted waved his hand, cutting Rajesh's apology short. He signaled the waiter to bring out the food, trays with meat, cheese, fruit and bread. We were served bottles of Chateau wines, starting with the good pinot noir; next, the fair champagne with the overwhelming carbonation, and ending with the excellent pinotage, the Chateau's strongest wine. Then he served a decanted red wine, which I took for a merlot, which didn't seem nearly good enough for its fancy cut glass vessel.

"You shouldn't have gone to all this trouble," I said.

"To the contrary, I plan for you all to stay here for as long as it takes."

"Takes to do what?" I asked.

"For as long as it takes to find out why these two lieutenants of mine, Mr. Kassie and Mr. Hassan, have recently failed to get the Gazelle workers back up to speed."

Raj and Hassan stopped eating and looked at each other apprehensively, like children who had to account for themselves. I'd been telling Ted we could commence to replace the ruined Gazelle plant with a modern one. First, by buying the German dismantled plant we already had an option to buy, then by dispatching the already packed shipping containers containing the plant, sitting in Europe, ready to sail to South Africa. Not having to build it from scratch would be a great advantage. It was waiting in a warehouse in Hamburg, Germany, waiting for transport.

It was easier to speak numbers and equipment to Ted than about personnel matters, such as why he was still using Hassan, whose services appeared to be one step removed from that of a street fighter.

"No problem, sir," Hassan said. "I am working with the Kassies to get back the workers who have been taken from Raj."

"Whatever we decide," Ted said, "Rajesh needs to relay our decisions to Chandra. He should be here this evening.

"My father is busy standing guard," Raj said. "That's because someone must keep an eye on things, especially after dark. That's why he's at home."

"I understand that you and your friends have been on sentry duty ever since the fire, and since Sunitha grew tired of you." Raj didn't answer, but looked at me, pained, as if I were responsible for Sunitha's choice to leave him. "But it seems to me, Rajesh, that if you don't know exactly who you are guarding against, then perhaps you need to find out from Hassan's friend Arendse."

Another uncomfortable silence, with all our eyes on Hassan. "You mean who makes the trouble for Gazelle?" Hassan asked softly. "It's Mafumo and Ozeer that don't want us in their neighborhoods anymore. They're gangsters, but not so bad we can't stop them."

"Stop them from what, Hassan?" Ted asked.

Hassan turned to me, as if looking to me for permission to continue. "Mr. Cooper, you already see everything you need to know about the townships. If you go home soon to America, you have no need to know more about the gangsters."

"To the contrary," Ted said, "Mr. Cooper needs to know exactly what these gangsters do to make their money, and so do I, Larabie."

"They make it through the taxicab fares, more than anything else," Hassan said. "Mr. Cooper already knows never to take a taxi van and to let me drive him instead."

"Sorry to interrupt," Raj said, "but I hear that you allowed your taxi friend Mikah Booley to drive around Mr. Cooper instead."

Hassan set his mouth in a scowl and would have

preferred to say no more. Ted nodded to him to continue, but he didn't take orders as readily as Tembo.

"Now that you think you see gangsters behind every streetlamp in Cape Town, how did the taxi man Booley impress you, Leon?" Ted asked.

"He's someone I'd rather have on my side than against me. It was Mongrel who had a face I'll never forget."

"Moegemat Mongrel, with his red hair and freckles, yes," Ted said with a smile, "I don't judge a man by his looks, but by his loyalty. Will Mongrel make a loyal pet, Larabie? Or should his master worry that he'll turn against him?"

"If Booley and Mongrel drive their own taxis," Rajesh said. "I would not be afraid to travel with them. But with their black drivers, never would I dare. They carry guns with the passengers, and between passengers they pick up and drop drugs to—"

Ted signaled Tembo to cut short the details of the dirty business in the townships. "The old story, the competition between the coloureds and the blacks—and the whites get flak from the crossfire. Unless, of course, we shoot back. Enough said!"

I suspected Ted knew more than he was willing to acknowledge, especially in front of me. He confused me. I couldn't blame him for not wanting to talk anymore about the townships so remote from this Stellenbosch Chateau dreamworld. Stellenbosch looked to me more like rural Holland than Africa. I was also confused about Ighaam and the van taxis. They were pretty much black-owned and driven, yet I was finding out that Booley and Mongrel were taxi owners. If true, why were they so closely associated with Ighaam? Was the taxi business merely a front for more lucrative enterprises? And why, if the black Ozeer Boys were the enemies of Ighaam's gang, would Ighaam's front men Booley and Ozeer rely on black taxi drivers for their livelihoods?

Hassan had been telling me all along he was fighting for the community, for PAGAD, People Against Drugs and Violence. Fighting the gangsters of CORE, Community Outreach Forum, gangsters who told the newspaper reporters that they'd permanently retired from the drug trade. PAGAD evidently consisted of both Moslems and coloureds, while CORE seemed to be black. I suspected I was in the middle of a turf war between coloured and black drug players. I'd been caught in the crossfire once, and next time I might not be so lucky. And what was the extent of Ted Nichols' involvement with Hassan and PAGAD?

"Please excuse me," I said to Ted. "You've given me some new variables to work with. If you don't mind, I'll be stepping outside for some fresh air."

I stepped onto the flagstone patio, which was the outdoor extension of the tasting room, where the public was served the Chateau wine and bar snacks. I was relieved to be alone, but in a couple of minutes Ted joined me with a couple of glasses.

"Unwanted guests," he said, cocking his ear to voices not far from us.

He walked to the hedgerow separating the public area from the fields. He passed through a break in the hedge and rousted out the four men in overalls behind it. One was holding a jug, from which Ted drew off a sample.

He dismissed these drinking employees, returned to

me, then poured half his glass of their rough native beer into mine.

"Taste this, Leon. What kind of beer do these black workers drink?"

"It's harsh. Like nothing I've ever had, too bitter for my liking."

"They brew this sorghum beer themselves. Many of them bring it home from the shebeens. With Chateau's entry into the shebeen market we gave them the Gazelle brand, which had been a minor player. The shebeens these days prefer to buy from breweries of Lion and Castle. They prove formidable rivals, but I believe they are they are big and slow-moving and defeatable."

"The KWV cooperative has been the major power here in the wine business. You've never been a member, yet you seem to thrive in spite of the competition," I complimented him. "Some players are big and powerful, and some are faster and stealthier, survival of the fittest."

"Is that why Cooper has been so persistent to expand the South African portion of Werner-Nichols? Because we managed to fight the KWV wine cooperative head-to-head?"

"Yes, one reason. We like to ally ourselves with the best, Ted."

"But if Cooper has a background in spirits, I don't understand why you've ventured into the wine business."

"For the same reason you've ventured from the wine business and over into the brewing business," I said, not willing to admit that when we linked with Werner-Nichols German distilleries, the wine operations were a small part of a package deal. We were flush with stock market cash, mindlessly buying in the name of diversification. "I think we may be more similar than we realize. We each go where the markets lead us."

"I see you fancy yourself as a man who can make things happen, Leon, a rainmaker. But instead of bringing a shower, you caused a bad storm, a hurricane which nearly destroyed the Cooper Company. But here you are, safe and dry on my estate, my trusted advisor and major partner."

He filled another glass with red wine from the decanter and watched me as I tasted it. "What do you think of this?"

"Quite pleasant. One of the Chateau's table varieties?"

"You think I've served you an ordinary mixed varietal wine? You must be teasing me."

"Sorry, Ted, I'm a whiskey and bourbon distiller by training, and you're the vintner, unlike me. You also don't do things accidentally. There must be a reason you want me to sample this merlot while your boys are waiting inside."

"Merlot? This is our premier cabernet, aged five years, and no ordinary table wine," he said, revealing my ignorance in wines. "Five years is a long time wait to see the fruits of our labor. Five long years, during which a beermaker could make a goodly amount of money producing and selling dozens of batches. While Cooper's whiskey is excellent and the Chateau's best wines are world-class, you and I are both eager to expand our horizons into the higher turnover beer market. Now that you've had a chance to orient yourself to the Chateau, do you see any reason why we shouldn't finalize our tentative plans and break ground?"

I made no secret of my search throughout Cape Town

for future business alliances. Evidently my meetings with other businessmen now had him concerned Cooper might back away from its plans to finally build the new Gazelle brewery from the waiting plant, in partnership with the Chateau.

"One problem, Ted." I finally spoke up, "I don't do business with gangsters, but I think your boy Hassan does."

"The Chateau doesn't have any direct business with them, but this is South Africa. We need to know their movements so we can avoid problems as we build our network in their territory. And for the record, keep in mind Hassan's no more my boy than Colin is."

Ted couldn't expect me to believe that PAGAD and Ighaam's men weren't gangsters simply masquerading as righteous vigilantes against Ozeer's drug organization. Obviously, he was using Hassan and Tembo as his liaisons. Since my arrival I still wasn't entirely sure didn't why he was throwing me in the company of low-level Tembo, Hassan and Rajesh. Had this been part of some sort of initiation or orientation he set out for me?

"I'm confused, Ted. You agreed to accept me as your advisor, yet I barely see you, not unless it's to report on the Gazelle project, which has stalled for months now. And thanks to your boys, I've been on one grand time-consuming tour of the underworld!"

"We've been giving you time to get acquainted. Now perhaps it's time for us to move to the construction phase, though I'm a bit confused about a recent phone conversation with your brother. He was suggesting, off-the-record, that the Cooper board is having second thoughts about the final cost of building our new facility. I was looking forward to Cooper's making good on its promises for financing, since we both know Werner-Nichols never had any intention of going it alone."

Was Harry crazy? Sharing the board's concerns with Nichols rather than with me? Perhaps he was undercutting me because if I failed in this mission, he would be justified in asking me to resign. On the other hand, if it was one of Harry's signature head fakes, I would make Nichols nervous enough about Cooper's wavering financing to want him to begin pouring concrete before the board changed its mind.

"A wise decision. Time is money. Frankly, Ted, the home office was beginning to wonder whether your commitment to the new Gazelle plant matched ours."

"Money, of course, is an issue. Your brother mentioned how much it's been costing the Cooper company to carry you, Leon, even before he dispatched you to charm us into a joint venture."

"It sounds as if you've been speaking with Harry almost as often as I have, Ted."

"Don't worry, I haven't suggested to him that you've gone native."

Harry's complaint about the cost of my stay in South Africa was a strategic mistake. If I couldn't trust my own brother to back me up in negotiating for Chateau Drakenstein, maybe I should have cut this project loose. Then for good measure I could have left Cooper altogether—that is, if my brother didn't stand to advance his career with me out of the way. If only I could speak to him directly face-to-face, I'd be able to find out whether he was behind me, whether he wanted to help me succeed here, or whether he was setting me up for failure. Or maybe I'd been isolated long enough to become paranoid and couldn't discern my friends from my enemies.

"If you tell him any more about how I've been enjoying my stay, he may want to come see what he's been missing."

"Please don't tease me, Leon."

We already signed an option on the beer plant waiting for us in the port of Hamburg, and based on shares each of us held, participation would be 51%Werner-Nichols to 49% Cooper. We had all the South African contractors' bids in hand, and I believe I could have a signed contract with construction bridge loans by the end of the month. I wanted details, but Ted was distracted by an unwanted guest. I saw Hassan, who was standing in the quarter-opened door, but Ted didn't seem to mind that he was eavesdropping on us. I was led to believe Ted wanted me as a consultant, yet since I set foot in South Africa, he seemed to be consulting primarily with a street tough chauffeur and an Indian fighting off nightly raids—emissaries to the South African streets, rather than with international businessmen. It was weird that how much he relied on their opinions and allowed them closer access than the wealthy and influential set that was at his poolside party the first night I met him. It was odd that these idlers were always on hand whenever I got a chance to speak with him. But most of all, I wished I knew whether he set them the task of dragging me through the townships to test my endurance.

"Hassan, your ears have grown too big for your head!" Ted said loudly, making sure I heard his protest. "Mr.

Cooper and I have one small matter to discuss in private. Be gone!"

He stared at me. "I believe your American-style marketing will work for Chateau Drakenstein, which is why I value you so highly, Leon. First, I'm not pleased that Rajesh took it upon himself to guard the old Gazelle plant. He will need another assignment, now that we have new plans for it."

"You've been speaking of this organization for some time without giving me anything specific to go on," I prompted Ted.

"Here on the Cape, we live on the tip of the continent where two oceans meet," he said, as we moved to the tasting room. "In aligning my business with yours, I'm setting course toward America, with you sailing with me as my navigator. We're setting out from the Cape of Good Hope to cross the Atlantic Ocean, overburdened with too much cargo. That's why you must help me jettison what we don't need." He motioned for Rajesh to join us.

He wanted me to think of him as a ship's captain, but, for my part, I couldn't help picturing him as a slave ship captain. Worse, I feared he was preparing to throw Raj overboard. I wanted no part of his conversation with Raj, yet he insisted that Raj participate on my first assignment as his consultant.

"Rajesh, let me get to the point. I couldn't help noticing that since the riot at Gazelle, production has seriously fallen off. You made quite a few enemies on that day."

Now anger came over Raj's face, and he shook his fist at the sky. Ted took Raj's fist into his hands and looked squarely at him, but not before he glanced at me with concern.

"Rajesh, I've learned a great deal from my enemies. You have made many new enemies since your workers turned on you."

"Tell him what you saw, Mr. Cooper," Rajesh said, turning to me, "that it was Mafumo, his friends and the Ozeer troublemakers, not my workers!"

"I can't tell the good guys from the bad guys," I said. "Don't ask me,"

"No matter, I don't care about the faces, but it's the declining production that concerns me, which has made Mr. Cooper and me reconsider whether we will be rebuilding the Gazelle label from your father's crippled facility."

Raj seemed astonished. I saw fear in his eyes as he looked at me to intervene on his behalf, as if I had had the influence to save his white elephant.

"Sir, to the Kassies Gazelle is more than a label on a bottle. The brewery is part of our home. When we rebuild, we'll put up a stronger gate with more guards, so I can sleep instead of stand guard all the time."

"Yes, we have a problem at Gazelle, and I must recoup my losses."

"You will be glad to know those refrigerated curing vats you purchased for Gazelle came through unharmed. Since I am good with brick and mortar, you might not need to hire a masonry foreman, once you release the insurance money to us."

"Mr. Cooper, should I commit fresh funds to a plant with so much deferred maintenance?" Ted asked me.

"I'll have to take a closer look, Ted, before I could advise either way," I said tactfully. We both knew as soon as our new plant was in production, the old one would be scrapped.

"Don't be afraid to tell him what changes he will have to make," said Ted, looking at me sternly.

"I'm sorry for what happened," Rajesh apologized, "but I had no control over—"

"That's correct. Things are out of control at Gazelle, Rajesh," Ted interrupted. "We're not saying the Kassie management is entirely responsible for the wreckage of Gazelle, but it's obvious that it's time to shovel yourself out of the rubble."

When Tembo and Hassan then joined us, Ted led Raj and me away from the bar to a table. A waiter immediately arrived with wine glasses on a tray.

"Nice, smooth sparkling wine," I commented, giving Ted a chance to demonstrate his vast wine expertise and my own ignorance. "Chateau label?"

"The Chateau's best champagne, naturally fermented, no harsh forced carbonation used to cut costs!"

Ted paced strangely around us. We watched him as we sipped our drinks. Suddenly he took Tembo's glass from him, held it up to the light, sniffed it and studied the bubbles. Then he collected the half-finished glasses from everyone, returned them to the tray, and led the waiter to the stairs away from us. Ted dragged a chair across the floor ten feet in front of us, turned it backwards, draped his arms over the back and commenced to rock on just two of its legs.

"Don't get too comfortable, Rajesh, because we are running out of time," Nichols said.

"To the contrary, sir, I am very uncomfortable. If not myself and my team, who else would stand guard for you?"

"In America, what would they call Rajesh's guarding?"

Ted asked, looking up at me, laughing, "The fox guard-ing the henhouse?"

"Sir, we do our best to protect your interests! Hassan knows if we don't stop the night raiders, next time they will destroy your investment in Gazelle. And along with it, our family home."

Ted stood and took Raj by the shoulders, smiling. "Rajesh, you think like a shopkeeper living over your store, not like a brewer who can help develop the finest beer in South Africa. Hassan, do you think Rajesh has enough Indian friends to fight off gangsters raiding Rajesh's plant?"

Hassan didn't answer, but continued whispering with Tembo. "Do you have any better advice for Raj?" Ted asked like a displeased teacher.

"I could always go to Durban," Hassan said, "and get busloads of Indians if you don't think there's enough of them on the Cape."

"You Arabs are very good at rounding up unwilling workers, my father tells me," Raj said to Hassan with a bitter smile.

"Then send your father to me so I can teach him that you need to trust me more!" Hassan laughed.

"What kind of slaves did your relatives prefer, black, Indian or white?" Raj taunted.

"No more fairy tales about my people!" Hassan shouted.

"Hassan, tell us the truth," Tembo started. "What did you Arab traders do with your white slave women when you were done with them?"

Ted waved his hands dismissively and rolled his eyes. He didn't like what he was hearing and wanted him to be quiet. "I don't have time to read history books to know whether to believe this foolishness. Nor do I really care, Rajesh, but I am curious. Were they white prisoners of war, these white women taken as companions by the Arabs?"

"No, sir, the Arabs needed half-men and half-boys to mind their harems," Rajesh said, "so they made them eunuchs! The black eunuchs were Africans, and the white eunuchs were from the mountains of Russia and northern Europe."

"You should not speak lies about my people, Rajesh!" Hassan demanded.

"Then you should not speak to me as if I were one of your coolies!"

"Careful, Raj, or next time I won't send my friends to help you when the Ozeer Boys come through the gate at Gazelle to finish you off!"

Ted was disgusted with talk of slaves and slave traders, especially when it grew heated. Tembo attempted to calm them. Ted led us outdoors again, where we could watch without being seen ourselves.

"I know what you're thinking, Leon, what can these young men do for Drakenstein? Why don't I fire them, especially Rajesh who could be a liability? It's a good solution where you come from, but not in the Chateau's best interests. They're important as scouts, our liaisons to the black, coloured and Indian communities. My European managers would not be suitable for the task, because they are family men, not crazy. Hassan and Tembo have been educated on the streets, but my managers are better schooled and will make you as good company in our organization as Alicia. A shame she couldn't be at today's briefing. But I assume you'll be passing what you know to her shortly, next time she comes back down from the sky to earth."

"I apologize for this bickering between my men. But now we have a minute before we return to them, so you might tell me how friction-free business works."

It was an impossible task, explaining to a traditional vintner about the new friction-free digital economy. But he was staring at me, waiting for me to begin, and an explanation was overdue.

"The friction-free economy depends on the principle that when you catapult a product into the mainstream, it becomes very difficult to dislodge it. The more market share you have, the more you continue to get because you build a momentum favoring the success of your product in the marketplace."

"Obviously."

"Mainstreaming may involve selling below cost or distributing for free the first generation of the product, even if you initially lose money doing it, as when you give away internet service in order to make money on advertising."

"If you plan to give away our product, I'm afraid—"

"Ted, people tend to fear the friction-free economy because they don't understand it. Traditional business-people may not understand it because it seems upside down. The friction-free economy turns upside down the old business equation 'supply equals demand,' because now demand will follow production—with almost no friction and no gravity. It's opposed to traditional economics, where prices are expected to go down after demand goes down. In the friction-free economy, when prices go down supply will go up, forcing increasing demand. In other words, it's a new way of moving goods and services at terminal velocity."

"It sounds like forcing a product in quantity before the market's quite ready for it, like trying to sew the tail back on the dog, even though he's rejecting it. You think that sort of surgery can work here?"

I couldn't tell whether he was curious to know more or just baffled. In the States Harry had done a good job discrediting my friction-free methods as the reason for my stock debacle. He must have briefed Ted, so without giving me a chance to explain, Ted evidently distrusted them in advance! Cooper's problem wasn't that our new wine and spirit line wasn't accepted, just that we catapulted ourselves into the marketplace too quickly. We didn't have enough time to turn profits before the public shareholders began dumping us. There was no use dwelling on the past though. I was focused on the man before me, on how I must have looked in Ted's eyes. He wasn't hinting whether he would have any further interest in my new age friction-free methods, not before we could rejoin the three men in the tasting room.

Finally, I got Ted to agree in principle to reorganiza-tion and expansion with my guidance. That left me to make good on some very ambitious plans, attempting to introduce friction-free business into a country where there was friction between every left-over apartheid group, where the friction had morphed into the unde-clared Cape Flats War. Did Harry know what he was doing when setting me up to accomplish this almost impossible task?

CHAPTER 9

THE CHIEF OF THE SHEBEENS

Once I had signatures on all agreements from Cooper in St. Louis and from Werner-Nichols in Bonn, we began site work, although the existing financing was insufficient to complete our expansion. The dismantled brewery arrived by ship in Cape Town and was trucked to the Chateau. The first earthmoving and concrete work employed dozens of day laborers, many with shovels, working around the heavy equipment—twice as many workers as I'd see on a similar job in the States. The foremen seemed to spend their time explaining the most obvious assignments several times, then having to return to correct errors. I had a limited background in construction and was no help on the site. I continued with my most pressing task, which took me into the poorer districts of Cape Town, where I helped to set up our network of mini breweries. Since I would be in South Africa indefinitely, I moved from the Inter-Continental to more suitable quarters, a flat in Rondebosch with the great advantage of being five minutes from our new brewpub. It was in a prosperous and relatively safe neighborhood where, with Alicia's help, I had set up our new flagship, Wandi Dadla's Place.

I was located near the University of Cape Town and enjoyed a distant view of the Atlantic. I could see the piers at Woodstock, and bought a neighbor's telescope, with which I could see the iconic statue of Cecil Rhodes. I could have learned what Rhodes was doing in Rhodesia long enough to have the country named after him, or what he did in South Africa to motivate the laborers to dig enough gold and diamonds to build his and DeBeers enormous wealth. But the challenge of making good on my promises to the Drakenstein and Cooper companies disallowed me the distraction of digging into the history books of South Africa. The country made less sense to me, the more I heard competing versions from people that had historical grudges, fanned on by the lefties in the colleges who were inordinately proud to have birthed the Rainbow Nation. I focused my attention on what I saw firsthand. From my porch there at Barclay Mews, I could see no sign of Maraville, even with the telescope. In my spacious apartment with a yard big enough for grills and lawn furniture, I felt a universe away from that neighborhood.

Barclay Mews hired armed guards around the clock and had coded locks for the automobile gate and pedestrian doors of the tenants. I suppose that's why from her first visit to my flat, Sunitha felt protected. It helped being in the university district where mixed couples were not that uncommon. We knew we wouldn't be welcome everywhere, so I relied on her judgment which restaurants and neighborhoods we should avoid when together. I was careful not to lead her to believe our alliance was more than temporary. It could last no longer than my assignment to South Africa. But for the immediate future, I had no intention of separating from someone as beautiful, spiritually conscious, and business-wise as her—disparate qualities that converged very well in her.

One Saturday I cancelled our standing Saturday evening date, since Wandi Dadla's was having problems with its new cooler which had failed. I needed the vendor to send a man out to repair it, or else find my own repairman that evening. I needed an onsite manager, but hadn't hired one yet. This problem should have been handled by Chandra, but lately he'd been impossible to find evenings, preoccupied as he was with keeping track of Rajesh.

"It's been a day and night process to boost Gazelle's production, and get the extra product distributed to the additional shebeens that were working with us," I explained to Sunitha on the telephone.

"I know how you dislike traveling at night in regions where you do not belong," she remarked accurately.

"That's why I bring Hassan or a bodyguard he knows, or Tembo or that driver DeWitt."

"Because Mr. DeWitt is quite a light-coloured man," Sunitha said. "I believe he was able to move over to the white camp, now that we have no race passes here in South Africa. I used to wonder how on the hottest of days he would wear not only the dark suit Mr. Nichols requires of his drivers, but that Greek fisherman's cap of wool. He told me he wore it because his cap reminds him that he's descended from a Dutch sea captain."

I didn't know what point she was making. To my

eyes, DeWitt appeared to be of European descent, maybe Mediterranean Italian or Greek or Spanish. But he wasn't European to South African eyes like hers, trained from years of apartheid to put people into four categories: white, coloured, black and Indian, based on subtle cues like the shape of eyelids and the texture of hair.

"Descended from a sea captain? Maybe I should look him up if I want to hire someone to sail me to the other side of the Atlantic, where I probably belong right now. Excuse me," I said and muffled the phone from my sneezing.

"Once you take care of the problem at Wandi Dadla's, I can come to your flat so I can cook for you," she suggested.

I needed to keep Ted's driver away from her because I couldn't take the chance of his spotting Sunitha and reporting back to Ted on the extent of our private-hours friendship.

"Sunitha, you know I don't like you traveling by yourself in strange cabs at night, especially from Valhalla Park. As for DeWitt, I can't call on him anymore since he destroyed Drakenstein's Audi. He did that during his off-duty hours while leaving a pub, other than one of our new shebeens."

I told her more than she needed to know about a fellow employee, but Sunitha had always been a source of invaluable information to me. I needed her to feel I was reciprocating, even if it was no more than gossip.

"His injuries required just a couple of days in the hospital," I said, "but unfortunately, Ted sacked him. And with DeWitt out of the picture, when I can't reach Chandra, Hassan, or Tembo. Where did that leave me but at the mercy of unreliable cab drivers? That's why I plan to lease a car and drive myself when possible."

"You realize, Leon, that the maps don't cover the townships. Even if they did, in the worst ones there are few street signs left standing. I'm afraid by yourself in a rented car you'd be like a rat in a maze, unable to find an exit. Don't be foolish. I don't want to worry about you. So, for now I'll be over and feed you better than your mother."

"She's passed on."

"But she's no doubt left behind many memories to ease your sadness, if you still miss her. I sense that her death has made you more cautious, although in your family you are certainly the risk taker."

Without having met my mother, she was offering me advice on how I should remember her! She spoke of feeding me better than her, and I wondered if she also divined our family's suspicions that the tap water with which Mother cooked proved to be a cocktail of industrial chemicals—water which might have given her cancer, and which I avoided in my adulthood by drinking only filtered water, a habit I know struck Sunitha as peculiarly cautious.

"Your concern is appreciated, but I don't feel like eating. The best thing I can do for myself right now is to sleep. Please understand."

"I understand you are sometimes cautious and sometimes reckless, and you tend to feel sorry for yourself, as right now."

She'd evidently managed to weave my life story from the confidences I'd been sharing with her, and was reciting them to me, drawing some broad conclusions.

She had a big heart, and I trusted her, but nevertheless I didn't care to be analyzed by her, and certainly not over the telephone.

"Well, hold those thoughts, Sunitha, until we see each other."

"Our thoughts are formed into the bodies of Leon and of Sunitha, which from time to time join harmoniously, but that won't be tonight. I don't think you want to see me. I sense you'll need a couple of days to solve your immediate problems before you're ready to ride with me. In the meantime, I'll be with you in your dreams."

It wasn't until late Saturday that she arrived, unannounced and unexpected. I took her to Uncle Solli's Shoreside Restaurant where they brought fish directly to the table, sizzling in an iron skillet.

"Sometimes I feel I've jumped from the frying pan into the fire," I said.

Her face was blank. That expression meant nothing to her. She waited until we were back at the flat to reply. "You mean eat or be eaten, that the big fish consume the little fish?"

I nodded my head yes, the path of least resistance, an acknowledgment that as an American I could only make myself partially understood.

"One creature dying so the other might live—that's not how we see the chain of life," she finally said when we were together in bed. "For the meaning of your life, Leon, or mine, I need to find where you float in the universe."

"Float? Sunitha, how could you fail to see I'm a man with a plan?"

"Our practical plans are no more than human vanity

and ego, the shell of our spirit that you must allow to float away."

"Drop my plan A? Not unless I have a Plan B!"

"There's no place for your plans in the universe we see," Sunitha said.

"The Hindu universe?"

"The Hindu universe, yes," she said. "In it we see the universe as an enormous egg, divided into twenty-one zones. The Earth is seventh from the top. Above the Earth hang six heavens. Below the earth lay seven nether-worlds, and below that, seven hells. Snake-creatures live in this netherworld. They have cobra head snake heads and a boa heads for tails. They are white with long horns, and their bodies are those of white oxen."

Now that she'd been officially reassigned for the duration of my stay from the old Gazelle plant's office manager to my personal assistant, we had few subjects that were off bounds. I'd given her Darwin's notion of the world, which she countered with her picture of the universe as an egg populated with fantastic creatures. As someone who understood the details of running a business office, I wish she wouldn't make me defend my survival-of-the-fittest businessman's view of human behavior. But despite the happiness of a fresh romance, she still seemed melancholy and preoccupied.

"Enough!" I said.

"Because we're here for love, not talk?" she asked as she reached beneath the table and squeezed my leg provocatively. "Hold the thought, please."

Through dinner I held those thoughts of immortality, and afterwards back at the flat. I had powerful new thoughts that took hold of me that night when I was asleep.

In my dream I'd abandoned my familiar view of the world. A force greater than the earth's gravity pulled me upwards off my familiar green planet. I rose through clouds, through the last of the cold, thin atmosphere and from there into black space, accelerating so fast my arms remained pressed to the sides of my naked, frozen body. I was able to see the pattern of the universe, its egg shape. I was traveling infinitely faster than the speed of light to a place where the stars were few and far apart, the outer bounds of all creation. Now I passed between a pair of planets at one of the edges of this universe. My progress was diverted. I took a new direction and went into orbit between a blue planet and a green planet. I had come close enough to the blue world to see the sacred snakes with cobra heads. Then when I approached the green world, I could see white oxen grazing on green grass, just like on earth, as well as Sunitha, naked on the back of an enormous white bull! I was suspended between invisible forces, and desperately wanted to land near Sunitha. But I was in a ping-pong trajectory, powerless to land on either of these Hindu nether worlds. I'd traveled further than I should, to the edge, the shell of the egg that was but one of many universes. Despite my extraordinary journey, I hadn't the ability to do the one thing I desired—to land on the green world of white oxen and rejoin Sunitha.

"I'm pleased to see some pink in your pale face this morning. I'm sorry to awaken you, but if we don't hurry, we'll be late!" she said.

I sat up, suddenly ejected into the ordinary world,

opened my eyes and saw it was truly her, sitting on the edge of my bed. My mind was still filled with a picture of the Hindu universe and eternity she'd inspired. It was 7:00 A.M. on Sunday morning. She then went to my closet and took out a suit, tie, and a white shirt.

"You promised to take me to a Dutch Reform Church this morning, remember?"

"This Mercedes is different from the one you used to drive," I said to Tembo once we were on the way to church. "Did Mr. Nichols loan me your services and this car for the day?"

"You must smell the new leather. I am the only driver he trusts with his most valuable vehicles, and I am at your disposal with this car for the duration of your stay with us."

"A shame about losing DeWitt," Sunitha said, sitting in the front seat. "Is that his Greek fisherman's hat he left behind?" she asked and put it on her own head.

"He must have others, but this one he give me for good luck. I told him he need it more than me because he's not a clever enough coloured man to outsmart Mr. Nichols. Then he tells me there will be bad fortune on me if I don't leave it here on the dashboard to remind me." Sunitha patted the hat she'd placed on her head.

"But if this cap is really good luck, Sunitha, then you should have been wearing it last week when Ozeer's gangsters come with their torches and hate in their heart."

"That's okay. They are ignorant men. They destroyed nothing of mine I cannot replace," Sunitha said.

She turned away and quickly wiped tears from her

face, another sign that something had been weighing on her mind, a visit by gangsters with torches! If she weren't scared to stay alone, maybe she wouldn't have shown up on my doorstep.

"I told Hassan he should have never placed you in one of Ighaam houses," Tembo said, "not in that part of Valhalla Park. It belongs to Ozeer's Boys. There's shootings enough between Ozeer's CORE gangsters and Ighaam's PAGAD over the drug business. Now Hassan's helping Gazelle by trying to take some of Ozeer's shebeen business and give it over to Mr. Arendse, who's a very strong man."

"Isn't this gang war really about the difference between the blacks and the Moslems? The longer I'm here, the less I understand. What's at stake in this Cape Flats War? What's it really all about, Tembo?"

"Drugs, sir, who controls the drug trade."

"But doesn't CORE claim it's reformed gangsters?" I asked. "Don't the Moslems advertise themselves as People Against Drugs and Violence? Aren't drugs against their religion?"

Both he and Sunitha laughed at the same time, glancing at one another. "Instead of using them, it's common knowledge in Maraville those Koran-readers sell drugs wherever they can," Tembo said.

I suspected the Moslems wanted to stop the spreading influence of the black gangsters' illegal business, particularly in the coloured territories where the Moslems themselves live. The black gangster leaders billed themselves as the CORE organization, as retired and repentant gangsters. The Moslems billed themselves as PAGAD, righteous citizens against drugs and violence.

Cape Town citizens like Tembo and Sunitha, for their parts, believed neither side. As an outsider I wasn't sure what to believe. I was dealing most directly with Arendse's PAGAD Moslem gang through Hassan, and now indirectly through Ted Nichols. Whether or not drugs were their core business, they certainly also had a substantial piece of the liquor trade.

I was determined to carve out a chunk of the market, to be able to successfully compete against the giant Lion and Castle corporate beer brands. They currently took 75% of the market. Ted didn't let KWV's 85% share of South Africa's wine volume intimidate him. I was concerned, though, about putting myself and Cooper in the crossfire of the Cape Flats War. The more I learned about the Arab and the black gangsters fighting over territory, the more I wondered about the side effects of building Gazelle's visibility in increasing numbers of existing shebeens. Tembo claimed the shebeens were paying protection money to thugs on both sides. I vowed I would not allow myself to be drawn into corruption. If Ted wouldn't let me build a reasonably clean organization for him, he'd have to attempt it with someone's help other than mine.

"Isn't this car quiet as a hearse, Leon?" Sunitha asked me.

"This car weighs two and a half long tons," Tembo said proudly. "Growing up I walked a kilometer from our house to the well. Now I am driving you in this big car. I make progress for my family."

"Do you have a family in the country?" Sunitha asked him. "Do they remain in Transkei, your homeland? You never told me you were married. Have you children?"

"No more married than Rajesh or Mr. Cooper is married to you!"

I didn't care to touch the subject of the ending of Sunitha's engagement with Raj. I sensed her discomfort as well. She asked him a question he didn't care to answer, so he struck back at her. She responded by asking him to bring the car to a stop on the shoulder, where she let herself out and moved to the back seat with me. Once beside me, she leaned forward and whispered so Tembo couldn't hear her.

"Leon, if I have brought shame to you, perhaps we should separate before we become too close," she offered.

"Nonsense," I reflexively protested, realizing my close association with an employee was bound to have repercussions, even in South Africa where America's legalistic and bothersome rules of office behavior hardly seemed to apply.

"Thanks for the reassurance. Has Tembo surprised you with reports on the drugs?" she asked, now loud enough to include Tembo in our conversation. "Let me assure you I would never use drugs. I must have a clear head for myself and for my closest friends. Am I right that you too are clean of drugs, Tembo?"

"I have to say I never used them, but that don't make me clean of them. I must deal with gangsters who do. To avoid drug scoundrels, I would have to take up another trade, such as schoolteacher, or better yet, Sunday School teacher."

"Sunitha, you are nagging him with a moral question with no clean answer," I said. "Perhaps you hope to find it at church this morning. I'm perplexed however, why you want to bring me not only to a Christian church, but an Afrikaner one at that."

"We Hindus need never go into a temple and can practice perfectly well at home, if we make our home our shrine."

"That will not be possible for her anymore," Tembo interrupted, "Mr. Cooper, now that her home and her gods are charcoal."

Did that mean she'd been through a fire in Valhalla Park! I turned and saw her silent tears. She turned away from me.

"I don't understand why you have entrusted me with your secrets," I began, but I saw her shaking and stopped short, not wishing to add to her distress. This morning, she was wearing a rose-colored silk scarf, covering the neckline of her long clinging black dress. I questioned whether my eyes had been tricking me, wondering exactly what there was about her that I found so attractive. Her long neck, big eyes, and high cheeks gave her a universal kind of beauty. Had I been from a generation earlier, I might feel differently about her dark cocoa skin, but today it added one more exotic attribute. Rather than create an unbridgeable difference between us, it attracted me even more to her.

"I'm sorry," I added, without knowing the cause of her tears,

"Just because I have been through fire, neither of you gentlemen need to feel sorrow for me," she said, leaning forward towards Tembo, draping her arms on the front seat beside him. "Don't worry about me, I can shed an old life like the skin of an onion."

"I have trouble understanding riddles," I said. "When

you say you've been through fire, you mean you've been through hell?"

"In all that time I was waiting, Sunitha did not tell you what happened to her?" Tembo asked, looking first at her, then back to me. "Then I will. Of her two gods, the one made of bronze, the fire was not hot enough to melt. The one of wood was charcoal, gone."

"I don't worship idols, Tembo!" she said with uncharacteristic testiness. "I would prefer that you forget about me for now. Welcome to Paarl," she said to me, "where they will make believe they don't understand you if you don't speak to them in Afrikaans."

We passed a billboard with an image of European settlers traveling in heavy wagons similar to the Conestoga wagons of the American pioneers, an advertisement for the Afrikaans shrine. "They look like could be crossing the plains of Nebraska in our country," I said.

"But this still Africa," Tembo said. "These Dutchmen called themselves voortrekkers—and make up stories from the Bible they was crossing into their promised land."

"You Americans killed almost all the Indians who got in your way," Sunitha said, taking up the argument. "These Dutchmen who first called themselves Afrikaners, tried it, but they were outnumbered and failed to find the promised land."

I could have asked her opinion about the connection between the North American Indians and Africa, but I don't want to encourage an abrasive grievance history lesson. I let it go.

The town of Paarl wasn't what I expected with its commercial signs and plate glass storefronts. But just outside the central business district, it transitioned to a classic Dutch town. Huge yellowwood Africarpus trees lined the street, with trunks twice the size of any two-century oak, forming a dense canopy across the road. We parked in front of the tallest building with a tiled roof and fake gables. Small stained-glass windows faced the street, so I guessed it was a church, although I couldn't see whether it had a cross or a steeple.

"Tembo, you can help us by finding out when their services begin," Sunitha instructed. So, it was a church, after all.

Tembo smiled and followed her suggestion and left us, reluctantly. Outside the church a huge man in shirt-sleeves and tie walked towards Tembo then stopped, his arms crossed. He had leathery skin and a deeply lined face. I couldn't understand a single word of the language he spoke with Tembo.

"Everyone here in Paarl speaks Afrikaans," Sunitha whispered. "They made us learn it in school, but it's a dying language that they unfortunately refuse to bury."

A fair-haired clergyman with a similarly weathered face noticed us, and he waved us toward him. Sunitha offered her hand, but he shook mine instead. I realized he did not talk to a man's driver or his house-girl, but to the man in charge.

"Welcome to our Dutch Reform Church," he greeted me. "You can follow me up the mountain."

Returning to the car, he pulled me aside. "Do you enjoy our country?"

I had been asked that leading question countless times since I arrived. "You've certainly built yourselves a picture book town."

He stopped me short. "Well, it's no fairy tale for some of us settlers!" He looked toward the others waiting in the car. "If you don't mind my asking," he whispered, "if your housekeeper rides in the back seat, where does that leave you?"

He walked to the front of our car and rested his foot on the bumper. "You know we built this car of yours in this country, better than the Germans produce them in Germany. In Germany they made the mistake of using Turks in their factories. We have our coloureds, but with the right training and supervision, they can build or fix most anything." He followed me to the rear door, opening it for me. "If you get to the flock before me, tell them Reverend Dieter DuToit sent you! Nice to meet you, Yankee Doodle!" he shouted, waving pleasantly to me as if he were saying goodbye to a friend.

"He looks like a farmer who's worked hard in the sun," I said to Sunitha as soon as we drove toward Paarl's Monument to the Afrikaans Language and Afrikaner people.

"These Dutch men still act like farmers. Some of them don't know a potato from an orange, but they all believe the land belongs to them. They teach the children in school that they were the first permanent settlers in this part of Africa, a myth!"

"His first name's Dieter, German, but his surname DuToit is French," I said.

"Understand that the Frenchmen have been here since the 16th century when the Catholic king kicked the Protestants out of France. The French Protestants sailed to South Africa, took up farming, and married the Dutch women. That's why you can't tell these French South Africans from the German ones or the Dutch ones. If they've been here long enough, they speak and think the same, like Germans with boots!"

Germans with boots? I hesitated to ask. Did she mean German soldiers in high polished jackboots or German farmers in low dusty work boots. But I didn't care to hear any more depressing South African history, especially when it was so hard for me to separate the historical myths from the facts.

"If what you say is true and this man DuToit is no friend," I questioned her, "why in God's name would you bring me to this church, where they don't know you any more than they do me?"

"Would that be your god or my God?" she responded, without directly answering my question.

The winding road up the mountain ended a few hundred yards below the monument. Once out of the car, the three of us climbed steep winding stairs. I could see the tips of several three-story concrete spikes above. I paused to look at the panorama from Paarl Mountain. Within the distant grayish blue mountains, I could see Bergkloof Pass, which dominated Jan and Peter LeRoux's Inn. Looking south, at the foot of the Drakenstein range was Stellenbosch and the Chateau. There at the foot of Paarl Mountain, were planted fields, separated by scattered farms. And directly west was the city of Cape Town; and behind it, Table Bay, beautiful and peaceful from this distance. If only I could get my bearings with these unpredictable South Africans as easily as I could orient myself to their landmarks.

We climbed on and reached a plaza of white stone,

the Afrikaner Monument itself. The concrete spikes I had seen were white stone obelisks, three streamlined shafts pointing to the sky. On the edge of this elliptical plaza, seats were carved into the white stone, creating a three-tiered amphitheater. Churchgoers in their Sunday clothes sat in the shady portion of these seats, while a man in a formal black robe spoke to them in Afrikaans. I got no more than a few glances because I looked like them, but when Tembo and Sunitha came into view of these people, they attracted attention. Though there were several shady places left near the listeners, Sunitha placed herself apart from them and instead placed herself in the blazing sun. Meanwhile, Tembo and I retreated enough to take ourselves out of their sight.

I felt a tap on my shoulder. "My Yankee friend, next time I'll put some of the sermon in English, if you care to stay and to pray with us." It was Dieter DuToit.

"A fine place to gather the flock, high on the mountain, like Mt. Sinai up here," I whispered.

"Ah, you are familiar with scripture. In that case, do you think I would be worthy to receive the holy tablets on this mountain?" he whispered, so close I could feel his breath. "Excuse me, I should not be speaking while my assistant pastor is preaching. Tell me, does this driver of yours speak Afrikaans?"

He looked over towards Tembo, but when DuToit walked toward him, Tembo quickly walked away, as if to avoid conversation. "Most of them can't even read, you know," Dieter said, returning to me. "I don't know about that driver of yours, but I shouldn't trust him for translating from Afrikaans to English. We must speak directly. Why did you come here, and what do you want to know?"

"As long as are doing questions and answers, as a minister, why you aren't dressed like the one delivering the sermon?"

"Even preachers take holidays. That's why I have time to visit with you now. He's my lieutenant minister. Anything else?"

"What about these three beautiful shafts?" I queried.

"One is for the Western languages, two for the black bush languages, and the third for the Malays, not the Indian rice-eater types. Each contributed over the years to Afrikaans, the greatest language of them all."

Another history lesson! Everywhere I turned, someone else seemed determined to present me with his version of the past. The more I knew about this country, the less I understood; not only the reasons for their battles, but who was winning and who was losing. Sunitha told me the language was dying, while DuToit would have me believe it was greater than ever. I really didn't care either way, and I just want to get back to the car.

"If you'll excuse us," I said, backing away from him and towards Tembo.

"Are you planning to leave her with us then?"

"Mr. DuToit, if you are speaking of the young lady who is a colleague as well as a personal friend of mine and who has asked me to bring her from Cape Town specifically to hear a sermon in your church—"

"No problem," he said, "if she belongs to you."

I moved so Sunitha could see me and motioned that I was leaving. She held up ten fingers three times, meaning she wouldn't be ready to leave for thirty minutes.

Again, eyes turned to her, and then toward me. I hadn't come here to disturb the church meeting and attract attention, so I ducked away and retreated to the car.

In the car, Tembo switched on the radio to a report of a robbery in Pretoria, the capital, twelve hours to the north. A gang of twenty had hijacked a ten-ton truck and used it to annihilate an armored bank truck, ramming it at high speed head-on, killing all four guards, and escaping with sixteen million rands of cash.

"I think I've heard enough, Tembo," I said, but he didn't hear me.

The grim news report gave details of another armored car robbery. The robbers had laid a spiked chain across the road, shredding the tires, and bringing it to a stop. After a swift machine gun battle, five guards and one of the bandits lay dead. This one happened at twelve noon on the main road between Pretoria and Johannesburg.

"How could the gang escape in full daylight?" I shouted to Tembo. "Where were the police to pursue them?" He turned off the radio.

"When I was a young man in the struggle, the police were everywhere, detaining black people, beating them, or worse. These days are different because now we have more gangsters than policeman. That is why you best take care of yourself, instead of waiting until after you're shot dead for policemen to shield you from gangsters. Do you understand?"

"Do you think the law's a joke?"

"It doesn't matter what I think. Please ask Sunitha what she thinks about the gangsters and the law since they burned her out. She was lucky she smelled the smoke in time, but she carries fear in her heart. You can see it in her eyes."

Burned out! The truth was coming out days after she could have told me herself, directly! Of course, that's why she appeared in an odd state of mind, as if walking around in shock. Why did she tell Tembo before me, because she's known him for a longer time? But her eyes—how could I have missed the pain in them when she came last night without calling first? I didn't appreciate getting the news secondhand. Was she testing me? Was she dropping clues I'd failed to retrieve?

"Burned out—how bad?"

"The interior, completely gone. Only the walls remain," Tembo said. "It's better they did it during the day before she got home."

It was no accident. Her house was owned by Ighaam Arendse, so more than likely it was burned by an enemy of his.

"Hassan knows it was Ozeer. Once he knew that one of Arendse's people, one of Kassie's worker's—Sunitha—was staying in his district, Ozeer sent his boys out with the matches."

"When did this happen?"

"Three nights ago. I move her and those heavy ruined dummies to her auntie's home in India Town in Athlone."

Through the open window of the car, I felt a gentle hand on my shoulder. "Tembo, you must remember those dummies are Brahma and Vishnu. One survived the fire, like myself."

"I'm sorry, Sunitha. If you had told me, if I had known..." I backtracked. "Don't just stand there."

She pointed behind her to Dieter DuToit. She walked around the car to the door opposite DuToit to avoid him, while I got out to see what he wanted. He led me to the center of the parking lot.

"Mr. Yankee Doodle, now that you and Ted Nichols are in business together, will you treat your workers like they do in America?"

"You don't know me any more than you do Mr. Nichols."

He looked me over carefully, with a smile. If Sunitha had hunted up a shrine or a church closer to home instead of this monument to besieged Boers, I would have never met him in the first place.

"South Africa is a big country," DuToit said, "but the strong and important people know each other and stick together."

"Are you strong and important? In that case, I'm honored to meet you." I began walking away from him.

"No, Mr. Yankee, I meant Ted Nichols. He was very important to our cause."

"What cause?"

"The cause of peace and security. He was one of our bravest commandos."

"I don't know much more about Mr. Nichols' private life than yours, Mr. DuToit!"

"Your Indian girl Sunitha tells me she works for him and you because you're his partner."

"How does that concern you?" I asked.

"Shouldn't I be concerned about what the savages are doing to Ted Nichols, my old squad lieutenant? I have not seen him for years, but I'm concerned with him more now than when he left the squad on account of that woman Jan. I could have fallen for her myself, if she wasn't a kaffir-lover! Ted's a good man who made a big mistake, allowing her to get too close to the enemy."

I couldn't believe Ted served as a vigilante with a search and destroy squad, alongside this Boer minister! Was this Alicia's friend Jan of Bergkloof? More deceptions and more inexplicable coincidences! Not wishing to hear more, I returned to the car, but this talkative Samaritan, if that's what he was, followed me.

"Aren't you going to say goodbye, Mr. Cooper?" Dieter DuToit asked. I was in the seat beside Sunitha, but he held my door open so we couldn't leave.

"These savages you speak of, Mr. DuToit, that's a bad thing to call men," I said to let him know I stood on the side of truth and justice.

"Doesn't your companion tell you anything?" he asked, staring at Sunitha. "When I saw her tears and asked what was troubling her, she told me about her bonfire. If you are planning to keep good help, you need to keep your people safe. And if you're not careful, the savages will soon be at your own door."

"Thanks for your concern, Reverend. It's been good meeting you," I said.

"But not for the last time, I assure you."

CHAPTER 10

AUNT GIRI

I felt closer to Sunitha than to any other woman, ever. By nature, I myself have always been a practical problem solver, but in her personality, I felt the intensity of a mystic. Though we were an unlikely match, I had come to regard her as essential in my life, and evenings without her seemed lonely. After a couple of overnight stays, I asked her to remain longer, especially since I knew she was staying with her Aunt Giri Bala, who offered plenty of unsolicited I-told-you-so's after the fire. I realized taking her into my flat might prove a questionable proposition. If I were back in St. Louis under the constant scrutiny of my family, I wouldn't consider inviting an employee to live with me. But in Cape Town I was in a gray area, since I still drew my salary from Cooper, and none from Chateau Drakenstein. In South Africa the distinction between what was acceptable in business and what was discouraged seemed far looser than in the States.

I had learned conclusively she was assaulted during the raid on her flat, and I didn't want Sunitha to think I was taking her in as an act of kindness. Neither did I want her to assume our arrangement was more than temporary.

The next time we visited her at her home, Aunt Giri was wearing a sari dyed in long sunlike rays of orange, red and yellow.

The next time we visited her she was wearing a sari dyed in long, sunlike rays of red, orange and yellow.

"That's an attractive design," I complimented her.

"If I give this to you, Sunitha, would you promise not to wear it about Mr. Cooper's flat as your house dress?"

She cast me a stern and disapproving look which changed to a radiant smile when Chandra arrived and squeezed her hand. Hands folded, she bowed her head toward him gracefully, obviously glad to see him.

"Giri, you must understand Mr. Cooper is a powerful businessman who lives behind secure gates and will keep Sunitha very safe. I approve of this gentleman, as should you. We must pray for him because he will do good things for our families. I pray that you will welcome him as one of our own."

This wasn't my plan, arriving as the evening's conversation piece. Chandra's admiration made me uneasy, and I was glad when Giri and Sunitha retreated to the kitchen to begin serving him and me at the table.

"I've never eaten anything like this," I said, midway through the main fish course.

"Then our fish is not familiar to you?" Giri asked.

"This is mussel cracker, a South African fish and very fierce. The next time Giri cooks for you, ask her to not cut off his head. Then you will be able to see teeth so powerful they easily crack through the shell of the mussel."

"I have always loved your stories, Chandra, and would like to hear them more often."

"That is why I am here for you now," Chandra replied, bowing his head politely to her.

"Not because you knew Mr. Cooper would be present? Not to learn how Sunitha has recovered from her attack?"

"Since Mr. Cooper must know even less about it than I do, don't you owe him an explanation?" Chandra asked, no doubt assuming Sunitha hadn't yet told me the full truth about the attack.

Sunitha left the table for the kitchen. Her aunt followed, leaving us alone at the table. Chandra and I said nothing for the moment. Sunitha returned, holding the refilled tea pot, her hand shaking.

"Would you like me to pour?" I offered Sunitha.

She dismissed my offer with a simple shake of her head, very unlike her. Chandra took the pot from her after she nervously overfilled his cup, dripping tea on the tablecloth. Aunt Giri attended to the stain.

"Well?" Chandra asked, looking directly at Sunitha.

She still looked away from him. I moved closer towards her, but she pushed me away.

"Those cowardly men, hiding behind ski masks!" Chandra said. "The evil they released will be revisited upon them."

"I told her," Giri Bala said, "that nobody, much less a young Indian lady, should live in Valhalla Park in the middle of the flying bullets!"

"We're not quite at war yet, Giri," Chandra said. "And we shouldn't worry Mr. Cooper unnecessarily."

"Aunt, you must keep out of my affairs," Sunitha said. "Those gangsters who tried to set you afire should be burned alive!"

"They were blacks, not Indians like us, Leon," Chandra explained.

"You must remember, Mr. Kassie," Sunitha said, "that in India not long ago we threw our women on the fire. Have you told Leon that my great-great-grandmother died in my grandfather's funeral pyre in Bombay, because it was expected a widow immediately follow her husband out of this life?"

"Chandra, do you think my niece is suggesting that I best have died like an honorable Indian woman, immediately after my beloved husband?"

"Of course not," Chandra said, "you are much too valuable alive, Giri. Also, Sunitha and I would miss you too much if you were departed. Now if you don't mind, I have something at home I must show Mr. Cooper. Excuse us."

Chandra and I walked away from Aunt Giri's home down the street towards his own house, I assumed. Lost in my own thoughts, I was late to realize he was no longer with me. Before I noticed I was alone, he pulled alongside me in his car.

"Excuse me, but I cannot allow you to walk these streets," Chandra said. "The sun has set, you are a white man here in the new black South Africa, and we are in Athlone township. Have you not learned from your travels with Hassan you must rely on us to protect you?"

Chandra had already helped me more than he knew by taking me away from Aunt Giri's tense supper table. This gentleman attempted to keep me out of harm's way again, but I would have been a fool to rely on a peaceful gray-haired gentleman of his age to keep me away from stealthy enemies, invisible in the night.

"I believe you are laughing at me," Chandra lamented.

"No, I'm pleased with your ingenuity. I noticed spray paint on the side panels, covering up the Kassie Gazelle Beer logo. You could have covered over it with our new Drakenstein Gazelle logo, but that would be waving a red flag at the bulls, the beasts who want to gore us."

He shut off the interior light and the headlights of the truck before we arrived at a gate at the rear of the Gazelle plant. He parked across the road, no closer than necessary to allow us to view what remained of the operation. The main building was relatively intact, though the outbuildings hadn't survived the vandalism nearly so well.

"About Sunitha," he began, looking through his binoculars at the compound lit by a few high-powered blue lights, "has she told you about what they did to her before they pushed her through the window?"

This was the reason he took me away so abruptly from the table, to avoid embarrassing them by speaking details about the evil Sunitha suffered. Now that we were alone, he seemed eager to fill me in.

"No need to tell me, Chandra, because I already know. It sounds like a police matter, though I'm also hearing that they have little interest in investigating it."

"Leon, I'm disappointed with the police, as Sunitha was when she made her report. She's young and had to learn for herself that these days our people have few friends in the police stations."

"Because there are so few Indian policemen?"

"Let me say, sir, it was not pleasant for Sunitha amongst the coppers, especially the white ones, questioning whether she was violated before the house was set on fire. They questioned why she had waited a full day before making her report to them. Not only did they doubt her, but they also mocked the idea of tracking down the enemies of her landlord Ighaam Arendse, especially since Ozeer's Boys were smart arsonists who knew how to burn up any evidence that could be traced to themselves. She's convinced those policemen didn't care what happened to her because she wasn't white or black or coloured, but Indian. Therefore, it has fallen to you to protect her. Do you agree?"

"I thought that was Rajesh's assignment as her fiancé."

"Speaking of Rajesh," Chandra said, evidently relieved to talk about anything other than what really happened to Sunitha, "I didn't see him on watch tonight. Lately he's been standing guard with a couple of men that Hassan introduced to him. I do not worry about him during the daylight hours when he helps me to set up the new microbreweries. It's the after-hours that trouble me, when he makes deliveries to Hassan at the warehouse in Bergkloof. He understands this Gazelle plant will never be rebuilt, but he still stands watch over it most nights."

I knew little about Hassan's connection with Bergkloof, other than his moonlighting part-time at the drostdy, a job I thought Ted made him quit when he found out. For what little money he made as groundskeeper, this quiet and isolated job hardly suited his street hustler personality. I didn't understand Hassan any better than I did Rajesh.

"Ah, my son is nowhere to be found out here," he said, "and the women are back waiting for us."

He started the truck and drove to Aunt Giri's house. Upon our return, Sunitha smiled broadly, as if Chandra had somehow accomplished a great act of healing in the wake of her terrible humiliation. Chandra, in response, placed his hand around each of our waists, pulling each of us closer to him.

He released us from his embrace, and walked inside, where he gave Giri Bala a kiss on her cheek, transforming her frown into a smile. I regarded Sunitha as an uncomplaining survivor. I took the opportunity to pull her into the shadows, out of their line of vision, and I kissed her. She responded passionately, as if looking for reassurance of my intentions, now that the news of the attack on her had been shared. I pulled away, just as Chandra returned, asking us to come into the house. He remained on the porch while we rejoined Aunt Giri to eat the rice and coconut milk desserts prepared for us.

"You like sweets, as well as we do?" I heard Chandra speaking outside.

"No time for that, Mr. Kassie," Tembo said.

I excused myself from the women. Tembo had, in fact, arrived for an obviously prearranged meeting with Chandra. I watched them remove the charred Buddha and relatively intact brass statue from their truck and tie them down in the back of a black Volkswagen. I wondered where they were taking these idols.

"What's this?" I finally asked.

"A safer car for nights in dark neighborhoods as tonight," Tembo explained. "Mr. Nichols might want to issue it to you.

Sunitha said amicable goodbyes to Aunt Giri and took

a seat in Chandra's truck, ready to return home with me to Rondebosch.

"It appears you and your aunt have come to an understanding," I observed.

"Understanding," she said in a hesitant voice. "Leon, I couldn't bring myself to return to my flat in Valhalla Park, but Tembo did, and by a miracle found one statue, a very good omen. I didn't think you'd mind if I kept him, the intact Brahma, with me."

"Of course not," I said reflexively.

I had questions but this wasn't the time or the place for them. How did she come to me with clothes and books and dishes and flatware, if all her possessions were destroyed in the fire? Perhaps she went back to Aunt Giri's after the fire to retrieve her personal things, along with dishes and pots and pans for the two of us. Was this because she had she assumed in advance we'd be living fulltime under the same roof?

Bringing Sunitha into my flat was the right thing, but it took some adjustment on my part. She rose before 5 A.M. to do her devotions, seated cross-legged on the floor, facing her pair of gods that passed through the fire, as she has. From time to time, she'd break her meditation to quietly check the progress of my sleep. If I had an early appointment, then she'd prepare our breakfast; if not, she'd slip back into bed, snuggling.

I'd been careful about approaching and touching her. I did not know the details of what the thugs did to her before setting the fire, and I didn't want to press her. I tended to avoid making love to her if she showed me signs of depression or if I sensed her withdrawing from me.

I hadn't seen her shed a tear since that Sunday I took her to the Afrikaner monument. It seemed she had great powers of meditation, forgiveness, and concentration to put her nightmare out of her mind as well as she had, yet I couldn't help feeling the more intensely she loved me, or made love to me, the harder she was trying to forget the terrible event.

It was another Sunday. I felt fortunate to awaken beside this Hindu beauty who thought like a philosopher—a fine woman who truly cared for me. She was calmer this Sunday morning than six weeks ago when she pulled me from bed, insistent that Tembo take us to the monument on Paarl Mountain for that strange meeting with Dieter DuToit. She was on the balcony looking out over the town of Rondebosch to the sea, leaning on the round metal table.

"Do you like my view?" I asked.

"Barclay Mews," she said, pointing to the carved wooden sign facing the street in front of the guard's office by the gate entrance. "Was this place named after a pussy cat?" she asked, turning back to me with a playful smile, "or after a big cat, a lion, such as yourself?"

"Some are calling me King of the Pubs, and now you flatter me that I'm king of the jungle. I don't feel very powerful though in parts of Cape Town, which is more dangerous than any jungle."

"Lions can make love for days at a time. The most powerful lion, the one who has won his harem, as you have won me, must have a lot of work to do."

She understood since I'd arrived in this country, nothing was more important than building my business.

I hoped I hadn't come across as a businessman in matters of love, that she didn't see me as writing a businesslike daily balance sheet for how well I'd been performing. Sunitha was unlike other women in my life. With her I didn't have to apologize or change what I'd become, a competitor. She always complemented me and never competed with me.

"Don't worry about my energy, sweetheart," I said.

She'd been listening to me attentively, not taking her eyes away from me. Now she turned and leaned forward on the edge of the waist-high wall, looking over the balcony rather than at me. With her hindquarters facing me, I wondered how much of the front part of her the neighbors might be simultaneously viewing.

"Do you feel like a lion now?" she teased.

"Actually, I feel like we may be watched by the neighbors now."

"Well, if you don't feel like a lion, then do you at least feel like a bull?"

"My trouble is trying to understand how you South Africans think, and sometimes I feel dumb as an ox."

"Then forget about thinking," she said, and made a rotation of her hips. "If you feel like a bull, then I'm your heifer."

I looked over the balcony wall at the windows of all the flats in Barclay Mews which were facing us. I put myself into their perspective, imagining how much of us they might be able to see with their eyes focused on us. Or worse, they could have been looking at us with binoculars as strong as Ighaam used in Maraville. Maybe I was worrying for nothing, and the low wall was enough to block them from spying on us.

Nevertheless, I acted on the desire she initially inflamed in me. Strangely, I felt first like a lion, then more like a lost boy in a cave. At her suggestion, I gave up thinking in order to concentrate on exactly what I was feeling. I stopped worrying about the neighbors.

With no need to rush, our rhythm became perfect. I heard a ring, which startled me out of my dream of slow lovemaking, as if timed by a magic clock spewing out stretched toffee minutes.

"Are you hearing things? Didn't I have your undivided attention?"

"You know you do," I agreed, choosing to ignore the noises behind us as I chose to ignore the windows facing us.

Sunitha was a combination of parts, including her belief that she was an incarnated bodiless traveler passing between successive lives. Though I assumed I was hardly one of her first men, I also believed the powerful love she was showing me was genuine. I wondered though why she was attracted to someone like me without any strong spiritual beliefs.

These happy thoughts of Sunitha's character and the nature of my attraction to her came to a stop, once I realized that we weren't alone. On the kitchen table there were several sealed sample jars of Gazelle beer that weren't there before. Someone had turned on the flame under the kettle for long enough to have brought a kettle of water to a slow boil.

"No, I wasn't hearing things. We have company," I said to Sunitha. It was Rajesh.

"What brings you here this morning, Raj?" I asked him. "Did I leave the door open?"

"No, sir, it was locked. As a hobby I have learned the locksmith's art, so I thought I'd let myself in, rather than disturb you two. I just came to say hello to Sunitha, Mr. Cooper."

Raj looked at the floor, rather than at either of us, then raised his eyes, until he was viewing only Sunitha. She was wearing her robe over her nightgown, revealing nothing to him, yet I imagined his eyes boring through the cloth to her flesh beneath. It was an intimate view of her I didn't care for him to share, now that she had broken away from him. I wasn't pleased with his intrusion, but I tried to keep my annoyance to myself.

"Excuse me for not stating my true purpose visiting," Raj began, "but with so much to fix I do not always know where to begin."

"Sorry to hear that, Raj. After the fire at the old Gazelle plant, I thought you and your father were doing well, setting up the Mombasa and Yellow Fin mini breweries. If you feel you're in over your head, I can always reassign you."

He raised his head toward the ceiling, as if he was looking to the heavens for guidance. His head shook in a barely perceptible shudder, either in inspiration from God above, or fear of me, his boss whose home he'd invaded.

"If I caught you by surprise, please forgive me, but Chandra and Tembo know early weekends would be the best time to find you at home," he said, filling our cups with water and tea bags which he took from his pocket. "I come to you with jasmine tea, Sunitha, your favorite. I'll make it sweet, as you always liked it."

He produced a plastic bottle of honey, which he

squeezed into her cup. She grabbed the bottle from him and shoved it, still dripping with honey, into his pants pocket.

"You needn't have bothered, Raj," I said.

"Rajesh, you stick to me like glue, not sweet and nice like this honey of yours." Sunitha said, calmly sipping her tea. "If you thought better of me, you would stay separate and not follow me to Mr. Cooper's."

"Then my cousin—she no longer wishes to marry?" Raj turned and asked me.

She told me a dozen times she had no intention of seeing him outside of work anymore, much less becoming his wife. I wasn't sure why he hadn't gotten the message yet. Either she hadn't told him directly, or he didn't care to believe it. Nor did I know why he called her cousin, unless that's what all Indians of the same age called each other.

"Don't let him confuse you, Leon," she whispered to me.

Sunitha retreated to the bedroom, rather than stay to help clear up the confusion. I didn't appreciate being left alone with him, especially since it was obvious that he was there for personal reasons, probably hoping to win her back from me. I didn't like to be challenged by him for a woman, especially by one of my employees.

"These Gazelle samples of yours are here a day early," I said, unscrewing one of the tops and pouring a taste into my empty teacup. "I prefer not doing business on Sundays."

"Please continue with the rest of the samples. Mr. Cooper, I assure you I would not normally bother you when you are busy with your new secretary." Again,

I made an effort not to show my annoyance. "I mean this must be the day you work together, planning your appointments for the week," he added, I suppose to save face for both of us.

"One of these beers tastes harsh, another watery," I said. "In one I taste the malt, and another tastes like it's lacking hops, like it's an ale. None of these tastes bad, but they are noticeably different from one another."

"I agree with you, Mr. Cooper, that they are too inconsistent," Raj said with a broad flash of white teeth. "I agree with my father we need to keep the taste uniform. Our customers don't like surprises. I do not mean to cause you friction, only to make your machines run smoother."

He looked at me carefully, trying to gauge whether I accepted his reason for this unexpected visit. I didn't, but it would have been a mistake for me to turn him back for pursuing his lost fiancé that morning. As much as I was tempted, I figured it best to forgive him and hear his report, especially if he had information about the business which I needed to know.

"I'm impressed with your dedication, Raj, going to all this trouble to report to me on some machinery that needs to be repaired. I suggest you figure out whether it's a plumbing, mechanical, or electrical problem and call in someone to come with an estimate of what it will cost to repair it. Okay?"

"If it was so simple, sir, I would not be so depressed."

He'd been thrown off-balance since the first riot in the plant, and I knew he was having trouble accepting the imminent shutdown of the old Kassie plant. Nevertheless, I gave him the benefit of my doubts, assuming he was under the stress of his futile sentry duty, and that he had a good reason for showing up in my kitchen that morning.

"Let's prioritize our problems. Which of our micro-breweries has produced these samples?"

"Ames, Laager Wheel, Chester's, and Pink Fynbos, four out of the dozen we've set up to date," he said. "See, each bottle has a number attached to the lid, and I have on this card the name of each of these shebeens."

Taught by his master brewer father, he knew far more about beer brewing than I ever would, yet he was coming to me for advice. Perhaps it was just an excuse to place himself before Sunitha.

"I see you've been taking pains to collect these samples."

"Thank you, sir. My father has taught me to take great care when taking samples. He has taught me not to take chances."

He was not looking at me, but over my shoulder at the bedroom. He was entirely too curious about this house and Sunitha's place in it. I caught him stealing a glimpse at Sunitha's nightclothes when he inadvertently placed his sleeve in a puddle of beer he dripped on the table.

"That red scarf you're wearing—is it silk like your shirt?" He nodded yes. "Since you don't take Sundays for church, what's the occasion for dressing up this morning, just to visit us? You might want to rinse the beer out of your shirt in the sink."

"Very sorry, Mr. Cooper. I did not come here to make a mess, but to help you."

After mopping up the table, he went to the sink to

daub his sleeve with water. I noticed blood caked on his neck beneath his bandana.

"Something heavy fall on you?" I asked, pointing to his neck.

He tried to conceal his wound by readjusting his scarf, but it was no use because I'd already seen his oozing gash.

"No, sir. Sometimes things are not as they appear."

"It would appear to me peculiar that a peaceful man like you is so ready to fight."

"I'm only fighting for us, Mr. Cooper. We caught Mafumo and his associates trespassing in our shebeen at Surrey Estate. The next time Hassan and me must be better prepared."

Mafumo was the black worker whose ankles his buddy held while he leaned into the vat of beer he had contaminated, the one who Raj and Chandra fired and who in retaliation joined forces with Ozeer's gang and organized our workers into striking.

"Rajesh, I hired you to make beer, not war!"

"Of course not, sir. I am here only to ask you how we should fix the way we do things in the plant until it becomes friction-free."

"You come with ideas about the old plant when you know it's beyond salvage?"

"I thought together we could discover the best course. That is why I come with bad samples."

He was undeniably clever, and evidently muddied up his problem, so I wouldn't know whether it originated in the old Kassie plant or in the new shebeens. I believed he had a plan in mind, but that he was introducing it bit by bit, trying to involve me so I'd accept it. If his father Chandra weren't so important to us in setting up the microbreweries in the shebeens, I might have terminated him. I knew Raj was manipulating me, with his excessive deference, even standing by the head of the table, as if waiting to serve me.

"You have a busy schedule, so I will take little more of your time. When my father and I used to work out of our Gazelle plant, we had great pride in quality control. Now, quality is low, and we have no control. There is too much variation in the processing. When the yeast is brought from shebeen to shebeen, we suspect it suffers not only in the travel, but in the refrigerators. We're afraid it's been getting too hot or too cold. Also, the batch sizes are not the same, so how can the flavor remain the same? And in each location the water is different."

"Raj, when the customer comes to the shebeen, he is looking for a beer with more personality than he would find in the grocery store. We have found in the States, the customer not only accepts but welcomes variations in taste."

He was shifting in his chair, looking into the bedroom again. Sunitha had changed into flowing pants of shiny fabric of the same eggshell color as the nightclothes I'd bought her. She, then Raj, looked to me for guidance, but I was not feeling generous enough to invite him to disturb us any further. My Sunday wasn't reserved for him, but for her.

"You have so many problems. I can't tell you where to start, but not this morning. I'll get back to you with an exit strategy."

"Because we are not first world like America or Europe, Mr. Cooper, we must therefore make a more consistent product," he said, not taking my hint that he leave. "If we are to continue supplying the accounts my father and I have developed over the years, we need to work out of a single plant. If we're trying to make a lighter beer, we can't do it with hard water with a lot of minerals. If we want to even begin to compete with the Lion or the Castle brands, we must wean our black customers away from the strong sorghum brews they used to make in their country villages. We must work out of a central plant. It's impossible to brew light beer using water piped in from God knows where. Typical shebeen water has too many minerals, and none of the shebeens, except Alicia's here in Rondebosch, filter the water to remove them."

He was not taking the hint that I didn't want to talk business now. Instead, he was continuing to yammer on about the old Gazelle processing methods, refusing to see that his days there were numbered.

"Filtered water, equal batch sizes, more careful handling of the yeast, excellent," I said. "Anything else?"

"I assure you, my father and I would not mind moving our stainless-steel vats to another facility of your choosing, where we could begin—"

I was not about to tell him that we would be using the very low-production microbrew shebeens as a frontline advertising promotion to gain credibility in the townships. I couldn't tell him because I couldn't trust him to keep our master plan confidential. In fact, unless he shaped up, I'd have to see to it that he got progressively less responsibility.

"Anything else on your mind, other than the faults in our brewing, which only you know how to correct?"

"I have too much on my mind, ever since Cousin Sunitha Bala has abandoned me."

"Sunitha and you aren't really cousins, I trust," I said pleasantly, working hard to avoid a confrontation with him. Sunitha seemed uneasy and left the room.

"You must see some resemblance between us, Mr. Cooper, unless we Indians all look alike to you. Sunitha and I are indeed cousins. That is the trouble between us."

"Come on, she wouldn't consider marrying a cousin like me unlike the Pakistanis in London do all the time!"

"Not anymore, not since you replaced me. The real problem between us is that we have come too close and know each other too deeply."

"Good, then you haven't married your cousin yet, and I hope you haven't already done anything with her you might both regret!"

"No problem. We're second cousins."

Cousins! He was patting my arm, as if soothing me. I was horrified but tried not to show my reaction. When we heard Sunitha's footsteps in the hallway, I was glad for the distraction, hoping when she returned we wouldn't have to talk about that unpleasant subject anymore.

"I know you've been talking about me, Rajesh," she said, standing behind him. She put her hands under his arms and eased him from the chair and began walking him out of the room. "That's why I've returned early, so you will stop making up stories about me now."

"I think about you day and night, Sunitha, but I come here today to bring a message from Alicia. She wants to see Mr. Cooper this evening at ten at her pub club here in Rondebosch. I should remember its new name, but I have too much on my mind."

"That would be Wandi Dadla's Place. Now, cousin," Sunitha said, looking for my reaction, for some reason. "Tell her our lord and master knows the way and that we'll be there."

Lord and master? That was a strange description of me coming from Sunitha, who I certainly didn't have to coerce to move in with me! We both knew the choice had been voluntary, yet she spoke to Raj as if I had control over her. Perhaps she saw him as a traditional Indian man who did not argue with his masters and accepted their authority.

Now that Rajesh had delivered Alicia's request to see me and left us alone, Sunitha and I were free to follow our original plan. That was a Sunday outing to the sandy beaches on the rocky coast. She remembered from when she was a little girl that most of the coast near Cape Town was rocky and inhospitable. Southward from Cape Town, the forbidding coastline was broken only by occasional stretches of sand.

We stopped at Llandudno, a lovely beach at the foot of a spectacular rise of mountains. Sunitha led us over to a spot with swimmers in a wide color range of skins, which pleased her. The parading women with their breasts bared interested me. Within a couple of hours my own pale skin started to burn beneath the sunscreen. We drove further south and eastward across the Cape peninsula to False Bay, to the rugged harbor of Simon's Town with its main street of restored two-story facades.

After lunch, we passed the off-limits navy compound

with guard sentries, which housed South Africa's submarines. "This decommissioned base was a holdover from World War II when the U-boats would prowl just offshore," she explained.

The next stop on this tour was Simon's Town, where she showed me a building with a phoenix rising from the flames and a Masonic emblem.

"This Masonic lodge was a holdover from 19th century slavers," Sunitha explained. "Welcome to Black Town, which was really Brown Town. Once slavery in England was banned, here the slave men, women and children captured by the British Royal Navy on the high seas were brought. They could have been my lost cousins."

I thought her relatives and the Kassies' were indentured servants, contract workers. Just as Rajesh did early in the day, she was confusing me. We ended the day's driving tour with dinner at the Ambassador Hotel, where I had previously been entertained by Rolf.

"Do you know that south of False Bay at the very tip of Africa, it was originally called the Cape of Storms, where many boats sank? Then for false advertising it was changed to the Cape of Good Hope. But here we are at the end of a beautiful day, high, dry and safe. What better viewpoint for us to share both today's sunset and tomorrow's sunrise?"

"To many more," I affirmed, raising my wine glass to her.

"Which we see together, or which you see by yourself?"

"Both," I said, looking past her at the clock on the wall.

"You didn't answer my question about us, which I'll

now withdraw. Besides, your mind is more on your 10
P.M. rendezvous with your dear friend Alicia, courtesy of
Rajesh," Sunitha remarked.

As far as I was concerned, Sunitha was late in object-
ing to my meeting with her, considering Alicia was
interested in me from the moment I got off the plane in
South Africa, long before I first met her. It also seemed
as if she suspected Raj's motives in encouraging me
to see another woman was to drive a wedge between
Sunitha and me.

"I think about you first, Sunitha, and if you want to
join us, please feel free to do so."

"We can't be free in this country, Leon, so long as
we must duck lead bullets. There must be another way
for us."

By its looks this block of Rondebosch, it could have
been an American college town. There was a photo-
copy store, bookstores, clothing stores, coffee houses,
restaurants, banks, and the crown jewel of the Chateau's
urban holdings, Wandi Dadla's. Inside, overwhelming
sounds pumped at us through massive speakers. The disc
jockey sat godlike in a glass booth suspended above the
dance floor and played eclectic tunes—traditional tangos,
waltzes and swing, with a hip-hop beat underneath it.
He built layers of sound and shifting rhythms, controlling
the motion of the dancers below him, as if he were a
puppeteer. I took Sunitha away from the punishing volume of the speakers, but even at that distance, I had to
speak into her ear. I asked her to help me find Alicia in
the packed dance club.

After several minutes of searching without finding
Alicia, Sunitha led me onto the dance floor. The dancers

around us were young, many from the university up the hill. I had trouble dancing to this music, not simply because I was older, but because the DJ was playing tricks, layering track on top of track of sounds. Nevertheless, I got myself in synch with her churning motion and locked myself into a groove with her. It was impossible not to bump into people, so I tried to keep my steps small, my elbows close to my sides.

I felt nudged from behind, ignored it, then felt another nudge. The third time I lost my balance and it made me trip into Sunitha. She thought I was embracing her and hugged me in return and kissed me. When I felt more tapping on my shoulder, I turned and saw it wasn't Sunitha, but Alicia. She motioned for us to follow. She was talking into her cell phone, plugging one ear with her index finger as she led us out of her club and onto the street. She stopped under the canvas awning, pocketed her phone, and smiled at Sunitha.

"Am I keeping you up too late?" Alicia asked, gave Sunitha a hug, then looked to me for an answer.

"Not at all," I said. "I figure it must have been important if you had to send Raj."

"Let me buy you a cup of coffee at least, for the inconvenience." She looked at her watch. "The way it works here is they save a parking spot for me across the street at ten o'clock whenever I'm playing disco coordinator, like I am tonight."

We walked across the street to the Olympia Restaurant, a glass front building with plastic laminate tables and bright fluorescent lights. Alicia seated us at the front window and scanned the street outside, rather than look at me.

"There's a nice view of the club from here," I said. "Sometimes we have to take a few steps back to gain perspective, don't we Alicia?"

"That's exactly why I had to consult with you tonight regarding my shebeen, Leon," Alicia said, "to gain perspective on my business."

"You know Ted's put more money into this upscale operation you're running than any other," I said. "He regards it as his showcase."

"Excuse me," Sunitha said, "but you should know that there was never a true shebeen here in wealthy Rondebosch. You may give it a Zulu name to make it sound authentic and African, but your place is really a European dance club."

"Why are you telling this to Leon?" Alicia asked sharply, moving her eyes from the street to Sunitha.

"Because as the Chief of Pubs, isn't it important for him to know the truth of how we do things in South Africa?"

"Sunitha, my friend," Alicia said, "your perspective doesn't matter anymore than mine. But, Leon, your advice does," she said, looking toward me. "I need your perspective on my direction. Since Wandi's means so much to Ted and the Chateau, you must help me understand how big I need to grow and what improvements we must make."

She stood up suddenly and rushed to the back of the restaurant, returning with the owner in a white uniform. She pointed out to him some young men milling around a white BMW with a magnetic sign on the door with our new Chateau Gazelle logo. He borrowed her cell phone to call one of the pub employees across the street to keep an eye on it.

"Where were we?" she asked, sitting at our table. "How much volume will I have to do to please him?"

"I think in dollars, say two million, by the end of the fiscal year, and in two or three years maybe four million. But for now, Ted's spent enough here," I continued, "not just on the sound system and the dance floor, but on the grand mahogany and brass bar."

"Ted's investing in me, Leon, a relative and not some stranger, someone who will be here long after you are gone!"

"In that case, you don't need my advice, Alicia. I'll be going right now!" I was halfway to the door with Sunitha before Alicia could intercept me.

"Stay, please," Alicia said. "I have only this question. Sunitha says we're not a shebeen, and her uncle has called us a microbrewery, since we sell all our beer on site, but in your professional opinion, what should we call ourselves?"

"Call it a pub or a tavern or a microbrewery or a shebeen. It doesn't matter. Your function here is to build name recognition, then brand royalty."

"To the contrary, it matters if Ted expects me to give up my airline career to run this place full-time."

"I believe that this place was more your idea than his, Alicia. Frankly, he told me the other day he doesn't care whether you stay in the air or come down to earth."

"You Yankees can be so blunt, but I trust we have no personal problem between us. So, if I may still count you a friend, will you tell me what I'll need to do to succeed here? How can I grow my business?"

"First, get to a positive cash flow. I've been checking

your figures, and I think you should be there within six months if you can control your expenses," I said.

"Can you be more specific?" she asked, placing her hands on mine. "I want to run this friction-free. I'll do whatever it takes to please Ted and you, whichever one of you is in charge of the Chateau's new beer business.

"Then keep doing what you're doing for the time being," I said.

"No, Leon, I'm afraid that won't be good enough. I must build my business considerably bigger than your projections. What would I need to do to develop this into a full-out brewery?"

It never made sense to me that Ted had thrown so much money into renovating this club, and especially why he put Alicia in charge. She knew how to serve passengers on an airplane, rather than how to run a profitable business.

"All the microbreweries make the same beer, whether we call it the old Gazelle with the logo of a herd or the new Chateau Gazelle with a single graceful animal. Wouldn't it make sense for me to augment the beer that will be produced at the new Drakenstein plant?" she reasoned. "If this were a real brewery instead of a microbrewery, then we could sell to outside markets. Even the Kassies agree not only we could sell more to the wholesalers but could also sell directly to retail out-lets such as supermarkets, restaurants and other bars."

Her request for me to authorize and divert more of the Chateau's resources to this already over-budget project resembled the one I'd previously received from Raj. The Kassies knew all about the art of brewing, but not enough about management. Against my advice,

Ted handed her everything she requested to set up this showplace money pit. Regardless, we couldn't afford to let her expand out of this location. Chateau wasn't about to take bad advice from employees like her who were incapable of seeing the big picture. She presented her case and now she was waiting for my judgment. She sat across the table, staring at me.

"Well?" she asked.

"I'm curious, Alicia. Was this idea of expanding out from Wandi Dadla's entirely your own plan?"

"Who else's?"

"It sounded similar to a scheme Raj just pitched to me."

"Leon, you should understand me well enough to know I'm not a schemer!"

I really didn't know her very well, other than one brief interlude in the Inter-Continental. I wouldn't embarrass her further though by questioning her about her impossible proposal, especially with Sunitha present.

But she had a more immediate problem. Two men had broken into her BMW and were attempting to start the engine! The moment the car alarm began to wail, the restaurant owner burst through the door. Before he got to the other side of the street, he was met by another man. With weapons drawn, the two of them now approached the robbers!

"The gentleman who owns this cafe runs so fast because he used to be a football champion, like Hassan always wished to be," Alicia said admiringly, strangely calm as if she were used to seeing car thefts.

The man and the restaurant owner prevailed, managing to pull both intruders out of the rear hatchway of the car. When we saw the would-be thieves quickly duck into an alley, Alicia laughed, pleased at the victory of her men, one of whom I now recognized as Tembo!

"You must have more friends than you realize, risking their lives for you," I said.

Her attention shifted from her car to her ringing cell phone. I used the interruption to get away from Alicia and her impossible proposals and crossed the street back to Wandi Dadla's. I wanted to check up on these two good Samaritans. But looking back, I saw I'd missed the Greek restaurant owner, who was back behind the cash register. That left me free to speak to Tembo alone, who I caught as he was entering the club.

"Tembo, I didn't expect to find you out here, chasing random thugs," I said. "That's not your job description. You're lucky someone didn't get hurt, or worse. From now on I forbid—"

"It's okay, Leon," Alicia interrupted breathlessly, herself having run across the street with Sunitha following. "Ted said I could borrow Tembo for a few nights until we find out who's been breaking into the cars of our customers parked on the street."

"Who were they, Tembo, these thieves?" I asked.

"Ozeer must have sent them. We had to chase them out of our neighborhood. I tell you, Miss Nichols, those yellow Chateau Beer signs on the side of Mr. Kruger's fancy car drew them to you like a moth to a flame. You should lose them signs."

Why was Alica driving Otto Kruger's car anyway? Was it her car, or was it a gift? That was a sign to me we were more than friends. Did this happen after I met him, or were they already lovers that night in the Inter-Continental when Alicia and I briefly came together. I had no personal interest in Alicia's love life, unless her arrangement with Kruger would affect her work for Drakenstein. But rather than take the time to probe into Ted's motives in lending her Tembo's armed services, it seemed best to leave right then.

I was anxious to protect Sunitha from these thugs, in case they intended to return. Alicia's cell phone rang again, and she talked behind us as we walked to the car. As we were pulling away, she rapped on my window, still on her phone.

"Leon were you really going to drive off without saying goodbye?" she asked once I lowered the window.

"Well, neither have you said goodbye to your friend on the phone," I said.

"It's Janice LeRoux. They want to invite you to Bergkloof next Saturday at noon."

"I'll have to check and get back to you. Take care," I said, closing the window.

"Not so fast," Alicia said. "Ted's the one speaking." She handed me her phone. "He expects you to be there with him. Myself as well."

"Since it's all been planned, I won't do anything to spoil it," I acquiesced. "We'll see you there."

"Just yourself, Leon," Alicia whispered. She looked at Sunitha, then kissed me on the cheek. "Promise?"

CHAPTER 11

LUNCH AT
THE BERGKLOOF INN

I didn't see why I had to accompany Ted to a meeting with Janice and Alicia in the white tribe village. We could have easily arranged a lunch meeting during the week in Cape Town or at the Chateau instead. Every time I tried to phone Ted with my suggestions for a more convenient time and place, he was unavailable. Saturday arrived, and Tembo called for me at 9 A.M., two hours earlier than I expected, to leave for our meeting. Just a week ago, without my approval, Raj had committed me to see Alicia in her club. Now she took her turn setting me up in an appointment arranged by others. I didn't appreciate arrangements being made without consulting me.

"Why are we arriving so early? Because you don't think I should keep Mr. Nichols waiting?" I asked Tembo once we were on the road.

"Because Mr. Nichols wants you to arrive early, at the same time as him."

"You know quite a bit about this meeting."

"Thank you, sir. I try to earn his trust, like with you."

"Good, then I trust you'll tell me why Mr. Nichols

hasn't been answering my calls and also why you're taking me to the Chateau instead of to Bergkloof."

"That's the trouble, Mr. Cooper, I know many of Mr. Nichols secrets, and yours as well. I don't dare mix them up, so I will say nothing more until I deliver you. Do you understand?"

I understood his fear of alienating Ted Nichols, his permanent boss, or me, his temporary one. It couldn't have been easy for him, trying to serve two masters. Perhaps he had no loyalty to me at all. That morning, he seemed to be concealing a plan he'd made with his first master, Ted Nichols.

We didn't speak for the balance of the trip to the Chateau. As far as I was concerned, that was better if he was going to avoid answering my questions. Nor did I ask why he drove a quarter mile past the big house to an equipment repair building. Behind it, Ted sat in the back seat of a white Cadillac from the early 50s, door open and his feet on the ground as he smoked a cigarette. He was wearing a beige jacket and a red silk scarf at the throat of his open shirt.

"Leon, I don't take this American car on the road often, but in your honor, I wanted you to enjoy riding with me today."

I might have appreciated it more if Ted hadn't used Alicia to deliver his message, then used Tembo to deliver me like cargo. There were no satisfactory explanations from them. I really had no complaints how Ted was treating me lately. He seemed to be taking me more seriously as his consultant, implementing almost all my suggestions. However, outside our scheduled, and often cancelled, weekly business meetings, he had been quite unsociable, keeping his distance from me. Today he was in a sociable mood, playing host, rolling out this restored automobile. Once we were moving, he poured me a stainless-steel cup of orange juice with ice, prepared from the limousine's bar.

"I must apologize for this product. It's neither Cooper's nor the Chateau's," he said, pointing to a bottle of Russian vodka. "If you wish, I can pour a couple of splashes into our glasses," he offered and glanced at his watch. "Tembo, it's 10 o'clock. You can turn on the news now."

On the radio came a report about a passenger on a packed train who had been sitting by an open window and was blinded by a rock thrown from beside the track. Maybe if I stayed here long enough, eventually such terrible events might have become normal to me!

"Another station, please. We don't want to give our American guest the idea that he's living amongst bloody spear-throwers!" Tembo switched to another news show, this one an interview of the survivors of a petrol bomb attack of a mosque in Bishop Laws.

"Who do you think is going to win, Tembo? Them or us?" Ted interjected.

I had no idea who Ted counted as his allies, nor what were the stakes of that bombing sabotage that killed half a dozen Moslems. Ted didn't wait long enough for me to think of an answer.

"Please turn it down a bit. We don't need any more bad news." He then raised the electric window separating us from Tembo.

"Recently I've been concerned about you as an American here in our country. We're traveling in this

American auto because I want you to feel a bit more at home, also because this car has a trunk big enough for a couple of paintings I'll be releasing to Janice."

"That's very considerate, Ted, a Cadillac in my honor."

"It was the only choice for this morning, since I have no other vehicle with a partition. We don't need my driver overhearing any more of your story than has become common knowledge, do we?" he asked with a wink.

How much had Ted been hearing from Tembo? Had Chandra been telling him more than he needed to know about Sunitha and me? Perhaps Ted was fishing for information about my private life, though I realized I myself had been probing into the affairs of him and everyone around him.

"You're a purposeful man, Ted. I suspect there is a method to your madness."

He leaned forward and pulled out the jump seat for me. He leaned close, arms on his knees, hands clasped and stared at me. "Speaking of madness, Leon, I understand how it creeps into a man, particularly one who has no friends or worse, the wrong friends. I know how lonely a young man can be in a new country, traveling alone. With all due respect to my brilliant consultant, I believe you may have gone a bit mad from your loneliness."

"No need to worry, Ted. I'm on track making measurable progress converting the old Gazelle to the Chateau label and setting up the shebeens as microbrew outlets."

"That's why I've been giving you better grades for performance whenever I speak with your brother about you. There's no doubt you've been successful in securing Chateau a foothold where we haven't dared venture before. But permit me to speak on a more personal level about where you've been venturing after hours."

"I'm afraid I can't permit you to cross that line, Ted."

"Aren't we talking about the color line, sleeping with them on a habitual basis?"

He leaned so close to me I could feel his breath on my face and bared his teeth at me, which I believe he intended as a smile. I wanted him off my trail, but I refused to lie to him or deny anything. Flustered, I offered no plausible explanation. Rather than honor my silence, he probed further into my life.

"We wouldn't be human if we didn't feel temptation. But yielding to it can topple the structure a man's worked hard to build."

"I have no intention of doing that, Ted. I've been assigned to add value to the structure of the Chateau, not detract from it. It looks as though with me representing Cooper and yourself, the Chateau can continue working quite well together. What do you think?"

"I think you gave in to temptation," said Ted with a consoling hand on my shoulder, "and you don't realize the complications that may cause."

The white South Africans wouldn't have had to be so vigilant to keep all whites from socializing with coloureds, blacks, and Indians if they didn't feel desperately outnumbered. On one hand, Ted wanted to reach into the townships to capture their business. On the other, he seemed displeased that I'd befriended Sunitha. He didn't realize how competent she was in the old Gazelle office, nor how useful she could be as office manager, if he were to give her more responsibility once I was gone.

"Ted, I don't understand what's bothering you. What complications?"

He poured himself another drink. I forewent the vodka to keep my head level and my tongue under control.

"It's sometimes mixed friendships that cause the complications. You see, mixing is nothing new to us, ever since the first ships came ashore looking for food, fresh water, ship provisions and indigineous women. Please don't misunderstand me. I have strong ties to England and empire and know how the world works far better than these Afrikaners do. To this day they've been trying to regain the power and the land they lost to us Brits in the Boer War better than a century ago. The peace we Englishmen made with them was far more generous than they deserved. Instead of having to fight with England, they've been waging a quiet hundred years' war with a new enemy here in South Africa—and that's anyone who gives them a hard time who's not a European.

"As an Anglophile who knows about building an empire, I believe there's more to be gained by trading with the non-Europeans than with fighting with them. Personally, I've always felt if the coloureds and blacks insist on fighting amongst themselves, that's their business. Unless, of course, their fighting interferes with Chateau's business, in which case we have Hassan to watch our interests."

"Is that why you sent for me this morning, Ted, to set me straight on the complications of doing business in South Africa?"

"No, it's about the complications you've introduced into our business union. Believe me, I've personally seen the troubles this sort of mixing can introduce into a family."

"Then consider yourself fortunate, Ted, that I'm your consultant, not your son."

His cell phone rang, and he rapped on the partition window, motioning Tembo to pull over. He quickly exited the car, shouting and cradling the phone against his neck, and began waving both arms. As he paced back and forth, he worked his way further and further from the car, approaching a line of trees. Tembo flung open the door, walked quickly towards him and stayed with him until they returned together.

"Care to say hello to my former wife?" he asked me and pushed the phone into my hand without giving me the chance to refuse.

"Jan LeRoux here. Who's this?"

Ted's former wife? Strange that in all the days I stayed at the Inn, Jan never mentioned that detail. Neither did Alicia, who would be Jan's sister-in-law. Either their silence was a coincidence, or the three of them had reasons to keep Ted and Jan's relationship a secret.

"Leon Cooper at your service," I greeted her, once we were back on the highway.

"First, Ted was going to visit by himself for lunch. Then he called to tell me he was bringing a friend, but he didn't want to tell me who. If it were anyone but you, Leon, I'd turn both of you away. But he's so busy if I break our engagement, I don't know when I could meet him again, and I really must update Ted now on what his family's doing here in Bergkloof. Leon, do you think Ted's brought you along because he's afraid to face me alone?"

"He's sitting beside me. If you want to speak to him directly, Jan, I'll say goodbye now."

She must have realized she'd already said too much and terminated the conversation with a click. I didn't want to put myself in the middle of a dispute between a divorced husband and wife. That left Ted again in the back seat scrutinizing me.

"Don't get the wrong idea about me and Jan. We had our differences before our family had a non-European introduced into it."

"You don't have to tell me anymore, Ted. This doesn't concern me."

"I only try to advise you because you need to know what happens in South Africa when you cross the line and mix with them, just as Janice did when we were first married," Ted said. "I'm speaking of Larabie Hassan. You need to know, regardless of who his Moslem father might be, I would have treated Larabie as a son if he hadn't kept such dangerous company since Jan brought him under our roof."

"Hassan, your son?" I asked.

"You can't really know a man unless you know his origins. You've been around long enough for me to take you into our Chateau family. But make no mistake about Larabie. He's Janice's. I've treated him very well over the years, even after Jan and I went our separate ways, but none of my blood runs in his veins."

It was a mid-December summer day in Bergkloof, the air muggy after the evening's rain showers, unusually heavy for the season. The still damp streets were filling with tourists, as the summer sun tried breaking through the clouds. On the main street, sightseers were entering a white masonry building in the restored Dutch style as all of Bergkloof. They paid their admission, and proceeded with maps to historical buildings, ambling on the cobblestone streets, buying mementos along their tour. The highlight of the tour, which I took the first day I stayed in Bergkloof, was the church which stood opposite the Bergkloof Inn.

"I had Tembo cruise around the village because we're ahead of schedule," Ted said.

We parked near the drostdy, which looked different from my initial visit. There was a ditch dug around the front of the building, revealing the foundation. A temporary fence had a CLOSED FOR RESTORATION sign. Behind that was an outbuilding, the size of a small house, built in the same Dutch style as the other restored buildings. All windows and doors were ret-rofitted with thick steel bars, and steel shutters. The building posted NO ENTRY! KEEP OUT!

"Hassan told me you and Kassie visited him here some months ago," Ted continued, standing beside the car, smoking a cigarette. "When I found out Larabie was working here, I wanted to know whether he came to get away from people, or whether he was looking for a kind of clubhouse for his friends. Do you know how he found time to work here at half the rate the Chateau pays him?"

Ted sounded like he was keeping something from me and wanted to find out how much I knew. It seemed strange to me that we paused at the drostdy, rather than go directly to the Inn. He seemed on edge, proba-bly because he was suspicious of all of Hassan's friends. Or was I detecting edginess about our meeting with Jan

239

and how this detour was designed as a means of post-poning it a few minutes more.

"I feel like a tourist in your country. Hassan baffles me as much as nearly everyone here."

"Even as much as your new girlfriend Sunitha? Does she baffle you, or does she give you the illusion she understands you?"

"That's quite personal, Ted."

"Leon, if I didn't trust you, would I have identified Larabie as my son and Janice as my former wife, his natural mother?"

Since I met him, Ted maintained a cool distance between us. Now he was pressing me with most personal information, and I was not quite sure how to respond.

"Associating with the non-Europeans," he continued without waiting for me to respond, "has cost me my family. I don't know what mixing will cost you, Leon. But I do know, like me, you will have to make peace with how you feel when and if you father rainbow children. I've brought you with me today, not just to pester you with my advice, but to take some advice from you regarding my former wife!"

The gravel lot in front of the Bergkloof Inn was full. We waited for a convertible BMW to leave, driven by an attractive woman dressed in a stylish tennis outfit that matched that of her tall, bronzed companion.

"The tourist trade does a big stroke of business for the year-end holiday," Ted said, inspecting the license plates of the Inn's guests. "Most of these cars are from Johannesburg. For their big yearly holiday, a lot of the whites, and lately blacks and coloureds who can afford it, travel to the Cape. Compared to Jo'burg, it's safe here, but we know how quickly that's changing! We can't let fear get the better of us, can we?"

I never had to answer his query about fear because someone captured his attention.

"Mr. Nichols," greeted the young coloured clerk, stepping from behind the reception desk to shake his hand. "We have been expecting you,"

The clerk was wearing a khaki bush outfit with epaulettes and button-down flaps over multiple pockets. "You look like you stole this from a British army grunt or are you a tracker from one of the game parks up north? Does Mrs. LeRoux have all you employees wear this uniform?"

"Yes, the overseas tourists like it very much and think we have lions raiding us at night, carrying off our livestock, sir," he explained.

It was a rude thing to say to the clerk, especially since Ted himself favored these safari vests. The young man took it well. Perhaps I simply didn't understand their sense of humor. The clerk led us from the front lobby on to the middle bridge of the H-shaped building, and finally to the patio and garden in the interior courtyard.

"So where are you from, Mohammed?" Ted asked, reading the clerk's brass name tag.

"The same place as my friend Larabie Hassan."

"Then you must be indebted to him for bringing you to this beautiful village," Ted said. "Where did you first meet him?"

"We've known each other since we were boys, Mr. Nichols. We first met when he was cast out of his home and onto the streets."

"Mohammed, don't you believe any such thing happened to Larabie, never! Take my advice and don't believe everything you hear. And don't be passing on any more foolish rumors about him!"

Ted began to say more but stopped short, threw up his hands, and lit a cigarette, which he smoked in fast puffs. I was accustomed to seeing him calm and fully in control, but now he seemed transformed, angry at a desk clerk he'd never met before.

Mohammed seemed nonplussed by Ted's criticism, and he seated us at a table furnished with linen tablecloth and napkins, a generous platter of fruit, and wine in a crystal decanter. Ted's hand shook as he poured our water, then he accidentally knocked over my glass of wine, which shattered on the patio floor and left a red streak on the white tablecloth. Sunitha's table mishap at Aunt Giri Bala's was oddly similar.

"I am sorry! Please sit at this table instead," Mohammed said, quickly moving us. "Please do not tell Mrs. LeRoux how clumsy I am today, diplomatically blaming himself for Ted's mishap."

"I'll tell you what," Ted said, "if you leave us now, I'll forget about you and all the false rumors you've been spreading about Hassan.

"I am sorry to remind you of Hassan's family, Mr. Nichols. I should have said nothing. I must forget everything Hassan told me. I promise he never said who was his father. If I did hear about it, I was too young to remember, alright? But please, do not tell Mrs. LeRoux you don't wish me to serve you! I must go now because we have a full house, and I'm needed in the dining room."

Again alone, Ted carefully poured us a fresh glass of wine. He sipped his and looked closely through the glass doors separating us from the main dining room, which was filled with holiday guests. Some mistakenly tried to enter the patio and garden where only Ted and I were present, but the door was locked for them.

"The way that crowd's looking in on us, I feel like we're fish in a bowl," Ted muttered once he had rejoined me.

"These roses weren't in bloom the last time I stayed here. We could easily be in paradise," I said, trying to cheer him. "Jan certainly has a way with plants."

Then in perfect timing, Jan emerged from between two Ficus plants, whose fronds had been concealing her. She produced a hose with a sprayer, indicating she wasn't spying, but watering the plants. Ted gave her a hug, then held her at arm's length, inspecting her.

"Have you gone native?" he asked, holding the sleeve of her brightly decorated earth-toned dress. He walked slowly around her, studying its orange and red pattern. "In your dress I see men with spears. Does this represent a primitive ceremony, or does it have a more current meaning?"

"You've always been so literal-minded, Ted!" she reacted, and pulled away from him.

"You never understood how intuitive I am, Janice. I look at your lovely dress and instinctively sense you are advertising for the next war, which, for all I know, you may somehow be assisting."

Jan took me by the arm and allowed me to help seat her at the table. Ted moved to unlock the glass door to greet Alicia, who was on the way to the dining room with menus in one hand. He took a vase of flowers from her other hand and embraced her in a far warmer greeting than he had for Jan, then followed her into the dining room, where he remained for an uncomfortably long time.

"Ted can be a charmer when the mood strikes him," Jan said as we waited. "Tell me, Leon, is he a better mentor to you than he is to his daughter Alicia out there?"

"Excuse me?"

"I mean, how can you work with him? What's your secret? Tell me."

Jan was asking me a personal question about Ted, whose answers she should have known herself! She was encouraging me to criticize him, which was inappropriate for me to do. I refused to speak poorly of him to anyone, especially with the new alliance between Cooper and Chateau, which I could not afford to jeopardize. He was certainly not my mentor, any more than he was Alicia's father, no matter what Jan might be implying about his domination of her or of me.

Now Ted was bringing in the two paintings that I saw on the Chateau wall. In the first, the French peasants were harvesting grapes.

"I know just the place I'll display that landscape," Jan said. "I've always loved it more than anything."

The second, the portrait of her sitting at the glass table by the cherry tree, her bathing suit hanging from the low tree limb, brought her to her feet as Ted stood it against the wall.

"Ted, you know this was meant for our bedroom, not for public display!" she said tersely.

She grabbed the nude and hustled it out of the room. When she returned to the table where Ted, Alicia and I were waiting for her, she placed her hands gently, maternally on Alicia's cheeks.

"You know, I never intended for you to wait on our guests when you come home," Jan said.

"And you never intended that two of your staff wouldn't show up this morning when you most needed them, did you? Nor that I'd have to dig up Mohammed, Larabie's friend, to take up the slack. While I'm here, I can make myself useful. After all, I don't have to be at the airport until Tuesday morning, and in the meantime, they can get along fine without me tonight at Wandi Dadla's. You've always done the same for me whenever I needed help."

"Of everybody in the family you were the only one I knew would always be there to help me," Jan said.

Alicia looked back and forth between Ted and Jan expectantly, then quickly returned to serve guests in the other rooms. Jan looked at Ted disapprovingly, then walked behind him, placed her hands on his shoulders and swept them all the way down his arms. She knelt beside him, now looking more closely at his cufflinks.

"A nice pair of emeralds, green like your eyes," she said, touching the cufflinks, "You've always been a formal man, wearing long sleeves on hot days, or perhaps you're simply cold-blooded. These are the same emerald green as Leon's girlfriend's cat eyes."

I was surprised she remembered Sunitha's intense green eyes, and still didn't know why I'd been brought to the meeting and having to witness their longstanding bickering. I hoped Ted didn't expect me to offer my opinion about the artwork he'd brought, obviously a source of contention between them. For now, they had no further comments on each other's appearance. She was fiddling with her ring when Ted suddenly took her hand, and turned it to see her ring, now worn on the middle finger, rather than allow her to slide it upside down and hide it.

"A marquis cut, nearly four carats, excellent color," Ted said, holding her hand for me to see. "Proof that no one more generous to her than I was. Do you like it, Leon? Do you wear it to impress your guests, Jan?"

Annoyed, she yanked her hand away. "Neither this ring, nor I, belong to you anymore, Ted."

"And I thought there was still some connection between us, and that you invited me to lunch because we're still friends."

Rather than respond to him, Jan quickly walked away. She rapped on the glass to call the waitresses, who brought a tray of cold cuts. We made sandwiches, filled our plates and ate without speaking. Jan finally pushed her plate aside.

"Ted told you of Larabie's situation?" she asked me.

I wished they had sorted their differences without me present. She was fishing for information, but I didn't dare slip up and tell her any more than Ted would want her to know.

"I told Leon that Larabie was raised as our son," Ted shouted, pounding his fist on the table, "but he doesn't know any more than I do of your Moslem independence fighter who fathered him! Instead of separating from you the minute I found out, I've raised Larabie as my own! I'm not a saint, but I am certainly not a fool!"

"A saint? Never!" Jan shouted back. "I wish your daughter could hear your empty boast! You were always a lady's man with anyone but me. You never bothered staying home enough to be much of a father to either Larabie or our daughter."

Ted watched me while she spoke, probably gauging how much of her complaints I believed, then left me alone at the table, and walked outside to light a cigarette. Jan moved in her own direction and grabbed the hose to water the roses.

"We don't allow smoking here!" Jan called out without turning around to look at him. "I didn't ask you here to insult me or to kill my plants! I must apologize, Leon, for the unpleasant interruption of our meal."

Rather than answer, Ted rushed to her and seized the sprayer, which he threw to the ground, soaking his shoes. This was becoming unpleasant.

"You told me you urgently needed to speak to me about Larabie," said Ted finally, "yet suddenly you have nothing to offer, other than anger and frustration. You have guests waiting, and I've run out of patience. We'll be on our way!"

He stepped away and nodded his head towards the nearest door. As I stood, Jan flung a stainless-steel pail, striking Ted's leg. He took it by the handle and slammed it back into her hands, striking something hard.

"Now you've done it, Ted! You've chipped my ring!"

"Remember that next time you throw your chamber pot at me!"

"I was merely returning that bucket of yours. Didn't you notice the Chateau label on the back?" she asked, turning the pail so its logo faced him. "And just because it smells like ammonia, it doesn't mean it was a chamber pot! There was fertilizer in here, chemical nitrate fertilizer! One of my staff saw it fall out of Larabie's truck on the way to the drostdy. He wanted to return it to him. My man also found these outside the drostdy outbuilding."

From her pocket she removed a handful of spent rifle shells and dropped them into the bucket one by one. She stared at him as if she'd caught him with a secret to hide.

"What's your complaint, Jan? Didn't you figure out a way to make Larabie visit you more often other than to have him play groundskeeper at the drostdy? Or was it your plan to hire him away from me?"

"Well, it wasn't my plan that he concoct God-knows-what explosives and go out on the veld at night target practicing!" Jan said. "I never liked the looks of the construction men Larabie brought here! I don't like—" she turned to me.

"Leon, we never should have burdened you with our family matters. Now I believe Tembo needs to speak with you." Her apology made, she led me to the storage room where Tembo was waiting for me, patient as usual.

"Alicia needs to see you right now," Tembo said, and came out of the pantry.

I followed him outside the main building to a garage and apartment above it. Unlike the town's historic buildings, its style looked more Teutonic than Cape Dutch. He spoke into an intercom, then led me up the stairs, where Alicia was waiting for me, coffee

cup in hand. She sent Tembo away and took me into her apartment, apparently another planned hand-off completed.

"Am I being delivered into the mouth of the whale?" I asked, planning to exit soon without offending her. "A strange location for a guest room, away from the main building and over a garage."

"It's not strange for a private person like me. Besides, I've always love it here. It was converted from a carriage barn. Jan's been very kind to let me use this suite whenever I visit."

"This furniture seems unlike any of the other pieces at the Inn."

"That's because it's all made from railroad ties, pallets, driftwood, yard sales, and such. See the nail holes?" She guided my finger to the nearest hole, which looked like a worm hole. "This furniture is a bit too countrified for Jan and Peter, but I don't care. This is my room when I'm visiting, and the adjoining one is Larabie's. They call this the railroad flat, though Larabie's room is different, with a nautical theme. I understand he's the reason you're visiting Bergkloof."

"So, between flights and when you can get away, this is where you stay? And this adjoining one is his?"

"Now you know the last of my secrets, Leon."

I headed for Hassan's room, but she blocked my way.

"His walls are dark wood," I observed from a distance, straining to investigate the forbidden room, "while yours are neutral. I also see a model boat out there."

"Larabie's always been an overgrown boy. He still doesn't let anybody in there except me, not even his friends, including Mohammed, who you've already met."

"Alicia, I'd like to talk to you"

"Quiet, we don't have much time. Don't look so alarmed." She sat me at her dining table and poured herself another cup of coffee. "I know you've been enjoying Sunitha. She's my best Indian friend, and you're my best Yank friend. Like my father, I have an international point of view."

Before I met Ted, my brother Harry described him as a man with an international point of view, the exact description of him Alicia just gave me. This information was consistent with the rumors circulating but calling Ted her father—that was absolute confirmation! Ted and Alicia have revealed the deep secrets of their family tree.

"I'm flattered by the trust you and your immediate family have shown me, but I don't understand why neither Jan nor Ted mentioned they were once married, that you and Hassan are their children."

I was disoriented by what Alicia had revealed, and she looked different from the way she did downstairs. Serving guests she wore a modest blue suit; she was now clothed in a sheer blouse with no underwear.

Since the short hours we'd spent in the Inter-Continental, I couldn't forget how she'd looked minus clothes. Perhaps she wanted to continue what we finished so quickly. She smiled at me.

"Ted told you how we're related?" she asked. I nodded yes. "He's already admitted to being my father and Larabie's stepfather, so why are you here? To torment my mother?"

"I wouldn't worry too much about Janice," I said. "She's a formidable contender in the sparring match with your father, fighting over Larabie and his construction friends at the drostdy. Can you tell me why they're digging up the foundation?"

"To repair hidden damage from the earthquake that leveled everything forty years ago. The cracks in the walls, especially the foundation, were growing wider."

"Another question, if you don't mind, Alicia—if Hassan grew up at the Chateau when Ted and Jan were married and living there, how did he end up on the streets?"

"That would be a long story."

I was sitting in a wing chair when Alicia leaned over and rested her hand on my knee. "It's too bad we didn't finish what we started when we were together at the hotel. But today we have time for a short one."

"If they're shorthanded on help today, shouldn't you be downstairs helping, rather than entertaining me?"

I knew I would not go further with Alicia, as I was bound to Sunitha. When she sensed it, she backed away, leaving me free to exit her flat. I got as far as the threshold of Hassan's quarters.

"If my intent was to amuse you, Leon, I'm failing miserably," she said, again blocking my way into the next room.

"I'm sorry if I disappoint you, Alicia. At least tell me the short version of how your brother ended up on the streets, or else show me more of that model ship. Otherwise, I'll get back to Ted."

I eased my way to the outside door, but she still wasn't letting me leave. My hand was on the knob, and her hand was on mine. She stared at me, then put her arm around my waist and led me into Hassan's room.

"This isn't a model of a boat, but of a submarine, a replica of an American submarine that sank in the Atlantic. As soon as he was old enough, Larabie tried to join our Navy. They would not take him for submarine duty because he wasn't Anglo or Boer. A shame because he'd have been a very brave sailor and it would have taken him off the streets. Does that answer your question?"

She took me into Hassan's off-limits boyhood room to show me his collection of fighting boats and soldiers. His shelves were lined with Greek soldiers in tunics, Romans in armor, soldiers with World War I wide-brimmed helmets, as well as World War II soldiers with Maltese crosses.

"The other night outside Wandi Dadla's, we were fortunate the thieves were after your car and not you, Alicia. I see why your father worries so much about Gazelle's security, even more than about the Chateau's. It always seemed to me uncanny how Hassan knows how our enemies think, as if he's lived with them all his life. Now I see he's always been a student of war."

I was holding a model tank from the World War II shelf, relieved at the redirection of her love-seeking energies. "Why did you do that?" she asked, putting it back in its place and treating me like a child in a curio shop.

"If the Army or the Navy was Larabie's ambition, I'm surprised that with all of his high connections, Ted was unable to place him in officer's training," I had nothing to substantiate my theory.

"Speaking of place, we're quite out of place here," she added, pulling me away before I could find anything more specific and useful to answer my questions.

"I'm the one who doesn't belong here," I said, helping her save face, "and I'm sorry I've made you uncomfortable."

"Please, we both know that lately Ted has been taking your advice far more seriously than mine."

"Give yourself more credit. You'll be important to the Chateau's operations long after I've gone. You're not putting in your time at the brewpub because you like loud music and drunks, but to train yourself for a career out of the air and on the ground. Right?"

"Thank you." She smiled, pleased with my acknowledgment of her influence.

The phone rang, but she seemed more interested in keeping me close. Rather than allow me to leave, she interlocked her fingers in mine, a grip difficult to break, and insisted I stay for coffee.

The phone rang again. This time she cradled it to her ear as she made us coffee.

"Mr. Nichols left Mrs. LeRoux to drink with the guests? Tembo, the trip will be a waste of Mr. Nichols' time if you can't bring them back into the same room to finish their session.... Don't tell me you're just his chauffeur, we all know better... We know how loyal to the family you've been, but I'm not at liberty to tell you family business... Then ask him directly."

"Did you need to speak to Tembo?" she asked me, muffling the mouthpiece.

"For now, I'm far more interested in hearing from you," I said.

"Mr. Cooper has no further instructions," she said to Tembo.

Alicia offered sequentially a coffee, a glass of wine,

and a variety of snacks, each of which I declined. It was time to for me to go.

"Mr. Cooper, what's your real agenda?" she queried as if we were strangers.

"I'm not here to talk business with you, Alicia." I was now seated at the table looking at one of her South African history books.

She was pacing behind me. "If you were facing me, it would be easier to hear you."

She sat down and nervously motioned to me, spilling her coffee, like what Mohammed did serving wine downstairs, as well as what Sunitha did at my dinner with Aunt Giri! I wondered whether I had an aura about me making people so jittery they couldn't hold drinks without dropping them. She quickly returned from the kitchen and cleaned up the mess with a cloth.

"So much for me. As an American, Leon, it won't be easy for you to understand a typical South African family like ours."

"It's been hard to figure out how you and Hassan are related to Ted and Janice or get an idea of how you lived together or apart and when."

"Leon, what you can't understand is if my half-brother Larabie grew up in this room, privileged, how can he know the underworld so well, correct? I wonder that myself. I could blame my mother as Ted does, but I won't because she's always had a big heart. When Ted brought her to the Chateau as a bride, the workers, especially the coloured and the black ones, trusted her. She made sure all of them ate well and had housing, no matter what their hourly wage. The problem was she made Ted quite nervous because she upset the fine

balance we maintained in apartheid days. It was hard for him to go along with her costly generosity, but quite another when she began siding with the ANC."

"The ANC? Nelson Mandela's disciples?"

"Ted used to call him King Kaffir. Today someone could be jailed for saying that. The landholders were none too pleased with the revolution which the international communists and ANC won. No matter how hard and how often the government forces raided their strongholds, there was no stopping them. To Father it was bad enough to be losing control of the country, but even worse to be losing my mother."

"Losing her to divorce?"

"It's not easy telling this to you, especially now that you're the power behind the throne at the Chateau."

"Not at all. We're all working as a team, and I value everyone's—"

"Please, Leon," she countered. "You're the key player making the game plan these days. But since we're not talking business anymore and we have a moment alone, let me satisfy your curiosity about my parents' differences. I can only guess the truth of the conflicting accounts Jan and Ted have told Larabie and me, separately. Mother will never tell me exactly what she did for the ANC and the revolution, but while she was assisting them, she made it a point of pride that she would never stay away overnight from the Chateau and Father and me.

"My father suspected that Jan was spending at least a day a week away from the Chateau to meet with people she would be afraid to bring home. His sources found out her Moslem friends were not part of the black ANC, but were their cohorts, coloureds working to bring down the apartheid government. In those days the whites saw the ANC as a direct threat not only to the government, but to their lives, and regarded sympathizers with the ANC as traitors.

"The Moslems, especially those my mother knew, they were not willing to allow their young men to defy the national government by looting, burning, and violently demonstrating. That's because the Moslems as coloureds, unlike the blacks, were allowed to learn trades and were afraid of going to jail and losing their livelihood as artisans. My mother will claim to her last breath that her Moslem friends always had their government ID documents in order and honored the curfews, and that she never expected they would be hunted down as a direct threat to the government. She'll have you believe she had no idea what a dangerous game her revolutionary friends were playing.

"Anyway, she was at a meeting in the Malay section in Cape Town when the inevitable happened. The police swooped down upon a house meeting of her and her friends and beat some of them senseless. The police were courteous to my mother, allowing her to ride in the front of the van to the police station. They locked up the ringleaders separately. And over the next couple of days, they were all interrogated."

"They interrogated Jan as well?"

"Not exactly."

"Because she was a woman?" I asked.

"In general, they did not treat women harshly, especially white women. Nevertheless, they regarded Jan as a conspirator and would have held her overnight if she weren't the wife of an important businessman. They didn't want to hold her as criminal, or even as a minor offender. As my mother describes it, the police simply wanted to humiliate her in front of Father. That is why they offered a deal to return home with no charges. She tried to refuse and be jailed like her subversive friends, but she had no choice and was delivered to the Chateau in a police car. The police must have known Ted was returning from a business trip to Johannesburg and wouldn't be home until ten in the evening. How else could they have timed their departure with Mother so that they arrived within a few minutes of him? They repeated the charges against illegal meetings and conspiracy and warned Ted that next time they wouldn't give his wife special treatment, then released her under the condition that he keep her under his control and in his custody."

"Did she give up meeting with her fellow travelers after that?"

Alicia nodded, but instead of answering, she just smiled as me.

"I know what you're thinking," she finally spoke. "I hope you don't judge us too poorly."

"Not at all," I reassured her.

Alicia came to me to put her hand on my shoulder. "You've been such an understanding friend, and I appreciate it. Because I know I can trust you, I'll share the rest with you about Larabie. Let's start at the beginning. When my mother fell pregnant with him, I was ten. When Larabie was born he looked nothing like Ted. For the sake of peace, my mother would have been wiser to never admit that he was fathered by another man."

I was embarrassed that she was telling me their most intimate family secrets, yet I needed to know as much as I could if I was to continue dealing with the Nichols family. I had only a short time with her, and I wasn't sure I'd have this opportunity again.

"So have you any idea who Larabie's father might be?"

"Larabie hardly looks like my mother and nothing like my father. They used to joke about him being switched at birth in the hospital. But by the time he was in school it wasn't a joke anymore. My mother won't tell me how Ted learned that he wasn't the father. He learned the truth when Larabie failed to return from school. Father sent a couple of his trusted coloured workers after him who found him in Mitchell's Plain in Cape Town with the sons of her old Moslem ANC friends.

"As a teenager it got harder and harder to keep him in school and away from the ANC controlled districts. Dad did his best acting like a good father, even though he knew he wasn't his natural son. Jan did her best to avoid Ted, spending a lot of time with other women who lived on vineyards like she did. They usually met in Stellenbosch for lunch. One afternoon they decided to try the Bergkloof Inn, which had been the LeRoux family farm for over a hundred years. Peter LeRoux was a handsome young man and developed a close friendship with my mother. He gave my mother a place to stay while she was separating from Ted. It was about that time that my brother came of age and foolishly had his name changed from James Nichols to Larabie Hassan. Believe it or not, he decided to rejoin his coolie tribe."

She stopped short, unsure whether to continue. When

the phone rang, she smiled, apparently relieved for the interruption.

"Tembo, you haven't been able to get Mr. Nichols to leave the bar...? Really, Mrs. LeRoux came to him there...? They were drinking together and laughing, no fighting...?"

I listened to her conversation. Ted wanted to leave in five minutes, but Alicia didn't.

"No, that's not enough time. We need twenty... Then you can tell him I said for once he can wait for someone else! Go ahead, blame it on me!" Frustrated, she turned to me.

"So little time—and I've spent almost all of it speaking of my family."

"About everyone but yourself, Alicia. You're still a mystery."

"How can I be a mystery after what you've seen of me already?" She rose to close the blinds, then went into the bedroom. "Now what do you want to know?"

"You've been very quiet about Colin and that side of the family," I remarked. "I've hardly seen him outside the office, and I get the impression there's no love lost between you and him. Am I imagining it, or is Ted trying to keep him out of sight and bury him in paperwork?"

"Let's just say Ted and I agree he'll continue to serve us well in his present capacity. He knows I'm more suited for dealing with the public." She came to me and took my head in her hands, then stepped back. "Sometimes it's hard to see ourselves as others see us." She studied my expression. I tried to keep a pleasant face, especially since she'd entrusted me with her most intimate family secrets.

"It's a pity we haven't more time," I said, providing a reason that might help her save face. "Under different circumstances I could help you better enjoy your furlough."

"Leon, I'm never sure whether I amuse or annoy you. No need to be polite, my offer's withdrawn."

"That's okay, no need to explain," I reassured.

"No, Leon, I want to account to you, as my friend, not as my boss. I know I've been tempting you, but that wasn't my intention. And I didn't intend to test your loyalty to Sunitha. She's a good companion for the duration of your layover in our scary country. Just remember we don't have nearly as many Indians here in Cape Town as north in Durban, so consider wherever you go as a mixed couple, you'll be noticed by strangers."

The advice about being seen in public with Sunitha was like Ted's, not helpful at all, but from her it sounded like it was coming from a rejected woman. I tried hard to hide my annoyance, since, after all, she had been helpful in putting together the missing pieces of her family puzzle.

"I understand why the Inn is your destination whenever you're in South Africa. It will always be your home. You look so different from Larabie, no one would ever guess you're even distantly related, but now I see how closely you resemble Ted."

"I have a good reason to see more of Father, now that the Chateau has set up Wandi Dadla's. He's helping bring me back home, and I love him for it. Leon, before you came to set the Chateau on a new track, I dreaded signing up for layovers in South Africa. In fact, I was debating quitting flying and emigrating to England, but it rains too much there. I also considered moving here to Bergkloof to be close to my mother, but who wants to live in a village turned into a museum?"

"So, you wouldn't want to live in a wet country like England or a dry village like Bergkloof? Maybe you've traveled so much you forgot where you want to go. Travel can be frightening."

She was in the bedroom changing into the third outfit since my arrival, a plain blue dress with brass buttons, her flight uniform. When she returned, she asked me to attach the hook and eye above the zipper, though she must have been able to do it by herself.

"Traveling here has frightened you?" she asked, turning my observation back on me. "How exactly?"

"Only in a dream which has repeated itself a couple of times. In it I booked passage on a ship that was not going to complete its crossing. First, an iceberg that punctured it. In the next dream, a tidal wave swallowed the ship. Then it was a reef. In another, a torpedo."

"You felt by returning home you were booking passage on a ship doomed to sink? Or it's our country that's doomed? You've escaped, but feel you must return despite grave danger? That's why you will do well to team up with my brother Larabie," she surmised.

"Why?"

"Because since he was a little boy, he dreamed of patrolling the sea and fighting for our country in a submarine. If water's your worst nightmare, it's his first love. He's strong where you're weak."

"Team up with him for what, Alicia?"

"I know you need to make a success here before you can go home. That's also why you might do well to

THE CHIEF OF PUBS

team up with a business-minded woman like me, not just with bodyguards like my brother and Indians— unless all your talk of the friction-free American way of business is a fraud."

"I believe in win-win solutions, that's all. What I care most about these days is making my relationship with your father work smoothly. I believe we can help each other."

She walked to the window, opened the blinds and looked outside. "The car's waiting below, and we're out of time, Leon. You know what you want, but if we're to cooperate, you need to know what I require. Ted's made it clear I have an essential position at the Chateau once I've proved my merit at the pub. With your help I can look forward to the day I can get away from pushing service trays along skinny aisles at 30,000 feet."

"Alicia, all of you and the Chateau staff could carry on without me. I could be the one checking in on a quarterly basis, while you're permanently and happily employed here. Don't worry, I'll be setting a timetable for my exit with Ted."

"All I know is the car's ready and Tembo promised to take me to the airport, which isn't too far out of your way. I'm glad you know I'm Ted's daughter, but you must keep it as privileged information!"

The car horn sounded as she emerged in her uniform, hat, scarf and airplane pin on her lapel, rolling her suitcase.

"I can help with that," I offered as she bounced it down the steps.

"I'll take a rain check," she said. "Save it for something important, if I ever have a big load to carry."

When we finally arrived Ted was busy reading business reports in the back seat of the Cadillac. Alicia leaned inside and pulled him outside to hug him. She embraced Ted, rocking from side to side, and looked for my reaction, as if still teasing me. Ted seemed comfortable with her and was laughing, which I'd rarely seen before.

"Leon, Ted knows that old American car's far too wide for our roads, but he's running it to please you. Aren't you, Father?"

For the first time I saw Ted at a loss for words. He looked at Tembo in the mirror, who didn't seem to hear. I still didn't understand why he'd been so reluctant to acknowledge her as his daughter. Maybe for the same reason he had for not openly acknowledging Larabie. It occurred to me if Jan LeRoux wasn't Alicia's mother, that would mean Larabie and Alicia weren't even half-siblings. Maybe the whole family was being held together by some private code of honor and deception.

I felt naïve and overwhelmed but didn't want to spoil the pleasant conversation she initiated as we rode to the airport. Ted opened up about his plans—our plans—for a bigger and more prosperous Chateau with Alicia's willing help. Ted offered her a glass of wine, though he knew she couldn't ink it before reporting for duty. When we came to the terminal, I wanted to ask her whether she had any fears before she travels but was superstitious enough to avoid introducing bad luck by bad suggestions.

CHAPTER 12
LOST CAUSE

Without delegation I couldn't have extended Chateau's reach as far as I had in such a short time. We already had twenty-three new outlets, which meant about $2.5 million per month additional sales. Hassan, with Tembo's backup, continued to be invaluable in giving me access into the toughest townships. Some of the regular staff, especially those assigned to maintenance of buildings, I redirected to assist me in our expansion campaign of renovating existing shebeens. I gave Chandra final supervision of the brewing equipment in the big new Gazelle plant, which had just come online, though at 40% capacity.

Our first total pub renovation, Wandi Dadla's, was originally a Woolworth's department store. Alicia, against my advice but with Ted's indulgence, insisted on doing the renovation her way, in the end hiring some of her friends in the building trades. It would have been better for her to follow the architect's original advice, but she changed her mind and modified the plan so frequently, he ended up quitting. It therefore came as no surprise to me her pub was running way over budget. That one outlet took more attention than I myself would have given.

As the Chateau's advisor, I had a reasonable amount of discretion. Even before Wandi Dadla's renovation was complete, Ted let me take charge of subcontracting all township brew equipment installation and minor renovations. He trusted me to take on the bigger renovations in the better neighborhoods, where we believed our investment would be more secure.

Often when I was supervising a shebeen or pub renovation, the people living nearby would stop to question me about our project, then quickly be on their way. One afternoon there was a spectator of pensioner age who had questions about our progress on the brewpub.

"Welcome to the neighborhood. I'm Frederick De Villiers," he said and handed me a business card. "Ted suggested I come see you, Mr. Cooper."

"Beautiful town you have here," I said awkwardly, off-guard because Ted had mentioned nothing about this banker, if that's what he was.

"You should have seen it before we improved it. It was a shanty town until it was leveled, and the squatters were relocated. If we're not careful, they'll be back. Eternal vigilance is the price of liberty, as they say in your America, is it not?"

I wondered what happened to the squatters, how far away they were relocated, and whether they simply built a new shanty town, but that was none of my concern. I didn't have the time to pursue a discussion about liberty with a stranger.

"Right," I responded. "We also say, 'What goes around, comes around.'"

"So, from an American point of view, how do you like South Africa?"

"When God made the Southern Cape with mountains that meet the ocean and with such a beautiful climate, He blessed you," I remarked, refusing to take his bait.

I shook his hand and headed inside to check on the day's progress. He followed me. He held a stud to his eye to inspect it for straightness, as I imagined he was inspecting me. "You referred to God, so you must have some faith. As long as you've stayed on the Cape, no doubt you've been tested. So, if you still truly see us as beautiful, thank you for the compliment, young man."

"I call it like I see it."

"Excellent, Mr. Cooper. That's the way I prefer to deal and how I would treat you if I were backing you. That is, whenever you've depleted your existing sources."

"You've gone through the trouble to track me down this morning. What exactly has Ted been saying to you about our needs?"

"Simply that you may have been pumping your existing wells dry, so to speak."

He was right. Our financing, while not critical yet, was bound to fall short within the coming year. To put up the initial phase of our new Gazelle plant so quickly, we had to pay a lot of overtime hours. I didn't like hearing about my business from a man I just met. I wasn't ready to tell him anything more.

Right then I was more focused on finding out from the workers on that job why they were behind schedule. Only one of the three of them was doing any visible work. He was installing an electrical box in the wall while the other two were sitting on milk crates eating sweet rolls and drinking coffee. Wires protruded through the holes in the unfinished plaster. Incomplete electrical work meant the finish carpenters couldn't start, which placed us a good two months behind schedule. I needed to get these men moving.

"I know what I'd do if they answered to me," Frederick proffered.

I didn't ask what he meant, though I suspected he sensed my frustration with this crew. Before I could escort him out of there, he disappeared behind a half-plastered partition, and returned with the electrical subcontractor, the one responsible for this particular logjam. Upon seeing the contractor, the two idle workers got to their feet. Each of the workers took an end of the blueprint plan and studied it as if it were entirely new to them. The contractor had a checkbook in his coveralls, wrote a check, folded it, and tucked it into Frederick DeVilliers' breast pocket, leaving me with an uneasy feeling about his connection with this subcontractor we'd hired.

"In case you're wondering, Mr. Cooper," the banker said, having taken me aside, "many letters, especially checks, get lost or stolen, such as his monthly payment to our bank. This contractor of yours wanted me to physically return the lost check, since I was here, or that was his excuse."

It seemed DeVilliers and his bank had cast a wide net! But instead of being wary of him, I was strangely impressed and envisioned his value as an ally.

"I had a question about why your boys were installing the electrical boxes before they'd run all the wires," Frederick said to the contractor.

"And I had a question about lighting fixtures, Mr. Cooper—" our contractor said, sidestepping DeVillier's criticism, "but that can wait until you are finished speaking with your banker."

"I can see how busy you are, Mr. Cooper, so I'll be on my way," DeVilliers said, excusing himself.

My first inclination was to simply let him go, but then decided I wasn't quite done with him yet. I caught up with him half a block down the street. I offered my hand, he shook it slowly and scrutinized me under his canopy-like eyebrows.

"You've helped me see some things as an American I might have missed, Mr. DeVilliers. It was good meeting with you."

"We Afrikaners are a lot like you Americans. Neither of us can hide the truth behind manners like an Englishman!"

"If that's a compliment, I thank you, especially coming from a banker."

"People used to blame bankers for foreclosing on homes and having no heart, but I assure you, though I resemble a banker, I'm not, strictly speaking, one of them. Business leaders like my friend and your partner Ted Nichols blame the money men because they can't help the rand. At the rate the rand is declining, someday it won't be worth any more than a paper towel. But that's not your problem, since you can run your business in dollars instead, which appears to be the chief reason Ted joined forces with Cooper."

Partnering with Cooper, an American company, in order to be able to shift rand revenue into dollars was a fable Ted must have told DeVilliers to save face, rather than tell the truth that he'd been pressured by minority shareholders to expand and reorganize his traditional business! A fable reassuring to me if it meant Nichols had spread it to keep DeVilliers guessing, rather than tell him more than he needed to know for now.

"A partnership is like a marriage, potentially rewarding, but challenging on a day-to-day basis, Frederick. These workers for example—"

"Acting like bad children? You must watch them closely to get a day's work out of them."

"I have a reasonably good working relation with our subcontractors. I have no big complaints. So, who's your boss?" I asked.

"Did I give you the wrong impression, Mr. Cooper? I'm an insurance man with our great Afrikaner company, Sanlaam Insurance. With that resolved, I would like to invite you this Saturday for dinner." He shook my hand and gave me a detailed map to his house and wrote the date and time.

"Are you trying to sell me insurance, Frederick?"

"Not at all, you're too much of a risk," he laughed. "But I may be able to prepare a favorable loan package for the Chateau's growing enterprises."

"I'll keep that in mind," I said and returned to the jobsite.

Since Sunitha moved in with me, she wasn't seeing Aunt Giri, nor her Indian friends. I wasn't sure how we came to decide to spend all our free time together. However it happened, we'd become inseparable, spending a great deal of time on Gazelle and Chateau business, yet trying to set aside at least one day of the week for a climb up Table Mountain. Sunitha was making it easier for me as a visitor to her country. Since coming to South Africa, I was driving myself crazy overthinking my strategies. I believed in the paradigm of friction-free commerce, the art of creating demand for new markets in smart new ways. Sometimes these clever new ideas didn't apply, and I was realizing I did better with a bit more direct approach, more suited to negotiating between rival factions.

In this mad country a trusted ally was a great asset, especially one who truly had my back. I would have been a fool to walk away from Sunitha, the deepest and kindest woman I'd ever known. Aside from help in sorting out my business affairs, I also needed to make sure it was in her best interest for us to continue our arrangement.

The subject of trust came up during dinner at home. When I cut into my ostrich steak, it was undercooked, and I asked her to cook it some more. "As you please, but it will become quite tough if I cook it more. It looks raw, but this is the best way to prepare it. Try eating it with your eyes closed." I followed her suggestion, and it did taste better. "Trust me."

"I do, but sometimes I wonder if you are trusting me too much, Sunitha. It's wonderful that we trust each other, but I don't want you to become too dependent on me. You haven't seen your friends or family since we've been together, which seems odd to me. I don't want to come between you and them."

"It's kind of you to worry, but I assure you my people aren't going anywhere. I can always return to them once you are gone."

I wasn't sure whether she was glad to have left her people behind, nor why she was predicting my departure so matter-of-factly.

"Do you feel I've cut you off from your past?"

"Is there something else on your mind, Leon?"

"Parties. I bring you to the parties I've been invited to by business associates, but I'm not sure you should go along with me."

"Do you mean whether I should associate with your people?" she asked, looking at me with piercing eyes. If she was asking about the differences in our origins, I needed to reassure her that I believed in us.

"I've received an invitation for tomorrow night from a Sanlaam insurance man, Frederick DeVilliers. I wondered if you'd want me to take you to a party of Afrikaners. I know you can be uncomfortable with the Afrikaans language with Afrikaans speaking people, other than Raj."

"To the contrary, while we are living together, your friends are mine. I would enjoy going. It's funny you should mention Rajesh because he's been on my mind since this morning."

The map Frederick DeVilliers drew to his home in Kirstenbosch led us through Claremont, close to our new pub where I met him. We passed the Kirstenbosch Botanical Reserve, set at the edge of Table Mountain with its walkways lined with ancient fig and camphor trees.

"It's an incredible place, set between a valley and a mountain," I said, glancing at the entrance. "They have hundreds of kinds of fynbos plants."

"You must have visited, because I can see none of that from here. Cecil Rhodes wouldn't recognize this estate of his if you brought him back to life. I've heard they have a restaurant that makes a wonderful breakfast on weekends. Will you please bring me to it sometime?"

Adjacent to Kirstenbosch Gardens, once Cecil Rhodes' estate, we came to a private estate. Frederick DeVilliers' driveway was bordered with stately overhanging camphors. We began walking from the car when Sunitha offered me her hand, which was cold, and she seemed nervous. We walked to an impressive brick house with white columns. Waiting for us on the porch was a smiling woman, who insisted on taking Sunitha aside.

"I'm off-duty now, family emergency," said the servant, a pleasant looking coloured woman in her forties. "I'm glad you're here to help in the kitchen. I think we have a uniform that will fit you."

"That won't be necessary," Sunitha said, clinging to my arm, "since I'm here as a guest."

A tradesman's truck with a ladder across the top arrived right behind us, the servant's personal ride home. "I don't care; we're the Rainbow Nation now!" she said and greeted her driver with a kiss. "Let them serve themselves. It's a braii, after all."

Sunitha's grip stiffened. She was moving so slowly around the building that I was pulling her, motivating her to continue. "If it's a bring-braii, we're not prepared," she said.

"A bring-braii?" I repeated.

Before she could answer, Frederick appeared, carrying a tray with a stack of beefsteaks, as well as a long fork and a carving knife. He stared at me, at Sunitha, then at me again, as if trying to imagine us together. He handed the tray to a tall woman with short salt-and-pepper hair. She was wearing trendy bohemian style suede sandals that tipped a bit backwards on their cork soles, making her stand slightly off balance and walk like a duck.

"Ilsa, this is Leon Cooper, the whiskey man from America," Frederick introduced me as he handed her the tray.

"Mr. Cooper, I've heard about you from DeeDee, Frederick's sister. Do you remember meeting her at Ted's party? She told me we should be expecting you once you needed some fresh funds," Ilsa DeVilliers said, looking Sunitha over closely. "Welcome to you, and to your companion."

"I'll be your companion for this afternoon as well, if you do not mind," Sunitha finally said.

"Have you told Mr. Cooper that a braii is a barbecue?" Ilsa asked her.

"You can also tell him," Frederick said, "that for a bring-braii the guests bring the dishes, but that here we would be shamed if we couldn't properly entertain all our invited guests without such a request. You do speak Afrikaans?"

I could tell Sunitha was uneasy by the way she was repeatedly glancing at me. I wouldn't give her any cues on how she should read them, since they might have been making a genuine effort to accept her.

"A little bit," she said awkwardly.

"Great," Ilsa said. "Say something."

"*Van sensitewe ontwerp en bekwame vakmanskap,*" Sunitha said, pointing to the house.

"She says she likes the design and craftsmanship of our house, Leon," Ilsa said with a beaming smile, and took Sunitha by the arm.

"Te wees op hul handewerk geen ander begraafplas in die land so 'n pragtigue..."

"She says we should be proud of ourselves, because this is the prettiest part of the country," Frederick translated for me, smiling as broadly as his wife, obviously pleased Sunitha was speaking to them in their first language.

Sunitha pulled away from Ilse's grip, walked to a bed of fynbos flowers and dug out a handful of the loose soil. *"Maar aangesien dit 'n verkwisting sou wees om op vrugbare tuingrond te bou."*

"You are very perceptive, young lady, our soil is very rich," Ilsa said, pleased with Sunitha's self-conscious performance. She took her by her arm, and walked her briskly around the house, with Frederick and me following.

"You can see we save the most fertile of the land for our garden," Frederick said when we arrived at the trimmed hedgerow bordering it. "Our family has been in this valley many generations, and at one time held more land than now remains in Kirstenbosch Gardens. In those days our workers were loyal, unlike these troubled times, when we're controlled by our help. What remains is a shadow of its former self. Would you care to see more?"

He sounded like the son of an antebellum plantation, owner repeating old stories of the glory days before the American Civil War and their defeat. I was too much a Yankee, too much an American, or else I hadn't been in this country long enough to offer him the sympathy he wanted. I accompanied him on the tour of his scaled-down gardens, keeping my opinions to myself.

I wasn't interested in hearing about a hundred years of his family's loss of land. I had my own losses to reverse or lose what was left of the possessions I still had in storage in St. Louis.

But instead of showing me more of his garden and home, his attention shifted to the little boy who'd been crashing in and out of the hedgerows. Frequently the child darted back towards his father, taunting him with mugging faces. Though Frederick couldn't begin to slip through child-size gaps in the hedges, he responded to the challenge by hiding behind a fountain, a concrete statue of a winged Venus, and a tree. The game became more boisterous with Frederick matching the child's hoots and cries. When the child fell on a flat stone walkway, he yelped, but Ilsa rushed over to comfort him, and he darted away, his Superman cape flying behind him.

Along with his parents, Sunitha and I took up the chase, trying to force him into the corner where the stone wall connected with the building. He raced across the patio and circled a hearth where a pork was turning on a spit over the flames. His circles diminished as Sunitha closed in on him. When the boy's cape dragged on the ground, she jumped on it, and she brought him to a sudden halt. He fell on the ground again, this time laughing instead of howling, apparently pleased with the adults' attention.

"If you and I help the women, we can catch him in a minute," I suggested to Frederick.

"Then what would we do with him?" Frederick asked. "I know that when a child is exhausted, he's easier to handle. If you were a horse trainer, you'd run your horse hard before you attempted to ride him. So, let's forget about him for the time being. First things first: I'll show you the orchard, my own pride and joy."

I wondered if Ilse was giving Sunitha reasons to leave the youngster alone. I wasn't about to challenge this ridiculous situation, where four adults were unable to restrain one rambunctious child, who was now dancing by the fire like a dwarf shaman. Instead, we took the path of least resistance, leaving it to the women to collect the boy, while Frederick and I moved on to view his trees.

He showed me his specimens of apple, pear, cherry, and plum trees, many with species names on identifying signs. He saw me admiring the fat pears, pulled one off and sliced it in half with his pocketknife for us. He led me to a gazebo where we sat opposite one another, eating cherries he picked, tossing the pits and stems onto the ground.

"I have left many messages for Ted Nichols, but evidently he's too busy to return them," Frederick finally said. "That is why I'd like you to convey this one in person."

"Believe me, it's just as hard for me to get time with him."

"Is there any particular one you want to relay to Ted?" I asked, if only to be polite.

"You must tell him that we are available to assist Drakenstein's ambitious expansion. I am available with any additional capital you may need. We can offer you more generous terms than you can possibly receive from Standard Bank, which you know is merely an extension of the Bank of England, domiciled in the heart of the beast, in City of London."

Ted and I agreed not to talk about our tentative

arrangements with Standard, since it might be possible to finance ourselves outside of South Africa and America. If Ted had kept his promise of silence, then Frederick must have heard his news from a source within the bank. He was charming, but a bit too inquisitive for my comfort.

"I hope you and Ted don't have the wrong impression," he continued, "that Sanlaam as an Afrikaner founded company favors Afrikaner businesses over Anglo business. If you can provide us with your business plan, I think you'll be surprised how we might accommodate you at a rate two or three percent lower than anyone else."

"That sounds generous. Why are you so anxious to do business with us?"

"Let's just say we have a strong interest in seeing your Gazelle line succeed against Lion and Castle. With our help you might be able to build yourself to a competitive size that would enable you to withstand their campaigns against you. What do you think?"

It bothered me that at our initial meeting Frederick claimed he was Ted's longstanding acquaintance, yet now it appeared he was trying to recruit me to deliver messages to him. He might have been making educated guesses about our operation, based on gossip circulating among his banker friends. I could have confronted him with this suspicion, but not while Sunitha and I were his houseguests. I would have preferred a lighter subject, such as his obvious success with fruit trees. While it might have been tempting to accept his offer of cheap financing, perhaps he was offering easy terms to make Sanlaam our principal creditor rather than Standard

Bank. If we expanded too fast and defaulted, he would then be positioned to take over part of the production facilities and distribution work we'd built.

He was offering us a bite of cheese, and perhaps a trap was attached to it. There was no way to evaluate a deal before knowing the details. A serious proposal, no matter what his long-term motives might be, was worth consideration. But that wasn't the time or the place to evaluate it. Frederick told me about what he called his second love, his oceangoing boat which enabled him to fish as far offshore as many commercial fishermen. Some distant shouting took his attention from me, and when it became louder, Ilsa appeared from behind the nearest hedges.

"Water, Frederick! Bring water! Dietlets's on fire!" Ilsa called to us before disappearing.

"What did she want—a bucket or a hose!" Frederick shouted.

He ran off with surprising speed for a man his age, and I followed close behind him, like two-man fire brigade responding to an alarm. When we arrived at the barbecue pit, fear turned to horror when I saw Sunitha rolling on the ground with the child. His cape was in flames, which she was trying to extinguish by rolling on the ground with him. The flames caught the hem of Sunitha's dress, and I stamped on it with no effect. Sunitha grabbed the boy again, clutching him and rolling with him until she managed to subdue the flame. Ilsa and another woman arrived with two buckets of water and doused the smoldering cape. They used the very same stainless-steel buckets we used at Chateau, which Jan LeRoux had returned to

Ted. Too many coincidences, too many inexplicable connections!

Sunitha had charcoal streaks on her torso, face, and limbs. When I touched a gash on her arm, she motioned me away, so I wouldn't call attention to it.

Ilsa disappeared again, returning with wash rags and another Chateau stainless- steel bucket. She began gently cleaning Sunitha, despite her attempt to walk away and be left alone.

"This young lady Sunitha has saved my grandson!" Ilsa declared, to a handsome woman with perfect tiny white teeth. "Sunitha, please meet my daughter Marlena."

Marlena looked almost identical to her sister DeeDee, as I remembered her from Ted's party, the one who originally gave me Frederick's business card. Sunitha though wasn't looking at Marlena, Ilsa, the boy, Frederick, or the arriving guests—just at me.

"Will you take me home please?" Sunitha asked me, having submitted to Ilsa's motherly attention.

Sunitha, their undeniable heroine, kissed the rescued boy goodbye, and we walked away from the stone braii. The two DeVilliers women must have taken a shortcut directly through the house, because they were waiting for us at the car.

Marlena was carrying little Dietlets in one arm, and with her free arm gave Sunitha a hug. "We owe you our son's life, and if there's any way we can repay it, you must let us know."

"Our lives all hang in balance between our births and deaths," Sunitha said. "I am owed nothing."

"Naturally, but if you don't go after what you want,

you have no one to blame but yourself. That is why we must seize the day."

Sunitha, hardly a New Age person, turned to me anxiously, unsure whether to respond to Marlena's flippant bit of philosophy. I was relieved she didn't even begin to explain her own complicated beliefs in consecutive lives, or about having to bear the consequences of our current life through countless millennia. She smiled and said nothing.

"I saw how brave she was," Ilsa added. "My guests all wanted to see you. Here, I've brought you fresh clothes."

Ilsa had a black dress on a hanger and tried giving it to Sunitha. Instead of accepting it and having to go back into the house to change her ruined dress, she thanked her and insisted I take her home, which I did after we exchanged goodbyes with her and Frederick who'd just joined us. Sunitha seemed dazed and didn't say a word the entire drive home. I wanted to know what was bothering her, but I was not going to press her, not then.

When we arrived at my flat, I prepared sandwiches. Sunitha had no more interest in eating than in speaking, evidently alone with her thoughts. She excused herself, withdrew to the porch, and looked over the balcony at the sunset.

"Frederick and Ilsa were disappointed to see us leave," I ventured.

"And were you, Leon, because you didn't have enough time to make a pact with him?"

Was she saying that I was about to make a pact with the devil? That was the same question I asked myself while he was trying to throw money at me. How could she have known what Frederick was offering me at the gazebo, other than through her intuition?

"If it weren't for your quick response, Sunitha," I reassured her, intentionally avoiding a business discussion with her, "the DeVilliers boy would be in the hospital with burns. He's very fortunate you got to him in time. If that's what you have on your mind, I understand."

"I don't, and you can't," she said.

It wasn't like her to dismiss me. Perhaps she was still in shock.

"I can still see him in flames, seconds from terrible burns!"

"The boy was spared, but perhaps the man will not be so fortunate!"

I was beginning to understand her pattern of long-term thinking. Though she never saw Dietlets DeVilliers before, she was worried about his well-being when he was grown into a man, concerned for the future of a boy she just rescued. Unlike me, she felt compelled to be her brother's keeper and had a more generous nature than mine.

I returned to the living room and began reading one of her books, *The Tibetan Book of the Great Liberation.* Had she been more approachable right then, I'd ask her whether the Tibetan Dalai Lama was a latter-day Buddha, or if the Buddhist Indians regarded the Buddhist Tibetans as their cousins. But why would I need more information about religions so different from the Christian one I'd forsaken? Sunitha's Indian beliefs were relevant only to the tiny diaspora of South African

Indians. There was no need to further confuse myself, so I put her book down. I had more concerns than trying to make sense of her complicated beliefs, which had just allowed her to reach out to her fellow man, despite her close brush with fire. Perhaps the unwelcome ordeal by fire was troubling her because it came so soon after she was burned out of her house and into mine.

A little past nine she was asleep, early for her, making me wonder if she was subconsciously trying to end a trying day. I followed her to sleep, but my mind raced, unable to stop reviewing the events at the DeVilliers' estate. I was impressed by Sunitha's bravery, the way she handled herself with grace and dignity, despite our host's initial reservation about my arrival with an Indian girlfriend. I wondered though whether it was a good idea to continue bringing her to my strategic meetings, and whether she would continue making early exits before I could use my opportunities to negotiate.

"I know what you're thinking," she said, suddenly turning towards me. "You are split in your loyalties between your business interests and me. For all your concerned words, you may be reluctant for me to accompany you to your associates. I sense your sleep is troubled, and I feel your tension."

"Not at all!" I disagreed.

She began massaging me, then stopped to turn on the nightstand light. She rolled towards me, pulled me closer to her, and explored for special pressure points on my toes. From her fingers, pulses of warmth radiated throughout my entire body. She sincerely wished to please me, but I worried that I'd been letting my appreciation of her beauty and intuition cloud my judgment.

"Remember our first night together? My promise that no matter what our troubles, we could overcome them?"

"With love, Leon?"

Love—the very word passing through my resistant and skeptical businessman's mind as well. Sunitha and I had a bad day, and we'd be wise to put it behind us. It was a good choice for this night in which we remained separately preoccupied with our own views of the world.

When I was living in New York I put in long days, beginning at 5:00 A.M. and often ending after midnight. But now I'd come under Sunitha's calming influence. She convinced me I was succeeding in my mission to build on the Chateau and Gazelle platforms, proving my value not only to myself, but to Cooper and my family. That meant that I no longer had to work like a driven man. Since she first entered my life, she became a top priority, causing me to synchronize my schedule with hers. Now I wanted to awaken when she did, rather than stealing off to my office to do paperwork as I used to do when I was alone.

One morning at first light, she was not there beside me. As I was awakening, an image of our family home flashed through my mind, a plantation-style home in St. Louis, the home of five generations of Coopers. Still disoriented between sleep and consciousness, it came to me where I really was, living in a strange land without friends or family in Barclay Mews. In a few moments I regained my bearings and realized that I was an oddity—a Caucasian with an Indian lover in black Africa.

I saw no sign of Sunitha but heard her voice coming from my office. On the door handle she'd hung a Do Not Disturb sign she'd brought with her from Gazelle, she said, intended for me to use, so I could reclaim my privacy and work or think or daydream.

"Chandra's here, Leon," Sunitha called to me from inside, her voice broken by sobbing. "I'll be with you directly."

Chandra arrived unannounced, even though many times I made it clear that he needed to be calling me beforehand! I didn't appreciate being locked out of my own office while the two of them were talking behind closed doors. It was annoying, but rather than make an issue of this secret meeting, I went to the kitchen and made a pot of Sunitha's jasmine tea. Chandra opened the door wide enough to take the tray from me, but I wasn't about to be turned away. Sunitha was sitting on the mat on the floor, her legs crossed under her, her torso erect, a posture of self-control. She was very upset and working hard to compose herself, looking away from me every time she dried another tear.

"There's bad news at the warehouse in Bergkloof." Chandra wasn't looking at me as he spoke, but at her instead. "Remember the evening we spent at Giri Bala's, what I showed you at Gazelle? Afterwards we were sitting in front of my home, watching Rajesh's comings and goings with his political friends."

Like Sunitha, he had tears in his eyes and looked to her to continue what he was having trouble explaining. She motioned me closer, and she pulled me beside her on the mat. As I remembered, neither Raj nor his friends were at the compound that evening to guard it against PAGAD invaders. This was no time to challenge his memory if I wanted him to get to the reason he'd invaded my privacy again.

"The warehouse exploded, and Rajesh went missing," she blurted.

"Terrible!" I mumbled. I wanted to know about other casualties and the extent of the damage but held my questions.

"Yes, the fault of Rajesh's bad friends which Hassan introduced to him," Chandra interrupted. "If only I could find Hassan to know the cause."

"Rajesh..." Sunitha said, looking stunned and speaking in a detached eerie voice, "if he wasn't destined to be carried away, then we must all blame ourselves for ignoring his cry for help. We must carry our responsibility, whether we know the cause."

"Chandra, are you saying Rajesh is dead?" I asked him.

My straightforward query set her lower lip quivering. I didn't know what had happened, yet I was making it more difficult for her. Chandra gently helped her to her feet, led her out of my study and locked the door, leaving only him and me.

"You know we once almost had a daughter, but she would have not been satisfactory," Chandra said. "While my departed wife bore me Rajesh, my only son, she passed to the other side."

He was telling me that his wife died in childbirth. I was unsure about the fate of Rajesh's baby sister. Was she born dead or did she die shortly after her birth? Perhaps she had been terminated beforehand because they predicted a birth defect or wanted a boy instead. I didn't want to know if she was born alive at nine months, then terminated as an infant like they did in India. He must have trusted me as a friend, sharing with me these sad stories of the deaths of his baby daughter, then his wife and now Rajesh! But why was he bringing up these old losses now, unless the older losses were easier for him to absorb than the fresh loss of his son.

"I know firsthand how it is to lose someone close to you," I said.

Why did Chandra's tragedy bring thoughts of my own family, my mother at her best, when she had her charming smile, a calming influence on my father, and able to moderate his naturally volatile temper. We never knew for sure what killed her. A death of her own making, some believed, due to her heavy smoking, preferring that explanation to acknowledging that we'd all been drinking the same tap water, and it hadn't killed us!

"My mother was taken from us when I was young," I explained, and let it stop there.

Though I'd known Chandra for some time, it wasn't easy discussing my mother's death with him. He was a man I admired in many ways, yet I was uncertain how much he communicated with my brother. I was careful how much of my personal life I confided in him. I wouldn't want him to misquote me and unintentionally give Harry some new ammunition to use against me. So instead of speaking about myself, it seemed far more productive learning what happened to Rajesh. If his bad judgment in friends killed him, that was in no way the fault of Chandra or Sunitha, though we might have each felt guilty for the simple fact that we were the survivors.

"Like yourself, Leon, but for different reasons, we are a nation of orphans here in South Africa, because doctors here are too costly and the cheap ones too ignorant," Chandra said, entirely missing my comparison, but thankfully not pressing me for details. "In this particular life you or I may be assigned to parents not truly our own, don't you agree?"

Any response I could give to his Hindu view of the migration of souls would sound foolish, especially coming from me, a lapsed Christian American. That left me speechless while he proceeded with his show-and-tell. He brought a large Gazelle stainless steel pail and gave me the lid to hold. He pulled me closer, pointing to its contents before he removed a red-stained sheet.

"This was once the bedsheet of my only son Rajesh, and now, I'm afraid, it has become his shroud."

He behaved like a magician trying to arouse some interest in me, his meager audience, and he succeeded! With a flourish he pulled out a pair of work boots, joined by the laces, flecked with red, and draped them over my shoulder, sending a shiver through my back, as if a dead man's soul had entered my body. He pulled out a cap with the old Gazelle logo which Raj wore all the time, put this on his head, and moved close to me so I could see the red smears on the hat as well.

"That's the exact color of the Chateau's pinotage wine," I observed. "Remember when we first brought Raj up to the Chateau a few times to give him a better acquaintance with winemaking after the marriage of Cooper and Drakenstein?"

"Thank you for trying to give me reason for hope, Leon. Have I not proven to you my son, if not in the grave, is in grave trouble?"

"I'm as troubled as you are!" I protested. "We must get to the bottom of this!"

"That's easier said than done. If you're standing by me, sir, beware. We're in quicksand, and there is no bottom."

"Chandra, we can't afford to exaggerate. What do you know, except that your son is missing? The night he was playing sentry with his comrades-in-arms, he was under great stress. When I was growing up, I remember when my friends had trouble at home they'd run away or threaten to. In my country we don't have your problems, yet we are easily dissatisfied, looking for greener pastures, wishing for better parents, then later looking for a better spouse, if we dared to marry in the first place."

"Terribly sad people, you rich Americans, if you don't mind my saying so."

I did mind Chandra's poor opinion of my country, especially since I'd suspended my entire former life to come here to show them how to build market share. Whatever he thought we Americans lacked in character and loyalty, he must have seen I'd compensated for my shortcomings by my devotion to our project. I not only trained him as my protege, I shared everything I knew about marketing alcoholic beverages. Under my direction, we were closing in on my $50 million per year target increase in volume and hoped to double that next year. It was a good plan, and a successful one.

"I know how upset you must be, Chandra, under the circumstances, so I'll try not to take that personally."

"Leon, you speak of my son as if he was a memory and that trying to find him would be a lost cause. Instead of speaking of him as if he were no longer with us, we must do something!"

"Of course!" I agreed. I hadn't noticed Hassan's

arrival, but there he was, attempting to find evidence that might help us.

"It will not matter to him where he rests now," Hassan said. "Inside his book you will find an envelope. Open it carefully." I thought he was speaking of the *Kama Sutra*, which I had told him to avoid at all costs. Instead, it was a lightly damaged *Siddhartha*, by a modern German writer.

As soon as Sunitha saw it, she took it from him and clasped it reverently to her chest. "Siddhartha Gautama, the Buddha. Perhaps it is not too late, Leon, to take his example and devote your life to find meaning."

"That was a long time ago," I responded lamely.

Chandra took the book from her, which had a torn out empty front page with some scrawls. "It's all here," Chandra said. "Look more closely and tell me which letters you find."

"A goose egg, a zero," I said, inspecting the lines more closely.

"Not a zero, but the letter O," he said, stabbing the page with his finger.

That was a stretch of the imagination, but there was nothing to be gained by challenging him. He opened the jeweler's magnifier from the chain around his neck, set the book down on the coffee table, and dropped to his knees so he could inspect the red mark more closely.

"And these letters on either side of the letter O— when you look at them closely, what do you see?" Chandra asked.

"Those lines? Like the peaks of a mountain?"

"Now you are thinking like my son, letting the

appearance of things deceive you. I want you to see this as the letter M standing upright. I recognize it as Mafumo's handwriting. The letter O he meant as the calling card of his boss, Ozeer."

"I'm amazed you can read so much into a few scrawl marks," I said.

"Red scrawl marks, did you notice, written in blood? Ozeer doesn't always leave his marker, only when it suits his purpose."

"Or red ink," I suggested, challenging Chandra's interpretation.

Chandra had more evidence in an accordion envelope. In it was a lock of black hair, held together with a red satin ribbon, exactly like the one that had fastened the box of the eggshell nightgown I had bought Sunitha when she gift moved into my flat! I hoped it was just a coincidence. But if was the same ribbon, how did Raj get it? I had to be careful not to expect logical answers, where few seemed to exist in this crazy land!

"I brought Rajesh's hair for you to see. I don't under-stand why he was wearing these, unless he wished to die in his good shoes," he said. Sunitha had left us, unwilling to look at more evidence. She went to her prayer mat and assumed her customary yoga pose.

Hassan produced a pair of dress loafers and a pair of bloody socks, and then they were done with their presentation. Had Hassan found these things inde-pendently, or had Chandra divided Raj's clothes with Hassan to strengthen his case for a big search?

"In pursuit of peace, I trust you are willing to con-front the evil ones. I too am a peaceful man, Leon, but we have been challenged. Our enemies are ruthless, and they must not mistake our tolerance for weakness. That is why we must do something."

"I agree! But this is a matter for the police, not for us."

"Not the very same police who refused to assist Sunitha after Ozeer's men burned out her flat and damaged her!" Chandra said with uncharacteristic anger.

"Do you care to rejoin us now?" I asked Sunitha as she entered the room.

"I heard you men speak of his fate," Sunitha said, back with the rest of us. "Mr. Kassie is urging you not to regard Raj as a lost cause. And now you both know my secret that I've become a lost cause as well."

"Not at all, Sunitha," I reassured her, discreetly into her ear. "Why don't we speak about this later when we're alone?"

She pushed me away from her and walked towards Chandra.

"No, Leon, all our minds are on what happened to me that drove me to your arms. As a Christian, Leon, you might believe I was assaulted by the agents of Satan. Mr. Kassie, as an honorable son of India, you might now worry that I can bring only shame to the family as a soiled woman. So where does that leave us?"

She was standing before me, looking directly into my eyes, trying to gauge my reaction to her admission she was raped by Ozeer's brigands. If we were alone, I'd tell her I was sorry, though my sympathy would not avenge the crime against her nor return Rajesh to us. If only she and Chandra had let me take this matter to the police! On second thought, that might not have been advisable, not with Ted's, Rajesh's and Hassan's connections with Ighaam, which could have proved embarrassing. Before I came here, I took pride in my ethics, personal and business, but here applying such distinctions too rigidly seemed likely to also harm the good people who personally mattered to me.

"It's time to set the hounds on the fox," I said.

"No! if they find him, they'll tear apart the body of my son!" Chandra said.

"He's afraid the police will use the wrong dogs, attack dogs like you Americans use in your race riots and which they used in the townships during apartheid," Sunitha said.

It was no surprise that Chandra took me literally, but I would have expected better from Sunitha! I suppose I should have been more careful choosing my words, though in Sunitha's case she often seemed to understand me better than I did myself. I could have told them we don't have race riots in my country, or bootleggers, but as anxious as they both were over Raj's disappearance, what they needed was to hear possible solutions to the immediate problem.

"I'm sorry for the inconvenience this morning," Chandra apologized, pressing his palms together in namaste Indian fashion, bowing his head slightly.

"When she was a young bride, my wife was as limber as a snake." He pointed to the position where the woman wrapped her legs behind her head. "And through me passed the love force of the lion." He thought about what he said and waved his hand. "Though, of course, no man has the lion's power to mate continuously days and nights straight." He paced across the room, hands clasped behind his back. "Do you not agree my son chose well in Sunitha as wife?"

"I trust you two haven't been speaking of me while I've been off serving you," Sunitha said.

"Not at all," Chandra said as we took our teacups from the tray she held for us.

"In any event, I do not matter right now," she said. She was sitting between us on the couch. "We must depend on you, Leon, because you can achieve results impossible for us Indians." I saw Chandra looking uncomfortably away as if he'd been betrayed.

"I appreciate your vote of confidence, but I'm afraid—"

"To the contrary," she said. "We are the ones who are afraid. We don't have the resources to defend ourselves, Leon, but you do. Chandra and I need your help."

Until this morning Sunitha had refused to fully acknowledge the assault against her. But now that Chandra arrived, she put aside her inhibitions enough to ask for help from me to pursue justice or vengeance—I couldn't tell what she really wanted. I wished her request had come directly from her to me. Regardless, she had been telling him more intimate details about this rape incident than she'd confided in me. I believed she trusted me but could have been holding back for a different reason. Maybe she thought I'd blame her for the rape, and rather than risk losing me kept her pain to herself.

"I think of myself like you," I said, "servants of Drakenstein and Gazelle. We serve the same master."

"And you fear for the master?" Chandra asked.

"No, I fear you may have planned something drastic for retaliation."

"Not at all," he slowly answered, looking to Sunitha,

whose attention was focused on me. "I have served Mr. Nichols faithfully, just as my Sunitha serves you well as a woman. Don't you agree?"

My Sunitha? He spoke of her as if he had a proprietary interest. He should not have spoken of her serving me as if I had hired myself an all-purpose gal Friday—worst of all, speaking of our private relationship in her presence.

"No, we are not in agreement, Chandra."

"I'm very, sorry, sir. You can forget about myself and your lady for now. If we no longer please you, forgive us. However, I urge you to consider my son. Has he not proven his value to you? Can you agree he was willing to give his life to preserve and protect our mutual interests?"

"Mutual interests, Mr. Kassie?" Sunitha continued to address him formally. "Leon has no more responsibility for Rajesh than you do for me."

"Quite true, Sunitha," Chandra said. "That is why I must use all means possible to find my son, dead or alive. Larabie Hassan knows important people, and he should be a great help. Do you agree, Leon?"

By important people he meant gangsters, from street level to Ighaam at the top of the feeding chain. He was asking me for consent to go outside the law to rescue Rajesh, my employee. Had I known for myself what bad company he was keeping, I might have terminated Raj as a security risk after the last raid at the old plant. But with Chandra so firmly bound to Ted Nichols after the takeover of the Gazelle operations, Ted would have never allowed me to fire either of the Kassies. It would be even less likely I could remove Hassan. I strongly suspected Rajesh had been assisting Hassan in build-ing an arsenal at Bergkloof under Ighaam's direction. My suggestions for what to do next depended on Ted's cooperation.

Ozeer was playing a no-holds-barred South African game with Ighaam, having blown up Hassan's cache of weapons at Bergkloof. This situation was rapidly get-ting out of hand. Whether or not I approved of Hassan's tactics, Chandra's instincts to involve him and Ighaam's men might prove the most effective way to retrieve Rajesh's body, even if we had to exhume it.

"For the record, it's our policy to follow the laws, not bypass them," I said, causing Sunitha to smile, "so we'll proceed carefully."

"Yes, Leon," Chandra said, shaking my hand as if to secure my promise before I had a chance to change my mind. I look forward to the progress we will make together."

CHAPTER 13

THE HEAVY HITTER

I recalled the details of my last interaction with Rajesh a couple of weeks earlier. One of the Gazelle beer deliveries had consisted of a few cases to a new pub in a shopping center in Belville, a suburb twenty minutes east of Cape Town center. I remember I was reluctant to ride with him after the recent debacle at his plant. Nevertheless, almost against my better judgment, I decided to would spend a few hours with him, as if on a surveillance mission.

I remember Raj introduced me as our consultant from America to a customer in a white uniform, though I'd never suggested any such thing to Raj. Perhaps Chandra planted that idea in his head. Or else Harry had pledged my time to Gazelle before I even stepped on the plane.

"Mr. Cooper is expert on how to do business without friction," Raj added.

Now a worker in dark coveralls made an obscene gesture, grinning at me! "Friction free! But more fun with friction!"

I was being mocked in this saloon! My friction-free economic theory turned into a dirty third-hand joke by my own brother—one that evidently had followed me to the other end of the world!

"I've got to go. This isn't a good use of my time," I

said as calmly as possible to Raj, once we were on the
road to his next customer.

"We think the same, Mr. Cooper. Managers like you
and me must use our brains instead of our backs."

"We must leave soon," I reminded him. "I must
return to prepare a report."

"A report on Gazelle?" Raj quizzed. "Will you give our
company bad report?"

"Look, Rajesh, I never saw your brewery has issues,
but as I've told your father, your legacy business is not
my direct concern!"

"I'm sorry you do not like our company, but Gazelle
is my father's life, and that is why he stayed. Maybe
he was wrong to make Sunitha and me leave his side.
Sorry for our change in plans. I had it planned to
take you to show our good customers today. Then my
father instructed me to keep our appointment with Mr.
Nichols, who will be waiting to relax with you. One
hand washes the other, does it not?"

When Ted Nichols heard about the disturbance at the
Gazelle plant, he was not pleased, especially hearing
that Raj had left his father behind to deal with the mob
alone. It seemed to him and me that if it was Gazelle's
beer-drinking customers that Cooper was considering
adding to Cooper's holdings, then I could not avoid
meeting them on their own turf.

After that I was done with Raj, with Ted instead
assigning Tembo to bring me on deliveries, acting as driver and guide, showing me not only existing accounts, but possible new clients. MITCHELL'S
PLAIN—FREE PEOPLE IN A FREE LAND said a sign by
the road shot full of bullet holes. We passed squatters'

homes cobbled together with cardboard, plastic and cloth. Then came the more permanent ones of sheet steel, boards and bits of plywood. After that, a food market, with chickens cooking on grills fashioned of split oil drums and sheep's heads hanging in rows, their eye sockets empty.

"This is the better part of Mitchell's Plain," Tembo explained. We passed a collection of concrete block buildings, with sound steel roofs, and double-hung windows on each side of six-paneled front doors. "Here you see the homes of the black Africa National Congress party men, built by the new government for their favorite supporters."

MAYFAIR SHEBEEN, our destination, was the biggest of Gazelle's customers. Our arrival had been expected, for as soon as the truck stopped, two men were there to help unload the dozens of cases. This shebeen also served as a Gazelle distribution building. Tembo presented the invoice, but neither worker accepted it, instead escorting Tembo and me to their boss, Sahid, a man with a weightlifter's build.

"You bring us the American, Tembo, for international trade, very good," Sahid Kosane said, flexing his arm muscles by making each hand into a fist, alternately. He showed Leon his knockoff Rolex, after noticing my dress-for-business Piaget. "Tembo, you must tell him they cut off his arm for such a watch as he wears."

Appearing from the side door, Larabie Hassan joined them, wearing a Springbok national team warmup suit with patches of his wins across the back. Kosane had friends with him, all wearing pillbox hats of the same colors—yellow, green and red. Leon tried to remember whether those were the colors of the New South Africa flag, or whether they were colors from some all-Moslem country.

"Inshallah!" they each greeted Hassan, awaiting their turns. They were Arabs of the southern Cape, a world away from the nomads in burnooses traveling the northern Africa Sahel desert.

Hassan looked to me and held both hands together in kind of a prayer sign. He pointed to me, garnering unwanted attention. He turned and brought from the cooler a cold keg of Gazelle, which he began drawing into paper cups.

"All my friends who visit this shebeen drink Raj's beer," Hassan said, "and now I will find you customers in other shebeens that know me. The blacks drink Lion and Castle, a shame. The hard Moslems, the ones who send their boys to the madrassa, they don't drink at all."

Tembo and I followed him outdoors behind the shebeen to a table chained to a concrete slab. Hassan sat on the table. He heard a truck engine turn over, whispered to Sahid, who in turn ordered his boys, one with a Glock and another with a .44 Magnum drawn, to accompany Tembo. Soon I heard two gunshots.

"What was that all about?" Leon asked Kosane.

"The truck thieves work fast, but we are faster, Mr. Cooper," said Kosane. "We need that truck because we will be traveling along with your Gazelle truck this afternoon to check on our friends."

"What about those shots?"

"I didn't hear anything, did you boys?" he asked, and everyone listening shook their heads no.

I wanted to know where Kosane planned to go before

committing myself to accompany them. Soon we came to a group of men and half a dozen young women dressed in revealing clothes. The Kosanes stopped to speak with them and wanted me to join them. He had Tembo go instead, and one of the girls reached through the window and slipped her hand under his shirt. The attention from the men, as well as from the girls, seemed to be focused on him. The more Tembo spoke, the more the women laughed. But as the Kosanes and Tembo and his admirers approached the Chateau truck, his expression altered from happy to more serious.

"I asked these people about Rajesh, Mr. Cooper," Tembo said.

"And?"

"The girls think you worry too much. With all due respect, sir, the girl in the red offered her services to soothe you."

"Tembo, I don't care about them any more than I do about your girlfriends in Maraville. Let's go!"

"Yes, that man who caught your eye, he was once a soldier," he said, pointing to the man with the duffle bag who had jumped from the back of the Kosanes' truck to meet the pretty girls. He had camouflage pants. "He might be useful to us."

"Tembo," I said, once we were underway again, "We're no closer to finding Raj than when we left my flat, so why don't you turn around and take me home?"

"Because Hassan wanted to see you before dark. Do you think it's wise for us to keep him waiting?"

"No, I'll call him and tell him to meet me Monday when it's more convenient," I said, then began dialing him on my cell phone.

"The trouble is that if Mr. Nichols knows where Hassan's been the past few days since Rajesh vanished," Tembo said, "he's not telling anyone. There must be a reason why Hassan's not answering your call. That's why we're lucky to have an appointment to meet him this afternoon, with your permission, of course."

"Why, because Hassan has some kind of a search plan?"

"He does not share such important matters with a chauffeur," Tembo said, looking for my reaction.

"We both know better than that, Tembo. I can tell you don't care to tell me if Mr. Nichols approves of Hassan's actions. Okay, you win. Why don't we go directly to him now, rather than continue any further in this foolish caravan."

"Directly," he repeated.

In response to my request Tembo made a sharp U-turn, leaving the rest of the caravan behind, which included the Kosane truck, a sedan taxi, and a white van containing a dozen men. We left the gravel roads of Belhar township for the main highway, but our followers reversed direction and raced to catch us. We passed the commercial district of Sea Point, where there were many restaurants and bars, two or three of which were Chateau accounts. Rather than visit them, Tembo continued onto a wide tree-lined boulevard, driving on the service road toward a section of residential apartment flats. In the dim afternoon light, he strained to read the numbers on the buildings. It was late enough to bring out the women in tight shorts and tops revealing their assets, displaying themselves for hire. When Tembo turned to park the truck, one of them jumped back from a nearby car and made an obscene gesture at him. He hit the brakes, bringing us to a screeching stop.

"We don't need to waste any time with prostitutes. Let's keep going," I said.

But she was fast and ran to our truck. She reached through Tembo's window and lowered the window the rest of the way.

"You dumb kaffir! Were you trying to kill me out-right?" she shouted, then giggled.

"So, are you having a slow day or what?" he asked.

"I'm waiting for you two blokes. Does that make me a common streetwalker? I could have waited inside, but Hassan wanted to make sure you didn't get lost tonight, Okay?"

"In that case, please accept my apologies," I said.

"Don't bother, Leon Cooper. Polite men don't turn me on. Are you coming back to me for a second helping?" she said, extending me her hand.

"You must have me confused with some other man," I said.

"No, Mr. Cooper, you came to see me at Maraville, remember? You brought my favorite black man with you, the one Ighaam won't let me see anymore. I'm Katie Ann Arendse, Ighaam's cousin, and I brought you up to the rooftop where he perches, watching down on troublemakers with his eagle eyes, day and night. Can you remember now?"

"How could I forget? It's all coming back to me."

"If you promise to stop giving me a hard time, I'll take you to Hassan, as he wishes."

"I'm confused, Katie Ann. How do you know what he wishes?"

"Like my friend Tembo, he practically lives with me in Maraville. We're one big family and look out for each other. He sent me ahead because he knows you'd never find him without my help. You see, ever since you lost Rajesh, Hassan's been kind of hard to find, if you know what I mean."

I didn't know what she meant, and I was not asking. I didn't need a hooker, an honorary member of Ighaam's gang, to act as intermediary between me and my man Tembo.

"Thanks, but we know where we're going, so I don't really think we need your help."

"Mr. Cooper, face it. You'll always be a stranger in need of help in South Africa. And Tembo, you must not forget your friends," she said, and slid onto the seat beside him, her hand on his leg. "Is he your friend, Mr. Cooper, or just someone who drives you from place to place and waits for you in between?"

Before I could arrive at an answer that wouldn't offend either one of them, Katie Ann signaled Tembo to turn into a driveway. She had a remote door control and opened the garage. Tembo parked the truck, and he and I emerged into the attached apartment building. She led, and I followed with Tembo behind. We went to the basement and walked through a utility room and storage room with lockers for the tenants. Katie Ann used her key, admitting us into a room with metal storage boxes of all sizes.

"You're a hard man to find these days," I said to Hassan. "Is this your new bunker?"

"No, just a quiet place for my friends and me to hang our hats," Hassan said, pointing to several Moslem caps and Moslem gowns.

"They don't like having women at their meetings," Katie Ann said, "but they use me when it suits them."

"Katie Ann is a woman who feels sorry for herself if she doesn't have a man's attention," Tembo explained to me.

"My time's my bread and butter," she said, "yet you waste it and don't appreciate that I stand out in the road, only for your boss to call me a streetwalker! If it wasn't for my Uncle Ighaam, I'd throw you men to the sharks!"

"What do you think, Mr. Cooper, that I should thank a woman who's all the time complaining?" Tembo asked me, trying to involve me in what seemed a petty quarrel with Katie Ann.

"Tell me about these meetings, Larabie. Is this bunker your meeting place since Ozeer blew up your headquarters at Bergkloof?"

"I have no headquarters. This is just where my friends store their things."

"Larabie, I don't know what you're planning, but this little turf war has gone far enough!" I said.

Katie Ann looked at Tembo and giggled like a young child. "That's easy for your master to say because he hasn't been here long enough."

"I agree it's gone far enough, the reason why we must stop them!" Hassan shouted, pounding one of the olive drab storage boxes hard enough to dent it. "Mr. Cooper, I sent for you now that we are hot on Rajesh's trail. If I seem jumpy, that's because my friends and me slept little, making plans to show them they cannot capture Rajesh without big trouble for them."

Hot on Rajesh's trail! I was excited Hassan could

possibly bring Rajesh back. He opened a camou-flage-colored steel ammunition box.

"How about this?" Hassan asked, holding up a gold chain with Buddha of green jade.

"He once told me he wore that to bring him luck," I said.

"Then I guess his luck ran out," Katie Ann said with another laugh. "Was this Indian so important to you fellows?"

"Didn't your Uncle Arendse teach you why we must keep score? Rajesh was one of our players!" Hassan said, placing a ring on his finger. "He wore this ring on his pointing finger," he said, pointing at an old pocket watch on a chain. "And this watch he never wore because it belonged to his grandfather, a jeweler, who taught him to like jewelry more than girls."

"You saying he liked boys and not girls?" Katie Ann asked.

"No, Raj's jewelry, that's what I'm talking about! Rajesh never played the rabbit!" Hassan insisted. "Raj was telling me he dreamed all the time of her, a woman. How could he be any kind of rabbit, if this was his favorite book." He was speaking of the destroyed *Kama Sutra, Guide to the Art of Love*. Inside its cover was inscribed, *"Love makes the world go 'round. To our future. From Rajesh to Sunitha."* The front and back covers were separated from the contents and the pages pulled apart, stained red.

I was bothered looking at it. "A rabbit?" I asked.

"That's what we call men who don't like girls, Mr. Cooper, but this proves Raj was a regular man like me, no rabbit!"

It bothered me that he was speaking of Raj in the past tense. How could I even mention the ruined sex manual? Some regarded it as an uninhibited world classic that had withstood the test of time, but that didn't make it as any less of a problem for me. I'd been caught in the middle, knowing it was possible that Raj and Sunitha had been learning tantric yogic lovemaking together. Had I inadvertently displaced him to become was part of her continuing education? I was letting this string of life and death events rattle me and probably unfairly questioning her motives. Evidence of Raj's end or not, there was no way I could ever mention to Sunitha the meaning of the book in her life, for she could have no good answer for me.

Even if Rajesh had brought his troubles on himself by trying to be a one-man army, Hassan couldn't bring back the dead by leading a strike force, if this was the true purpose of his meetings in this bunker.

I couldn't ask Chandra whether he was thanking me for coming between Rajesh and Sunitha by setting me up with her, the night he'd left me stranded at her flat in Valhalla Park while the bullets were flying! I didn't know what to think. Was there ever much fire between Raj and her? She couldn't have been too fond of him, or why else did she consistently tell me their engagement was a delusion of Raj's?

"Booley, where are you now...?" Hassan spoke into his cell phone. "Are you secure where you are...? You think Mafumo's with them...? He's bringing his friends...? I'll be there in half an hour with the American, and I expect you to take good care of him, understand?"

I was a little frightened where they might be taking

me. I still had the opportunity to back out, but didn't take it, instead hoping we were closer to solving the mystery of Ozeer and his soldiers in the townships.

Hassan made arrangements with Booley, then threw Rajesh's things in a drawer and led Tembo and me to the garage. He gave Tembo the keys to his car, which still had the old Gazelle logo of the herd of gazelles visible under a cover-up of spray paint. He helped Katie Ann to the passenger seat.

"Wait a minute!" I said, once the garage door was raised and Tembo had started Hassan's car. "Why is Tembo in your car with Katie Ann, rather than with me? Are you taking his job away from him, Larabie?"

"No, I am trying to make sure she gets home safe," Hassan said. "If anything happens to Katie Ann, I answer to her Uncle Ighaam."

"Larabie, you have it wrong. We both work for Chateau, and you answer to me."

"Mr. Cooper, are you forgetting Ted's my father?"

He wanted me to remember his father, quite a change! Until recently neither he nor his mother nor his half-sister nor his father hinted they were all one family, yet now he was using his relationship to Ted as a shield. He was unpredictable, a loose cannon. It made me uneasy, how he habitually resisted following directions. If anyone was going to rein in Hassan and make him more accountable, it had to be Ted. I wished I could turn back, but if he didn't show up at this meeting, I might never know Booley's real connection to Hassan. Quitting might have sent the wrong message to Hassan, that I didn't care and couldn't control the Gazelle distribution deals I'd been making in the townships. I couldn't allow him to think he had carte blanche to use his private army to do the company's business off-record!

Hassan drove me past the remains of the big Sea Point weekend market, where the vendors were still breaking down the stalls and packing up their unsold goods. One of these vendors stood by the road, displaying folding sun covers for dashboards, another sunglasses, and another cut flowers.

"See that man standing by the tree?" Hassan asked me, pointing with his thumb. "He doesn't mean us well."

Hassan was jumpy. Lately he seemed to attract mean-hearted characters, without looking under trees for more. Had I known it would be so much trouble trying to make sense of these dangerous alliances, I would never have gotten on the plane to help build the Chateau's new distribution network. We came to a ball field, and Hassan drove with great caution, circling it. The Kosane brothers were among a group of men kicking around a soccer ball. I thought we'd left them behind earlier! Hassan pointed to a sign—Green Point Rugby Club. Members Only. Behind it was a two-story clubhouse with an upstairs screened porch.

"So, have you ever played any tournaments here?" I asked him.

"Rugby looks like your football they used to play in white man's schools and here at the club. This was a white players' club while I was growing up. That's why it looks abandoned this afternoon. I played my soccer here in the streets, like these poor boys. Right?"

Again, Larabie was trying to present himself as a poor

boy, but from what his mother Janice said, he grew up pampered, at least until she took up with his secret father. Even after Ted realized Hassan wasn't his, he still treated him as a son. But now it was convenient for Larabie to forget about his privileged origins to pander to his poor following in the inner townships.

Hassan pointed to a young man watching the players from a distance, his cell phone in his hand. Suddenly he jerked the wheel, so the car hopped the curb and headed directly for him. At the last moment the young man bolted out of harm's way. Hassan ejected himself from the car, took off after this young man with impressive speed. I lost sight of them once they reached an empty overgrown lot. In a couple of minutes Hassan returned, his clothes torn and filthy.

"You used this car as a weapon!" I shouted. "You could have killed him!"

"He was calling ahead with this phone to spy on us, Mr. Cooper! He's one of Ozeer's Boys!"

"I don't care!" I said. "I'll be driving now, so I won't be needing you any more tonight."

He didn't have a conscience, and it didn't matter to him that he almost ran over a man with a company car. Monday, I planned to tell Ted about this incident, that Hassan was out of control.

"I know you're angry at me," Hassan said. "I'm sorry you don't like me or my friends."

"I didn't say that. It's nothing personal."

"Good, we're still friends," he said with a smile, underestimating my disapproval. "That's why I feel good to take you to meet my other friends before you go to your nice flat and your pretty lady."

When I started this affair with Sunitha, I did it with my eyes open, breaking an American corporate taboo against consorting with direct subordinates. But here in South Africa, I was being scrutinized by people who hardly knew me, some who have never met me face-to-face. I should have expected that as part of a mixed couple, I was an oddity, especially as an American, and should have become used to the attention. But I was just as curious about this ragtag collection of followers as they were curious about me. On this ball field I was seeing not only the Kosanes, but their pals from the caravan that followed us from Mitchell's Plain and Belhar to Green Point.

We moved across the ball field to the rugby clubhouse. Hassan looked through a window, saw no one was inside, then broke out pocket tools and quickly used them to open the lock and enter the building, a fast break-in done with the confidence of an expert lock breaker.

"I don't do this without a good reason," he explained after he let in the followers, "but I knew the boys would enjoy saying their prayers here."

He had opened the clubhouse not for his black followers, who continued playing ball by the dim streetlights, but for his Moslem cohort, who made their way to the second-story porch where they took positions on their knees, bowing to the east, and chanted prayers. They wore the same white robes I noticed hanging in his basement office.

One of the men stood and led me into the main building and sat on a stool at the bar next to Hassan. I stepped away from him. "I'm ready for whatever may come, but right now I'm ready for a drink," Hassan's follower requested.

Hassan closed the door to the porch. "Don't let them hear about drink! Prayer will make a man strong, while drink will make him slow. All our men must be dead sober."

"Yet drink is your business and the American's. Is this what we are defending?"

I didn't like the direction of this conversation. Hassan was supposed to act as my liaison to the townships, yet I didn't hear him saying a word promoting the company. This man wore the same green-trimmed robe but was now pacing and nervous. Maybe I should have found out from him what was spooking him, and whether Hassan was placing him, his friends, and me in a dangerous situation.

"I know you," I said, seeing his face in better light.

He had reddish hair, freckles and green eyes, a coloured man with skin like coffee with three teaspoons of cream. It was Mongrel, who I saw after he left Ighaam Arendse's apartment at the top of Maraville! The rest of the men returned from the porch in street clothes, carrying their robes, and all set their eyes on me.

"You're the one with the hot little car with the fat wheels. Mongrel, right?"

"You hear what your boss called me?" Mongrel asked Tembo. "He tells me I'm an ugly mongrel dog!"

For a tough-looking guy it didn't take much to upset his feelings, not what I intended. I was relieved once he retreated with the other praying men.

"Forget about Mongrel," Hassan said, "This is Booley,

who I just spoke to on the phone; the man who will be in charge of our tour this evening."

I didn't know how long Booley had been here. Maybe he had slipped past me to first join the praying Moslems and was now ready to speak with me.

"And this is the man who you call the chief of the shebeens?" Booley bellowed to the delight of everyone watching me, rubbing the top of my head. "You ask me to take good care of him because you bring him to the wrong place where he don't belong?"

"Keep your hands off Mr. Cooper!" Hassan shouted and pulled me away from Booley. "You know what you must do. We'll catch up with you."

I couldn't see what drew these newcomers here, other than the two obvious events happening here—the soccer game of the blacks and the prayer session of the coloured Moslems. Why had Hassan brought them together and what had Booley planned to do with them, now that they'd unwound? What was the true reason for bringing together himself, Tembo, Katie Ann, and the Kosane brothers, as well as these three dozen men?

The Kosanes and the black soccer players intercepted me at the front door of the club. They cornered me with questions I wouldn't be answering, if Hassan were doing his job to keep me out of trouble. I refused to answer this crowd's intrusive questions about why I was working in South Africa. I was relieved when Hassan returned with Katie Ann and Tembo and was standing between me and his aggressive friends.

They allowed none of this group to pass and demanded to know why Hassan placed Booley and Mongrel in charge of the evening's work and wasn't remaining with them. He explained I was an important man, and he had to take care of me, similar to the reason he gave me for putting Katie Ann in the car with Tembo. Apparently, his answer satisfied them. Released, Hassan and I made our way to where Big Al Kosane waited for him at the Chateau's Volkswagen. A black soccer player also waited, defiantly sitting on the hood with his feet on the bumper.

"Are you scared to go with us, Hassan?" Kosane's follower asked insubordinately.

"Toloki, I'll make believe I didn't hear talk of fear," Hassan said.

Hassan got in the car with me, but the soccer player wasn't moving from the hood. He stood on the bumper and began jumping on it. Hassan put the car in gear and pulled forward then suddenly hit the brakes, making the young man slide onto the ground. Hassan began backing away from him as he lay on the ground, but he didn't get far before he had to stop for more of Kosane's black friends who were blocking the way. Hassan jumped out of the car.

"We don't have time for this!" Hassan shouted. "I told Booley I'd catch up with you guys!"

Toloki made his way next to Hassan and towered over him. Toloki kept tapping Hassan from behind, but Hassan did his best to ignore him.

"I was asking if you're scared to go with my fellows!" Toloki bellowed, pointing to the black faction of soccer players who were encircling him.

While Toloki tried to draw attention to himself, two or three of the Moslem contingents came from behind, grabbed him and began pulling him away from the road and towards the woods at the border of the ball-field. When he began to throw punches, a couple of the black Kosane group subdued their comrade Tolki. They threw him into the cab of a Lion Beer truck and sped off before the confrontation between the factions had the chance to grow uglier.

"Stay united! Black men with coloured men!" Mongrel shouted with an upraised fist, intending to restore morale. "Together we can keep Ozeer's Boys out of our neighborhoods, but we must follow Hassan's lead. If it was not for him, we wouldn't be speaking with Mr. Arendse about what to do to stop this big gangster! If a man like Toloki does not show respect to Hassan, then we must cast him out! We only need men who are will-ing to protect their homes from these bad gangsters!"

Like Mongrel, they responded by raising their fists and cheering their approval. Mongrel was promising to protect them from bad gangsters like Ozeer's men with the help of a good gangster like Arendse. That was how he enticed them here! I came as an observer and consented to none of this, yet I felt as though I'd unwittingly made a pact with the devil! Once Mongrel had pacified the followers, he and Hassan got moving with me driving.

"Where shall I bring you?" I asked. "I've had enough touring for one day."

"I know you must feel out of place, Mr. Cooper, like a zebra in a herd of wildebeest," Hassan said. "I never want to return living here with these poor people with their troubles and fears, but my father taught me never to rise too high in the world that you forget where you came from."

He was trying to deflect my anger by telling me what he believed I wanted to hear. It was hard to believe Ted knew anything firsthand about township poverty, much less ever encouraged his stepson Hassan to remember it!

"Really? I'll mention it to Ted when I meet with him Monday to give him a progress report about today."

"No, that's not a good idea," he said, shaking his finger at me.

"Why?"

"Because we have not made enough progress yet today."

"Any other reason?"

"Because we'll be meeting my father before then."

Hassan could be evasive, but I'd never known him to speak frivolously. Could he intend that we go to his natural father that evening, Jan LeRoux's unnamed lover, a Moslem from the townships?

"Great, I'd like to meet him, if I haven't already," I probed, though he wasn't telling me any more about his true father right then. "So where do you want me to drop you, Larabie?" I asked again, trying not to show him my growing impatience.

He still wasn't telling me where he wanted me to take him. After ten minutes he gave me the first set of directions. "That's it... Keep going... I'll let you know the route." Finally, in Bantry Bay he had me stop in front of the Ambassador Hotel. "I wanted to keep this a surprise, Mr. Cooper," he said with a big grin. "I have friends in this hotel. They like me, so I make them a Chateau customer and already we ship them plenty of cases."

"Nice work, Hassan."

"You should thank Rajesh too because he came with me the day I called on them for their business."

"From what you've shown me, Larabie, I won't be speaking with Raj anymore."

"No problem," Hassan said. "We won't speak of Rajesh to the manager, just of yourself, Mr. Cooper. I bragged to the manger about you, the American bringing the special American beer formula here to Cape Town."

"But you know that's not true!"

"In our country we don't know from one minute to the next what's true. Mr. Cooper, with all respect, you cannot even guess what's true unless I show you!"

He was not at all respectful, and we both knew it! I couldn't afford to ignore him because he was quite right, without him I was on my own. I could never understand these people and their shifting alliances, but I tried to play fair in my dealings. Evidently, I had agents in the townships I never knew about, except through him directly, and his followers and acquaintances. The more I learned about how our designated agents and invisible subagents promoted themselves, the more I wanted to cut them loose. The trouble was, we couldn't be too selective in choosing our associates and clients, now that we'd built a plant in the Chateau and the satellite breweries in the shebeens, all continuously turning out cases of our product that we had to sell somewhere.

"No, I can't even guess what you want, Larabie."

"I want to introduce you to the manager of the Ambassador. He'd be disappointed if we don't show our faces."

"You have it all planned, don't you?" I said as we passed through the lobby.

"His name's Rolf," Hassan said, avoiding my question, "and he likes Americans."

"Hassan, this must be the American!" the receptionist greeted me. She was an attractive dark woman and had a big smile for me when she came to shake my hand and give me her calling card.

"Word travels fast," I said afterward.

Hassan brought me to the bar and restaurant, which was decorated with a nautical theme. He had a particular table where he wanted to seat me. People at the other tables had paper placemats; our table had a white linen cloth.

"You finally brought him," said a man with a tattoo of a creature half fish but with the torso of a woman. "I'm Rolf."

A waitress began to serve our meal, starting with steaming hot fish soup. I politely asked about his life before working in that hotel. Rolf came from the sea, first as a navy man, then as a ship's captain. But rather than about himself, he wanted to talk about America— our cities in warm climates, asking whether I might have a job for him there. Hassan seemed preoccupied, and he glanced frequently at his watch.

CHAPTER 14
BARGAINING CHIPS

A couple of days after Raj's disappearance, I met Chandra at the new Gazelle plant. He was wearing a hard hat with the updated Gazelle logo, identifying him as our master brewing manager. At lunch we ate in the managers' dining area, off the main tourists' dining room, which was crowded due to the Christmas holiday.

"Chandra, there's a rumor going around that you're looking to get even for what happened to Raj."

"Truly?"

"Yes, some are saying that you're organizing a vigilante gang."

"As in the cowboy movies?"

He cocked his hands like a couple of six shooters, as if I were a potential target. He needed to understand I couldn't consent to his jeopardizing the company's reputation for any personal reprisals. My disapproval must have upset him, because he wasn't eating his curry and rice lunch.

"You have been a great asset," I started, "but you must understand if you get into trouble, we will have to deny any connection on the part of the company for your actions. In other words, you'd be entirely on your own."

Now he responded by pantomiming cutting his own throat. "A good caution, which Hassan too must heed. Thank you too for Sunitha's support." He packed up his uneaten lunch, directed to me another traditional bow, and left me as confused about his intentions as before I delivered my warning.

As for Sunitha, I admired her loyalty to Rajesh, though I was not sure whether she was remembering him every day out of guilt, or because she truly believed she could bring him back by chanting daily mantras for him and by lighting incense in his honor. One day I asked why she was so quiet and withdrawn and what was the meaning of the Indian words she was chanting. Wishing Rajesh a smooth journey, she said. She was vague on whether that would happen between this life and the next life after death, or whether she was trying to merge her soul with his right then.

Part of her ritual was to cook pungent foods, then set them out on the dining room table in tiny brass bowls with matching lids, the offerings part of *chadra*, a ceremony for the peace of a departed soul. She wouldn't accept my offer to help her perform these rights, explaining she had to use a man of her faith, rather than me. She offered the same reason one evening when she packed the bowls, plates, incense, and foods and waited on the porch for Chandra. I helped by carrying her crates out to Chandra's vehicle. Rather than argue about unexplained plans, I gave her an enthusiastic hug goodbye. I wanted to make a statement in front of Chandra about my loyalty towards her. Wherever she was going with departed Rajesh, it seemed I was launching her on an arduous journey.

Once she was gone, I felt oddly relieved that I was free develop a plan. Earlier in the week, after Chandra and Hassan had produced their bloody evidence, I told Ted of the loss of our man. He took it calmly, calling it thinning the forest. Maybe it was normal to become numb amid Cape Town's continuous street war, where casualties were expected. I hadn't developed his detachment. Reprisals didn't seem to be the answer. Whether the Kassies and their allies had acted stupidly in challenging Ozeer's Boys, and whether Raj should have put the loss of the old, functionally obsolete Gazelle plant behind him, I had to agree with Chandra that Raj was struck down fighting for the Château, that perhaps it was up to the company to organize an investigation to learn who were the thugs involved.

With Sunitha gone, I bought a copy of Herman Hesse's *Siddhartha*, and studied the journey of his life. It was arrogant of me to be make comparisons of myself to a great spiritual seeker, or worse, to excuse my own shortcomings. I was not a hero to be emulated, but I was an honorable man. I ceased trying to rate my character and instead concerned myself with eating. I built a sandwich with the last night's king clip fish— unique to South Africa. I ate on the porch, looking to the ocean, imagining Sunitha and me cruising up the coast to Durban port. I remember her telling me she'd never been on a ship, though she spent her life close to the ocean.

I believed perhaps a few days traveling alone with her might help me overcome her somber mood. If she was with me, we would agree it was not my role to amuse and distract her from legitimate cares. Since we first became an item, I worked hard to understand her spiritual view of the world. I now realized that when Chandra dropped me at her bunker in Valhalla Park, I should have immediately confronted the reasons for her withdrawal to her miserable quarters. I could have removed her then and there, instead of waiting until Ozeer's Boys got to her. But how could I have known the attack was not only intended against her house and property, but against herself? I believed she'd been using diplomatic skills, as well as the strength of her character in the face of adversity, to avoid involving me in her ordeal.

With many troubling questions rushing to my mind, I'd given up concentrating on the story of the Buddhist path toward enlightenment, and instead turned on the television to watch a tribal ceremonial dance. There was a knocking on my door, but when I turned to answer it, I saw that Tembo had bypassed the guard. I felt like a goldfish in an aquarium. It was obvious that I had no privacy.

"I could've waited until I picked you up Monday to inspect the shebeens in the townships," Tembo said, "but we wanted to get to you sooner."

"We? What's this all about?"

"Not about you, sir, but about Rajesh. We can't find him, but we must look for him in the right places."

"Where did you have in mind?" I queried.

"We will be glad for your help, Mr. Cooper. Let me show you," he said, easing me out of my chair.

"Wait a minute! I want to know who's behind your visit."

"Sir, the truth is Sunitha Bala and Chandra Kassie cannot afford to lose Rajesh, since the Indians are so few here in South Africa. Mr. Nichols said the Kassies are not strong enough on their own, and authorized us to form a search party, provided we take measures."

Sunitha and Chandra had been gone only a few hours, but evidently they'd already relayed their plans to Tembo. I suspected Tembo was proposing a vigilante reprisal in disguise. It was puzzling that he could locate and explain this all to Ted, who in turn rushed here to enlist me to search for a dead man! I wish I could take at face value the story he was presenting, rather than suspecting Tembo or Chandra, or even Sunitha, had set in motion an illogical non-rescue plan.

"A search party? Did Ted authorize bloodhounds?" I asked about Ted's plan, who had recently been rather indifferent to Raj's fate.

"Rajesh shed blood on his bed clothes days ago. He may have blood left to fill the noses of search dogs, but Mr. Nichols doesn't like dogs. That's why you will see no dogs at the Château.

Tembo had completely misunderstood my quip and given it a grotesque turn.

"When you find some leads, Tembo, you can return to me."

He handed me an envelope marked:

TO: L. COOPER
FROM: T. NICHOLS
CONTENTS: SALES REPORTS, TO BE VERIFIED WITHOUT
DELAY

"No need to bother you, sir. Mr. Nichols told me he will not be available, and you should only go during daylight to Mitchell's Plain and Belhar to check on our black shebeen owners, the ones we are selling cases of canned beer to."

"This is a Sunday, Tembo."

"Exactly, the day my friends like to hang around the shebeens after church. They may be help, but if you care doing it some other time—"

"Okay, Tembo, I'll assume it's important enough for you to be hunting me down this morning."

"Yes, sir," he said with a grin. "I am a good hunter, but sometimes human game is hardest to bring down."

I made it a practice to spend no more than a quarter of my time at the office. Ted had great confidence in his staff at the Stellenbosch estate, as well as those transferred to the new plant. Chandra was an excellent teacher and was invaluable in applying what he knew to a modern plant. That left me primarily working with the satellite brewpubs. They were key to spreading our revamped brand into the market, especially in the bigger, higher volume brewpubs such as Alicia's Wandi Dadla's—the ones located in the European and more secure coloured districts. My strategy was to continue to buy old taverns in decent locations where we could obtain insurance at an acceptable rate. Frederick's Sanlaam insurance company was working closely with us, setting them up as microbreweries, organizing them to turn profits, all the while putting our product friction-free into an expanding market. As planned, we were establishing our niche for Gazelle as a premium artisan beer, though the bulk of our output would be mass-produced in our new plant. The daunting task was selling in high-risk zones. We had to compete with

Lion and Castle brands with homebrew no-name brands made in wooden barrels and very cheaply out of their shebeens.

If I was the Chief of Pubs, as Hassan claimed, I was a reluctant ruler over the poorest and most dangerous of our territory. This occurred to me as Tembo took me into Mitchell's Plain to inspect several of our customers' operations. I had been avoiding these bottom tier shebeen customers, and realized I'd been over-delegating their businesses to a couple of black shift managers from the Château, and to Chandra. No matter if I were accompanied by several black employees, I felt uneasy entering these poor black townships. My anxiety took hold when we passed from the paved roads to the unmaintained gravel roads, full of potholes. I asked Tembo to stop to give me the chance to compose myself before going further.

"Our new government promised us houses," Tembo explained. "This is one of them, but the government has no more money. They built very few model houses, but if you want, we'll stop at a house you should see."

"That's not necessary," I said.

We stopped in front of another structure unlike anything I've seen. It was a steel box, with a couple of cutouts for windows and a door, all fitted with burglar bars. Attached to it, at right angles, there was an identical box.

"Truck trailers?" I asked.

"No, ocean shipping containers, carried on the piggy's back." He then kicked one of the steel walls. "Very strong and secure, very good for Mr. Kosane to keep out thieves at night."

Frank Kosane, the shebeen owner, yelled from the window to a well-dressed couple. "Jonathan, I see you are walking a straight line, without a blue Monday hangover." Kosane spoke in a basso profundo voice, impossible to ignore. "You are a lucky man to have a pretty lady this afternoon after the morning's church service." The passing couple laughed in response. "Don't mind me. Come on in. We have a game going."

He came out and led us inside. Sitting at a wooden utility cable reel, repurposed as a table, a couple of men watched a soccer match on TV. In the rear room, others were playing pool. They stopped their game to look us over.

"Is he your boss?" asked one of the men, who was so big he twirled his pool stick like a baton. "Are you on the job?"

"This is Big Albert, my brother," Frank interrupted, sweeping his hand over his brother's cropped head, causing him to drop the cue, which he retrieved and handed to me.

My cell phone rang, and I moved to a corner to answer it. "Leon, it's me."

"Bernie, who else calls me in the middle of your night?" I asked.

"Actually, it's 4:00 A.M. I couldn't sleep because I was dreaming about you."

"You're dreaming of me again?" The men, overhearing my side of the conversation, began to whistle and cackle, no doubt believing I was speaking to my lover, a man.

"I hear your pals, Leon," she said. "Are you in a party?"

"Why? Do you think you're missing something?"

"Hardly. I wouldn't get along with those people as well as you do."

"You didn't call to tell me that, Bernice."

"Stop calling me that."

"Sorry. You were dreaming about me?" I whispered, but the walls of the shipping container amplified my voice. Again, they hooted.

"Not about you—about the Truth and Reconciliation Commission trial. I saw an article in the paper about the bodies of people who were buried or burned to cinders."

"We get the news here too. What's your point?"

"Don't say anything to get yourself into trouble."

"Pleasant dreams, Bernie. I'm sure you'll stay in touch."

"That was my secretary in the States," I said, realizing it was ridiculous to explain my conversation to the pool players. They looked me over, and Big Albert handed me a can of Gazelle beer.

"You come here, Mr. America, to see what poor people drink?" Big Albert said. "You should be pleased with my brother, who sells this watery beer of yours. I think he loses customers this way. Sir, does my brother work for you like this warrior, Tembo?"

As a deal maker in the States, I had to make small talk with almost anyone. But here I was confronted with the people I had no way to read. I wanted to hear what they had to say about Tembo. I tried to interact with them the best I could.

"You have a big reputation. Is that how you got your name, Big Albert?"

"What are they calling me?" Big Al asked.

"If you really want to know, tough, strong, and when

you are in battle—vicious." "Don't listen to these bar-
flies, Mr. Cooper. I make enemies no more."

"Not so fast!" said one of the players, who had a
nasty raised scar across his chest and wore a shirt open,
revealing it as if it were medallion. "Once we were warriors together and fought beside you, Tembo. We have
not changed into flies you can swat dead."

"Tembo's a bit younger, and a bit tougher than me. He
was a lion in his younger days," Frank Kosane boomed,
"a commando fighting to take back our country."

"But I'm not a soldier anymore." Tembo said. "I'm
done with fighting! War was in the past. I must make
a living, so I live in the present, like Mr. Cooper does."

"That's easy for you, now that you make so much
money as Mr. Cooper's servant," Big Albert said.

"This time you go too far, man," Tembo said. With
astonishing speed he lifted this loudmouth off the floor
and threw him across a table. Big Albert reappeared,
helped the man to his feet, and hustled him out of the
shebeen. Frank then brought Tembo and me to the area
in the back where he stored cases of beer. We took a
seat on a keg.

"I am sorry if he makes trouble, Mr. Cooper. I know
your time is valuable."

Tembo got down to business. He presented an invoice
for his purchase of Gazelle product, prepared at the
Château office. Kosane studied it for a minute before
speaking.

"I know you don't give up your Sunday to talk with
me about beer I bought from your company. You know
if you give me a cut and make me your distributor,
I sell more beer for you. Here, look at my figures,"

he said, scribbling some numbers on the back of an envelope.

I believed I was on a fool's errand. The last thing our company needed was to set up Kosane as one of our distributors. Even if, by some miracle, he were able to move a reasonable amount of beer out of this little shebeen, I had no reason to believe he'd succeed as a distributor, certainly not based on the modest figures on the back of his envelope. They were tallies of how much per month he sold of other brands of beer and of bottles of liquor. It proved nothing about his ability to move the Gazelle brand. Did he think we had such deep pockets that we would to fill up this building with our product, and then trust he could control it from pilferage and theft? I wouldn't consider it, certainly not in that part of town.

Big Albert joined us. He grabbed his brother's scribbled numbers, tore up the paper and threw it on the floor. "No need to say anything more. The Kosanes do not need you, and we do not need Gazelle in our district!"

"What we do need, Mr. Cooper, is to find your coolie Rajesh," Frank said. "If Ozeer's Boys grabbed him, you'll see we are powerful warriors who will make them pay!"

I had nothing more to discuss with them, and their converted shipping containers were feeling like a coffin. In seconds I was out the nearest door. Once in our company truck, Frank got our attention by pounding on the hood. "I promise, if we don't find our man Rajesh alive, there will be trouble!"

Without waiting to hear what kind of trouble he was

predicting, Tembo quickly got us underway. But before Tembo could reply, we were pushed from behind. The next time it was a hard jolt. Through the rear window I saw it was the Kosane brothers in the cab and their friends in the rear of their pickup truck, bumping into us. We slowed down and they passed us and locked their brakes, forcing us to bump into them. We were in front of vendors at a market with dozens of tables of produce and prepared food. Frank bolted into the marketplace, while Big Al rushed back to our truck.

"We stop so Frank finds a toilet," he told me through the window. "Also, he wants to know if you mind waiting while he buys something for dinner. No harm done, boss! You have a strong bumper... So now that you have time to think it over, you decide the Kosane brothers make a good distributor?"

Meanwhile, Frank rapped on Tembo's window. "I brought something for dinner." He hoisted a heavy plastic bag and threw it between us. "This is the kaffir food Tembo and me grow up on when we was little and mama's milk go dry."

Tembo looked inside the bag at the gift and immediately threw it out the window, hitting Frank on the shoulder, leaving a bloody stain on his shirt. A bloody goat's head rolled on the ground! Big Al retrieved it and threw it in their truck, where his friends were seated in the box, waiting.

"Savage," Tembo muttered when we were underway. "A poor man can be a gentleman, but a man with no manners, rich or poor, is no better than a savage. Don't you agree?"

I realized he could string together English words well

when it suited him. His intent was clear—he wanted to give me the impression that he was a different kind of poor South African, one with a more European point of view.

"There's a lot of wisdom in that. I didn't know you're a philosopher."

"No, sir, I have a little education." He pointed to some children on a street corner. "I grew up in Transeki, in the countryside, far from the city where the older boys show them bad things."

The Kosanes were following us, and Tembo brought our truck to an abrupt stop. His target was another group of kids, no more than ten years old. The Kosanes stopped as well. These boys began cursing the interfering adults, when Big Al lifted the two loudest ones off the ground, limbs thrashing, then dropped them onto the ground. When another of the boys began to punch Tembo, he grabbed him by his belt and twirled him over his head. This gave Tembo the opportunity to gather the lethal playthings the boys had scattered on the ground. After a short consultation Big Al bellowed a warning. "If that glue you're huffing don't kill you boys, the next time we find you with it, we beat you hard!"

One of the boys produced a hunting knife, which Frank quickly wrestled out of his hand and kicked him in the butt. The others escaped into an alley. Tembo showed me what they left behind—lighters, cigarette papers, straws, a can of benzene and some tubes of glue. He made a flourish over these objects, with the brothers watching. "This poison make them crazy. That's why the youngsters are so mean. And they don't get any smarter when they grow up."

"Cold beer is better for them because it's natural!" said Big Al. "And if they don't have enough money to buy it by the bottle, they can always go to a shebeen and buy sorghum beer out of the barrel. That's why we do a good thing, Mr. Cooper, giving them our better natural beer."

"In my country the tavern owner is supposed to stop serving when they become drunk," I said. They laughed at me.

"Here, if you cannot get drunk and forget your troubles, you become crazy and extra dangerous!" Frank said. "If I was you, Mr. Cooper, I would go home where you belong before you too become crazy!"

The brothers seemed much like clowns, but they understood my precarious situation, especially Big Al. I felt forces beyond my control acting on me. If I were to stay in this country long enough, I probably would be crazy, if not from fear, then from anticipation of the next trap.

Earlier that day I agreed to listen to Tembo and visit our shebeens. We mixed Chateau Business with inquiries about Raj to see if we could pick up any useful leads for where he was last seen. Every few minutes Tembo and the Kosanes' friends would make stops to talk with men on the streets, always asking about Raj. No one had any information about him, and the Kosanes repeatedly suggested to anyone listening that Ozeer's organization was nothing more than kidnappers and killers.

"It's been interesting meeting the friends you seem to have everywhere," I said to Frank after a few more stops, "but does it make any sense for you to stir them up?"

"It's dangerous to forget when your enemy attacks," Big Al said. "We don't care much about your Indian girl, but we will never forget Ozeer as long as he lives."

"I'm not here to see fighting, but to bring people together without friction."

"Shouldn't we fight the man who wants to rob us and make us as slaves—Ozeer?"

Ozeer the gangster, the man I've heard so much about, but hoped to never meet, had a feudal power in the townships. He was in a death struggle with Ighaam Arendse for control. My words of reconciliation must have seemed hollow to them.

"I love watching American cowboy movies, Mr. Cooper," said Frank. "On the stagecoach they always have lookout with a rifle. How do you call, riding the shotgun? That's what we are doing, riding the shotgun for you."

The talk about rifles and shotguns didn't please me, especially if he meant to use firepower to defend his territory. Before I could question the brothers any further to gauge their real intentions, we continued this stop-and-go journey, and he continued to introduce me along the way.

At one stop, we came to a group of young women, dressed in working girl clothes. Tembo seemed to attract female hustlers. This insistent group wanted us to join them, but I sent Tembo to lose them. One girl wasted no time, reaching her hand under his shirt and flirting with him.

"These ladies think you worry too much," he said when he returned, "and they offer you their services."

"Forget it! My advice is that street walkers will never

do you any good and may cause you a great deal of harm. We are no closer to finding Raj than when we left my flat, so why don't you turn around and take me home?"

"Mr. Cooper, are you forgetting that Hassan is expecting to see us before dark? It is not right for us to keep him waiting."

"No, I'll call and tell him to meet me tomorrow afternoon, normal business hours." I dialed him on my cell phone several times, with no success.

"If Mr. Nichols knows where his son hides since Rajesh vanished, then maybe he has a reason not to tell anyone. He must also have a reason for not answering your call. I believe we should try to find him before the sun sets, with your permission."

"You believe Hassan has some kind of search plan?"

"If he does, he would not share such important matters with a driver like myself." he said, looking at me out of the corner of his eye to gauge my reaction.

"Okay, but don't play dumb. Rather than continue with this foolish caravan, let's go directly to him now."

"Directly."

He made a quick U-turn and left the gravel roads of Belhar township for the main tarmac highway. Our followers reversed direction and were right behind us. We passed through the commercial district of Sea Point, where four restaurants were our accounts. We continued to a boulevard and drove on the service road until we reached a section of residential flats. In the fading afternoon light, between the apartments and the businesses, was a gathering place for another herd of women for hire. Tembo slowed down, then stopped.

"Damn it, let's get out of here. You're stalling now, Tembo, and Hassan's been stalling me all day."

"Correct, sir. Now please let's go to Maraville."

"Didn't Hassan say we'd be meeting his father?"

"Yes, sir, we'll be seeing Mr. Arendse in Maraville."

Ighaam Arendse was Larabie's natural father! Ighaam, the man who's evidently taught him lessons on how to control a territory! I wondered how Tembo knew he was the father. Did he find it out directly from Ted, or indirectly from gossip within Maraville, where boss Ighaam perched on his roof like a bird of prey? Why had I been kept in the dark so long about the connection between him and Larabie?

When we arrived in Woodstock, Tembo spotted some men standing in the road at the intersection, just before Vortrekker Road, the main commercial street. He slammed on the brakes before we had fully stopped and spun around 180 degrees. He quickly turned off that street and onto a parallel one. When he noticed a couple of men pacing on this street, he again violently reversed our direction. He raced into a church parking lot, cut off the headlights, and hid us between the sanctuary and the rectory.

"Trying to get us killed?"

"In Cape Town, sometimes it's best to keep going, regardless."

"What are you hiding from anyway?"

"It's a long story," he began. His cell phone rang. "I had to take a different route to get away from them, Larabie. It was too dark to see their dark faces, but it had to be them... No, don't go without us! We'll be there in a couple minutes."

We drove down the second alternate street, until we were on another part of Vortrekker Road. He pulled into an alley next to Ebrahim's Halal Market and quickly entered through the back door. Once inside, while white-bearded Ebrahim offered us bottles of soda pop, his son moved to the front of the store, listening to repeated distant explosions. The reality was Larabie had been waiting for us. I could not understand what he was doing, why he'd appeared and disappeared three times in the last few hours, first in Mitchell's Plain at the shebeen, then at Sea Point in his bunker, and now here in Woodstock at the halal grocery.

"Hassan, are you playing hide and seek, or a deadly serious game, running away from the war zone?"

"Those shots are coming from just a few blocks away! We need to make sure our people are okay. I don't play around, Mr. Cooper, and I don't run away from nothing!" Despite his bravado, I could see the fear in his face. "So, are we ready to roll?"

My first inclination was to stay put, but this was his territory not mine, and I had to let him make the calls. Larabie led the way in his car, and we followed until we were nearly hit by a minivan taxi, traveling the wrong way on a narrow street, forcing Tembo onto the sidewalk. When we arrived at Maraville, he stopped on the far side of the street, debating whether to go through the open gateway, now that the steel gate lay twisted alongside it. It was strangely quiet, with no tenants anywhere to be seen, as if the place had been evacuated! He pulled a little closer, in front of the guard shack. With his flashlight he lit up a man inside, slumped on the floor, moaning. The wall was pocked with bullet holes.

"What's happened?" I asked stupidly. "Let's get out of here!"

"It's too late now, sir," he said and proceeded inside. Some men pulled out the injured man who was speaking.

"What's he saying? Why don't they pack him up and take him to the hospital?"

"It's not Zulu, and it's no language that I know," Tembo said. They tore a shirt to use as tourniquets on a leg and arm. "This guard was a first-class medic in the liberation army. He saved more than he lost. This one, I don't think he have family anyway, in case things go bad for him. The trouble is we need all the fighters we can get, just in case lightning strikes here twice."

Now that Tembo had given me his opinion, Big Al was next. "Ozeer's Boys play dirty," Mr. Cooper said. "Hassan brings us here to make a final peace with them, so what do they do? They try to ambush us! Pigs! Good thing Ighaam had plenty of men to back us up. And they was lucky Ighaam's Boys wasn't shooting to kill everyone, except at the ones trying to get us! Dirty rats! We treated them better than they deserve, sending out the truce flag, and letting them take their casualties with them! Take my advice, Mr. Cooper, I wouldn't be hanging around this place too much longer!"

How could I know the truth, whether the rabble Hassan had collected from the townships and brought here to Maraville were looking for a truce, or for a pitched battle? Or was the offer of peace really intended to trap them in the Maraville compound, which would account for why it had been evacuated?

"Hang on a minute, sir," Tembo requested. Evidently,

they found another casualty, a man who they laid down in the back of the truck, his head on the tailgate. I looked up at one of the balconies and was surprised to see a couple small children, and saw a woman pull them back indoors. Could Ighaam have ordered everyone in the compound to evacuate, but missed that particular family? Perhaps there were other residents hunkered down inside their flats, terrified to show their faces.

"Hassan, we was stupid to listen to you and let them carry off their casualties," said a man carrying a khaki military issue bag like I'd been seeing during our wild ride, duffels I now suspected had been carrying weapons. "We should have evacuated our own casualties to that doctor friend of yours."

"Who's this one you planning to haul away?" Big Al asked. Tembo shined the torch on his face. "Isn't this the scoundrel who set fire to the Indians' brewery to get back at them after he was fired?"

"Right, he's Mafumo," Larabie confirmed.

"I give him a better resting place," one of the Kosanes' followers laughed and yanked him off the truck and onto the ground.

Mafumo managed to sit up and said in clear English. "Then you leave me here to die?"

"You're a clever one, Hassan, leading us into this slaughter pen," Big Al shouted, pounding the side of his truck for emphasis. "Next time don't be calling me, you coward!"

"Did he expect we wouldn't take a few casualties?" Larabie asked me, once we were back in our truck.

"Never mind that, we can't just leave this poor man here to bleed out."

Tembo got out to confer with the Kosanes. "Mafumo's either Gazelle's property—or else Ozeer's. We can't touch him. We must go. There'll be consequences if we stay."

"Then it's on you, Tembo. You're going to have a hell of a time explaining to the authorities about him!"

"Authorities? In the Rainbow Nation? It doesn't work like that here, sir."

"Tell me, why not?" I demanded.

"Because Mafumo's a bargaining chip that's been cashed out!"

I was still a Christian, and I was about to dial for an ambulance, whether or not Mafumo, the subject of my prophetic dream, deserved to be saved. But before I could, we heard sirens in the distance. I feared the authorities as much as I did the gangsters! We moved quickly out the gate, and in a few blocks Tembo saw police cars coming and slowed down, so as not to attract attention. Fortunately, they did not intercept us and we managed to slip away from Maraville.

CHAPTER 15

OASIS SECURITY

A quarter hour later we were at the entrance to my flat. The guard came out of the guard shack, slowly walked behind the car, hand on his nightstick and looked in Tembo's window. He didn't recognize the truck, nor did he seem to notice me sitting in the back seat. A career military man, he was partially deaf from artillery explosions. He put his ear closer to Tembo's face and in the meantime could not hear me identifying myself. It seemed to me a deaf security guard could be a hazard, not only to himself, but to those he was hired to protect! In the spirit of charity, I made it a point to see what I could do to get him fitted for a first-rate hearing aid. He returned to the shack to make a call, then let the motorized gate roll aside, allowing us to pass. Tembo accompanied me into the elevator, then into my flat.

"Tembo, I never asked for a 24/7 bodyguard, but under the circumstances, I might take up your offer. I'll let you know soon."

"As we saw tonight, we have no security at Maraville. If you were me, would you care to sleep in such a place tonight, sir?"

I didn't really know much about Tembo's background,

except what he told me of his journey from a country village into the townships. Ted trusted him, not only as a driver, but as a confidant, yet Tembo's friends in Mitchell's Plain remembered him as a tough freedom fighter. It seemed to me he played multiple roles well as obedient servant or lover, as the situation demanded. But tonight he was not trying to hide his terror of returning to Maraville.

"Of course not. You're too valuable to us," I reassured him with as much enthusiasm as I could muster. "The couch over there makes out into a bed. Make yourself at home."

"I am a man without a true home—I can never return to my village, except to visit," he spoke, his vulnerability surprising me.

Bad dreams brought me fitful sleep. By 2 A.M., and the wind coming out of Table Bay was shaking the windows, forcing its way through the cracks. I was cold, but didn't want to disturb Tembo by going in the living room to turn on the heat. For some reason, I couldn't get comfortable. Trying to get back to sleep, I imagined Tembo speaking to me: "*I am a man without a true home of my own.... Your home tonight would be far too nice for me.*" Despite his sycophancy, inviting him to stay felt like me like the right thing to do, especially with Sunitha gone.

In my dream, I was lying on my back in the dark, while Tembo slept on his belly in the living room, mumbling to himself. When I went to arouse him, he was rocking side to side and bobbing up and down and seemed more troubled than me.

I tried again to sleep but couldn't get him out of my mind. I dreamed he was floating face down in the water, dying, myself helpless to save him! Soon the wind off the Bay died down, and I was finally able to sleep. Then I heard knocking.

Tembo was outside the door. "Mr. Cooper, are you okay?"

"Insomnia. I'll get over it."

"That makes both of us, sir." he responded, then left, though it was only 3:30 A.M. He didn't return until the next evening.

Alone again but too agitated to sleep, I picked up a new book of Sunitha's, the Robben Island prison writings of Nelson Mandela. I fell back asleep after half an hour, now dreaming I was on Robben Island, not as a prisoner myself, but as his special guard. I didn't mind taking care of Mandela because he was a gentleman. It was my job to deliver him his meals and take him out of his cell for work assignments—field work during the growing season, hard labor in the quarry the rest of the year, pounding big rocks into little rocks.

At the last prison cell check of my midnight watch, I didn't report him missing and instead took the next 24 hours off-duty to look for him. I searched for Mandela from dawn until the sun was overhead and heating the rock quarry like a kiln. In the blinding sun, prisoners were breaking and hauling rocks, periodically retreating to an overhang where the stone had been undercut and which the men were using as a latrine. I heard a noise, a groaning.

Someone seized my ankle. I shook myself loose and saw a hand protruding from the rock debris! I asked for help and with a couple of inmates managed to free the gasping man. The trustees dragged him into the open and gave him some water, which sent him wheezing. He sounded like a man with only a few breaths left, a man resisting imminent death. I cleaned the limestone dust off his dark face with my shirt, believing we'd found Mandela. But instead, it was a street tough of the Ozeer gang—Mafumo!

I heard the whistle announcing the start of my shift. I had to leave immediately. I darted to the main prison building, reporting late for duty. I had a sinking feeling that in my haste I'd done the wrong thing and should have brought Mafumo with me, even though he didn't have much life left. I shouldn't have left him for dead under the rubble.

This time it wasn't the whistle I heard, but the clock beside my bed. The sun had risen, and I wasn't alone in my room. Sunitha was sitting in the chair at the foot of my bed, watching me.

"I was wondering when you'd return, Sunitha. It's been too many days."

"You must have had a nightmare, though I couldn't hear everything you were saying."

"I was talking in my sleep?"

"And crying. Had I known earlier you needed me, I'd have been here for you, dear."

It wasn't Sunitha's nature to lie, so I knew she really had heard me cry. I hadn't done that since I was a small boy. Maraville rattled me more than I realized. I wondered how much of my dream she overheard. She came and held my head between her hands, as if trying to feel the dream that filled my head, trying to exorcise it from me. I hoped she didn't feel sorry for me, simply because she found me sleeping poorly.

Soon she was beneath the covers with me. I realized

how much I'd missed her in the week since she'd been gone to search and mourn for Rajesh. I couldn't get Raj out of my mind, nor Mafumo, nor the half-dead man Big Al Kosane retrieved from the Maraville guard shack. Sunitha sensed my distraction and massaged nodes on my feet, stimulating them until the three men's faces left my mind. We knew each other's pleasures and needs, and I vowed we would not have to be separated again anytime soon.

It was time for breakfast, but I didn't respond to Tembo's call for us to eat. When I didn't answer, he opened our door a crack.

"Tembo, get out of here!"

"Sorry, sir. Would you prefer I reheat everything in a bit?"

He had prepared a fine breakfast—eggs, ham and sliced meats, cheeses, crackers, mushrooms, porridge and fried bread, as well as juice and coffee.

"Sunitha said you would like a full English breakfast, Mr. Cooper."

I looked at her for an explanation. "I thought this would celebrate your safe return," she said and kissed me, in front of Tembo. "Tembo, you've been more than attentive this morning."

There was tension at the table as the three of us sat down eating. "Did something keep you up last night?" Tembo asked.

"I just got caught up in an interesting book I've been reading, a prison diary."

Sunitha went to the bedroom and returned with the book, Mandela's picture on the cover. "Tembo, do you like our ex-leader? Do you think he does a good job?"

"When he was in charge I had a good job, almost as good as I have at Drakenstein," Tembo said with a smile.

"Mandella tried his best to keep a semblance of peace," she said, looking at him. "Otherwise, the bad boys would surely have burned the Boer farmers and this entire country to the ground!"

"I know you heard the rumor that I was once of those bad boys, a street fighter, but so was Mandela! We did what was necessary to do to bring down the old government! But he was a good man, otherwise he would have been a snarling dog after thirty years in jail!"

"Leon, what do you think of the Rainbow Nation's spiritual leader since reading his book and living In South Africa?"

"I've not been here long enough to understand you people!"

Tembo held the book toward me with both hands, as if it were the Bible. "Mandela was telling the way he saw things, how the apartheid government benefited no one except the whites and made a lot of poor people starve to death. What do you think, Mr. Cooper?"

"As they say in my country, you may have thrown out the baby with the bathwater. You may have replaced one set of masters for a far worse set. No matter how long I am a guest in your country, I don't believe I'll be able to sort out your differences."

There was more I could have discussed, but there was no point. Mandella was writing about an old regime and I couldn't see what difference the past made. Unlike my indifference to history, Sunitha thought we needed to first know the past to understand the present condition in South Africa. I never liked discussing politics, even with my best friends, but there in South Africa I'd been intentionally avoiding the subject, except when alone with Sunitha, and now this morning with Tembo at the table. In the bedroom she got me to talk about my dreams, then at breakfast managed to bring out what was on Tembo's mind.

Tembo's immediate concern was his living conditions in Maraville, not politics. I couldn't blame him for not wanting to return to his flat there, but after tossing, turning, and snoring on my couch a few nights, he thankfully left me alone with Sunitha. After he was gone, my mind was filled with the gang war and its aftermath at Maraville. Hers was preoccupied with Rajesh's migrating soul. She saw the evidence report, including his clothes and hair, and finally accepted that he was truly dead. Still, she remained loyal to his memory, offering prayers and incense to his departed spirit when I was still asleep, or else when she was home alone.

Rather than speak about the demons bothering us, we kept our troubles to ourselves and enjoyed our time together. She spent more time cooking dinners, buying fresh meats and fish and vegetables a couple of times a week to create meals rarely twice the same. She said cooking was good because it helped her forget and had the same soothing effect on me, so most evenings I offered to assist her with the preparations.

I believed Sunitha had given up a great deal to be with me—not that I minded, since I needed her companionship every bit as much as she needed mine. We were a fine but peculiar match. I wondered whether it might flourish more if we weren't in such a hostile environment.

The success I built for the Nichols' Chateau label and the Cooper companies came at a price to those associated with me. I saw a pattern that bothered me. It was more than a coincidence that gangsters burned out the Kassie's old Gazelle Brewery, then Sunitha's flat. Unfolding the unpleasant truth had been confirmed by the collections of Rajesh's jewelry and bloodstained clothes. Once Hassan led me to Maraville, it was hard to hold back my anticipation of the next shoe to drop. If I ventured out at night, now I vowed to make certain we were following a safe route. I was even more cautious during the days, especially when walking the busiest streets, watching on all sides for pickpockets, enforcers, and muggers.

One day I was on the phone in my office at the Chateau, speaking to one of our barley suppliers about why he was billing for shipping surcharges. I knew this man had been gouging us with high prices, exceeding the high fair market price. He used the excuse that his farmers had a poor crop, and the supply of barley was tight. Ted entered without knocking and listened to my unsuccessful attempts to get him to deliver at market price his special variety, which we needed and which he controlled.

"Stubborn chap, this greedy supplier of ours, Pretorius," Ted said when I was done. "He's doing this to all the beer makers, except Lion and Castle, blaming his extortion on acts of God. If you can't handle him, leave him to me, and I'll get him to treat us like the majors."

"Ted, you know him better than I do. I make it a point never to argue with an idiot."

"Speaking of acts of God, Leon, I hear you witnessed one at Maraville. Tembo tells me you were at the last meeting of the knife and gun club this past weekend."

"Actually, we got there after it was all over."

"We, including my boy Hassan, correct?"

Ted looked at me intently for my response. As if to lead by the power of suggestion into agreeing with him, he began nodding his head affirmatively, until I nodded as well, making him smile.

"Obviously you three couldn't be in two places at once. Those Arab shopkeepers will remember your visit while shots were fired, and if asked should place you, Tembo, and Larabie away from the scene. Well done!"

It seemed odd Ted hadn't brought up the Maraville incident before. I was suspected Ted had known about the plans for the ambush and wanted to make sure his son wasn't around for the shooting. I wondered if he knew Hassan had gone to such lengths to take me there immediately after the slaughter. Had it been Ted's plan to introduce me to the warring factions all along, knowing the Chateau would have to make peace in its expanded territory to survive? There were plenty of unspoken truths between Ted and me.

"When Tembo and I arrived at Maraville after the fighting, Hassan was already there. And remember Mafumo, the man the Kassies who destroyed a batch of Gazelle beer and burned—?"

"Stop right there! Maybe your memory is playing tricks on you. You wouldn't want to bear false witness to me, and especially not to those authorities who may ask you to explain your part in the next few days."

Ted seemed to be speaking in riddles, suggesting the

next time that my account of what I saw that night should be more to his liking. He was probably concerned if I spoke too much, I might expose the security arrangement between Ighaam Arendse's forces and the Chateau. Ted shook my hand and was about to leave without saying any more, but I held him back to get some answers.

"We've had a run of bad luck. Not only the loss of the old brewery, but the loss of Rajesh, as well as the attack on Sunitha."

"That's part of the high cost of doing business in South Africa," Ted reassured me.

"But this war between Arendse and Ozeer appears to have taken a worse turn. Not only has Rajesh been murdered, but we've failed to honor him with a memorial service. And another issue—don't you think we'd be better off without Arendse's protection, and staying neutral, now that this showdown at Maraville has involved Mafumo and Hassan?"

"That has nothing to do with us! And remember, we know nothing of any murder, and we're certainly not at war!"

"Okay, rather than concerning us, Ted, let's say it concerns only me. Perhaps I should take the blame for implementing the expansion into the worst townships after our deal between Chateau and Cooper."

"Is this the advice you are offering the Chateau? Having me avoid a war that doesn't exist!" he laughed. "My advice to you is to be careful about exaggerating. Now excuse me."

Late Friday afternoon I was at my office gathering unfinished paperwork to bring home. I'd received a couple of calls from Oasis Spring Water, Ltd., from a salesman then from a saleswoman, but didn't bother answering them, assuming they were trying to sell the company water coolers. Overall, it had been a week of solid progress. As for Sunitha, thankfully she seemed stronger than before she left for her stay with Chandra. I'd at least begun discussing with Ted the meaning of the Maraville incident. Best of all, no authorities had materialized, demanding awkward explanations from me. Then came the annoying third soliciting call from Oasis, this time from the CEO, the Power-O man himself, Otto Kruger, the man I met at the Inter-Continental Hotel. He assured me he wasn't calling to sell anything, but to talk to me about our friend Alicia. He suggested some times for Saturday, but I wanted to close out the week and go home rather than hear a sales pitch.

"This evening would be best," he persisted. "Can I buy you dinner?"

"Actually, it's waiting for me at home."

"No doubt your table is set for you, Alicia told me. But I would be honored to dine with both you and your beautiful roommate."

"If Alicia knows so much, you should be speaking to her instead of to me," I said abruptly.

A minute after hanging up the phone rang again. I ignored it. But half an hour later in my car on the way to Rondebosch, I made the mistake of answering. It was Otto again.

"Where did you get my cell number?"

"I know you want to hang up again, Mr. Cooper, but you mustn't! I'm calling about my close friend Alicia!"

"If you're so close to her, you'd know you're asking the wrong man."

"You are the man. Please, we need your help to find her!"

Find her—what did that mean? I didn't know what the truth was anymore, but he'd gone through much effort to track me down. I didn't dare ignore his warning, not if it concerned Ted's daughter. So, I agreed to meet at the Greek restaurant opposite Wandi Dadla's brewpub.

"I'm pleased you joined us, Sunitha," Kruger said, taking her hand to kiss it. "Alicia speaks very highly of you. A very nice lady, Mr. Cooper," Kruger said to me and shook my hand, as if congratulating me on my choice of a lady friend.

He turned toward the restaurant owner, the man who helped Tembo chase the thieves who were about to take Alicia's automobile from the front of the tavern. He served us a tray of coffees and pastries. He sat down at our table and introduced himself.

"Please call me Nikos," he said, "and what name do you go by?" he asked Otto.

"Kruger like the krugerrand," Sunitha volunteered, "like the Kruger game park. Leon says you are related to Paul Kruger, the politician."

"My great-uncle Paul Kruger was a great statesman, not a thieving politician," Otto Kruger explained, turning the conversation to his prestigious family lineage. "He was a Boer himself who didn't care to be controlled by the English, no more than the tough Boer farmers did. But he didn't think the solution for the Boers was to give up on our country and trek toward the northern border, though many did. Because he was a well- respected Afrikaner himself, he could have turned around their wagons and sent them back to their farms. I'm stubborn like him, and like yourself, Mr. Cooper. We all know we must stand our ground."

"Many South Africans never had our own ground on which to stand," Sunitha added.

"If Alicia were here, she'd agree with you, my dear." Kruger said. "She's lost some ground, but we shall catch up with her."

"Now are you going to tell me what happened to her!" I insisted.

"It appears that without warning she became a player in your gangster's drug game," Kruger said.

"Who do you mean?"

"Ighaam Arendse, of course."

"He's a PAGAD leader, and that stands for People Against Gangs and Drugs. They do not approve of drugs," I reminded him.

Nikos laughed boisterously, thinking I was joking. He tried to speak, but I couldn't make out his words past a coughing fit that replaced his laughter.

"Get a grip on yourself," Kruger said, placing his hands firmly on Nikos' shoulders.

"PAGAD would like the newspapers to believe they are clearing out the drugs," Nikos said deliberately, "but all the Arab gangsters want is to take the drug trade away from the black gangsters for themselves!"

If what he was saying was true, then the Moslems were every bit as deep into the drug trade as the black Ozeer gangsters! That would suggest Ted made a bad gamble relying on Hassan's natural father Arendse to protect Gazelle interests in the most treacherous neighborhoods. If I had any idea about the games being played by these violent factions when Cooper and Werner-Nichols were at the negotiating stage with Ted to bring me over for the Gazelle project, I'd have never considered coming to South Africa. If Nikos' blunt explanation was true, then I'd fallen into a very dirty business! By working with Hassan to expand our distribution network in the townships, I may have unwittingly developed stronger ties with an organization that was a cover for the drug trade!

I tried not to show the regrets running through my mind as Nikos made me understand the dangerous alliance we were in. Our team in St. Louis believed they researched the Chateau and had a team of auditors draft a due diligence report, which unfortunately never alluded to how things worked in post-apartheid Cape Town. I noticed Kruger watching me as Nikos spoke about PAGAD, perhaps to read my distress.

"Of course, none of that has anything to do with you, Mr. Cooper," Kruger said, touching my arm. "I simply wanted you to hear what Nikos remembers about Alica, the final time anyone saw her."

When he spoke, I felt a familiar foreboding that hit me as when Chandra spoke of Rajesh in the past, reporting him as a lost cause.

"I never think a woman belongs in the shebeen business, especially not a pretty woman like Alicia Nichols," Nikos said.

"Nikos, you and Ted Nichols arranged for her safety," Otto Kruger said. "Unfortunately, no one was there when she needed you."

Ted had set up Alicia's in her own shebeen to appease

her, not because he wanted to put her into the liquor business. Intentionally or not, he gave her a business nearly impossible to run part-time while she continued flying for the airlines. Now I was about to find out what had gone wrong with her.

"Otto, you don't know me. Are you suggesting I've been negligent regarding Alicia in—"

"Leon, excuse me. She spoke well of you and depended on you more than you may realize, that's all. Did Alicia tell you we were engaged to be married?" he countered.

"So, while I have indirect business interest in Alicia, yours is a more personal interest? Interesting, but the only project I am interested in now is in getting her back."

I shouldn't have been so direct, but we didn't have time for subtle inferences, not if he had information that might lead us to her. I didn't know if he was once engaged to her and it was broken off, or whether he was currently engaged to her. He was probably trying to soothe me by telling me she spoke well of me.

"Nikos, if you don't mind," Kruger said, "please tell him how they took away Alicia, everything you told me."

"Remember the night Alicia, you, and me sat drinking coffee at this table, two men they break into her BMW and Tembo and me go after them, scared them, making them think we was going to shoot them?" I nodded my head in acknowledgment.

"That car was an engagement gift to her," Kruger added. "She loved it."

"Next time it wasn't two but three men that come after the car, and they took it with her in it. Gone!" Nikos said, snapping his fingers.

"What three?"

"Who they were?" Nikos asked. "Good question, Mr. Cooper. If they was car thieves, wouldn't they want to just take that new BMW? If they was kidnappers and just wanted to take a valuable person like Alicia Nichols, don't you think it been easier to sneak her away in their own car? If they was hijackers, wouldn't they take both the white BMW and the lady? But if they was killers—"

"Don't talk like that, Nikos!" Otto shouted. "We're going to stop those bastards in their tracks, whoever they are! What else did you see?"

"Not much. The streetlight was out where she parked. The minute I saw them pull her through the driver's window and throw her into the back seat, I run to her help. I got close enough to see it was the same two blokes we scared off before. But this time I was alone and barehanded and could do no more than watch them carry her off, then report it to the police."

"Shouldn't the police be able to get her back?"

"No better than they got your Indian man back," Otto said. "They have no chance, unless they get some help. That's why I'm here on behalf of the Oasis Group, as a security technician."

"But you're a soft drink man."

"No more than you're Chief of the Shebeens, the Chief of Pubs," he said with a grin, knowing as well as I my title didn't fit. "Sometimes how we make money and how we want to make money are two different things. In case you don't recall, our specialty beverage is not carbonated but oxygenated. But that's beside the point. For years I have been a security consultant and have expanded into another area, beverages, in hopes that in the non-alcoholic beverage business I would not have to deal with as many unpleasant characters as in security. That seems a move not unlike the move the Cooper Company made from American whiskey to kaffir beer."

"Auto burglar alarms and home alarms?" Kruger nodded yes. "As a security expert do you think an alarm with a siren would have slowed them down? Otto, it seems this talk of security systems is useless as shutting the barn door after the horse has escaped."

"No matter," he said with a dismissive wave of his hand, "we need to work together fast if Alicia's to have a chance. So, Leon, will you come with me to my security office? I'll show you what I showed the police. And Nikos, can you arrange to take this young lady home?"

"Not a chance," I said. "With all these unpleasant characters, as you call them, she's going wherever I go from now on."

Not only was I concerned about Sunitha's safety, I wanted to keep her near because I trusted her judgment. I was anxious to know her impression of Kruger. If Alicia didn't make it back unharmed, that would be a personal tragedy, and it could be the end of what I'd built in South Africa, perhaps the end of my career as well. Ted had done a good job of sandbagging Rajesh's disappearance, but Alicia's would become high profile news in a matter of days. I knew I'd make a likely scapegoat for any major incident during my work for the Chateau and perhaps might be forced to resign.

"Then I'll have to earn your confidence and support," he said, looking at Sunitha, not me, "if we're going to work together."

"Work together how?" she asked.

"Let me show you now, unless you have something more important this evening," he said, looking at me this time. He shook my hand, as if I'd consented to an agreement. "And, Nikos, thank you. I'll give you a call in case I need to bring the authorities to you."

I wanted to ask Otto whether he meant he had influence with the police. He seemed to know a great deal about the Nichols family and about my connection with the Chateau, understandable if he was truly engaged to Alicia. I excused myself to make a call to Ted, to confirm Kruger's relationship to Alicia, and whether he could be trusted. No answer. I had to make my own decision whether to follow him. I remembered though Alicia must have thought highly enough of him to originally set us up for a meeting in the Inter-Continental. Also in his favor, Kruger hadn't mentioned Maraville or Hassan's unsavory associates, perhaps meaning he had no underworld connections. Though I was annoyed with him for not setting out his search and rescue plan in advance, I felt compelled to accompany him, in case he had genuine leads.

Sunitha and I followed behind Kruger's car, winding through the streets of Rondebosch and Observatory, then stopped at a convenience store with a dozen pumps. Next to it was a two story commercial and a building that had been converted into the offices for Oasis Security. On the roof were a couple of satellite dish antennas, and the Oasis sign with date palms and a spurting geyser. The same logo was duplicated on some trucks and cars in front of the building, and on the uniforms of guards, who were sitting on the tailgate of one of the trucks. They were smoking cigarettes and drinking coffee, while monitoring scanner radios.

Otto rang the buzzer at the entrance, but no one responded. "Hello! Anybody home?"

Once inside, we passed a woman dispatcher who sat before an array of radios and a console, then on to the adjoining display room, where Otto opened a couple of glass showcases.

"Here we keep the products we've developed which could prove profitable to a marketing partner. This is mylar film we apply to windshields so they can't be cracked. And this is an immobilizer that stops an attacker dead in his tracks at twenty feet. Here are our microbugs, smaller than the head of a match, and for police use, this box can immobilize a car by scrambling its electrical system."

Also, on display were the night vision binoculars I'd seen both Chandra and Ighaam use to scan for enemies. This had to be more than a coincidence! As a security man it would make sense he'd be marketing these devices, which apparently, unfortunately, also helped the gangsters and their enemies keep track of one another in the dark. He was an effective salesman, saving the best of his presentation for last.

He then opened a heavy steel door with a touch number pad, then a biometric iris scanner afterward. Inside this vaultlike room was a weapon on a tripod supporting a missile. "I would rather you view this alone, Leon."

"As I said, Sunitha goes where I go."

"Is that truly necessary? Very well, but only under the condition that what you see goes no further than here. This piece belongs to our military line, very confidential. And in case you're wondering, we're completely licensed. It's the only way I operate, should we decide to do business together."

As we were walking to the next room, I knocked over a cordovan attaché standing by the wall. This gaffe bothered Otto, who quickly grabbed it and set it on the glass showcase.

"When we found this briefcase, it was filled with explosives and a detonator. We called in the police to disarm it. Schmidt and I tell our men at Oasis Security we don't hire them to be heroes, that we do security work, not police work. There's a fine line we try not to cross, except in situations like we have here."

Sunitha stayed behind, where she was working the tricky coded latches of the terrorists' already deactivated briefcase, while Otto took me to the shipping room. Its shelves were piled with boxes to the ceiling, addressed to and from all parts of the world. When Otto buzzed the security door to the next room, it immediately opened for him, and he was embraced by a tall, young towheaded man.

"As you see, I have access to products our customers may be hard pressed to find elsewhere."

"Good, you finally brought Mr. Cooper," the tall guard said, shaking my hand. His suit jacket to fell away so I could see his holstered Sig Sauer .40 caliber pistol.

"Don't worry," Kruger said. "You're in good hands with Schmidt, the best undercover man I've found. Welcome to Oasis World Headquarters."

"With these work hours, Mr. Kruger," Schmidt said, "you leave me no time for the ladies!"

"Not to rain on your parade, but your personal

schedule is of secondary interest to Mr. Cooper, who needs our security services immediately."

"Seriously, Mr. Cooper," Schmidt said, "give me a lead and I'll follow it anywhere in South Africa, through the gates of hell if necessary. We won't disappoint you."

Otto led us upstairs to a room full of monitors, computers, sound equipment, and black boxes with switches, lights, and gauges. He introduced me to a skinny young man, his long hair tied in a band.

"Meet Mister Satellite Man," Otto said. "He may be the brains of our organization, but that's all the name we give him."

That made no sense. I saw some security monitors with views of the front, rear and sides of the building, and an array of computers with their screens showing maps. This young man's attention wasn't directed to security work, but to the big screen on which he was watching a game show originating in England. Why was it so urgent for Kruger to arrange for us to meet tonight with Nikos, Schmidt, and now this computer geek? From what I knew of him, Kruger was a methodical man following some plan. I doubt he'd have troubled bringing us here if he didn't have something to show us.

Meanwhile satellite man looked between Sunitha and me, evidently trying to figure out whether we were a couple. He turned his attention to the maps displayed, each covering different territory with red broken lines, two of which were beeping an alert. The first screen showed the origin of the subject in Cape Town, and the third one terminated at the northern frontier. All of them had breaks and loops and reversals, routes someone would follow to throw off pursuers.

"These appear to be satellite maps. Where is this most recent one?" I asked.

"Fifteen hours' drive north of Cape Town, more or less. They made it there thirty-six hours after they grabbed her."

"How do you know that when the rest of us at Oasis don't know, son!" Otto shouted. "All we have to go on is some inconsistent position reports we've been monitoring on her since she was abducted. We know nothing more yet!"

He pointed to the top of the screen. Vehicle: BMW Series 735. Abductors: 2 Males, Black. Ozeer Link Suspected. Abductee: Alicia Nichols. Map Region: Free State, Bloemfontein. Uplink Frequency: 1.205 Gigahertz. Downlink: 1.140

My worst fears were being confirmed. It was starting to make sense why Ted was so edgy yesterday and why he refused to schedule even fifteen minutes to discuss some problems with our new hires. His immediate concern was for Alicia's wellbeing, as was mine. But his secondary concern must have been that the Chateau might be dragged into the cycle of attack and reprisal. I was concerned as well whether Cooper might pull me off the Gazelle project and out of South Africa altogether. Meanwhile, Kruger and his son were silent, staring and waiting for me to say something, as if my opinion mattered. I'd taken the bait. Now Kruger and satellite man were reeling me towards their boat, but I was going to surprise them by spitting out their lure.

"Mr. Cooper, this isn't the only location where we have satellite fixes from the transmitting unit we placed in Mr. Kruger's car," satellite man said. "Map one simply shows where we tracked her from Tuesday through Thursday. Map two, from Thursday through Monday, where they were further north in the Kimberly region, as you can see."

"If you get to Kimberly, you must tour the diamond and gold mines," Kruger said casually, "to see the greatest source of Cecil Rhodes' wealth. Leon, you and I may not have such natural resources at our disposal, but we do have our business talent as our most powerful assets. That's why we need to join forces, for greater leverage."

I didn't know whether this was another thinly veiled suggestion that I consider him for a business partner, or if Kruger was simply trying to distract me from the real- time alarming computer maps. Satellite man wasn't quite done with his orientation though. He showed me the map with the broken red line of Alicia's progress, particularly her movement through two days prior, which seemed to have the most gaps and twists. On the final map I saw her journey had terminated, for the time being just within the South Africa side of the border with Botswana. This didn't look promising. Sunitha studied this map which was so clear and three-dimensional that a layperson could easily visualize the terrain. She seized my hand with a startling and powerful grip, then released it, and instead took Otto's, bringing him closer to that last monitor, encouraging him to show us more.

"Mr. Kruger, this is where you must look," she said, pointing to an uninhabited spot in Botswana. Then she placed herself between him and the screen, looking into his eyes. "I can sense the personal concern in your heart. If they take her out of South Africa, then you will have to follow her. But you do not dare cross the border, unless you first have powerful men behind your rescue. I believe that is why you invited Leon, in order to convince Mr. Nichols to call up his strongest friends to cross the frontier and, if necessary, retake Alicia in Botswana."

Otto pulled away and turned toward me. "Does she always have such an active imagination?" he whispered.

"Sunitha makes up no fairy tales," I said so everyone could hear. "That is why I rely on her extraordinary judgment."

Otto looked at me with disbelief, then laughed. "Then you must rely on your assistant as I rely on my satellite man. Except I have the advantage of being able to send him home, so I don't have to pay him overtime. You understand, anything you might know about this search will continue to be confidential, right?" He took some rand notes from his wallet and tucked them into the young man's breast pocket. "That's partial payment in advance to verify the young lady's speculations about any possible interception we may decide to launch in Botswana, understood?"

"You shouldn't have hired me, Dad, if you trust this amateur more than me," young satellite man said.

"I told you not to call me that during business hours!"

"It's after hours though."

"Try to be more professional. Here, this should be enough for dinner in case you forgot to eat." Otto tucked another bill in his pocket. "Thanks for the overtime tonight. Now if you don't mind, Leon and I need to talk business alone."

When satellite man hugged Otto, I saw the family resemblance in their birdlike noses. Seeing them together made me recall my father and myself when I was little enough for him to hug me before bedtime. I was a kid, and he still believed in my brilliant future. I wondered if Harry had let Father know what I've accomplished here, and if I could mend fences with him. Incredibly, I was a world away, yet worrying about regaining my father's confidence. Once I was back in the States, there would be time to make it right between Father and me, maybe even with Harry. But that was the future. Right now we had to do everything to get back Alicia while we could. I didn't know what I could do to help her, but I did know I'd seen enough satellite maps to get the ugly picture that Ted must have been holding back from me the last couple of days.

"You're leaving us already, Mr. Cooper?" the tall blonde guard asked as we passed through the dispatch room. I paused to speak with him.

"I'd like to ask you about the injured people Mr. Kruger tells me you saw in Maraville."

"Would you? I don't know what you're talking about," I said, looking for Otto to dismiss him. I was perplexed that the rumors of the event had been dispersed so far.

"Please, Leon, allow me to properly introduce Sargent John Schmidt," Otto said, coming between both of us, making sure we shook hands, "formerly with the Cape Town Police."

When I heard he was a policeman, I wanted to escape from him, as if I'd broken the law at Maraville and been caught. Introducing me to Schmidt was evidently part of Otto's plan.

"Don't worry, Leon," Otto continued, "Schmidt is no public employee. He is my right-hand man, just as you are Ted Nichols' key man. He can work both for me in Oasis Security and you in the Chateau, and that's why he's important as liaison between us and Cape Town."

"If I caught you at a bad time," Schmidt said, "apologies. I'll catch up with you later, if you don't mind."

"Actually, I do mind. Nothing personal, Mr. Schmidt, but I don't see how you could be expected to serve two masters." With Sunitha in hand, I walked out of that suffocating building without windows over to the car.

Before we could drive away Otto let himself into the back seat. "I'm not sure you know your way back, so I wanted to make sure you follow me."

"That's very thoughtful," Sunitha said.

"We're ready whenever you are," I said and reached for the rear door latch to open it for Kruger to exit, but he wasn't going anywhere.

"Leon, now that I've taken you on my tour, are you better acquainted with our mutual problem?"

"To a point," I said, "only as much as you want me to know."

"Why do I get the impression that you are eager to part company?"

"Because I know little about you, except what you've told me, nor about you and Alicia."

"What about Alicia and me?"

"It seems that if you cared about Alicia, if she really was your fiancé, then you'd go to Ted rather than to me with your scheme to save her. We both know that Ted's much closer to her than I am."

"And we both know Ted can be a hard man to approach, even for you, his partner. As for me, he'd rather I'd disappear. Once Alicia and I told him about our wedding plans, he went out of his way to avoid me, hoping I would simply forget about marrying her. Colin hasn't helped my cause. When he learned Ted might be welcoming a new son-in-law, he worked overtime to make sure it wouldn't happen. Alicia tells me he's a good accountant, very clever with numbers, all business. I might have gotten along with him if he hadn't lied to Ted about me, making me out to be overextended, close to bankrupt. A lie he used to discredit me!"

I understood why Ted might distrust Otto. His entrepreneurial enthusiasm made him come across as a hustler, a man forever selling a questionable product. It made sense that Colin would want to keep him away from the Chateau, seeing him as a dangerous competitor.

As we drove behind him, returning to Rondebosch, Sunitha and I agreed we had to cooperate with him. He was the key to retrieving Alicia. I knew I had to make Ted understand that no matter what Ted thought of Kruger, it would be a bad idea to ignore him and Oasis Security if he wanted a chance at retrieving Alicia.

CHAPTER 16
BAD DREAMS

I was not in the habit of making hasty judgments of men, nor was I quick to make important decisions, but in the case of Otto Kruger I didn't haven't the luxury of time to sufficiently know him. After hearing him out, I chose to judge him an honest man. That's why I invited him to my flat for a drink. Sunitha was at the dining table with a customary cup of jasmine tea for herself, and Chateau Sauvignon for us.

"I hope I haven't interrupted any plans you two had for this evening," he said as Sunitha joined me on the couch. "I'm sure you had in mind a more intimate evening than the one I've provided." That word intimate startled Sunitha which Otto noticed. "Excuse me, but it's late," she said. "We need to call it a night."

"There's no rush to leave us just yet, Otto. Here, have another," I offered, but he pushed the bottle away before I could pour.

As he was leaving, he pulled out copies of the satellite maps of Bloemfontein, Kimberly, and the Botswana frontier. "You can show these to Ted—the sooner the better, before Alicia gets out of range."

Sunitha looked at me, then unexpectedly snatched the

maps out of my hand. "I don't understand how Alicia could possibly get out of range!"

"The way it works, we lost her when we lost her signal or when we heard an intermittent signal with too much noise."

"Lost her?" she whispered unsteadily. "I can't lose another person!"

Why was Sunitha upset now, as opposed to earlier in the evening when we first learned of Alicia's abduction? The same reason I'd been able to have a pleasant chat and a drink with Otto—denial of her dire prospects.

"Not if we can help it, young lady, not if we are quick. Take care of her, Leon,"

Kruger finally left before offering any more details. When we were alone, Sunitha released the tears she had been holding back for some time. "First Rajesh and now Alicia," she said in a choking voice.

Rajesh and Alicia. Sunitha was right, there had to be a connection—the PAGAD thugs who took them. I had brought her with me in order to see Otto because I thought between the both of them, they could help me sort out the facts of Alicia's disappearance. In retrospect, I probably should have kept her away from Oasis and Otto Kruger, rather than cause her additional worry. She had been withdrawn, saying little to me nor to Otto. Was that because she didn't trust him?

I tried to sleep that night, but it was Alicia on my mind, locked dead in her auto. Then, thankfully, I saw her as the pretty airplane attendant who first charmed me.

Sunitha pressed herself against me, her cold feet under my legs. "Bad dreams?" I whispered when I felt her shaking.

"She is walking through the desert at the height of the sun with no compass and no water and little life force remaining."

I could muster no credible words of encouragement and soon fell back into my own troubled sleep.

"Sunitha, Alicia's outcome will be different than Rajesh's," I said once awake in the dark at 2:30. "I believe that with the satellite pictures and Oasis Security and Schmidt's connections with the police she has an excellent chance. Don't you?"

"One of your Christian brothers once said we have to believe in something," she whispered in my ear, "even if it's the existence of the devil."

"I'm not going to let you talk about her as if she's gone!"

"Leon, I don't believe anyone can be truly gone. She will travel from life to life. But in this life, I'm afraid, though Alicia was a friend to me—she lived under the veil of delusion."

"And for yourself, Sunitha?" I asked, prompting her to continue.

"The fourth and greatest aim, greater than religious merit, prosperity or pleasure will be for me to win salvation, to free myself from the bounds of transmigration. But I believe you're too sleepy for this to make sense. You're trying to distract me. Thank you though," she whispered. I dropped back to sleep, soundly this time, a bit relieved by her message of hope.

Since arriving in South Africa I hadn't slept through a night continuously, though it improved since Sunitha came into my life. With her calming influence, I'd been dealing better with my bad dreams and sleeping but three hours at a time.

Now a familiar dream returned. In it I was alone on an impossible mission with no backup in desolate territory I didn't know how to navigate and questioned my ability to succeed. I was weak with exhaustion and didn't know how much longer I could survive on my failed one-man mission. With the power left in me, by force of will I brought myself back into my familiar bed. I awakened, oriented myself, and emerged uneasily from my dream, still not knowing what country my mission was in. Now another mystery, the sweet smell of a woman stirs my senses. My clock said 4:35.

I found Sunitha in the room where she meditated, the place where she'd been offering her prayers in earnest since returning from Chandra's. I cleared out the second bedroom for her rescued Brahma. It now sat on an inlaid rosewood bureau, and on the matching end table she lit her incense and slow-burning candle. Chanting, she faced the Brahma, cross-legged on her bamboo mat, prayer book beside her, her eyes closed. I stayed behind the threshold, peeking into the room from time to time, not wanting to disturb her.

"Leon, would you rather watch me from a distance than touch me?" she asked, suddenly turning to me with open eyes and a smile. I then sat by her on the mat and took her hand.

"What are you doing with these?" I asked. Along with her prayer things she also had the Oasis satellite maps!

"I know Alicia's still with us, and I'm communicating with her. But let's forget about her for a moment— what about you? Your heart's beating too fast. Have bad dreams awakened you too?"

"Maybe this war you people have been fighting in Cape

Town is making a tourist like me nervous. But your nerves, Sunitha, after how much you've already lost..."

"Leon, how devoted are you to me anyway?"

"You shouldn't have to ask me anymore."

"No? I wonder what will happen to us if you are recalled home suddenly by your family."

"My brother may try, but I'll never allow him to run my life! We're no longer strictly a family company. I can come and go as I please!"

"But how much longer will I please you enough for you to wish to continue with me?" Rather than press me for an answer, she led me back to our bed. "Your demons have been dancing around where we lay. If I'd been here to chase them away with you—Leon, you need me now."

I'd never known Sunitha to speak idly. Once joined with her, my dream returned to me for a moment. This time I felt trapped by an upwards force greater than the gravity trying to pull my body away from the earth below. I was suspended and amazed, but there was no person anywhere to witness my supernatural suspension.

Sunitha remained the true force energizing me. It occurred to me that together we were stronger, able to overcome forces that might destroy us individually. I wanted to do nothing to break the spell of the lovemaking she requested. The morning's dream of myself as a man lost and dying, suspended alone over hostile territory, I willingly left behind for this reality of Sunitha. My dream of helpless dangling had put in waking perspective her importance to me. I was happy just to be close to her. Our pleasure now complete, we separated and moved to the balcony to watch the sun rise.

"Sunitha, I should have told you long before now how much—"

Before I could get my words out, she stopped me with a kiss. "Leon, if I mean so much to you, will you help me this morning?"

"With what?"

She knew she could count on my help when she needed it. She smiled and went to prepare a big Sunday breakfast before we had to leave for the Chateau, her destination.

We were within a quarter hour of the Chateau, she still wouldn't explain the purpose of our trip, so I stopped the car. "This isn't like you, Sunitha, holding back on me. Again, it's Sunday and I'm being led on a tour I haven't booked!"

"I would have told you more, but I was afraid you'd change your mind if you heard we were going to a church once again. I should have known better than bring you to that Dutch Reform service in Afrikaans."

"Then you're telling me the preacher on Paarl Mountain didn't inspire you?" I asked and started the car. I was relieved that I had an excuse to break our deadlock and could continue towards the Chateau instead of to another remote church.

"This will be in English, so it should make more sense."

"And what about your home services for Rajesh, Sunitha, when will they end?"

"It depends on how long we stick together," she replied.

If she was suggesting our days together were numbered, I didn't want to hear it! If her generous spirit had the power to banish my nightmare, then she had to be the antidote for some of the troubles here in South Africa.

We understood each other's loyalty without the need for more words.

This church service was in Chateau Drakenstein's chapel, a building unlike the gabled buildings the wine-tasting tourists saw. This one had a domed roof and was three stories at its peak. A cross rose above the southern end; the Chateau coat-of- arms on the northern one. Its round windows were as big in diameter as a man's height.

"With its round portholes, this building looks like a cross between a warehouse and a ship," I said.

"Originally, there were no windows in the building, because it was built as a wine cellar a hundred or so years ago. What you might not know is during the war between Boers and the English, the Chateau couldn't keep their skilled help out of the national Army, which, in turn, forced them to cut back their operations. The roof was leaking in this particular building, so they closed it and left it without any care. Forty years ago the maintenance manager, who lived on site and was a former merchant marine sailor, took it upon himself to rebuild it as a chapel with the labor of his crew on their off hours. This is the result, something like a grounded ship."

Since starting with Chateau Drakenstein, I hadn't a clear explanation about how they came to build this odd chapel. Apparently, Ted was continuing to use it to make his skilled vintners feel like part of a self-contained community.

Van Staden, the senior plant operations manager, was waiting for us at the door with prayer books. "Did you come together this morning, Mr. Cooper, with Miss Bala?"

"Apparently," I said, intending to explain no more.

"At any rate, sir, we were hoping to see you here."

Many of those present were tourists, judging by their casual clothing. A Sunday service in a converted wine cellar must have drawn them between their breakfast and the noon wine tasting. There were maybe seventy-five worshippers, less than enough to half fill the chapel. Yet instead of taking us to the free pews at the rear, Van Staden took us upstairs to the balcony.

Once Sunitha and I were seated, he was tall enough so he could step over our row of chairs to the one behind, where he seated himself, and where he leaned forward between us, facing Sunitha. "We welcome you, Sunitha, Christian or non-Christian. Tell me, Mr. Cooper, have you come to worship? Or are you here in the hopes of finding Mr. Nichols with us on this Sabbath morning?"

Sunitha nodded yes to his last conjecture, mistakenly believing he had the right to ask me why I was in the chapel.

"Now, Mr. Van Staden, let me ask you a question. We are so far back here we can hardly see the minister, even though the chapel's half full. Why have you put us up here?"

"Frankly, sir, I must be concerned with the morale of our staff. She can tell you management and the workers at the Chateau don't fraternize after hours."

"Are you forgetting Miss Bala is management, like yourself?"

"Of course not. Please don't get me wrong. It doesn't matter to me which cover is on which pot because I been to London and seen what's cooking there. The reason I put you here is so you could talk without bothering anybody."

He seemed in a rush to get away from us, probably to avoid having to further explain his observations of London to me. Van Staden must have realized his advantage here in his church, where my responses to him had to be limited to whispers. He was trying to play his twenty-five-year seniority at the Chateau over me, not understanding my exact role. He had no way of knowing I was more than a nuts-and-bolts organizer, and that I represented the new direction in the company. But I kept calm and remembered that he commanded the respect of the men on the production line. He seemed to be speaking as the prime representative for our Caucasian staff, especially for the half dozen key Afrikaner foremen who, like himself, came from displaced farming families.

Long before I arrived, Hassan's function seemed to be controlling the coloured, especially the Moslem coloured hourly workers. Without him, how could we resist the lingering influence of the angry black friends of the Mafumo contingent? But there was one faction at Chateau who seemed loyal without compromise to the organization were the Indians. Maybe I felt that way because Chandra, and Raj in his own crazy way, had sacrificed so much for both the old and the new Gazelle, and no doubt because I was personally close to Sunitha. Whatever my reasons for trusting and relying on my Indian friends, to a besieged Afrikaner like Van Staden, they must have seemed like direct threats to his own influence. And, come to think of it, I must have seemed to him like Ted Nichols' courtier.

"Don't be upset on my account, Leon," she said, "because, as a rice-eater girl, I myself am used to low-level slights."

"I won't allow you to call yourself names!"

"Then would you rather I call him a bad name like a sausage-eater?"

"I'd rather we forget about Van Staden altogether." I looked below on the main floor, where I saw him working his way down the center aisle to the front where the higher-level Chateau staff had reserved a section for itself. For such a big man he moved with surprising agility. Between hymns he'd take a few long strides, then sit for a few minutes with a set of worshippers, speaking behind his hand before moving to the next ones.

"From a distance Van Staden looks like a politician collecting votes," I said, testing my impression of him with Sunitha. "But after twenty-odd years here, he should know that the only vote that counts belongs to Ted Nichols. Why do he and his listeners keep turning in our direction, looking up at us?"

"Because he hasn't forgotten his promise to bring us to Mr. Nichols this morning. You know how hard he can be to find, traveling so much, especially on the weekends with the calm seas. That's when Mr. Nichols invites his friends to ride on his seaworthy boat. But if anyone can find him, it's Mr. Van Staden and his crew, even if they have to swim after him."

It seemed I was the last to know key details about my associate's life. It occurred to me I shouldn't have bothered chasing after him on a Sunday, no matter how anxious Sunitha was to tell him about Alicia's abduction.

"You look upset," she whispered, "because you don't believe that we can find her?"

"Because I don't know what to believe. I don't understand why you decided to call on Van Staden if he doesn't respect you. Or why you brought me here blind."

"Leon, do you feel you've been misled by me, a poorly trained guide dog? You don't trust me to lead, yet you have no scent to follow the trail yourself."

Was she's telling me it was vision I was lacking? That was unlike her, criticizing me directly rather than supporting me. She might simply have meant I'd been deceived by appearances and ought to rely on her more as a liaison to these wily South Africans who were so good at camouflaging themselves.

"My eyes aren't good enough to see the altar from this distance, and I don't believe yours are any sharper, Sunitha. As for my ears, right now they are having trouble hearing both you and the sermon. We're leaving."

"We'll move wherever you want," she said, either misunderstanding or not accepting that I wouldn't be staying to the end.

It was her choice whether she wanted to remain on the balcony alone or else follow me out of the chapel. After Van Staden's lukewarm reception, she must have felt more out of place in this service than I did. I had enough and slowly walked across the balcony. I turned around and saw why she'd fallen behind. A little boy in a dark suit with short pants and knee socks was grasping her, as he might hold on to his mother.

As soon as the boy saw Sunitha was with me, he broke loose and quickly ran down the stairs. Before we reached the landing the boy, little Dietlets, was back, this time with his father Frederick DeVilliers!

"My son's been begging me to bring him to the lady

who pulled him from the fire and saved him," Frederick said to Sunitha. "You left our party too quickly for us to properly thank you. Rest assured, I will remember the great favor you have done...Are you leaving before the sermon? I'm not an usher, but let's find you better seats," he whispered, then led us to seats on the ground floor. "Now that I'm working with the Chateau to help finance your expansion, I thought I'd take a look at this lovely and unique chapel."

I was amazed that the overall morale at Chateau was as good as it was, since most of the workers seemed to owe their allegiance to their ethnic group first and to the company second. That morning, Frederick couldn't fail to see that the worshippers there were primarily from the white tribe, though I wasn't sure he knew they were virtually all management level. I remembered Ilsa telling me Frederick was a twelfth-generation Afrikaner, someone who could not have prospered in the insurance business without a realistic knowledge of how things operated in his country.

"It's a never-ending battle, keeping our men productive," I said, "just as I'm sure you found in keeping your insurance staff motivated."

"I'm sorry, Leon, but my wife won't let me talk business while I'm under the roof of the church. We can talk after the service."

"Excuse me, but do you need to take care of him?" I asked, pointing to his son as he was moved away from us, eating a candy bar and heading towards the stairs,

"Please don't get the wrong idea—we watch Dietlets more closely than ever after the fire. That's one of the reasons my wife's downstairs."

"And not because you want to keep her from hearing you talk business in church, Frederick?"

"Honestly, we didn't come here concerned with our son's whereabouts, so much as yours and Sunitha's, since I promised to meet her and you this morning, along with Ted in a four-way conference."

I looked away from DeVilliers and turned towards Sunitha. She smiled with a single nod, which I took for an acknowledgment. Had she been anxious to meet with Kruger and me at Oasis Security out of simple curiosity? Or had DeVilliers told her in advance about Alicia's disappearance? Was she behind the plan in which Kruger had enlisted me to convince Ted to help organize a dragnet, based on her visions, inspired by the satellite maps?

This morning's contact in the chapel with DeVilliers did not seem coincidental. I now suspected Sunitha called Frederick in advance and had prevailed upon him to come to the chapel with his family on short notice, due to the heroic rescue she had done. Was she now collecting a favor from him in return? No doubt, DeVilliers had better information about the Chateau's politics than I did when I had first arrived. I believed she had an agenda. She never told me a lie, but in this case appeared slow in telling me what I needed to know. The fault might be mine for not understanding the secret relationships among the people surrounding Ted. I found myself in a communications bottleneck, which Sunitha might have felt too cumbersome for her to sort out for me. I had to be patient and continued to remind myself she had no deception in her heart, that perhaps she just didn't feel like explaining what she thought should be obvious to me.

"You haven't been telling me everything, Sunitha, have you?"

"You'll know everything you need to know in time. I sense I've only succeeded in confusing you, Leon, for which I'm sorry. Now that we're closer to the pulpit, look at the guest minister. His face should be familiar to you."

"He's Reverend Dieter DuToit from Paarl, who you already know," DeVilliers said. "You must listen carefully to him, since he has come here this morning with important guidance."

Guidance for whom? For him or for me? This seemed like a show that had been prepared for my benefit. I understood the way they did business in South Africa enough to launch our expansion, but it was one thing to teach them how to work a business plan, quite another to understand them personally. If I wanted to get insight from our managers, I needed to listen carefully to DuToit, whom they had invited to deliver their sermon:

Not long ago, before the overthrow of our government, we felt more secure. What kind of citizens are we now in the New South Africa? In the Cape we're more apprehensive than we used to be, more like our brethren in Johannesburg—we have learned fear. How many of you will walk to the downtown railway station after dark, or for that matter, ride the train in daylight? How many of you have been traveling alone in your car, stopped and been surrounded by a gang of young men?

We live in fear of those who have no fear of God, those who have been preying on us. Criminals without a human heart who wait for their prey, then pounce, so they can play with them as a cat plays with the mouse. I'm talking about the great sin and crime of kidnapping.

My brothers and sisters in Christ, I had a dilemma in preparing today's sermon. The New Testament stands as the foundation of our faith and the guidance for our everyday lives, yet we cannot turn the other cheek to sadistic criminals who are measuring our resolve to fight back. I looked to the Old Testament for suggestions on how we might deal with the crime of kidnapping, the stealing of a person. In the spirit of seeking the truth, even from an unfamiliar source, I quote from the Bible of the Jews. In Exodus it is said, "He who steals a man, he shall surely be put to death." In Deuteronomy it is said, "If a man is found stealing any of his brethren of the children of Israel, then that thief shall die; and you shall put evil away from you."

I am talking to you about the kidnapping of a member of our community, Alicia Nichols. Right now, I am not interested in whatever justice may be meted out when the kidnappers are caught, only in bringing Alica Nichols back to us. I do this not to create fear and anxiety, but because I want you to pray for her, that we may become stronger. Let us now pray for Alicia's safe return.

I was astonished this minister was telling Alicia's story to the entire congregation! Already probably more people knew about this than I'd been led to believe. In my evening with Kruger, I thought he was confidentially sharing the details of the kidnapping with me. My understanding was I had to keep what I knew to myself, except to relay his recapture plan to Ted Nichols. Why was this sermon taking place at all, much less from the mouth of a guest preacher, and on the Chateau's grounds? To feed this congregation's curiosity?

If you feel fear in your heart, follow this advice, "Let not your hearts faint, fear not and do not tremble, neither be terrified because of your enemies, for the Lord God goes with you, to fight for you against your enemies, to save you." In

*strength and faith we will work to bring Alicia back to us.
Amen.*

I had no idea how many people found out about Alicia
before the minister's sermon, but now that her situation had been made public information, I wanted to
get out of this chapel, alone in a quiet place, so I could
think about the implications.

"Are you trying to leave us again? He's not quite
done..." DeVilliers commented.

He reached for my sleeve, but I brushed it away before
he could restrain me. I quickly made my way downstairs and out the back door with Sunitha behind me.

"We left too soon, Leon," Sunitha said.

"You find Ted Nichols then!" I stated. "This is more
than I bargained for, and I don't appreciate being the
last to know—"

"Excuse me, but I couldn't help but overhear," said
the man who had been running towards us. I recognized Peter LeRoux, and we shook hands. "I don't mean
to interrupt, Leon, but Janice wanted me to catch you
in time."

Jan was standing between two of the windows made
from the huge wine barrels, watching her husband,
before moving to join us. She hugged me, and I could
feel her tears against my cheek, which she quickly dried
with her sleeve.

"Sorry, I didn't mean to do that," Jan said, "but it's
been so difficult, waiting and wondering about my
daughter. Apparently, Ted has kept you so busy here at
Drakenstein that you haven't had time to visit us again
in Bergkloof. Frederick and I regard Dieter DuToit as
our guardian angel, and now Sunitha as well."

"Guardian angels?" I repeated, incredulous.

Since Alicia vanished, attempts had been made to partner me first with Kruger, and now with the part-time minister Dieter DuToit! I wasn't obligated to deal with anyone I didn't vet!

There were tourists when we arrived at the café after church. Those arriving from the chapel filled the remaining tables on the patio. When the LeRouxs showed up, they joined us, and despite the somber sermon on kidnapping, enjoyed their drinks and food.

"I'm acting foolishly this morning!" Jan apologized, "But the last time I set foot on these unhallowed grounds as Mrs. Nichols, there was no cafe, no tourists, and no offsite beer plant built! How things have changed since I was Ted's wife! So please understand if I'm disoriented."

"You've been divorced from him for how many years?" Peter asked. "Isn't it time to let go of the anger and the guilt?"

"This isn't the time or the place to discuss him, Peter. You know I wouldn't be here if Ted were on the premises. I came today to hear any news of Alicia, especially from you Dieter, our lead guardian angel," she added, loudly enough so Rev. DuToit could hear. He had completed his duties in the chapel and was joining us.

"I was simply suggesting you might set aside the baggage of your sense of betrayal. After all these years you could sit down with Ted and negotiate a resolution," Peter suggested.

The minister was close enough to overhear and took a chair at our table. "I may be a retired military man and now am an ordained country minister, but please don't mistake me for an angel. My name isn't Gabriel, but Dieter DuToit. Did you hear my message, Mr. Cooper."

"Just as I heard the message of your assistant preacher on Paarl Mountain," I said.

"That was in Afrikaans, and you couldn't have understood any of it. Mine was in English, so everyone could understand what we must do now for Alicia."

"What I don't understand though is your connection with the Nichols family."

"Let's just say I made some connections in my former career that might prove helpful in a limited campaign. Did I mention, Mr. Cooper, that Ted and I are old friends? He was under my command, a fighter without fear who dragged me out from under kaffir—excuse me, we don't say that anymore—enemy fire when we had to zoom across the border to mop up some rebels in Rhodesia."

"You don't like hearing that story, do you?" Peter asked, looking carefully at my face. "But you shouldn't feel too different from us. After all, in the 50s and 60s you Yanks were busy fighting wars in Asia. Going back further, I recall how your European forebears cleared the land of its original settlers to make way for their farms and towns. We may be more similar than you care to believe."

I didn't care to hear Peter's Yankee-bashing comparison. As I saw it, their wars had been self-inflicted civil wars to keep the ethnic groups separate, while our one civil war was fought for the opposite reason. I was looking to establish friendly working relationships, but Peter LeRoux was trying too hard to be an intellectual for me to attempt to show him I regarded myself simply a messenger of prosperity. I had no interest in their politics, which didn't parallel America's!

"Dieter, there's no need to make Ted Nichols out as the hero," Peter continued, "not when you deserve the glory. It was you, who led your men, despite your injury, to safety after your unit was ambushed while fighting the rebels. All that Ted did was drag you a few yards to safety after you were hit."

"For someone who wasn't there, you speak as though you were with us."

"You're right," Peter said, "I know nothing firsthand, just what the newspapers reported at the time. Forgive me, Dieter, for straying from the subject of Alicia. Let me see if I understand who's who and what's what. Jan has a proprietary interest in her, while I have no direct interest in her."

Once again, the push was on for a serious rescue plan. I didn't know what these people expected of me, but I wasn't planning to commit to anything open ended! Before I left the table though, I needed to ask DuToit directly about his contradictory careers.

"It seems you've led an interesting life, as a man of two very different parts, a soldier and a preacher."

"Either way, I try to have God on my side. I suppose if we weren't shorthanded in the field, Pretoria might have let our army build a chaplain corps such as you bring along with your American Army. As a young man, if I knew what I do now, I might have become a chaplain rather than a fighter and served to comfort our injured boys. But after my fighting stint, I became a better minister to confront the forces of evil for the life of me and my flock."

The forces of evil? Was he talking about the evil of war in general, or about the independence fighters he mopped up?

"You are very convincing from the pulpit, Dieter," I said, "and very interesting, quoting from the Jewish Bible."

"Before we can overcome a man, we must first understand what he believes."

"True, Dieter, but I'm not sure where you hope to lead the flock with your prayers."

"You must understand, it is our combined prayers that will guide me to Alicia. I've made promises to Janice, you see."

I still didn't see the connection between Dieter and her, but rather than question him any further, I refrained from challenging him.

"You're leaving us, before we've had a chance to eat?" Jan asked once she saw me shake Dieter's hand goodbye.

"I'm not very hungry," I said, helping Sunitha from her chair.

"That's too bad," Peter said, "because the ostrich steak here is quite good. Or so I've been told by my farmer friend who supplies this cafe from his ostrich farm."

Jan quietly came behind Peter and placed her hands on his shoulders, causing him to stop talking. "What we mean," she said, "is that we're not exactly welcome guests here at the Chateau. We don't anticipate returning anytime soon. Meanwhile, I'm sure Dieter and Leon have plans to make and their time is short, so why don't we find the waiter so we can order?"

Now that Jan and Peter had left Sunitha and me alone with DuToit, I had a few questions for him. "Where do you think Ted's hiding today?"

"I'm not my brother's keeper," Dieter said "Ted Nichols is a man who doesn't run away from things. He's gathering his strength. But as his advisor, Mr. Cooper, shouldn't you be his keeper?"

"What do you mean?"

I could have asked Dieter whether he served Ted as his spiritual advisor, or as a fellow comrade in war, but I saw by the way he crossed his arms, he'd shut down and didn't care to respond. I suspected that Ted was on his yacht with a lady, diverting himself, trying to escape Alicia's troubles. Ironically, we were sitting there trying to figure out his state of mind!

"If you were advising him, would you be asking me where he's hiding?" Dieter asked with a sly smile.

Dieter was right about Ted and me; sometimes I had to chase him just to get his attention! The Cooper Company had a substantial interest in the Chateau, yet he'd been treating me as casually as one of his hourly employees! But how could this fighting minister know so much of my relationship with Ted, if he'd never once seen us together? I decided Sunitha and I should simply leave without my making any more polite talk.

"What do we do now?" Sunitha asked, once we'd driven a few miles away from the Chateau.

"We just saw Kruger's maps, and attended DuToit's prayer meeting and heard Jan LeRoux's pep talk afterward. That leaves Ted, evidently the key man in your plan, the one with the best ability to get her back, other than the police."

"I won't be able to put her out of my mind until we get her back."

Without telling her my plan, I took a detour into the Hyperama big box store to buy us a couple pairs of sneakers, and a couple jugs of water for a walk up one of Table Mountain's trails. She was reluctant to hike in Sunday clothes, but it seemed more important to do something to help us think of more pleasant things than our stalemated search for Alicia.

That must have been the half-dozenth time we'd climbed Table Mountain. We worked our way up the trail, then at the summit looked down at Cape Town sitting below us at the edge of Table Bay. It was a city blessed with beauty, from a distance.

"In the airplane when we were descending, this mountain looked like it was raised by God's hand."

"But you weren't here long before you learned you were descending into the gates of your hell." she remarked.

"Not hell. You must see the extraordinary beauty of what you have here, or maybe you're too close to appreciate it."

"That's easy for you to say, Leon, because you'll leave Cape Town and me far behind."

"That's not fair," I protested. "You knew from the beginning I'd have to go back home. You know how I feel about you."

"No, Leon, sometimes I don't."

This wasn't the time or the place to pledge my loyalty again. After spending the last few hours slogging up and over the mountain to distract her from her worry over Alicia, I refused to spoil the pleasant mood by choosing the wrong words to explain my devotion. Instead of answering, I pulled her close to kiss her. That accomplished, we headed back down.

Driving away from the mountain, we watched the amber sun descend beyond Cape Town and touch the sea. "This day turned out better than I thought, Sunitha said. "Thank you for being here when I need you."

That evening, after a few hours of sleep, I awoke to feel Sunitha shaking beside me. "What's the matter?" I asked. "Did you have a nightmare about Alicia?" She was sobbing, not answering me. "About Rajesh?"

"My prayers for them remain unanswered," she said. "My prayers must include more than only them."

If it was not Alicia's life nor Rajesh's departed soul now in transit, then she could have been frightened for herself. In that case, it could mean a breakthrough, a chance to get to what was really troubling her. I was half awake, but there was no way I could return to sleep without getting her to share her latest fears.

"Then should we be praying for you instead, Sunitha?"

"Yes, if you have faith."

I was a modern man who believed in explainable cause and effect. My original faith in the powers of reason had been constantly tested from the moment I arrived in South Africa, which left me in a state of doubt. Her faith was stronger and more complicated than mine and served her well, connecting her insepa-rably with her forebears, acting as a bridge through this life into future ones.

"Later about me and my faith. About you, Sunitha, I'm surprised to find you still in bed with me."

"Why, Leon?"

"Because whenever you have a nightmare about Rajesh or Alicia, I find you at your shrine, before the Brahma."

"That's after the fact, just as in my nightmare tonight."

"After what fact?" I asked.

"After the fire that took my—"

She stopped suddenly. Again, I felt I was intruding on a secret she'd rather keep, but I pressed her to finish her story.

"The fire that destroyed your flat in hell, Valhalla?"

"I remembered you in this dream. You were standing in the street outside the house, watching it go up in flames without rescuing me."

"I'm sorry."

"Don't say that, Leon. I don't blame you for wanting to escape from this battlefield and from me."

It might have been unpleasant to hear how I'd let her down, nevertheless I needed to hear any complaints about me, if that's what was keeping her awake.

"If I was late in taking you into my flat, forgive me. If I was responsible for coming between you and your Aunt Giri by driving you to Valhalla, I'm sorry."

"Yes, I had to confront that fire alone and worse, the men who set it. As you already know, not so long ago in India it was an honorable thing for a widow to follow her beloved husband to the next world by joining him on the funeral pyre. I don't know why Ozeer's hyenas let me live! After they had their turns ripping into my body, perhaps I should have been consumed in the fire. But that was not my destiny—because I was destined to return to you, Leon!"

Ripping into my body. She must have been hurt more

than she cared to reveal to me or even admit to herself. She must have felt she was irrevocably damaged, even though she had the good fortune not to fall pregnant from the rape! I had to reason this out, and I had to think of her rather than myself. It had been more than twelve weeks since the fire, and by then I would have certainly seen the signs of a pregnancy or evidence of a termination of it. As careful as I'd been to protect her from pregnancy by me, that would offer her no protection from disease carried by Ozeer's Boys. What if her attackers had planted a deadly virus in her! I needed to learn if she'd been tested. But for first I needed to concern myself with the state of her mind rather than of her body.

"Do you want me?" she whispered.

"Of course."

"I mean more than anything else."

More than anything else? For how long did she mean? For as long as we shared this flat? Or was she suggesting for a very long time, for our natural lives? Or for an infinitely long time, the consecutive lives in which she believes? A heavy question, far too big for me to attempt answering then.

I showed my immediate response by my kisses. Yes, I wanted her, damaged goods or not. My own fears remained tied up in my persistent dream of my disastrous jump into this country without an escape. Hers was her still half-spoken fear of the arsonists returning to attack her again. We made love with a new intensity, exorcising our personal bad dreams and clinging to each other as if our lives depended on one another.

CHAPTER 17
BIRD OF PASSAGE

It was 8 A.M. and Sunitha and I were walking to my car to begin the workday, when a Chateau Drakenstein Mercedes pulled up to us, the one used to ferry guests to and from the airport. Tembo was driving with Chandra sitting beside him.

"We caught you just in time," Chandra said.

"I'm running a little late," I said, looking at my appointment calendar. "I must be in Mowbray this morning, then Newlands and Claremont this afternoon. But first I must drop off Sunitha at Wandi Dadla's."

"That's why I am here," Chandra said, "to help you and Sunitha manage Alicia's shebeen, since no one has been there to run it properly."

"Then you don't think Sunitha will be able to pick up the pieces, Chandra?"

"She knows I trust her abilities managing an office," Chandra said, taking both her hands and smiling fondly. "Who else would be sharp enough to spot the problems with the new cashier and the new manager that Mr. Wessels has so suddenly placed there?"

"Tembo, what's this talk about Colin Wessels?" I asked, wanting a second opinion.

"It seems Mr. Wessels has quickly taken on new

responsibility, especially since Mr. Nichols has so much on his mind about Alicia and has not been available," Tembo said.

Chandra was a science-based man who preferred to gather his facts before speaking. Like Sunitha, he was not prone to exaggeration, so I was inclined to pay attention to his suggestions.

"I still don't know why you're detaining us."

"Because we need to be ready for Mr. Nichols when he returns this afternoon. It is up to us to set him in the right direction toward Alicia. You need to pass what you learned from Mr. Kruger. We can't lose another person close to us."

Chandra turned away from me, looked to the ground, then wiped his eyes. "I understand," I said.

"No, you don't, sir," he said, looking sternly at me. "If Mr. Nichols had used his resources to crush Mafumo's vandals, I would have my only son! But my sadness gives me no excuse for anger. I must work to keep my perspective and continue to be Mr. Nichols' loyal servant, even though he might have been able to save my son, but did not try. Now I worry for his daughter Alicia. I won't let her be slaughtered like Rajesh. I know Mr. Nichols has the power to save her, but only if we can direct his forces."

It seemed Chandra overestimated Ted's resources, perhaps because several years ago Ted had rescued him financially from Gazelle's insoluble defects and put him on the Chateau's payroll. But that wouldn't account for Sunitha's, Kruger's and the LeRouxs' insistence that somehow Ted possessed the power to defeat an organized band of kidnappers.

"Excuse me, Sunitha," Tembo said. He directed her toward my Volkswagen. "With Mr. Cooper's permission, I will drive you today to Wandi Dadla's and to any of the people who we need to speak with who may have been stealing from the till."

"Tembo, please—we know no such thing yet. This is a sensitive matter. We'll let the figures speak for themselves."

Chandra understood figures and waved a sheet of numbers on graph paper at me. He knew how to use computers but never trusted them without verifying them with firsthand inspections.

"Do you have your copy of my figures and their figures and the discrepancies between the two?" Kassie asked Tembo.

"Right here, Mr. Kassie," Tembo said, tapping his breast pocket.

"Now, Leon, if you don't mind, I'll be your chauffeur today," Chandra said and opened the door to the Mercedes.

"I don't think you understand," I said, waving my appointment book at him. "I told you I have a tight schedule."

"Yes, you have taught us well to make efficient use of time. Therefore, I have rescheduled so you can come with me to Colin Wessels and then to Mr. Nichols, if we can locate him."

How did Chandra know where I was going today, unless Sunitha had told him? I didn't like him patting me on the shoulder, like a child he was trying to pacify. He seemed to forget I was his boss. Or maybe he saw me and my assignment as temporary, knowing that for the rest of his working life he would never be removed by Ted from the Chateau.

"I suspect that you may be blaming Sunitha for the changes I've made in your schedule," Chandra said, "but I assure you, sir, she and I will always have your best interests in mind, as if you were one of our family."

Apparently, Sunitha had gotten into my calendar and told Chandra who I was meeting that day. No matter how good their intentions, I couldn't run a business if my plans were to be altered without consulting me!

"You are angry and rightfully so. I have taken the liberty of rescheduling you to free you to attend to priority business. I take full responsibility for not consulting with you of any changes in your appointments."

I respected Chandra, for his skill as a brewmaster and for his powers of observation. He strove to lead his life honestly, but was given to flattery, especially when dealing with Ted or myself. I had no patience for it today. As far as I was concerned, he was interfering with my decisions. Though he must have realized he was overstepping his authority, he must have felt immune from consequences from me. As Sunitha's beloved godfather, and quite nearly her father-in-law, he must have believed I'd never reprimand him before her and cause him to lose face.

"Chandra, do you really believe you know my priorities better than I do?"

"Only because you have taught me well enough to think like you."

"Please, Chandra, it would be better if you would follow my directions rather than praise me."

"I am simply your student, Leon. You've taught me well how important it is to make your appointments run friction-free. That is why I could clearly see these lower priority meetings would have to wait."

"Wait for what Chandra?"

"I'll show you," he said, motioning Tembo who quickly opened the car door for me.

"Not so fast," I said, jangling my own car keys.

"I sense you are angry at me and prefer not travel with me today, but I must stay with you if you are to see how Colin has been mismanaging Alicia's brewpub in her absence."

"Chandra, you're aware that aside from Ted, while I am here, I have the final decision-making authority."

"Of course," he readily agreed.

"Well, at this point, it's too late to reverse what you've done. Just don't do it again, understood?"

"Very sorry. You can always rely on me, sir."

I didn't see why it was so important that we see Colin immediately, but I consented to that detour, provided he take me to Ted later. I didn't appreciate Chandra's interference, yet deferred to his plan, and let Tembo take the keys to my Volkswagen. Neither of them said anything more, as if afraid I might change my mind. Tembo was quick to drive away with Sunitha, while I became Chandra's passenger.

Once in the Chateau's gates, half-dozen government and police cars were gathered. Alongside the road I saw several men in light gray uniforms with shoulder patches I wasn't quite able to read.

"Who are these men, Chandra? Ted's troops you mentioned?"

"Do you think he has the Army at his command?" he asked, avoiding my question.

"Stop. I want to ask them why they are here."

"It may be a routine patrol, or they might be officials inspecting our facilities."

There was nothing routine from what I was seeing! Though they were not carrying sidearms, they looked like soldiers or cops, not food inspectors! I was sure Chandra had a good idea of what influence Ted had to use to get these men here. It looked as though the Chateau was under military occupation.

"I will stop as you wish, Leon," Chandra said, stopping the car in front of the cafe, a full half mile after I told him.

"We've already lost time, Chandra. They don't serve until noon, so why are we parked here?"

"Those men in uniform we saw, Leon—we are here to meet them if you will follow me."

Inside the entrance to the cafe, I was startled to see Colin Wessel's wife Amanda on a swiveling leather bar chair, rotating herself impatiently. I had only seen her a few times since the party at the Chateau, where I met Ted and his friends for the first time. When she saw me, she came closer and greeted me with a polite handshake.

"What an unexpected surprise," I said.

"If you expected me, then how could I surprise you?"

Her mind apparently ran in a straight track, very much like her linear-thinking husband, our comptroller, Colin Wessels. A perfect match, the Wessels, two very literal-minded people.

"Do I amuse you?" she asked. I must have revealed myself by my inadvertent smile.

"Of course. I always found you charming," I reassured her, realizing it wasn't that different from Chandra's more strategic flattery, which I didn't trust when used on me. Not sure how to respond, I laughed with her. I couldn't tell her the truth though. I was not amused at the ruse used to bring me there, which she'd obviously done in cooperation with Chandra.

I also wondered whether Sunitha had planned with Chandra for me to meet Otto Kruger. At least there had been a purpose for that meeting, to show me the workings of Oasis Security. Nevertheless, I didn't understand why Wessel's wife had been dragged into Chateau business. Because she was the wife of our comptroller or because, like Alicia, she was closely related to Ted? I was the one nominally in charge, yet here she was leading me to waste my time on their agenda, which still hadn't been revealed to me. It was also odd that Amanda then introduced me to the uniformed men. They wore either police gray or warm climate khaki uniforms. Seated at three tables, they seemed like joint occupying forces. There was no telling whether Chandra had told them in advance to make themselves at home, but this hardly felt to me like a social visit. Not only did their uniforms put me on edge, but also the liberties they took to feed themselves in our closed cafe. They helped themselves with generous plates of meat, cheeses, and fruit, as well as bottles of Gazelle beer. I felt I'd been led to a party that I had paid to cater, but to which I hadn't been invited.

"I didn't realize I was hosting this event, Chandra," I said, taking him aside to the bar where I poured us a couple of sodas. "Was this party your idea, Amanda?"

I added, annoyed that she had followed and was now trying to overhear us. "Or was it Colin's?"

"You'll have to ask him," Amanda said, "because I've always tried to stay out of his affairs, except when I'm asked to take up the slack, as now."

Take up the slack? She looked at Chandra as if she didn't want to be there any more than I did, yet was doing a favor with her presence. She walked towards the door, where stood the real object of her attention, a new visitor, Otto Kruger, who quickly came to me and shook my hand.

"Another surprise," I said when Kruger came to me.

"I assure you I didn't intend to set foot on Ted Nichols' grounds before you had a chance to present the plan we had discussed regarding Alicia," Kruger said, waving toward the only three men out of uniform. "That was before these turnkeys from Pollsmoor became involved."

"This makes no sense! What does Pollsmoor Prison have to do with Alicia's kidnapping?" I asked.

"Please, not so loud," Otto Kruger said, turning his back to the men whose attention I had attracted. "Rest assured we're working hard to figure all this out. We knew this was no simple carjacking. We thought Ozeer's purpose was revenge, to even the score with Ighaam. Now it looks as if they're keeping her as a bargaining chip in exchange for some of their prisoner friends who are being held in Pollsmoor. You see, these Ozeer Boys have been awaiting trial without bail for armed robbery and homicide."

"My God, this keeps on getting worse!" Amanda whispered to me. She watched Otto to make sure he was listening to her opinion of his fiancé's chances of survival. "Alicia shouldn't have let her guard down at the club. Since I've been filling in at Wandi Dadla's, I always have someone see me safely to my car. I don't know why she took such chances. As close as I was to Alicia, I must tell you confidentially that she had a reckless streak, especially when it came to men."

"Excuse me," Otto said to me. "We can't be wasting any more time setting out in the wrong direction. Mr. Cooper, that's why we're counting on your help. You must be as concerned as I am, but now that we're on the same team, we're formidable."

"Wait a minute, gentlemen, I can't accomplish miracles."

"We were hoping you'd do whatever it takes to get Ted and his men away from the Southern Cape, where they're searching the wrong area, and employ our superior maps to deploy them toward the Botswana border instead."

"...And furthermore, as an American on a work permit, I can't involve myself with this sort of thing."

I noticed a few laughing among themselves. If my disclaimer seemed funny to them, perhaps it was because they already knew of my involvement with extra-legal operations. From what I could see, they weren't much of a team, just a hastily assembled collection of soldiers, cops, and Pollsmoor prison guards. Now joining the party, a new arrival, John Schmidt. Like his boss Kruger, Schmidt was wearing an Oasis Security uniform. The lot of them represented a cross section of the private security forces, but I saw no one in charge of this rescue team. I wondered whether Kruger was justified in his confidence that this paramilitary band would allow him to lead them. Nevertheless, there he was, standing in the middle of the group and speaking to them like their rightful leader, thanking them for coming there to protect the Chateau.

Why were these motley troops gathered there? To use the Chateau as a convenient meeting place, or the staging point for raids? Could their mission be a defensive one, to prepare for an attack against us, unless we were another potential target in the ongoing war between the black and the coloured gangs? I could have used my position to take control of this meeting away from Schmidt and Kruger and chase them away, but now that they had assembled, and with great difficulty, I decided to use it to Chateau's advantage to get an idea of their true agendas. I was jumpy, in part, because I'd already been at the fringes of these skirmishes, which seemed to be getting progressively more lethal. Nor did I like the looks of the cordovan attaché Schmidt had set on the bar, which was just like the case Kruger had demonstrated as the one the black CORE gangsters used to transport a bomb! It made me uneasy how quick he was to pull the case toward himself, when Amanda inadvertently rested her elbow on it.

"If you want, Sergeant Schmidt," I said, "I'll watch this brief case for you while you assist Mr. Kruger with this dog and pony show."

"That will not be necessary, Mr. Cooper," Schmidt said, giving the case to Kruger for safekeeping. "Please don't call me Sergeant, not in front of them, since I'm on private duty now, and these blokes here today get a little touchy about calling a man by his right rank "

"If you don't mind my asking, are you carrying something very important in there—or dangerous?"

"No, nothing important, but I understand your man Kassie has something interesting to show us."

"I've told you no such thing. Now if you'll excuse us, Mr. Schmidt."

"No problem," Schmidt said and made his way back to the tables of enforcement, security and military men.

Chandra pulled from a file folder the sheets of graph paper with the Wandi Dadla accounting figures.

"Excuse me," Amanda said, "Chandra, you never told me I'd be waylaid in a room of policemen. Why you want me to watch you play coppers and robbers today?"

"Whose personal company makes you more nervous, Amanda," Otto asked, "these chaps, or myself, now that I wear an investigator's hat?"

"Why don't you leave me alone Otto, and we'll talk again if we have reason, if you manage to pull your pretty rabbit out of your hat."

The pretty rabbit to which she was referring must have been Alicia, her cousin, whom she must have seen as a threat to her husband Colin. Not only did her nerves seem frayed waiting with this crew of men, but there seemed to be personal issues, as if she were hoping Otto and his men might not be able to bring back Alicia. Otto looked over Chandra's shoulder at his green sheets. When Chandra noticed, he spun himself around to hide the papers.

"Very sorry, Mr. Kruger, but this is private Drakenstein business," Chandra said and stood up to hand the case to Otto, in the process sweeping it onto the floor.

Schmidt was looking hard at me, reading my near panic over the dropped case. Schmidt, Kruger and I must have been the only ones in this crowd familiar with the attaché bombs displayed at Oasis Security. Perhaps my fear of that brown case was groundless, but this wasn't the time or the place to discuss it. I turned to leave the room, but Otto rushed to me and brought me back to the table.

"You look like you've seen a ghost," Amanda said, picking up the briefcase and handing it to Schmidt. "Land, money, women, or a cheap briefcase that isn't even leather, you men can find a reason to fight over anything!"

"You needn't be nervous," Otto said, patting me on the back to soothe me. "We're fighting professionals, and our job is to protect you."

"Protect us from the brutes?" Amanda muttered. "Impossible, there are far more of them than of us."

"Then I'll assume you have no place more important to go than here with us," Otto said, as if he had a right to claim Chateau Drakenstein as territory for himself and his gaping associates, all of them focused on me. "Good, because until we find my fiancé, think of me as your right-hand man, just as Ted regards you as his right-hand man. We are both crucial links."

He could be persuasive, which must have been how he had managed to woo Alicia. He would have had to work his magic on her during her short layovers in South Africa, while she was busy managing Wandi Dadla's. I couldn't get it out of my mind that when I was new here, she'd offered herself in my hotel room, while she had already pledged herself to him. I wish Otto, the great persuader, would go away and forget about me, yet he reappeared in my life, and asked me not to forget I was a liaison between Ted and him! On the other hand, I was glad he organized this search party, since I believed, if nothing else, he had the ability to find her and bring her back.

With Alicia's life at stake, I wouldn't let any personal skepticism of Kruger prevent me from making a sound decision. I was becoming impressed how he managed to turn out this squad of law enforcement and prison bulls, with who knows how many more behind them. It was so important to recruit me in order to use my influence to redirect Ted to follow the satellite maps in attacking near the Botswana border.

"If I knew when Ted was returning, I could give you a better idea—" I said.

"We've been tracking him for the last few days, Mr. Cooper," Van Staden called to me.

Could it be everyone there knew Ted's whereabouts, and I was the only one who had been kept in the dark? Had I been intentionally kept from Ted for these extra days to give Otto extra time to assemble this strike force of mercenaries?

"Ted should be glad to meet with you after dinner at 1900 hours," Kruger said.

Otto appeared intent on reclaiming Alicia, his trophy. Did he court her from attraction, or love, or because her family had connections he was planning to turn to his own profit? As a master of criminal pursuits and investigations, he must have discovered her true family tree more quickly than I, that Ted was her natural father. I wondered if he knew that some woman other than Jan LeRoux was her mother. But the longer I dealt with the Nichols family and with the Chateau, the less I trusted I knew! I distrusted the expanding web of alliances that stretched all the way into the underworld, all linked back to Ted and the Chateau. I saw no way to disentangle myself from these people who had staked their claims on me.

"Amanda, I was expecting we were meeting with your husband," I said as Chandra walked us to Colin's office.

"Truthfully Leon, I don't keep any closer track of him than you do. I know what you're trying to do here during your brief stay with us, to make us work harder and faster."

She seemed to be telling me I was a newcomer, one who didn't fit in very well in South Africa. Though she was showing little respect for me, if she hadn't been told my true function at the Chateau for my assignment there, how could I fault her? Colin was secretive by nature, so it wouldn't have surprised me if he hadn't told his wife the details of the Cooper Company's status, nor about my true position in Cooper.

Perhaps I'd unintentionally brought upon myself such speculations by keeping too low a profile, and by letting everyone think Ted Nichols was the absolute lord and master of this domain. On the other hand, it was good diplomacy to downplay my status so as not to interfere with Ted's authority, even though it made it difficult for me to stop uninformed people like Amanda to throw shade and remind me she and others at Drakenstein regarded me as merely a bird of passage.

"Chandra, you didn't tell me you were going to bring me to cops, prison guards, and soldiers, as well as lead me to Amanda," I said to him once we stopped in front of the big house.

"I'm surprised you put me in the same category as these rough chaps. Do I look so poorly today?" Amanda asked me.

"No, as attractive as always," I complimented her, attempting not to show signs of ill humor.

"Chandra," she said, "you must have lost your way. Instead of taking us to my husband's office in the beer plant, we're going to the king's court."

By king's court, she was referring to Ted's main house, a disparaging thing to say about the man who provided her livelihood. Once we were inside the mansion, we came to a room by the kitchen which had been made over into an office. It was Colin's name was on a plaque on the desk!

"Leon, you know he never belonged at the beer plant," Amanda said, "unless you put him there to separate him from Ted. If he wished to work on an assembly line in that factory building where you were trying to assign him, I would have never consented to his career in the liquor trade, no matter how much Ted originally begged him to come onboard. He should have taken a position as actuary at Sanlaam Insurance. The benefits were better, and he would have been treated with more respect."

"Excuse me, Amanda," Chandra said, "but I have never known Mr. Nichols to beg anyone for anything."

"But, Chandra, how well could you know Mr. Nichols?" Amanda asked, "any better than our American guest? Everyone knows Mr. Nichols never cared for the taste of beer, yet you somehow convinced him to make all this beer so you could act as his beer meister. Please don't take my criticism personally."

Nevertheless, Chandra indeed appeared to take it personally, looking at me as if the wind had just been knocked
out of him. She implied that neither he nor his work were
important to Ted. I believe she was striking at Chandra for
calling her out for irregularities in how she and Colin were
running Wandi Dadla's Place since Alicia disappeared.

"Excuse me, Amanda," I said, "but I think you owe
my man Chandra an apology."

"Leon, didn't I say nothing personal intended? At any
rate, no more personal than you bringing us to my husband's office to rummage through his payroll papers.
But first, Colin asked that you give me your sheets of
numbers so he could look them over beforehand."

"Amanda, we can make this far pleasanter for us if
we to work together. I can't begin to cooperate with
you until you stop fighting me. If you have it in you,
I'd suggest you try to be a bit nicer to us."

Rather than pay attention to me, she seemed fixed
on the green sheets on the desk. "May I?" she asked
Chandra.

Chandra began to move the papers away from her,
but she was too fast and manage to snatch away a
handful of the accounting sheets. Before he could take
them back, she folded them and tucked them into her
blouse! She must have believed Chandra was too docile
to challenge her and that she was free to speak to us on
behalf of not only her husband but of Ted! I was angry
enough to get those accounting sheets back from her,
even if we had to take her by the ankles and shake her
upside down!

"Excuse me, Amanda," I said, trying to get past her
and out the door. Inside, I could see Colin waiting.

"You must appreciate that I need a few minutes to catch up with my husband," she said. Though we managed to escort her out of the office and into the hallway, she quickly reversed direction and scooted back inside, quickly locking herself in with him. I was at the limit of my patience, and knocked on the door hard, with the heel of my hand, until she answered.

"Amanda, you've gone past the limit! I have no idea what you think your function is here at Drakenstein, other than as Colin's wife, but I'm serving notice that he will be held accountable for your actions."

"Does your bean counter Sahib Kassie wish to speak with Colin? Only if you gentlemen will you allow us the time to look for the beans Chandra claims are missing. We'd love to cooperate, but only if you'll be patient with us and return after a long break for coffee." This time when she tried closing the door, Chandra held it back with his foot. She slammed it harder, and when he withdrew with a yelp of pain, she slammed it shut and locked it.

"That woman is too forward to make a good wife for any man," Chandra said, leading me out of the house. "It is best to allow her a bit of time so when we return the intelligence of her *moksha* may overcome her unpleasant *maya*."

"What do you mean, Chandra?" I asked.

"I talk of the prism of delusions we hold to our eyes and see the world around us distorted."

In front of the cafe, I saw neither Oasis, nor official vehicles. It looked as if Otto and his associates were gone. The café was serving, and we sat with the first tourists of the day. We were a stop on their itinerary of wineries, but I knew our Chateau's beauty compared well with any others they might visit. I remembered the first time I drove there how serene and removed from the world this place seemed. When I partnered with Ted, I took a personal and proprietary interest in this jewel of a winery. But what troubled me was his growing sphere of influence beyond the law, especially since I'd been central to increasing it—especially Drakenstein's influence by driving our product line into the poorest parts of Cape Town, where the laws were irrelevant. While it looked like a profitable move to expand the Chateau into high-risk township markets where the gangs happened to rule, the ultimate cost could prove higher than I ever intended. At that point, my regret regarding these alliances didn't matter. I could not pry the Chateau loose from its underworld allies as we continued doing business in hostile territories. I suppose I'd inadvertently made a pact with a devil in the form of Ighaam Arendse, if only to protect us from a worse devil, Ozeer and his gangsters.

"Excuse me, Leon, but I see you're concerned," Chandra said, leaning toward me to study me closely. "I believe you must be very upset with Mrs. Wessels for delaying you from your appointment, as I know you prefer to book your calendar yourself."

He had proven to be a good student of mine and learned to make much more efficient use of his time since Ted and I began using him to establish and supervise the brewing equipment in our new shebeens. He was once more telling me that I was busy and important because he thought that's what I wanted to hear.

"You're a good friend, and very perceptive," I said.

I hoped he didn't mistake that for flattery, which I avoided, especially with key people under me in any project. He was a good man and one I'd come to regard as a trusted friend, but I had to continue to relate to him first on a business level. I also needed to discuss with him as a lesson in how we could have better handled Amanda.

"Chandra, doesn't it make sense that she'd want to know the agenda of our meeting in advance in order to share it with him?" He nodded in agreement. "It must have been very important for her to steal your papers, stomp on your foot, and barricade you from her husband."

"Leon, I come from the race of Gandhi and am a man who needs not fight to win. Would you mistake a great man of peace such as him as a weak man? Or would my son Rajesh appear to you a foolish young man for fighting for our home?"

He made his point that he didn't believe in violence, only when necessary. He made a reasonably good argument, primarily by turning my question around with his own questions. Whatever the true extent of Gandhi's or my teaching had on him, I believed his powers of persuasion had improved, and I was proud of him.

"Why was Amanda so interested in rummaging through those notes and printouts of yours?"

"Of course, Leon, how could I miss it! With her husband, she must be trying to stitch together the pieces of their stories into one quilt!"

"Chandra, I'm more interested in how you've decided to handle her. If you remember one thing after I've departed, that is to negotiate from a position of strength."

I couldn't read the response in Chandra's face. I wondered whether he could see my frustration in my negotiations with Werner-Nichols. If he did, then my advice to negotiate from a position of strength must have seemed hollow indeed.

"I wouldn't worry about our position, Leon."

"What makes you so confident?"

"Confidence in you, now that you are the key man at the Drakenstein Company."

"Does anyone else know besides yourself, Hassan, and Sunitha, that I'm the one bringing sweeping changes in your organization? How about the managers, especially the Afrikaners from Van Staden on down?"

"Then, if I may ask, are you are feeling invisible?"

Again, he was turning my question back to me. As his mentor, I wanted to build on his strengths, rather distract him with explanations of my own shortfalls. It was time to return to Colin's office. This time the door was open.

"Please make yourself at home," Amanda said.

"That's nice of you, inviting me to your plush quarters here," I said and sat in one of the leather wingback chairs that were facing Colin's long, carved desk.

"What's the problem? Isn't this new office of Colin's to your liking?" she asked testily.

By now it should have been obvious to Colin and his wife that I was not pleased with his sudden move to this room next to Ted's private quarters, away from the more efficient office we originally earmarked for him in the new Gazelle plant, where he would have been better able to stay in touch with the men and any payroll problems.

"If it weren't for these few things," I said, pointing

to the computer equipment and the photocopier, "this would appear to be a comfortable flat, rather than the Chateau's accounting office."

"Don't be silly," she said, and to prove her point opened a pair of cabinet doors, revealing hidden filing cabinets. "You see, Colin can get more work done here, away from the dreadful racket in the factory, where you tried to convince Ted to stick him when you first arrived. I would appreciate it, Leon, if next time you gentlemen ask for our permission before running barefoot through our private quarters."

"I'm afraid if I had come barefoot, Mrs. Wessels," Chandra said, "you would have broken my right foot by stamping so hard on it." He then sat down in the other wingback chair, leaned back, and with a grin waved his foot at her.

Chandra went to Colin's desk and looked through a pile of folders sitting on top. When Amanda lurched for them, he pulled them back, just beyond her reach, then took them with him to the filing cabinet and opened one of the drawers. Colin appeared wearing white linen pants and a yellow shirt.

"What are you doing here, Chandra, really?" Colin asked.

"Ah, by the looks of your shoes you've been out boating today, Mr. Wessels," Chandra said. "I don't blame you for wanting to be elsewhere. Did you buy a boat, Mr. Wessels, or did Mr. Nichols invite you for a ride?"

I wondered if Chandra was challenging him directly for my benefit, to show me he wasn't passive. He was skillfully volleying his questions one after the other, controlling the conversation.

"Chandra's in the wrong place, Leon," Colin said to me pointedly. "If you're after some particular records, shouldn't you be looking for them in the payroll office? Now if he's done prowling through my files, I'd appreciate—"

"I'm just trying to be of help," Chandra said.

"Help me! By rifling through these folders and this file cabinet?

Chandra, why don't you stick to what you know best—cleaning your vats of beer?"

"A good idea, that's why I've brought Mr. Cooper with me."

"Why?" Colin asked and looked to Amanda sitting behind Chandra and me on a high stool, as if she were a referee watching a tennis match.

"Because if you don't have respect for my department, Mr. Wessels," Chandra said forcefully, "then I knew you would have to honor Mr. Cooper's."

"What department would that be, Leon?" Colin asked.

"In case you've misfiled this memo, this might help," Chandra said. From his jacket pocket he produced a paper, which he waved to all of us. "You remember, the memo in which Mr. Nichols requested that all departments cooperate with Mr. Cooper, including yours here in accounting."

Amanda quietly walked to Chandra, snatched the memo out of his hand and laid it on Colin's desk. He read to himself, then slid it to me. "Cooperate with what, gentlemen?" he asked.

"Our compliance inquiry is now in session," Chandra said, staring steadily at Colin. "That is, if you don't mind answering a few questions," he added tentatively, in an instant diminishing his negotiating posture.

"Leon, are you sure you're not here to see how my wife has decorated my office?"

"Your wife must have told you by now," Chandra continued, "we're here regarding Wandi Dadla's and about the funds that have allegedly come up short."

"So, as Ted's personal consultant, are you here with a specific complaint?" he asked, now on his feet. "What might be the problem?"

"We're looking at a substantial discrepancy between the funds allocated and disbursed to the Wandi Dadla account, and the receipts for construction costs and operating expenses."

"There's 5.5 million rand we cannot find," Chandra said, showing him a tally sheet, which Colin brushed aside without looking.

"We don't know what you mean," Amanda said. Colin was behind his desk rocking back and forth, tapping his pencil on his desk, and she was now pacing around the perimeter of the room.

"We mean that money is missing," I said. "If we can't account for it, you must help us find it. Have you any suggestions?"

I wanted to leave them an escape hatch, not corner them. But they had nothing to say, and fear shone in their eyes. Chandra looked at me with the hint of a smile. We had them off-balance.

"I know where we can begin looking for those funds: in the 90-, 120-, and 150-day accounts with our contractors," Chandra suggested. "Maybe the funds in question haven't had a chance to come down the pipeline yet. Of course, Alicia's method of running Wandi Dadla may have been at fault."

"How so?" I asked, sensing that Colin was trying to put the blame elsewhere.

"First, Alicia's trained as a stewardess, and her pub was no more than a part-time hobby for her," Amanda said. "Second, everyone knows how she always spent way over budget. Third, she was never good with figures."

"Yes," Colin added. "Perhaps she didn't record her expenditures promptly."

This was becoming complicated. Maybe Colin had been using Alicia's loose management as a screen to skim money off the large expenditures in getting Wandi Dadla up and running.

"Very sorry I bring you facts you did not care to hear, Mr. Wessels," Chandra said.

We'd hit Amanda hard, then afterward Colin, but were now shifting to easing our attacks on both. We'd given them plenty of reason to be angry at us for revealing their game. As a good negotiator, I planned to back off to allow them to blow off some more of their anger. After all, I was an imported American telling them what to do in the Drakenstein family business, which had existed for more years than my country! That left me sitting there for an uncomfortably long time, my eyes locked with Colin's. The first one of us to blink would lose this round of our match, and it was not going to be me.

"Quite frankly, Leon," he finally said, his eyes weirdly fluttering, "I never knew why you convinced Ted to put me next to the production floor where everyone thought I should be available throughout the day to hear their petty grievances."

"I've been over that already," Amanda interrupted him, "so why don't you ask him why he and Chandra insisted on dragging me into this mess?"

"Leon, I've given twenty-five years of my life to Chateau. My office used to be right next to this great house, a minute's walk from Ted's home office, and when you arrived, he wanted to ship me off to Siberia, where I would be completely cut off from his office. Someone owes me an explanation!"

Colin knew full well as Ted's troubleshooter, I had carte blanche access to all records, including his, yet he was insulting me. As much as I wished to confront him directly on his insubordination, I refrained. Instead, I decided to give him what he was looking for at this stage of the negotiations, a lukewarm apology that would allow him to save face, in front of his domineering wife.

"Thanks for calling this to my attention. I'm sorry I didn't get to you earlier to explain our intentions, but you know how close to the chest Ted likes to play his cards."

"This may be a game to you," Amanda shouted, placing her arm in solidarity around his shoulder, "but it doesn't amuse Colin and me!"

"Of course not," I said sympathetically. "This has been just as difficult for us but let me explain. When Ted hired me to help Drakenstein's expansion, we began working on plans for the Gazelle beer plant. It made sense to us to move key people like yourself, closer to the action, where you would be the most effective. Since you are responsible for payroll, it seemed logical to us that you might be more effective if we relocated you next to the production floor. In the plant building our workers would have been able to find you more easily every day, not just Friday afternoons. That way we believed we could better count you to supervise every paycheck you had to cut on the Chateau's account."

"We know that you intended to put distance between Ted and me because he was tired of my visits to his office during the day. Why else, Leon, was Ted too busy for morning tea break with me ever since you arrived?"

"Colin, you're overestimating me, a mere bird of passage. You and Amanda have a great advantage because you're permanently attached to Ted as family."

Amanda moved her chair forward, so she was alongside me and leaned on my armrest. "Who exactly do you think I am to Ted?"

"Weren't you introduced to me as his sister?" I answered.

"You must have poor Alicia on your mind, as we all do," Alicia said, not striking me as sincere, but looking at me closely to discern from my expression whether I was bluffing or knew her genealogical secrets. "You must have confused us because her name's so like mine. Unfortunately, Colin and I are not that close to our lord, or else we'd be more secure."

Was she speaking of the Lord God, or her master, Ted Nichols? Was she telling me that being closely related to him didn't give her much advantage, or that the problem was that she was too distantly related to give her an advantage? Again, working close to this crazy Nichols family baffled me! I'd retreated enough. It was time to end this diversion. I looked beyond Amanda to catch Chandra's attention and signaled with another discreet nod it was time to get down to business.

"Excuse me, Colin, maybe you can help me," Chandra said, and stood by the desk facing me, "The other day when Mr. Cooper asked me why you suddenly put your wife on the payroll after Alicia went missing, I didn't know what to tell him."

"Just a moment," Colin said.

To avoid Chandra's question Colin busied pulling manila folders from the desk drawer. Amanda came behind him they began hand they began whispering. Chandra looked at me for what to do, and I motioned to him for him to get closer to them and break the deadlock.

"Help us out, please," Chandra said, "by explaining why you've been allowing Mrs. Wessels to drive all the way from Wandi Dadla's to Stellenbosch by herself. With that late a schedule, I calculate she couldn't be arriving back home earlier than 3:00 A.M."

"What is your point?" Amanda asked, as Chandra laid his accounting numbers on the desk beside Colin's folders.

"I'm not sure I dare say any more right now," Chandra said.

"Please continue."

"I'd rather not, Colin, not in front of your wife."

"Then you shouldn't have brought her on this trivial mission. Dear, would you mind bringing coffee for Leon and teas for the rest of us?" he directed, effectively dispatching his wife.

"Now speak up, man!" he snapped at Kassie once she was gone.

"Frankly, Colin, if she were my wife, I couldn't pay

her enough to take the kind of risk you've encouraged her to take."

"For your information, Chandra, she's always well escorted. If you think what's happened to Alicia is going to happen to my wife, that I'd risk her life, think again."

"Actually, we weren't concerned with Mrs. Wessels' personal safety, so much as in the wellbeing of Wandi Dadla's and Drakenstein's. I notice you've brought your wife to run the place with a couple of portable computers."

"They're called laptops," Colin said with a wink. "It's no secret, Chandra, that you don't understand computers. Welcome to the computer age."

"Actually, I do miss the paper ledger system Alicia used at Wandi Dadla's. It helped me keep track of the money coming in as income and going out as expense."

"Are you forgetting I'm an auditor!"

"Forgive me if I have stated the obvious. I'm sure there's a logical reason why all the papers from the office, including the ledger books, have disappeared, and why you have replaced the ledgers with a couple of your tiny computers."

"Chandra, don't be a thorn on the ass of progress!" Colin shouted.

This confrontation had reached an inflection point, but this time Kassie was the one to blink first, which he did as a hearty laugh that built until his eyes were tearing.

"That was a good one, Colin. I love good jokes, even if I am the butt of them," Kassie said after his own good-natured laugh. "Now maybe you can help Mr. Cooper and me understand why all these paper records disappeared? Why did Mrs. Wessels start working at the brewpub the day after Alicia Nichols went missing? And why on that day were the old records removed before the new computers and software were introduced?"

Colin might have an innocent explanation, but I was concerned he put his wife quickly into the pub, hoping to cover his creative accounting or to expand his power within the Drakenstein organization. Colin's face was reddening, embarrassed, but I withheld final judgment for later.

"Have I missed anything important, gentlemen?" Amanda asked. None of us answered.

The interruption allowed us to sip in silence and gather our thoughts. Chandra produced a stack of computer printouts, which he set down in front of Colin.

"I got these from one of Wandi Dadla's new computers. You can compare your computer figures with my figures on the green sheets for any disagreements."

"This is ridiculous," Colin said. "What are you trying to do!"

"No need to worry, Mr. Wessels. For me this is an exercise to get used to your new computers, nothing more."

"A training exercise? What a waste of time!"

If there was any truth to the discrepancies Chandra unearthed, Colin knew he was in trouble. As for hiring his wife, perhaps he simply seized what he saw as a vacancy, assuming Alicia would never return alive. If nothing else came of this unpleasant meeting, at least they knew we'd be watching them closely.

CHAPTER 18

A TOUR OF OSTRICH COUNTRY

By the time we were done with Colin and Amanda, it was midafternoon, which left Chandra and me a few hours before Ted was due at Stellenbosch. It didn't make sense to drive all the way to Cape Town, so we made the best use of our time by dropping in on our nearest grape farmer. We found him on a ladder, scraping loose paint off his storage building, but he wasn't quite ready to drop his work. His stout wife met us on the porch of their house, then led us to the kitchen.

"My husband Franz is a hardworking man, but it's not easy to survive on what Chateau pays us for our grapes," she said to Chandra as she made us coffee. "I wish he were here, but he'll never talk business in a dirty shirt."

"We already pay a premium over market price if your quality matches that of our vineyard," Chandra said.

Franz returned with a fresh white shirt with sleeves that clung to his large biceps. "As a beer brewer, Mr. Kassie, do you think that qualifies you to speak about grapes and wine? Or do you believe you know about farming because your people up north not so long ago worked in the fields? It's never been easy farming, but this year with so little rain…"

For now, I ignored Franz's complaint. He should have treated Chandra with more respect. Eventually, Chandra was going to have to get better at asserting himself.

"I suppose we Indians should consider ourselves lucky because we never saw the inside of your camps."

Chandra was digging up unpleasant history from a century ago. Judging by his uneasy, irrelevant response, he didn't want to speak any more of camps. Instead, he turned his attention to me.

"I didn't get your name," Franz said.

"Cooper, Leon Cooper."

"Ah, the American! It's about time I met you. Has Mr. Kassie been serving you well?"

He treated Chandra like my manservant, winking at me as if to say we were both Chandra's masters. If he knew how much he was annoying me, he wouldn't be laying his whole sad story before me, complaining not only about the low prices for his grapes, but about high expenses, unfair taxes, and unreliable help. I wanted to cut him short, but it was important to treat him carefully because all the growers spoke to one another, and we didn't want to alienate even one of them.

"Sorry to put you through that," I said to Chandra when we broke away and moved on to the next grower.

"I'm a Hindu in exile. You're an American on a mission, Leon. Every man has a right to join a club that will accept him, including that hardheaded Franz, don't you think?"

The next grower was more welcoming. He greeted Chandra with a warm hug, then took my hands in his to greet me. His weren't rough farmer's hands like Franz's, but more like mine. He ran a different operation, bigger, more dependent on equipment than on manpower. This man seemed proud to show us a new design of grape picking-machine imported from Italy, which was being serviced by his hired hand,

We moved to his living room, where his wife served us a Cabernet Sauvignon of a label other than ours. Within a couple of minutes he began to query me about Drakenstein's expansion.

"Mr. Cooper, rumor has it that you're the man behind the beautiful new Gazelle beer plant. Congratulations," the farmer said.

"Actually, I can't take credit because I'm part of a team."

"Mr. Cooper, you're the lead horse, aren't you? You don't have to tell me, but since Chateau's been buying grapes from us for many years, I'd like to be sure you plan to continue."

"Continue what?" Chandra asked, as if he hadn't heard this question dozens of times since our expansion.

"Continue with your grape wines, or do you plan to sell that part of your business?"

"Where did you get that idea, Heinrich?"

"It's not my idea, but obvious to everyone in wine country, more so since Mr. Cooper come from America to work with Mr. Nichols. Are you planning to take a new direction away from wine, and leave producers like me behind?"

"Is that bothering you?" Chandra laughed. "Here's to a long and profitable relationship," he added, holding up his glass in a toast we all shared.

"Then I should forget everything I hear?" the grower asked.

"Hear what?" Chandra pressed him.

"I hear that Drakenstein has an American who make many changes. But now that I meet you, Mr. Cooper, I ask that we keep doing business together, even if you think some other growers give you the cheaper price than mine. You can find cheaper grapes than I grow, but never better. We do things different than America where your friends don't mean a thing. Do not be too quick to change the people who serve the Chateau for a long time."

I felt his suspicions were right about me, that perhaps I'd managed to muck up a long-established enterprise in the interest of efficiency. Before I could explain myself, Chandra spoke in my behalf.

"Heinrich, what would Drakenstein have without its good name? Have we not existed for two and a half centuries? Would we do anything to hurt our name? Think about it."

Chandra picked up his cell phone and made an outgoing call. "We'll be there in twenty minutes, sir. Sorry for the delay." To Heinrich he said, "Unfortunately, we're running late and must leave now. You understand." We said goodbye and escaped without further embarrassing and unadvisable explanations.

"That was a well-timed exit, Chandra."

"I trust we gave him confidence to know we're committed to the Chateau and the Chateau's committed to wine."

"Do you think he needed all that reassurance?" I asked.

"Are you asking whether I should let our suppliers set our agenda for us?" he asked. "If we lose our best suppliers, we are in trouble with our wines. That is why I had to reassure him the Chateau would carry on as long as he lives and well beyond. You die, I die, Rajesh dies, but our deeds live after we are gone and forgotten."

"If we look hard enough, we can find tragedy in any family," I said reflexively—foolishly. How could my troubles begin to approach the tragedy of Chandra's, whose son was presumed murdered?

"I thought it was a good idea for him to know that the Chateau will only grow stronger with your guidance."

First Chandra handled Heinrich, and now he seemed to be handling me, trying to calm me. I had good reason for my agitation, having been brought to Kruger's tough boys in the cafe with backup troops patrolling outside; the afternoon's visits to a hostile grower, then to an anxious one. I was uneasy about what to expect this evening when we'd catch up with Ted.

Ted was finishing his dinner when we arrived. "I expected you'd be here for a bite about now," he said, directing us to the places set for us.

"That wasn't necessary, sir," Chandra said, looking at the fish, still warm in their skillets on wooden plates that were served for us.

"I'll be the judge of that," Ted said.

"No, thanks. I'll pass," I said, waving off a coffee.

"Pass? You won't be poisoned at my table," he laughed. "My offering is uncontaminated, I assure you. As opposed to everything I've built here at the Chateau, which I've created for my people, not for my own vanity. Don't you agree, Leon?"

"Absolutely," I said, not knowing where his bizarre recital was leading.

"Leon, my people, from the lowest serving woman, to the most useful, such as Mr. Kassie, know I'm fair. I've had nothing to fear in this organization, at least to this point. So, what brings you here, Chandra? If it's some problem with Colin though, I'm not sure I care to mediate between him and anyone else."

"Nothing like that, Mr. Nichols," Chandra said. "We were of the same mind when we parted."

Ted rose and stood directly behind Chandra. "I know I can trust Mr. Cooper not to pass my opinions past these walls."

"Your secrets are safe with Mr. Cooper and with me, all the way to the grave, Mr. Nichols," Chandra assured him.

"I never rest, and I always require loyalty while you live in my vicinity," Ted said and drew back from Chandra with a smile and approached me. "Leon, as my consultant, could you advise me about Chandra? I've hired him for loyalty while he's here, not in the hereafter. Have we been paying him for more service than we need? Should we renegotiate with him?"

"As far as I'm concerned, he's indispensable," I said with a nod towards Chandra. "I'd be lost without him."

"But then what should I do with him when you're gone, Leon?"

Chandra looked at me to intervene. I saw he was upset; the joke had gone far enough.

"He goes with the territory, and he'll be your righthand man long after I'm gone. Since you made the original deal to take Mr. Kassie from his brewery, I should think you're bound to him, not just legally but as a point of honor."

Ted looked at me, then turned to Chandra and took his head in his hands and planted a loud kiss on his forehead. We all laughed, the tension broken. "A new family member? It could be worse, Kassie. You could be like Colin, I suppose."

"Ever since I joined forces with the Chateau," Chandra said, "Colin has worked full hours, diligently."

"Colin's very simple, gentlemen," Ted spoke softly. "His mind wanders, and he just goes along with it."

"Excuse me, I missed that," Chandra said.

"He may talk like a fool and act like a fool," Ted continued, loudly enough for us to both hear, "but don't get the wrong idea about him—he is a fool!"

"Sir, I'm very sorry my performance has disappointed you."

"I'm not talking about you, Chandra, but about Colin. What's your complaint about him? And don't give me gossip, because there's more than enough of that circulating around here."

"It's nothing personal, Mr. Nichols," Chandra said. "I try to get along with everyone. But when I discovered a seven-figure discrepancy at one of the brewpubs—"

"God help me, I have no time for Colin!"

"Yes, timing's everything, sir. With Alicia so much on everyone's mind, maybe we should postpone—"

Ted had pulled away from Chandra to talk to the black woman in the maid's uniform who'd been serving us. From what I could overhear, she seemed flustered that DeVilliers had arrived earlier than expected and that she had to keep him waiting outside. By the way Ted hustled Chandra out of the room, he placed a higher priority on meeting with DeVilliers, rather than get to the bottom of Chandra's complaint.

"Between you and me, Leon, there's no love lost between Colin and me," Ted said to me, once we were alone. "I would have found a replacement for him long ago, if he wasn't a family member I have no way of sacking."

"I just meant that it must be difficult to bring someone like Colin into any business, no matter how competent, him being a blood relative," I said.

"Make no mistake about it, there's no blood between us."

"I mean with Colin as your brother-in-law—"

"Enough, Leon, you have the Nichols family tree wrong!"

I'd been in South Africa for more than two years, and all the while he'd done his best to pile up sandbags to hold back the flow of information about the Nichols family! Ted said I don't know about his family tree, but only because he did a good job of hiding it, especially details of the arrangement Ted had made with Ighaam for protection in the townships. I didn't understand the payments Gazelle paid to expand business into dangerous markets, but that was one area I didn't want details. Nor did I want to pursue those shortfalls Chandra discovered in Wandi Dadla's books, especially if they weren't caused by pilferage by Colin, but rather used to pay the network of protectors authorized by Ted himself!

"Then maybe you can set me straight," I said.

"Let's just say, these discrepancies you are so anxious to push under my nose—"

"Wait a minute, Ted," I interrupted. "It's Chandra who came here to complain about Colin, not me. I don't care what Colin is to you!"

"Well, we both better care if he's dealing from under the deck."

"Let me make this clear, Ted, I may have suspicions, but it's Chandra who has the numbers."

"To the contrary, to accommodate Amanda's wishes I've stayed out of Colin's way, so long as he performed his duties at the Chateau. For a man who lives by the numbers you'd think he would have paid closer attention to his records. Good thing somebody caught him. From what news you've brought me, he's not playing by my rules. Don't you think it's time to put him out of the game for everyone's good?"

"If you're judging him in advance, you're probably misjudging him."

"Colin—you want to know about him? Do you ever notice how if he doesn't have papers to shuffle, he rubs his hands on his desk? That's because he has itchy palms!"

"If putting him out of the game means firing him, I don't think—"

"That's right, Leon, you're not thinking, so let me tell you as simply as I can about his game. When Colin lays his cards on the table, it's a good idea to count them! If he's cheating, we're at least going to warn him!"

Ted wasn't a man who suffered fools gladly, nor tolerated his subordinates to challenge him. But he needed to realize the situation had changed since Cooper bought into this enterprise. He was no longer the sole master of this kingdom with the final veto. A few minutes earlier, he sounded ready to fire Colin, but he backed away from that plan. Now he appeared satisfied to warn him, rather than to use Chandra's figures to eliminate him altogether. But in the end, he'd consented to keeping the longstanding truce between him and his brother-in-law, or however they might be related. There was nothing to be gained by talking about him anymore.

"Now what else was so bloody important that I had to shoehorn you in before DeVilliers and the gang?"

"You mean the Ighaam Arendse gang?" I asked.

"No! They've never set foot on Chateau property, and we never have and never will do business with gangsters! Don't talk to me about those gangsters!"

"Right, a case of mistaken identity," I agreed, the easiest course of action for the moment. "Okay, let's forget about our own gangster for a moment, and instead consider Ozeer, the gangster Ighaam would love to liquidate, the one who likes to set fires to our buildings and terrorize our people."

"When you have solid proof, show me," Ted said evasively.

"Yes, for now we'll forget about Ozeer, as we did about the man with the itchy palms. But getting back to Ighaam, you know he can be of great use to us, especially now that we're compelled to fight the thugs on two fronts, from what Otto Kruger tells me."

"Kruger, a man of promise—broken promise! Does he know anything I should know?"

"I'm confused. What has Kruger promised he couldn't deliver? Do you distrust him because you think he's scheming to get a piece of Werner-Nichols?"

"Is this speculation necessary in front of the help,

Leon?" he asked when he noticed the maid inside the door trying to get his attention. He sent her off with a message to DeVilliers that he'd be done in ten minutes, then led me to the dark library. "This room is more secure," he said, closing the doors. "Kruger has carved out his career by first-class chiseling. But we're running out of time. What has he told you about two fronts?"

"There's the battle against Ozeer's forces and the battle against the ex-convicts at Pollsmoor Prison, the ones making the extortion demands."

"Why do you think it's the Pollsmoor ex-convicts behind this, and not the jailed convicts as well, Leon? South Africa has prison walls that are porous. It's the guards who are well paid by the convicts and assist in their jailbreaks all the time."

Though he'd have me believe he didn't respect Kruger's opinion, he couldn't help wanting to know what it was, if only to discredit it. "Is there anything else you and Kruger think I should know?"

"Simply how to use better logistics and strategy to get Alicia back, that's all." Just as Chandra and I had done in our confrontation with Colin, I'd reached the strategic time to remain quiet and engage him with no more than my gaze.

"Kruger's too puffed up to remember Napoleon is now a cake."

"That was quite clever, Ted."

"You think so, Leon? Then I'll be serious. Kruger may think he's Napoleon because he has a few military and paramilitary friends who are loyal to him. But my sources tell me he and his security guard have been snooping around police stations, asking questions about

Alicia, as if he were her husband and had the right to know the details of her abduction. To make matters worse, he's been hinting that he might be willing to pay for her return—ransom, in other words! What do you think of Kruger now?"

"For trying to help find Alicia while there's still time?"

"No, we're short on time, and speaking of him is wasting it!"

He looked through his window in the twilight across the Chateau's grape arbors toward the Drakenstein Mountains, his holdings and beyond. He walked around his leather armchair, his hand shoved into his waistband, a Napoleonic pose, though he dismissed Kruger for his Napoleonic paramilitary entourage. Rather than risk laughing at the irony, I looked away so I wouldn't give myself away. My time was short, so I had to make Kruger's case succinctly, before it was too late.

"There, that's where you'll find Alicia!" I said. On the side table, I spread out the maps entrusted to me by Kruger, the ones with the sequential satellite fixes from the beacon carried in the stolen automobile. I saved for last the one satellite man drew freehand for Sunitha and me, the one showing the Botswana-South Africa frontier.

"What is this? Otto's best ten guesses?" he said, dropping the maps one by one at his feet after inspecting them.

"No, Ted, you're one-tenth right. You're looking at one very educated guess with no satellite fix, based on his intelligence, as well as nine with satellite fixes. The nine are accurate to within fifty yards, no guesswork involved. You see, his BMW that Alicia was borrowing had a transmitter and he's been able to follow her. I also believe they've somehow managed to bug a couple more vehicles."

"If the kidnappers have been on the move for days, why should we conclude they've suddenly stopped, based on these past-dated maps. Isn't it possible her car's in one place and Alicia's in another?" His questions seemed logical, questions that hadn't occurred to me.

"A dangerous gift," Ted continued, "that car she took from Kruger, a Trojan horse. First, he fools her into believing he's a sincere suitor, then he ups the ante, as you gambling Yanks would say. He no doubt thinks he can outsmart me through planting these wild ideas in your—my consultant's head. I see how you admire Kruger as intelligent—God help you—though he's a man with designs on not only the Chateau, but on Alicia herself!"

"Ted, with all due respect, we don't have time for your suspicions! Can't you see, if Kruger's brought any kind of gift, it may be the gift of your daughter's life! You better take a closer look at his suggested rendez-vous point and follow it!"

"No one talks to me like that!" Ted shouted, then returned to the satellite maps, reviewing them more carefully this time. "Where are you going?" he asked as I was picking up the maps from the floor.

I had to resist my urge to answer him. If I were to challenge him, I might push him to act stupidly just to defy me. "I'm going to find Chandra so he can take me home. It's obvious, Ted, that you don't want me at your meeting to pass along Kruger's findings, which you aren't taking seriously," I then eased from his hand Kruger's speculative map of the proposed capture in Botswana, marked with circles and crosses like the strategy of a sports match.

"Keep in mind I never said Kruger wasn't a clever character."

A double negative equals a positive, a positive statement about Kruger. That sounded to me as if he didn't have that much confidence in his own alternate plans, whatever they were, now that he was ready to consider Kruger's rescue plan laid out before him. Ted looked at me deliberately for my reaction to his low-key turnaround, in the form of his unexpected bit of praise for Kruger. I read his silence as a concession.

"Otto calls his security and rescue system Stop Jack," I said, "and I think it's going to prove Alicia's real guardian angel!"

"He's a clever salesman, isn't he?" Ted asked, neither praising nor insulting him.

"I would hate to be treated like a bothersome salesman. I would have preferred to have him here rather than myself. If only you could trust that he simply wants to show you how we can stop the gangsters, convicts, kidnappers—the whole lot of them—dead in their tracks!"

"Dead would be best!" Ted shouted.

The thought of the death of the abductors obviously excited Ted. He shook my hand, which I took as an agreement to pursue Kruger's plan to recapture Alicia, the full details of which I didn't know. Before he changed his mind, I left with Chandra, who had been entertaining DeVilliers prior to his appointment with Ted.

Driving back to Rondebosch, I recounted the day's work: the meeting with Kruger's forces, visits to two farms to handle complaints, then confronting Colin and his wife with their suspicious figures, then finally getting Ted to look at Kruger's commando strategy. It had been a productive day. My contentment was short-lived though, because when Chandra dropped me at my flat, Sunitha was gone, with no note of explanation!

Maybe that was part of her plan, allowing me to feel what it's like to live with her gone, to test my devotion to her. A cruel game, if that's what it was, one I was not about to break by trying to second guess her itinerary and wasting time searching after her. That left me with a lonely hole in my life, and I had looked to fill it by making extra appointments into the evening. A couple of nights later, expecting to return to my empty flat, I was surprised to see Chandra at my dining room table, sipping a Chardonnay, which the second grower Heinrich had produced himself and given us as a gift. He was drinking with Sunitha!

"This is quite good, Leon, better than the Chateau's. It seems if you really wanted to help this grower Fritz, you'd show him how to market his own grapes rather than supply us."

"Sunitha, I've missed you," I blurted. "I really don't want to speak business with you now though."

"Then you and Chandra should not have left me behind the evening you saw Mr. Nichols, though I understand why you didn't want your Indian girlfriend near him and his circle."

"So where did you vanish?"

"If I were to vanish, I'd be nowhere, at least nowhere visible to your eyes. Since you weren't available, I went to speak with Aunt Giri."

"Speak to her about what?" I asked.

"I'll tell you about my meeting with her, if you'll tell me about your meeting with the strong men." With a nod I agreed to her exchange. "I spoke to Aunt Giri for your sake. In case I weren't on hand to help you in the future, if trouble were to come your way, I needed to show her how she might be able to guide you, if you choose to speak with her again."

"Is there something in store for me that I should know about?"

"It's not entirely clear, and I don't know whether I'll be directly involved, or whether instead you'll leave me behind again as you and Chandra did to confer with your council of warriors."

"I hope you're not one of the current cohort of women who feel superior to all men who they regard as dangerous brutes. Are you?"

"By now you should know, Leon, that I have no such pride. Warriors, since they lived in caves, thought it bad luck to have a woman present while they made their battle plans. Now you must tell me what exactly happened."

She still hadn't told me why she'd involved Aunt Giri, but Sunitha must have been discussing my personal business with her. If that was the case, then I couldn't predict how far my confidences might travel and figured I probably shouldn't tell her what first happened with Kruger. Not unless she told me what might be coming my way.

"Not now," I said.

"I should have told you I was leaving and why, but I didn't know myself. I had to get away to think."

"Think? What about?"

"About how to make a peace with Aunt Giri. I now see

it was at the expense of peace with you, that right now you're not quite trusting me."

She sensed that I had a great deal on my mind, now that Chandra safely redelivered her and left. Our lovemaking was strong and trusting, powerful enough for me to forget about my problems. It occurred to me that lovemaking wasn't just the result of youthful hormones, but strangely therapeutic, ever since our lives first intersected. Could that magic continue indefinitely?

As we were rested in each other's arms, between consciousness and sleep, I recalled faces of women I'd known back home, memories from the past. Sunitha was the present, and far more devoted to me than any one of them ever was.

"I feel you have someone on your mind, other than me," she murmured.

There was no hiding from her, though she was not always on target with her interpretations of my thoughts. Women may cross my mind, but I was unable to remember a single one's name! "I've forgotten them all," I truthfully reported.

I willed myself to blank out their faces and replaced them with an image of Sunitha as a palace dancer with harem pants and jangling brass bells. As our session heated up once more, she responded to my pledge of devotion to her, showing me again that I could never find a better lover. If there were bounds to our trust, we needed to overcome them.

The next night after dinner, Sunitha and I were sitting in the living room reading. Her book was *The God of Small Things*, an Indian novel on a couple breaking the Brahmin-untouchable taboo against mixing. Mine was a journal by the nineteenth century explorer Robert Scott, who died trekking to the South Pole. In a way we were looking for the same thing: she, a way to escape her Indian community; myself, escape on a rigorous mission to prove my worth.

"Is this for a special occasion?" I asked when I looked at the label of the fine port wine she was serving, fifteen years old and imported from Spain.

"One of Mr. Nichols' favorites, which he gave to Chandra to try. I wanted to drink something like what you and the warriors might have been sipping during your meeting."

"They had to make some sober decisions, so they weren't drinking," I said, not eager to speak with her about what was decided, since I wasn't sure myself. "By the way, did you know Frederick DeVilliers dropped in on Ted at the Chateau, asking for you?"

"Of course I do, Leon. Mr. DeVilliers did so as a special favor to me for pulling his son away from the fire. Did he get on with you warriors?"

Before she spoke of the meeting with Kruger's fighters as warriors. Now she spoke of today's appointment with Ted, DeVilliers, Chandra, and me as another meeting of warriors. But what else should these strong and brave men do other than fight for Alicia's life?

"I hate to disappoint you, but it was largely a social visit. Chandra entertained our banker friend by playing ping pong with him, while waiting to speak to Ted and me."

"Table tennis?"

"Several games, almost a tournament. That was after we made sure Ted knew about the short funds at Wandi

Dadla's. Afterward Chandra entertained Frederick while I was brought Ted up to speed with Kruger's plan for retaking Alicia. In the meantime, I was with Ted while he was changing into his old uniform."

"Uniform?" she echoed. I had confused her.

"Khaki fatigues. Did you know he was once a commando? His fatigues were a bit tight after so many years of good living and good eating. DeVilliers wanted me to play with him, but I don't like to play in a game in which I can't make a good showing."

"The warmup games didn't matter, so much as the meeting."

"Which meeting, the visits with the wine growers, the late afternoon one with Colin and his wife for Chandra to check his suspicious figures, the dinnertime one with Ted and DeVilliers with table tennis in-between, or the earlier meeting with Kruger's warriors?"

"Yes, tell me everything, starting with what Kruger said."

"I was left with many questions in my own mind, but I've told you pretty much everything of importance."

She studied my face for a long time before she came to me and knelt before me. "I withhold nothing from you," she said.

Maybe she believed that, but certainly she could have told me more about her meeting with Aunt Giri. They discussed my fate, what I could expect ahead, and I was curious about the details. Perhaps she'd tell me soon and was simply waiting for the right time.

"I suspect you have a window into the future, especially mine,"

"I simply take the best ideas that come my way. But

now, you are peeved because I won't raise the shade from that window for you."

"The window looking out to my own future?"

"I'm reluctant to tell you what you may expect. The man who depends least upon tomorrow goes to meet tomorrow most happily."

Whether her wisdom was hers alone or borrowed, I didn't know. Either way, I felt I'd do well to heed her, since she had predicted both the arson against Rajesh, and the fire from which she rescued the DeVilliers boy. She was telling me I should plan on meeting with adversity without the benefit of her predictions, that I might go away happily blind to the future.

Whatever her reasons, neither would she advise me what course she thought Alicia's rescue mission might take. More unsettling, after work she would spend more and more hours in her room alone with Brahma, chanting prayers I could hear through her closed door. She said she was praying for Alicia, she said one evening when I asked who the subject of her prayers was. And she was praying especially hard for me, she added.

For me to be comfortable staying behind in Cape Town, it was essential to have good information about the rescue operation. The Reverend Dieter DuToit, Ted's old buddy from his commando days, was my best source. For a few days he telephoned me every morning with reports from the field. But every time I specifically asked DuToit for the current location of the mission, he'd refuse, afraid our calls would be intercepted by the enemy. I wondered whether I was being appeased with just a smattering of information.

Instead of continuing to depend on DuToit for their

progress, I had more confidence relying on satellite man for information. He was placed in charge of the Oasis Security office while Kruger and Schmidt were off on the campaign against Ozeer's forces. When I asked satellite man his age, he said he ran into trouble all the time for appearing so juvenile, that he was really twenty-five. No matter, he was proving to be a valuable confidant, presenting me not only with satellite maps, updated twice a day, but also with actual military satellite photos. They had such detail I could distinguish the models of vehicles in both Ozeer's gang and in Ted's and Kruger's combined forces trailing them ever northward.

"This is terrible, knowing where Alicia is without saving her!"

"What do you think they should do then?"

"Get Alicia now!"

"But, Mr. Cooper, they're in the middle of nowhere, just outside the Kalahari Desert. Between you and me, it wouldn't do much good to take them down now. When they move westward and north and cross the border to Gaborone on the Botswana side to link up with friendly forces, that will make the trip more worthwhile and allow them to take down a lot more bad men at once in a classic pincer move."

Evidently Alicia was regarded as little more than the winner's trophy of this game. Both Kruger, his fiancé Alicia and Ted, her father, were playing for a bigger haul of criminals than if they struck now. I didn't know if they and their collection of commandos and police had struck some kind of deal with the Botswana authorities to take out as many of the gang as possible. Apparently, they were now waiting to fill their net, even though Alicia was thrashing around in the water, close to going under for the final time! I was getting into my car and about to drive away, but satellite man followed me and continued talking to me.

"It must be tough, wondering" he said standing outside my car door, "and waiting so long for someone you really care about. If we do find her, don't you think she'll make a pretty bride for my father? Have you always liked blonde women like her, Mr. Cooper?"

When the phone rang, he answered it, and I took the opportunity to get moving. But I heard banging. Satellite man was pounding on the trunk, and before I could stop, he opened the passenger door.

"This is yours, Mr. Cooper," he said, handing me my cell phone. "I wouldn't have noticed but it was ringing. I told her to try again in a couple of minutes if I could catch you."

"I must have more on my mind than I realized. Thanks," I said, tucking it into my pocket.

"Well, are you going to answer it?" he asked the moment it began ringing again. "I believe it's your American girlfriend Bernice. I think she really wants to talk to you, Mr. Cooper to make sure you're not in danger, or else she just misses you."

"I'll be in touch the same time tomorrow," I said to satellite man standing outside the car. I wanted to roll up the window, but didn't want to alienate the source of the invaluable satellite maps.

"Only if you think I may still be of use to you, Mr. Cooper," he said mysteriously, leaving without being asked.

I waited to speak to her until Oasis Security and satellite

man were well behind me. "Bernie, if you come to South Africa, I could arrange a date with the young man you just spoke with. He likes the sound of your voice. So do I, but I wonder what's the news from St. Louis?"

"In a word—money."

I tried not to talk about personal finances with those who had much more or much less than me, but I had no time for protocol, since our phone link could drop at any minute.

"Henry Ford said, 'Money's like an arm or a leg. If you don't use it, you lose it.'"

"I don't drive a Ford, so it doesn't matter what Mr. Ford thinks about money," she said, misunderstanding me. "But confidentially, I am concerned about your money for South Africa drying up. Your brother will be notifying you that our bank wants to reduce its South Africa exposure. The truth is that he's turning back the spigot. Expect a drought, Mr. Cooper!"

"Another thing about money, Bernie; money talks, but it doesn't always make sense. If I run out of money, I'll take up collections in churches! Thanks for the warning! Be good. Don't forget to pray for me."

Maybe I shouldn't have made a joke to a churchgoing, religious Methodist like Bernice, who believed I might allow Harry to kill my project and take me down in the process! I may have downplayed Harry's latest action against me, but I was plenty worried Harry was working to cut off money beyond the initial amount pledged. No way I was going to allow Harry to hold me back, now that we were overcoming friction and finally building momentum would be grossing $90 million. Harry didn't understand that I'd primed the well, and we ought to keep pumping! I'd have to let the other board members know that if Cooper didn't want to commit to the continuing expansion, I had DeVilliers in our corner, ready and able to finance our already successful expansion. Frederick might prove be the key to the survival of this project and of myself as well!

Back at the flat, I heard Sunitha speaking a language I didn't understand. When I heard my name, I realized she'd been praying for me before the Brahma as promised. I was honored to be uppermost in her thoughts and perhaps under her protection. I could see how worry had taken its toll on her, and in my own case, revealing itself in my bad dreams. The two of us were waiting for Alicia to come back to us, not knowing whether dead or alive. Alicia's imminent loss had to be worse for Sunitha, after presumably losing Rajesh to the same Ozeer gang a few months back. It occurred to me it might be a good idea to organize a real memorial service for Rajesh in a church of her choice to help her with closure—before rather than after having to deal with bad news I was expecting about Alicia.

She needed a break, so I brought her into the living room where we sat facing each other.

"Now that you've spoken to the ascendant master, you can speak to me."

She looked at her watch. "Are you done speaking to your assistant or lady friend, or whatever she is, about the withdrawal of your brother's support?"

"It's not that dire," I said, though I wasn't quite sure. "But I'm far more concerned about what problem you're facing, Sunitha."

"Not just me, but something we may be facing together."

She seemed ready to share what was on her mind, but I refrained from asking her more about this prediction, should it become a self-fulfilling prophecy. Nor did I care to explain my vigilant American secretary, as I had for satellite man.

I feared if we stayed in my flat much longer, more gloominess would overcome us. If I could get her away from her mournful shrine, that might improve both our states of mind. I didn't want to spend another evening with her in the confines of the flat with her quiet tears and our troublesome dreams. I decided to take her away from Cape Town.

It was her country, so where we would spend our retreat was her choice. She had me drive north. She wanted to get further away and for longer than I had in mind, but I followed her lead without questioning it. All I asked was that we stop to make a calls to Chandra and a few others to make sure they'd know not to expect me for a few days and to notify me only for an emergency. By late evening we stopped at a motel familiar to her. I was careful to avoid asking her whether she had been there with Rajesh.

At first light she was eager to travel again. We had been on the road a couple of hours the next day, and were eating breakfast when I admitted, "I have no idea where we're going."

"We're at the edge of the Karoo. I've only been here a couple of times, but with you I'm sure it will be more special. This is the furthest from Cape Town I've ever been."

During the day the terrain became progressively drier and the villages further apart. "This is a vast desert!" I said when we hadn't met another vehicle for a quarter hour. "Where on God's earth are you taking me anyway?"

Late in the afternoon with the temperature over 100°, we arrived at a town on the edge of the Karoo Desert, Oudtshoorn. "You can stop here," she announced as we approached the Nel Museum. Inside the museum we saw collections of weapons, shells, old bottles, and other antiques. The main exhibit consisted of Victorian era ostrich feather ladies' fashions, housed in rooms of sumptuous drapes, flocked wallpaper, and overstuffed furniture.

"This is really our destination?" I asked once we finished touring the museum.

"Our first one. Did you know this ostrich palace was one of the first houses here to have indoor plumbing and electricity?"

After dinner I found a fine looking, turn-of-the-century house converted to a lodge. "This is beautiful. We can stay here tonight."

"I'd rather not stay in someone's house, rubbing elbows with the proprietor. What if he doesn't like me? Can we find a bigger, more private place? A room out of the way would be best."

I wasn't sure about the reason for her hesitation, but when I drove to a large modern hotel, she wanted me to drive the car to the side, out of view of the lobby and the clerk. I completed registering and parked in front of our rearmost room and brought in the bags while she stayed inside.

"I had no idea you are so shy," I said to her once we unpacked.

"This isn't like Cape Town where there are a lot of dark people. Here it's pretty much the blacks and the

Afrikaners, and they don't associate very much, in case you didn't notice. I was afraid they'd claim they had no rooms if they saw me with you."

I didn't know what to say, so I took her in my arms. "That's not necessary," she said, pulling away from me. I got up and turned on the news, but she came behind me. "Isn't that why we're here, to get away from bad news?"

"That wasn't the only reason," I said, and led her back to the bed and without resorting to words to assure her how much I valued her.

The next morning, we drove through rocky and barren country up a steep zig-zagging set of switchbacks to the summit of Swartberg Pass.

"First you brought me up Paarl Mountain to meet the Reverend. Now we're on another mountain, this one above a severe desert."

"This is the route the Afrikaners took in the nine-teenth century with their ox-drawn wagons on their trek to the interior to get away from the English. This road was built by convicts, with some of them buried in the tarmac. I wanted to see it just once with you before you move on. Are you impressed with our second destination? How would you like to end your days buried under that road like the uncompliant convicts? No more than you'd care to be buried with me?"

A startling question, impossible to answer. Was she really asking me how much longer I intended to stay with her? I wanted to reassure her and speak about forthcoming plans, but I held back speculations on our uncertain future, which most likely wouldn't make either of us feel any better. For the next stop there was a cool interlude at the Cango Caves. Its rooms of stalactites and stalagmites were a welcome relief from the intense desert heat. We moved on to an isolated homestead that farmed ostriches. It was meant for tourists, such as we'd become that day, and in a holiday spirit and we mounted a couple of the huge birds and rode them.

"Did that amuse you?" she asked at lunch.

"It was good to hear you laugh, riding the ostrich like a pony."

"Aren't we very clever at creating new beasts of burden?"

Another sober question I wasn't prepared to answer. We'd come many hours on this tour, undertaken to make us leave behind our preoccupations. I'd had enough sightseeing and driving and wanted to call it a day and return to the hotel. But since I hadn't yet completely succeeded in cheering her up, I pressed on with our journey, moving towards the capital of ostrich country, Oudtshoorn.

In the afternoon we toured several in-town feather palaces. By dinnertime we were tired, but not tired enough to retire to the room, where I feared her gloomy thoughts would overtake her again. I decided to cap the evening with a dinner of ostrich steaks, then a movie, a strange Afrikaner film with English titles about an itinerant performer ruined by the loss of the railroad station, droughts, storms and isolation.

"I took you to the wrong movie, Sunitha, too depressing," I said, back in our room.

"Not at all. They overcame their troubles, as I must do. Don't you think we should admire the Boer farmers for their toughness?"

I wasn't thinking about Boers, but about Sunitha,

and didn't know what to make of her sudden flip-flop. Maybe I'd been focusing too much on her persistent sadness, rather than on her increasing bravery. When we first arrived here she was afraid to be seen by any Afrikaans-speaking person. Overnight she'd apparently overcome her ancestral fear of Boer overseers and hadn't been afraid to be seen with me. Coming back to the motel, she didn't have to scan the entire parking lot before exiting the car and entering the motel room.

"I'll never fully understand how the Boers or the other factions in this country think, but I do know something about you, Sunitha."

"Really?" she asked with a playful smile. She signaled me to sit on the bed beside her.

"I know that you are tougher than your enemies."

"You too, Leon."

"Then we must be a matched pair," I said.

"Thank you for saying so, but I hope you aren't saying that to boost my spirits."

"Not at all Sunitha. I believe in you... and us," I said.

She smiled broadly, drew me to her for a long kiss. She pulled back, lifted her blouse over her head, then rose to remove her skirt.

"Do you believe together we're stronger than the people who don't wish us well?" she asked as we lay side-by-side.

"Can you doubt that?" I in turn asked.

I posed the question to reassure her of our bond. I hoped we weren't together simply as war buddies, that our association was based on more than adversity.

"Doubt is the curse of those without belief. Don't ever doubt my devotion to you, Leon, promise me?"

CHAPTER 19
BACINI'S CAFÉ

The night after we returned to Rondebosch, Sunitha retired early. A few minutes later, still asleep, I heard her laugh to herself, making me believe our morale-boosting trip had some success. But when I heard her chanting before her Brahma, I knew she hadn't left her sorrows very far behind.

Shortly after dropping off to sleep, my own dreams returned. This time I dreamed I was suspended over a forbidding, unknown land. In an instant I dropped to earth. At first I thought it was a church bell tolling for me, but the ring was too weak, too high pitched. It was my cell phone. By the third ring Sunitha handed it to me.

"Am I catching you at a bad time?" I asked.

"It depends on what you have to tell me, Bernie. You sound like you're in a cave, so please speak quickly before I lose you," I moved to get up, but Sunitha play-fully grabbed me by the waist and wrestled me backwards. We laughed as I landed on top of her.

"I hear your lady friend nearby. I hope I haven't awakened you."

"Bernice, you know my time is eight hours later than your time. Let me guess—you're calling me at dinner

time, since it's two in the morning here! I trust you
have an important reason."

"It's about your brother again. He'll be coming over
to Africa to take you on a safari. You must have a lot
of lions there."

"Tell him to stay at home because we have no animals
here, except for some aggressive baboons who like to
steal food out of cars on roadside turnoffs and who are
so bold they will grab the sandwich out of your hand."

"Really?"

"Yes, now why don't you tell me the real reason you
called me."

"About your other lady friend, Alicia Nichols—they've
found her."

I was overjoyed and wanted to know all the details,
but not with Sunitha next to me. There was no need
to raise her hopes, not until I could confirm that her
retrieval wasn't a rumor.

"You've been too busy to read a newspaper? Then you
couldn't have seen the photos of Ozeer's Last Stand."

"Is that what the newspapers called it, in honor of
Custer's Last Stand?"

"In their raid there was little honor, and no shortage
of bodies oozing life."

She was an ocean away, yet she seemed to know more
than I did about the capture I'd been supporting! She
seemed to have the idea I was living in a frontier amid
wild animals, rather than in urban zones of undeclared
but continuous raids and counterraids. She had read a
wire service generated report of a bloody ambush, but
she wasn't telling me straightaway whether Alicia got
caught in the crossfire. I couldn't wait to get my own

local newspaper. Patiently I coaxed from her what she remembered from the article.

"No shortage?" I asked, careful to choose my descriptive words so as not to alarm Sunitha. "What did they show in particular?"

"They're still sorting out who was Botswanan, who was South African, and who were the rogue Botswana paramilitary helping the drug gang. Twenty or thirty of them were reported dead. The gangster chief got away. What's his name?"

"Ozeer, is that who you mean?"

"It says Ozeer escaped with half a dozen of his best men further into Botswana, where Ted Nichols and his men decided not to give chase."

This didn't sound right! Ted, like Kruger, might have been able to influence the police and the soldiers they were accompanying, but beyond that, most likely they could have been the ones to give the final orders to the police and paramilitary on the recapture mission. But whoever had decided against pushing the gangsters further into the interior of Botswana, on second consideration, that might have been a smart political decision, one that would avoid the appearance of an invasion across the frontier.

"And about the captive?" I asked just loud enough to make myself heard by Bernice.

"What about her? Do you want me to offer consolation, or what?"

"For what!" I asked, a bit louder than I intended.

"She was pretty badly bruised and scratched."

"Great, just a few bruises and scratches?" I repeated, relieved that she was alive.

"Have you no sympathy in your heart, Mr. Cooper?" Bernie had misunderstood me and was exhausting my patience.

"I couldn't hear that," I said, muffling the phone with my hand. "Bad connection."

It was 3 A.M., and I managed to rouse satellite man from his sleep, hoping to find out the truth, or at least what he knew. Sunitha had tears streaming down her cheeks. I pulled her toward me.

"I know you've been talking about Alicia."

"But do you also know the worst may be behind her?"

"That she's jumped over her hurdle, yes," she said cryptically.

"Then why be so glum?"

"Because I'm concerned for her, as well as for you, Leon, and for us."

I reassured her again, but when I touched her lips, she wasn't responding, which was a reversal from her warm kisses earlier in the evening.

In the wake of the good news of Alicia's rescue, we needed to get to Chandra, since we each trusted him more than anyone else. I spent most of the next morning trying to telephone him, and when I finally spoke to him, I confirmed that there had to be some truth to Bernice's story.

Alicia had arrived back in Cape Town the previous day and was reported to be well-rested with no visible marks on her. Over the next few days she was ready to meet with well-wishers eager to greet her. Ted organized a welcome-home party at the Chateau for primarily his military associates who had traveled with him and Kruger to the northern frontier. I was also invited, as were the wives and girlfriends of the rescuers and those closest to the Nichols family, including the LeRouxs and the DeVilliers. Sunitha didn't think she belonged anywhere near that wealthy crowd. For my part, I thought I should have been notified immediately of Alicia's return and invited to the reception sooner. I called Ted to congratulate him on his successful mission and let him know we couldn't make it to his party on such short notice that evening.

There was another reception that Chandra and Hassan were organizing for the next afternoon which we would attend instead. It was to be held at a restaurant in Camp's Bay, with mostly ordinary wage-earning people as guests, an atmosphere more to Sunitha's liking. But by noontime she was having second thoughts about attending even this alternate homecoming party.

"You can't abandon me now," I said, taking her hands and pulling her up from her chair. "It would help me a great deal if you would appear with me, if only to introduce me to these strangers."

"Is that what this is all about, how we appear together? My problem is that I don't see the point of making an appearance if we won't be together afterwards."

"You're speaking in riddles again," I said impatiently. "I don't see how we can refuse to show up at either reception, especially since Alicia's been so much on our minds."

"Well, if it means that much to you," she said and hugged me, trembling, "I'll be with you, no matter what, Leon."

As the crow flies, it was a short distance from

Rondebosch to Camp's Bay, but the route we were driving didn't seem short. It took us on roads that wound through serpentine passes between huge Table Mountain on one side and Devil's Peak, and Signal Hill on the other. We were then descending towards Camp's Bay in a sharp and narrow switchback, when a couple of motorcycles zoomed by us. To avoid colliding with them, I slammed on my brakes, which threw my car into a skid! We came to a stop in the gravel at the edge of the road, with no guardrail to keep us from sliding off the mountain. I must have collided with one of the motorcycles! My heart was beating violently, and I started down the mountain to get away from them.

"Stop! We must go back to see how badly that poor man's hurt," she whispered, her fists curled up in her lap, obviously shaken as she looked out her window at the steep drop we barely avoided.

"They could have killed us! You don't stop for strangers in South Africa!"

"We must, in case this one needs to go to the hospital. I won't allow you to leave him!"

I wasn't my brother's keeper, and certainly not responsible for a rider that I'd already saved by swerving out of his out-of-control path, nearly forcing Sunitha and me to fly off the road to our deaths. I agreed with her, though it was the right thing to at least offer help. Reluctantly, I backed up and approached his uninjured riding buddy. He turned away from me to put on a helmet identical to the one the injured man was wearing. In a final step to conceal his identity, he dropped his black visor over his face. In my quick glimpse of him I could tell that he, like his buddy, had a dark skin;

the one on the ground almost black, and the other one in the range of coloured.

"Are you going to stand there, or are you going to help me?" the injured man asked. I didn't grab the motorcycle in the right place, and it was heavier than I realized, so on our first attempt to right it, we dropped it back onto its side.

"Damn it, if you keep bashing my motorcycle," he slightly injured man said, still sitting on the ground, "the panel beaters will charge plenty to fix her up!" His voice sounded familiar, but with so many new people I met every week, I couldn't quite place it.

"Next time why don't you get yourself a Japanese bike," the uninjured rider suggested, "instead of such a bloody heavy BMW that couldn't get you out of Mr. Charlie's way!" After the second attempt the two of us finally brought it onto its wheels.

The biker I struck raised his visor, and sniffed the gasoline tank. Sunitha saw he was okay, and began tooting the horn of the car. She waved to get me away from them, but I chose to take my time rather than show them how uneasy they were making us feel.

"No bones broken, and no hole in your gas tank. Now if your engine turns over, this is your lucky day," I said.

I had nothing more to say to these blokes. By this time Sunitha was standing behind me, with a firm grip on my hand, pulling me backward to the car. We continued toward Camp's Bay on the winding road for a few minutes, until we once again heard the roar of motorcycle engines closing on us.

"If they strike us again, this time we must stay on course," she whispered.

Coming into another sharp bend, the bikers overtook our car, barely missing us. Sunitha was looking straight ahead, as if in a trance, and trembling.

Ten minutes later I parked on the main street of Camp's Bay, the businesses on one side, and the beach and ocean on the other side. "Journey's end," I said. "Now let's find the restaurant before the party's over."

"Okay, this way," she said, firmly intertwining her arm in mine, and led me through a crowd of people moving between the beach and the stores and restaurants.

"They're back," she said, nodding to the men on the motorcycles, now without helmets. "The one who tried to run us off the road is Molefe, a member of Ozeer's gang they left behind in Cape Town rather than bring to Botswana. He's a friend of Mafumo, someone who doesn't mean you well."

If he really was a gangster and the collision on the mountain wasn't an accident, why were they in town with us? What else did they intend to do that day? If we were their target, why did they rush away from us after the collision? I wanted to get away from them, but if we did, what other mischief might they attempt that afternoon?

Instead of running away from Molefe and his pal though, we followed them to where they shielded themselves from view of the street behind a twenty-foot mobile sign on a trailer, which was hitched to a small truck. They had spread a couple of camouflage motorcycle rain covers so the motorcycles were hidden from the pedestrians' view.

"I don't think you're in the mood for this party," I

suggested. "I can take you home now if you're as shaky as you appear."

I took her hand, which was cold, though it was a hot day, and tried to lead her towards the car, but she wasn't following me.

"Leon, I sensed Rajesh was in grave danger before he was taken, yet didn't know what to do. I believe you sense the danger about us right now, as I do."

"Of course," I said, not sure to what I was agreeing. "If you're not ready to confront bad men again, I completely understand. If you want to go somewhere other than Alicia's homecoming party and meet me afterwards..."

"No, Leon, we must stay together."

I assured her and myself that they didn't have anything lethal in mind for us, or there would have been a different outcome on the mountain switchbacks. We followed these two thugs at a distance. They strolled with the crowd on the main street, drinking beers in brown bags and ogling women in skimpy bathing suits. After a couple of blocks, we came to Bacini's Cafe, and we were ready to get off the street.

"Not so fast," a man at the door said. "I need to see some ID before I let you in." You're not the police, are you?"

I wasn't about to show my American passport to this bouncer, if that's what he was. I began moving past him, but he held me from behind with both hands on my shoulders. He laughed at me when I spun around and broke free of his grip.

"What are you doing here when you could be with them on the beach getting a tan?" a man asked me.

"Ah, you are looking at me like you don't remember me."

On his forearm was a tattoo of a warship. He was one of Ighaam's Boys from the first night I visited Maraville, a tough man.

"Now I do," I said.

"I'm Mikah Booley, in case you forgot. But we remember you, Mr. Cooper," he said, then shook my hand and led us into the restaurant. "Remember my partner Mongrel? He drove you out of the danger zone. Remember how nervous you was? He says make sure I don't charge you and your girlfriend each fifty-rand admission since you be special guests. Before you leave, don't forget Mongrel want to speak to you one more time, to make sure you like to stay in South Africa. Got to go now." He hurried to the door to screen the next people and collect admission from them.

We took a table at the front of the restaurant so we could look out the window. As soon as I spotted Hassan, he took a chair by us. "I'm glad you're here, Leon," he said and hugged me, then Sunitha.

"Too bad though you didn't bring Alicia with you."

"That wasn't part of the plan, as far as I know," Hassan said. "No doubt I missed a lot while I was out of town."

It was strange no one I could reach on the phone mentioned this party to me until a few hours ago. One day I was key to the rescue, then when the rescue was a success, I became the invisible man.

"Too bad Alicia couldn't travel just half an hour to be with this poor people's celebration. Mr. Cooper, do you

464

think the authorities advised Alicia to stay away from my people?"

Chandra joined us, bringing a chair between him and me. "Hassan, what's the matter with you? Just because she and you grew up in adjoining rooms, does it surprise you that she feels most comfortable with her own kind, as you do with yours?"

"What does he know about Alicia, Mr. Nichols, and me?" Hassan asked. He looked hard at me, rather than at Chandra, confusing me. If Chandra wasn't supposed to know Hassan and Alicia were half-brother and sister, was Hassan suggesting I was the one who told him?

"So, Larabie, if this is a party, why aren't you showing our guests to the food before it is all gone?" Chandra asked, diverting attention away from questioning the inner workings of the Nichols family. To further dissipate the tension, he got Hassan to take me to the buffet, while he stayed at the table with Sunitha.

"You see something you like here, Mr. Cooper?" Hassan asked me once we were alone. He lifted the covers of the chafing dishes, allowing me to scoop out samples for my plate and Sunitha's. "Keeping a woman's like feeding a baby, hey? Most people think Bacini's is just pizza, but you also got lasagna, ravioli, cannelloni, salads, and for dessert... So how does this dish look to you?"

Hassan had his eye on a sensuous woman her skin the color of dark coffee. I noticed the only beer they were serving was Gazelle. This woman was at the bar flirting, holding the attention of two men simultaneously. When done speaking with them, she picked up two hard-sided travel cases labeled *MAMA AFRICA PRODUCTIONS*.

As she struggled past us, Hassan reached out his arm and stopped her, his hand wrapped around her breast!

"Mama Africa—is that the name you go by now?" Hassan asked her, though she wasn't responding to him. "Are you packed up for an overnight customer, Mama?"

"Shut up, Larabie.

"Sorry, Felicia, if you must go do something more important than visit with your old friend," Hassan said as she had a couple of waiters move the buffet aside, then hoisted her cases onto the table. "Now are you going to let my boss Mr. Leon Cooper have a look at you?"

Her large breasts were stuffed into her emerald green halter top, the same sort of outfit I remembered that was worn by one of the working girls at Maraville. Her mahogany skin was damp and glistened.

"I don't do that type of man-work anymore, Larabie, but I do like the looks of this one," she said to me, looking into my eyes. "Didn't we get together some time before?"

"Remember when you and your girlfriends were dropping bottles off your balcony? That was me walking below. You barely missed."

"No matter, life be full of near misses," she said, and turned away from me and towards Hassan. "For your information, Larabie, I'm not interested in men I don't know. I've taken up a new trade. You're looking at Mama Africa, the disc jockey queen of the Cape, not a shebeen queen like my friend Katy Ann over here," she said, pointing with her thumb to Ighaam's niece, who was now at the buffet, nibbling on a slice of pizza and smiling for me. "Now if you'll excuse me, I need to plug in." Felicia held up a handful of CD discs. "Why don't you two blokes go find yourself partners and prepare to dance in a few minutes once we're ready!"

We did as she suggested, leaving her to set up her turntable and equipment and had the waiters move tables off the dance floor. This left Sunitha and me to eat in silence at our table on the perimeter. Chandra watched us, refusing to take even a nibble we'd been offering him from our plates.

Through the speaker directly above our table I heard drums, too many of them to distinguish, drums powerful enough to reverberate in my chest. Brass pierced through the drums—trumpet, saxophones and trombones, but the real power was in the African drums, which created a wall of sound.

When Katy Ann came to our table, I couldn't help but see half dollar-size nipples through her sheer blouse. Against her black coffee skin, her clinging beige dress created a very alluring contrast.

"You're not just going to sit there, are you?" Katy Ann challenged me. "You don't mind if I take him for a while?" she asked Sunitha, who nodded her consent.

She led me to the dance floor and began to move her feet in both vertical jumps and fluid slides, accompanied by shaking of the shoulders. A fourth motion, a rotation of the hips, thrust every fourth beat. In school I had been a fair Saturday night dancer, so it shouldn't have been difficult for me to duplicate these motions, at least at half tempo. When I tried moving my hips like hers though, I realized it required a young woman's broad and flexible pelvis, and that I had best watch, rather than foolishly trying to follow. I stepped back and witnessed her match the pounding drums which I could feel radiating from my chest and through the rest of my body.

I spotted Hassan behind the disc jockey table, gesturing to his old friend Felicia, repackaged as Mama Africa, encouraging her to move onto the dance floor. After she began spinning the next recording, Hassan escorted her to a spot next to Katy Ann. Together the women's four dancing feet moved in a blur of high steps, tightly coordinated if they'd learned a routine from the same teacher! Their hips rotated and thrust in counterpoise with their bellies, accentuating their shaking shoulders. Everyone was watching their brilliant performance, especially Tembo, as well as a man with a big scar on his arm. I recognized him as Big Al Kosane, whom I had met with Hassan in the Mitchell's Plain shebeen with his brother and pool-playing friends.

Tembo approached me, but since I couldn't hear him over the drums, we moved to a quieter corner of the restaurant. Waiting for him was a girl who looked ethnically a lot like him, with a head as round as his, with similar strong, white teeth and small and symmetrical handsome features. She had a feather tucked behind one ear.

"These Cape Town girls have good motion," Tembo said, motioning to Katy Ann and Mama Africa, "but not so good as the girls from the tribe I showed you dancing on the TV in your room in the Inter-Continental. Remember?"

"The dancers with the bare breasts," I recalled, confirming the link between the TV dancers, the ones on the dance floor and Tembo, "the ones who you said were so primitive?"

"If I said that, Mr. Cooper, it was only because I knew you regarded some of us village people as savages. Do you remember what the savage women were wearing from the waist down?"

"I don't know. Grass skirts or beaded skirts?"

"No," he said shaking his head. "Those Zulu women wore skirts of leather, not ordinary cloth. Sometime you must see us Zulu men with plumes and feathers about our ankles, waists and heads! Mama Africa is from the Xosha tribe, yet she plays our Zulu music, giving us no credit! Do you hear the *ngoma* drums, the *djembe, ashiko, jun jun* and the *sekere* drums? I could have been a drummer of great power, Mr. Cooper! Do you hear my brothers whistling? Do you hear these other Zulu sounds too?"

Together Tembo and his female companion accompanied the music with weird ululations, sounds unlike anything I'd ever heard pass through human throats! Tembo was looking at me closely and smiling, seeing how their primordial singing was affecting me. This tribal side of him seemed so unlike Ted Nichol's polished chauffeur, I was having trouble reconciling both halves of him, as if he'd been acting a charade ever since he was first assigned as my driver. Still singing their Zulu songs, Tembo and his girlfriend turned away and walked together to the dance floor, where there were now half a dozen new women, led by Katy Arendse, with Mama Africa back at her DJ duties.

I found Sunitha at our front table by the window with Hassan, Mongrel, and Booley, all of them looking expectantly to the outside.

"Have you made new friends?" I asked Sunitha, once I got her attention away from that pair of Ighaam's gangsters, who seemed charmed by her beauty.

"Your reputation has preceded you. They speak very highly of the American," she said, once we had walked far enough away from the table so no one could hear, other than Tembo who stopped his singing to rejoin us.

"I was afraid I lost you, Mr. Cooper," Tembo said, leaning so close to me that his gold cross was dangling inches from my face. "Please, could you be so kind to watch my lady dance right now?" he asked and led me back toward the dance floor. "I need to know your opinion of Zulu dancing, because I have much Zulu blood in my veins. Now I bring you this Zulu girl to see if you like to watch her better than these pretender women from Maraville. Do you think they are as good on their feet as on their backs?"

Tembo was adaptable by nature and, like Chandra, could alter his opinions to tell me what he thought I wanted to hear. He was bordering on rudeness, as if he'd too much to drink. Underneath his chauffeur's polish, did he really see himself as a displaced Zulu warrior? He grew up in a village on such poor land that the strongest and brightest young men and women like him had to migrate from it to find work in the city. Did he see himself a point man and informant for Hassan, now based in Maraville? Or did he really live for his days off when he was free to drink and womanize? His role at the Chateau was a lot bigger than simply as Ted's driver. I made a resolution to learn the extent of his literacy and whether he could be used more effectively.

Had Tembo at last found in his exile in the Southern

Cape this pretty Zulu girl and was eager to show her off to me? He took her to the dance floor and turned her loose, making her the sixth woman to join Mary Ann Arendse and Mama Africa in a shoulder-to-shoulder stomping and shaking chorus line. After a minute, Tembo's woman broke free from the group and moved out on her own. She danced with an inspired and frantic abandon, weaving among other dancers and spectators, jumping high, and twirling. Tembo had a proprietary smile, proud of the performance representing his tribe, which delighted the applauding and hooting audience. Whether they had any notion about her Zulu inspiration, I did and was coming to appreciate how long and difficult a journey he made from his homeland to become Ted Nichol's driver, and both his and my confidant.

"Have you seen anything interesting?" Sunitha asked. She came behind me and greeted me with a kiss on the neck.

"I'm ready to leave whenever you are."

"Not before you buy me a Gazelle beer."

It was a strange request from someone who drank wine, never beer, other than the tiny batch samples in the Kassies' old Gazelle plant. She asked the bartender where the other bartender had gone and insisted on waiting until he returned. And strangely, she took me close to the kitchen door, and when the missing bartender returned, it swung open, striking her hard enough to unbalance her. When the bartender bent down to help her up with his free hand, she wasn't looking at him or at me, but downward at his motorcycle boots and the attaché he was carrying.

"Thanks," I said to him, helping her up.

I brought her to a booth, where I extended her legs to make her comfortable. "You didn't have to do that," she said. "That man was no help. Did you notice his boots? I wish we got a better look at the faces of the motorcycle men, but I believe he's one the one who tried to run us off the road and has been watching us from outside. He's not a bartender and does not belong here inside with us. You must do something to contain him." She was not looking at me, but behind me. When I turned and saw the waiter coming from the kitchen again, she poked me. "Careful, if you stare at him, he might get skittish enough to bolt. I'll be back. You watch that attaché he left by Mama Africa, while I get help from our new friends."

She returned to the front table, where I saw Mongrel, who was drinking with Booley. They were standing to one side of the window, looking outside at the passersby on the street.

"See Mafumo watching us from the curb?" Tembo said to me, pointing through the window. "He does not mean us good, and I need to find out why he spies on us."

By the time Tembo opened the glass door, Mafumo had moved close enough to look through it. What about Molefe, who Sunitha was sure she had spotted? Did she have the names confused? Tembo pulled his hat down over his eyes and managed to get to arm's length distance from him before he rushed out of the room.

Mongrel chased after him with Tembo behind him, zig-zagging through the crowd. When Tembo finally got his hand on Mafumo's sleeve, he managed to break away and duck into an alley.

I decided to follow them. Mafumo broke Mongrel's bear hug and landed a couple of punches. In retaliation, one powerful punch to his head sent him flying against a metal trash can and onto the ground. Tembo helped to move defeated Mafumo, and assisted in dragging him away, each taking one of his arms.

I had seen enough, and rather than follow them any further, left the alley and went around the block to use the rear entrance of Bacini's and keep a low profile. By that time, Booley and his friends had roughed up Mafumo's partner, the motorcycle rider who Sunitha caught posing as the waiter. They dragged him to Booley's car, a white BMW with a dented right fender. It had to be Kruger's, the one in which the gangsters had carried off Alicia! I watched Booley back up to the alley, where Mongrel emerged with battered Mafumo, stripped of his shoes. They heaved him into the back seat! I saw a flash of silver steel, as one of Ighaam's men waved a gun at Mafumo, perhaps this time to put him out of commission permanently!

That left me alone outside the service entrance of Bacini's with no visible evidence of the battle. I was shaking, as if I was the one who'd been beaten, rather than Mafumo, the man responsible for the destruction of the old plant and perhaps for Raj's disappearance, and the thrashing of one of the motorcycle men. Ozeer's Boys had evidently been sent to harass Alicia's homecoming guests. Perhaps I had just been watching the preliminaries to an execution or two by Booley and Mongrel!

"You look sad, Mr. Cooper," Tembo interrupted, "like you lost your best friend. The truth is, we just said goodbye to some of our worst enemies."

"I don't know what you're talking about," I said.

"Don't know?" he repeated.

Either Tembo didn't know or didn't care that he'd stepped into the criminal world by assisting a couple of Ighaam's Boys dispose of enemies. For both our sakes, I knew we shouldn't speak of this any further. I had to remind myself that in South Africa enemies, particularly from the townships, regularly settled their scores without bothering the authorities with the details. I was in no mood to celebrate, but if I stood there with him any longer, I was afraid the next thing Tembo would be explaining more than I needed to know. I simply wanted to collect Sunitha and Chandra and retreat behind the gated walls of my flat.

"Should we return to the party before it's all over?" I asked Sunitha, who had turned stunned and silent.

I hung back for a couple of minutes after Tembo returned to Bacini's, where a dozen guests seemed thrilled that he'd chased away Ozeer's gangsters before they could ruin the party. Tembo had become the center of attention for the fight with the motorcycle riding party-crashers, but I was relieved that he withheld details on what happened to the pair of them once they were caught. Nor did he report any more about Mongrel and Booley's disappearance, other than he didn't think they'd be back.

Chandra found me and took me to Mama Africa's

table. I was relieved to be out of earshot of Tembo's conversations, but didn't understand why Sunitha was clasping to her chest with both arms the attache case the bogus waiter had left.

"We must leave immediately!" she declared.

"I will catch up with you later, Mr. Cooper," Hassan said.

Alarmed at the unmistakable fear in Sunitha's voice, together we pushed our way through the crowd. Chandra was behind us as we stepped onto the crowded sidewalk.

"It started out as a nice party," I said.

"It would have been over in a few minutes," Sunitha gasped.

She looked at the top of the case, into a thumb-nail-sized window beneath a tiny leather flap where a timer displayed the count down. My heart began to pound wildly. This attaché was like the one shown me at Kruger's security office, the one filled with explosives— with the identical window that counted off the time remaining to detonation! It must have been left there by Mafumo and his motorcycle friend, with help from an accomplice in the kitchen—before Booley, Mongrel, and Tembo spotted them and neutralized them. An explosion was set to take out Katy Ann, Hassan, Mongrel, Booley, Tembo and no doubt Sunitha and me and whatever other friends of Ighaam Arendse happened to be in the restaurant! I yanked the time-bomb away from her and took charge. She pointed across the road to the beach where many people were lying on the sand at the end of a lovely day. I had to do something, but I was frozen where I was standing, my vision shrunk as if I was looking through the wrong end of a telescope. Chandra tried to get the case from me, but when I didn't release it, he looked at the little clock window.

"Four minutes thirty-five seconds, Leon!" Chandra shouted, bringing me to attention before grabbing my hand and Sunitha's, lurching the three of us into the street and dodging the moving cars.

Behind me I heard a car jam its brakes and skid to a stop. I turned and saw the bumper touching Sunitha's leg. She didn't stop, and instead pushed me forward, this time across the sidewalk and onto the beach. On the sand she and Chandra locked arms with me and we formed a three-person phalanx, advancing in a coordinated trot.

We came upon a couple of families of picnickers and ran past the blankets and umbrellas where the grownups were drinking, eating and laughing. The big children lost interest in their sand and shovel bury- ing game and followed the three of us, mimicking our awkward shuffle, as if we were playing some kind of grownup game, a more interesting one than theirs!

"Get away from us, children! This is a bomb!" Chandra hollered, turning backward as best he could while charging forwards, locked into our desperate momentum to haul the bomb away from people. "Run or you shall surely die!"

They ignored Chandra's grim warning, and hung dog- gedly close to us, still imitating our shuffling advance. When one of the boys came within arm's length of Chandra, he struck the child squarely in the chest, hard enough to knock him onto the sand. But the boy just scrambled to his feet and treated it as part of a game. With exuberant hoots and taunts, he and the other chil- dren darted around us like irritable bees.

We quickly crossed the beach among boys playing toss-and-catch, girls sunbathing, families on blankets, and older people asleep. Suddenly Sunitha stopped and knelt before the case I held tightly. Her hands were shaking as she fumbled with the leather flap, once again revealing the window of our time remaining.

"There may be enough time to drop it in the tidal pool a couple of minutes from here, rather than out in the ocean where many people are wading," she said looking at it, then at me, tears in her eyes.

Though not sure of her reasoning, whether panic or logic, it wasn't time for argument. With the case in my arms, I ran where she directed me, as fast as I could on the damp packed sand toward to a manmade tidal pool, a hundred-yard circle captured from the ocean, protected by a sea wall of huge boulders. At just one hundred feet away were lockers and showers. I dove into the shallow water, clutching the ticking case, then stood on it, holding it under the water as if it were an evil living thing I had to suffocate!

"We must get away from this bomb, Leon!" Sunitha shouted, jumping in after me, using her surprising panicky strength to pull me away from the danger. "When we were at Kruger's office, he told me these briefcase bombs are waterproof, so it will still explode! We must get these people out of here!"

"Attention!" Chandra shouted to everyone who had been suspiciously watching the three of us in street clothes in the tidal pool, and now Tembo as well. "You must exit now before this bomb explodes in your faces!"

Fortunately, the women at the edge listened, pulled their children out of the pool and rushed out of sight!

I worked quickly to grab several of the remaining children and hoisted them one by one onto the deck, where they scampered out of harm's way. That left some doubting teenagers asking a lot of questions, unconvinced of the danger. Those Tembo wrestled out of the water, some violently, against their protests.

"One minute to go, no more, Leon!" Sunitha shouted to me.

She had a two-year-old girl in her arms and passed her to her mother, who had just yanked her four-year-old boy out of the water. Tembo, having ejected the balking youths, saw two rambunctious coloured brothers rush from the lockers into the water—the bothersome ones who failed to heed Chandra's warning and had been trailing us since we passed their family picnic. Without hesitation, Tembo jumped into the water right after them and scooted up the ladder with one in each arm, as if they were no heavier than sacks of rice.

That left Sunitha between Chandra and me, the three of us hunched behind the half man-sized boulders of the seawall, waiting. As we watched Tembo's brave rescue, well past the margin of prudence, I felt her trembling fingers on my arm. But just after he bolted to the beach with the young boys under his arms, the third and biggest brother charged from the lockers toward the pool! The one that Chandra knocked down to try stopping him from trailing after us was now using up his second chance! When he ignored our shouts to him to turn back, I jumped up to make a sprint for him and save him, but Sunitha grabbed my ankle and held me with a fierce strength, tripping me until I fell back next to her and safety.

"You must not go there!" Chandra shouted one more time. "Turn around!" But the boy simply laughed and belly-flopped into the water and swam directly towards the attaché case.

Sunitha began to cry, and I pulled her towards me, her face in my chest so she could not watch. The boy came up from his dive below the water, emerging with the attaché case in his hand!

The explosion sent a geyser of water into the air. In that water chunks of concrete rained like an artillery barrage. They struck the wooden walls of the lockers, blowing out gaping holes. Miraculously, no one we'd evacuated from the pool was in the bomb's path. Without delay Chandra jumped into the water and with my help pulled the boy from the pool onto the deck. Sunitha walked reluctantly to the child's body.

"You need not go any closer," Chandra said.

He tried to guide her away from the gathering crowd, curious about the explosion, milling around the mutilated boy. I kept my distance, but she insisted on approaching what was left of the boy and knelt beside him. She placed her hands on his chest, then with tears in her eyes, turned to me for some kind of answer.

"Do you think he died in our place?"

I didn't know why she thought the bomb was destined for me! I just happened to be in the wrong place at the wrong time and certainly in the wrong country! Who was responsible for this despicable act besides Ozeer, or one of his men? And for what purpose, other than retaliation against the Botswana battle where they took so many casualties? Did they intend to take out the whole room of Ighaam's associates and sympathizers at Bacini's?

"I don't think so," was all I could manage to reply, hardly justifying to her or to me the question of our survival.

"Someone was bound to suffer, and it ended up being this boy."

We took a final look backwards at the curious crowd that was building.

"It is a shame he was so young," she said once we were halfway across the beach. "I could feel no evil in his heart when I touched it."

Tembo was waiting when we came off the beach and back to the road. When he spotted us, he whistled to Hassan, who had been looking for us from his position opposite Tembo and us. He hustled across the street to meet us and embraced Sunitha.

"Did you know Mr. Cooper would be such a hero?" he asked her.

"We can all be thankful for your bravery," she said, pulling away from him to hug me.

"What about Tembo?" I asked. "He was far braver than any of us, saving the two children at the last very last minute. He's the hero, if anyone."

Rather than look at me, Hassan had his eye on the cops gathering across the street. But before the police came, medics arrived, and two of the cops were rushing across the sand with a stretcher. Then a van taxi stopped at the curb. Katy Ann Arendse stuck her head out the window and whistled for Tembo.

"It looks like the party's over, Tembo," I said. "I think the police are going to want to know what we saw, and you need to tell them. Where are you going now?"

"With me," Hassan said. "Mr. Cooper, you must believe me that a police station would be no place for Tembo, innocent or not, even in the new Rainbow Nation. Besides our friends at Maraville have enough troubles without inviting a lot of police to ask them questions. The cops will believe an American like yourself a lot quicker than ordinary people like us. So I must go with Tembo while we can!"

By this time, he and Tembo were running to the van. "If we don't see you for a while, Mr. Cooper, goodbye!" he called back, then threw Sunitha a kiss. "Let me know if you need anything! Good luck!"

CHAPTER 20

VIEW FROM THE BRIDGE

Hassan understandably was in a big rush to leave Chandra, Sunitha and me at Camp's Bay main street. I didn't know why their sudden departure bothered me, whether it was because he took Tembo with him, as if protecting a criminal, while I believed he should have been honored as a hero. I suspected Hassan was making sure to get Tembo away before the police could make him answer questions that might ultimately lead them to Ighaam himself. But now that they'd driven away, my thoughts turned from them and instead to the parents of the dead boy, who were approaching the pool. Neither myself nor Tembo nor Chandra could have done anything to save the child from his own willfulness, yet just the same, I was compelled to offer my sympathy to the parents. I felt an odd sense of relief when the police got to Sunitha and me before I had to explain any gory details to the parents.

They brought us back to the damaged tidal pool, where the medics were lifting the body from the bloody spot on the concrete. With our arrival, the cops drove the spectators even further back, so they could interview us without an audience. When they learned I was Chandra's and Sunitha's employer, they were suddenly far more interested in hearing my own account than either of theirs.

I was careful to report to them on what I'd actually seen, with no speculations. As for the time bomb set in Bacini's Cafe, I could only guess it was Ozeer's payback for the defeat his forces took at the hands of Ighaam and Ted Nichols, after Alicia's failed kidnapping. However, that was a personal speculation I didn't care to make for the police. Nor was I prepared to speak to them about Booley's and Mongrel's seizing Mafumo, nor about the motorcycle man disguised as a waiter—especially where they might have taken them in the white BMW with the dented fender. To explain our suspicion of the contents of attaché case, I stuck to the important facts, that it resembled a time bomb case my employee Sunitha and I saw at Oasis Security, an enterprise belonging to someone who wanted me to buy into it, and that we grabbed the case and rushed it out of Bacini's, looking for a safe place to let it harmlessly explode. While they seemed to be paying particular attention to my initial account of events, a photographer was taking photos around the entire pool, especially of the bloody stain on the concrete, and then took many photos of me.

The police then brought us to Bacini's, where the photographer snapped pictures of me in front of the cafe alongside my police interviewers. There was no longer any sign of the partygoers inside, just a few people at the bar and at a couple of the tables.

"Are you going to tell us where the rest of your friends have disappeared?" the gray-haired police sergeant asked skeptically, with a look at me, then at Chandra and finally Sunitha.

"We came here as colleagues of Alicia Nichols," Chandra explained for me, "to share drinks of our Gazelle beer, celebrating her safe return from terrorists. The people that were here in the bar with us were lucky that we did not become impatient and leave when she did not arrive. They were even more fortunate Mr. Cooper was quick and brave enough to put his own life in danger, seize the bomb and save many lives."

Now that Chandra had stopped, Sunitha embellished the story that I was a brave man with the plan to detonate a bomb in a safe place, one that could have easily blown to pieces everyone within twenty-five yards. By building me up, probably far more than I deserved, that made me a hero, inspiring the photographer to take pictures of me in yet another setting, once again with cops on each side of me, this time pictured at the bar with a real bartender behind it.

Once the authorities heard our brief accounts of the party and the bomb, they walked us a couple of blocks to the police station, which faced directly onto the beach. Outside the building, a policeman was standing beside the front door, peering across the road through binoculars. As soon as I arrived, he set them down and shook my hand. He was a black man with a line of symmetrical forty-five degree ritual scars visible from under his shirt collar. The three of us were led inside the station.

"Quite a job you and that kaffir friend of yours from the PAGAD gang did, evacuating the pool," said the youngest of my interrogators as we stood facing him across his desk. "He must be the shy sort, or else why would he rush away so quick before we could see the whites of his eyes?" He too had binoculars, which he now used to look through the window in the direction of the tidal pool.

"I didn't think you could see quite everything from here. Rumors must travel fast," I said.

"PAGAD, what do you know about them?" another interrogator asked, a big blonde fellow with a square jaw. "And what about Ighaam's Boys?"

That was a leading question, one he was going to pursue, now that he had taken us to his cramped office and sat us in a row of chairs facing him across his desk. Now that he had thrown out those names, he tipped back in his chair and stared at me. For the first time since he started questioning me, I had the opportunity to look him over, trying to imagine whether he was a military man, whether his powerful good looks gave him success with the ladies. If he planned to conquer me by disorienting and outwaiting me, it was not going to work. I was careful not to show my apprehension, and turned to Sunitha for a moment, which she mistakenly took for a cue to speak on my behalf.

"You should congratulate him as a hero, Sergeant Vos, not interrogate him," she said, leaning forward to read his name tag.

"No, Ms. Bala, it's you and I who must chat now, alone. Come along," he said, and escorted her out of the room.

In the meantime, a coloured Malay-looking cop came for Chandra, while a third, the ritually scarified black one, after a quick whispered consultation with Sergeant Vos, remained in the room to finish the interview with me. We were separated like criminals with something to hide, rather than as good Samaritans. There was nothing to do but answer as many more questions as they cared to put to me!

Shortly after arriving at my office the next morning, Ted was waiting for me and threw a copy of *The Cape Argus* on my desk. In it was a picture of the medics removing the shrouded body of the boy blown up in the pool, as well as a photo of me in front of the bar. On one side I was flanked by the cops detaining and interrogating me, and on the other, a jukebox. At the time I had a grimace on my face, feeling trapped, yet oddly on the photograph this grimace appeared as a smile. *AMERICAN BUSINESSMAN FOILS C.O.R.E. GANGSTER BOMB!* the headline screamed, reporting an anonymous source crediting PAGAD with me as a hero defeating CORE. The photograph made me appear cocky, although I was anything but that.

"As I told you last night when you reported this incident to me, welcome to the heroes' club. Well done! A feather in our caps!"

"If I had been just one minute quicker, Ted, no one would have been hurt. It's a good thing Tembo was there. At the last minute, without any regard for his own life he..."

"That's quite a testimonial for a man who doesn't even have the courage to show up for work. Then again, I suppose, unlike you, Leon, he may be afraid to make himself known for fear of reprisals."

"I was thinking the bomb was Ozeer's payback for the raid into Botswana."

"Maybe."

"Then maybe Tembo's smart to have disappeared! And maybe I should follow in his footsteps! You know I've never condoned the Chateau's connection with gangs! So, if that's how you plan to continue protecting our assets, count me out of your battles!"

"Nonsense, I won't let you retreat, not after you've done so much to publicize Chateau. Cheer up, Leon. You didn't choose to be a hero, but that's what you now are, as far as the newspaper readers are concerned. There's no escaping your well-earned fame, unless you try to do what our hero Tembo's done—disappear. But for now, I won't let you get away so easily, so you may as well come along with me this morning."

We had coffee in his dining room in china cups on a sterling tray carried by a house servant into my office. Rather than speak business, he wanted me to repeat my story of the Camp's Bay mountain pass, Bacini's Cafe, the tidal pool, the bomb and the boy's death. I abbreviated the whole series of events for Ted, not proud, but apparently delighting him with the details. Now that he saw me as a kind of battle comrade, he told me the bloody details about the skirmishes he waged decades ago on the Botswana side of the border. To Ted it was as if I'd joined a club to which he'd belonged since he was a young man going on commando missions for the old regime's army. But rather than ask him what he meant by why he believed my rescue of some children from a pool was going to build the Chateau's image, I excused myself and got to work.

Sunitha wasn't saying much about the disaster at Camp's Bay. It seemed just as well that she was back to pursuing her devotions at the feet of the Brahma, especially late evenings and early mornings. For my part, I was careful to stay out of the room and to avoid questioning her about her renewed vigils. As a new addition to her prayer and meditation routine, she would bring her mat out to the porch where she'd also chant. From there she could take breaks to view the road with my hunter's daytime binoculars so high-powered they required a tripod. Rather than watching her on the porch through the glass door, I decided to join her. I noticed sometimes when I was with her on the porch, her attention would shift to the street eight stories below.

"What are you seeing?"

"Patterns in their comings and goings. There are men in a couple of cars, and I don't like it. Last night they were looking toward our flat with spy glasses." Lately it seemed everyone was watching someone else through field glasses; even Chandra now had a pair. Once I left Cape Town, I wouldn't miss all that spying and counterspying.

"It will seem very odd to live anywhere else. That is, if you truly take me with you." She wanted to believe that I wouldn't leave her behind, but in the immediate term I was too distracted by the men on the street below who might be a danger to us in order for me to take time to reassure her again about my intentions to stay with her. I wondered whether those people on the street had synchronized themselves with her schedule, whether we might truly be in their crosshairs and vulnerable.

That evening I received a call from Alicia herself. She congratulated me on my heroic rescue in the pool, but had a more specific reason for contacting me, to invite Sunitha and me to spend the balance of the weekend in Bergkloof with her.

We arrived at the big living room of the Inn, where a couple of elderly guests at the far end were playing cards. Sitting in a circle of leather chairs were our hosts, the LeRouxs, Otto Kruger and Alicia herself.

"We meet again," I said, greeting Kruger first, "but under more pleasant circumstances."

He stood up, gave Alicia a possessive hug as her new husband, supposedly having married her just before she was abducted, and looked at her affectionately. "Don't you think I should stay in the horse rider corral now?" he asked, looking for approval at the three of us in turn.

"I hope you take good care of my daughter, now that she's become your wife," Jan said with a self-conscious laugh, speaking openly of her relationship with Alicia.

Every time I came to the Inn, there seemed to be a new surprise, especially the last time when Jan confessed that not only was she Alicia's mother, but Hassan's as well, which still left unclear in my mind Ted's role. I believed Ted was Alicia's natural father, or why else would he have risked his resources, his credibility, and his life to rescue her?

"You seem sad, Leon. Could that be because you were too late to have her for yourself?"

Jan had apparently misread my confusion for disappointment that Alicia was taken by Kruger, rather than myself. How could she be so rude as to suggest that in front of Sunitha? Alicia, as if sensing my recollection as her single-evening former lover, approached and sat beside me.

"If I learned one thing after my close escape," Alicia began explaining quickly, "it's the importance of close friends. Sometimes we get lucky and get a second chance. I had no right to expect to survive the terror and get another chance at life with my new husband. I wanted to join the wellwishers at Bacini's, but Otto and I were just too exhausted. Now I feel guilty that I was indirectly responsible for the terrible damage that was done there."

Did she have any idea how much I'd done behind the scenes to support her rescue, perhaps the reason now for classifying me as a close friend? Wasn't Alicia told the Camp's Bay reception was held in her specifically in her honor, and that everyone assumed she'd have the courtesy to show up at Bacini's?

"Or was it because the crowd at Bacini's might not have been close friends you'd care to bring back to the Chateau, Alicia?" I blurted out, more annoyed than I realized that Alicia had not shown up at her own reception.

Alicia stood up and exchanged a bewildered look with Otto. Once she regained her composure, she leaned over close to me. "You don't mind if I have a word with your consort? And, Leon, while I have your ear, would you mind taking a rain check so we can invite you to my new residence at a better time?"

Alicia withdrew arm-in-arm with Sunitha into the next room. When Sunitha was back, she asked that we return before dark. I wasn't going to argue with her decision before the LeRouxs, who seemed genuinely disappointed we weren't going to spend the entire weekend at the Inn as planned.

We were twenty minutes from Bergkloof, when Sunitha put her hand on my shoulder. "I thought it was a good idea to get you away from this last round of mourning, Leon."

"Probably not a bad idea. Alicia's too focused on being saved herself to really care about the people we saved at Camp's Bay."

"Actually, she's more interested in us as a couple and was suggesting we don't belong together permanently. She thinks I'm no more than your consort."

"No, my consort would be my wife."

"Well, if I'm not a wife, then does that make me, your concubine?"

"A king or a sheik or a noble would keep a concubine; I'm a democratic American who doesn't believe in human bondage. It's not like you to look for rigid definitions. Do I need to tell you again that I'm—?"

"Please. No need to give me a loyalty statement."

When we arrived at the flat, we were crunching glass underfoot. Something was wrong! Sunitha looked at me apprehensively and insisted I stay where I was. She walked through the hallway and living room to the patio door with the blown out glass. "This was no accident! It was those men with their eyes on us!" she said. I got busy on the living room side of the patio door sweeping up the steel pellets I noticed mixed with the bits of glass.

"These pellets are from a shotgun," I said trying to be calm and analytical, "which couldn't have been done this from street level, so far away from here. Whoever shot out this door must have been on the neighbor's patio—or else broke into the flat, you know."

"No, I don't know any such thing, any more than I can account for why the neighbors wouldn't haven't noticed such shots, or why the guard at the gate wouldn't haven't seized the shooters!"

"Maybe they have. I'll call and see what I can find out."

I was shaken too but couldn't show it. We needed to get to the bottom of the intrusion, and we couldn't do it sitting there. I reached for the phone, but Sunitha wanted to talk to me, not anyone else.

"First losing Rajesh, then the burning of my house, then saving the DeVilliers boy from fire, then losing this last child to the bomb—I'm afraid, no matter how hard I try, I've brought you bad karma! That is why I will call Chandra and stay with him and release you."

"Sunitha, to somehow improve our bad luck, you intend to move out of the flat?"

"Believe me, Leon, this isn't my first choice. I'll miss you," she said and telephoned him.

"That's considerate of you, but you should realize you'll be of greater help to me at my side rather than with your uncle."

"Why?"

"Because the last time you vanished, I worried about your welfare. Actually, I was ready to fire you whenever you decided to return. Then I realized if I let you know that rather than your continuing at Drakenstein, I wanted you to eventually come with me back to America, which might come sooner than later if Harry manages—"

"I was taking unused vacation days. That wouldn't have been fair!"

"But do you now think it's fair to leave me alone again when I most need your help? What's really bothering you?"

"I'm afraid to stay here anymore. Next time they might find us at home."

"I suppose we both should be more cautious. So why don't we move out of Rondebosch to someplace where we can feel more secure, together. How about the Inter-Continental?"

We agreed to abandon the flat and began deciding which were the most important things we should take with us immediately, when Chandra arrived, appearing every bit as upset as Sunitha by evidence of the intrusion. His plan was not only to accompany us to the hotel, but to spend the night there with us. I didn't really want him to stay with us, but Sunitha welcomed his company as additional security. I suspected from the bulge beneath his jacket that he was now carrying a pistol.

"What's this, Chandra?

"A special Glock to protect you."

"Special how?"

"See this switch at the back of the slide? It makes it fully automatic, so it fires three rounds per second."

"At that rate you wouldn't really aim, but you'd pray and spray! And pushing your gun that hard, it wouldn't take too long for it to get too hot to handle and jam up. What else do you have in your arsenal," I asked, pointing to a leather pouch on his belt. From it he produced several extra loaded magazines.

"I'm a peaceful man. Sometimes we must fight fire with fire. That's why I am here, so neither of you worry too much." Without answering he smiled at me. "Leon, you may regard me as a poor bodyguard. If you refuse the security Mr. Nichols wishes me to provide you, I will trouble you no more. Though I assure you I would die to protect you, tomorrow we can look for a younger, faster, and stronger man you can better trust as your guardian for as long as you remain in Cape Town."

It seemed like more than a coincidence that both he and Ted and even Hassan had been giving me the same opinion, that my days were numbered in Cape Town, and that I should be ready for reprisals for which I would be no match. Their warnings made me more determined to stay, even though Bernice believed Harry had been working in St. Louis to get me out of South Africa.

To keep a low, safe profile I relocated our entourage away from my vulnerable flat and to the Inter-Continental with its substantial security staff. Tembo reappeared and took over from Chandra guard duty for me. He insisted on taking additional security measures, such as keeping us out of the hotel's public places, including the coffee shop, restaurant and especially the main lobby.

Late one afternoon between the hotel and the parking garage, Tembo was confronted with his first test when a man appeared behind him and grabbed my arm. Tembo quickly pulled him off me, taking no chance that he might be attempting a reprisal. Tembo restrained him by pinioning his arm behind his back and grabbing him around his neck. Oddly, the man looked at me with a stunned smile.

"Excuse me, aren't you the hero who saved the children from the bomb?"

"Sorry, you must have him confused with someone else," Tembo said angrily and hustled me away from this unwelcome admirer.

He shouldn't have been so violent with a wellwisher who simply meant to congratulate me, as if I were a hero. I couldn't blame him though for trying to protect me. I knew I was edgy myself. I didn't like relocating to a hotel suite with Tembo as my bodyguard, sleeping on the couch, leaving his radio on sometimes until the next morning. But bothering Sunitha's sleep more than Tembo's nightly radio were his trips to the bathroom via our bedroom!

Sunitha and I had been in close hotel quarters with Chandra or Tembo, and therefore readily accepted an invitation from Frederick DeVilliers to return to their estate for an overnight stay. When we arrived, Sunitha was greeted with a big hug from their boy Dietlets she had saved from the fire, then with thank yous from his parents. Soon I was talking business with Frederick. Then and there he offered me a virtually unlimited line of credit for future expansion, which interested me considerably, especially if Harry was working behind the scenes to make sure Cooper, Inc. itself would not pay for further Chateau expansion. He congratulated me on the successful Botswana mission, not believing that I was just a go-between, nor that my function was simply to help bring together the forces who needed to sit down and plan beforehand. Frederick, despite my denial, repeatedly praised me as a hero, because I grabbed the attaché case and ran to where it would do the least harm.

I was not comfortable being object of our hosts' praise,

and instead focused my attention on one of the servants, a pretty black girl, who was serving us hors d'oeuvres. Now that he'd offered me a big financing package, DeVilliers was also in a generous mood with Tembo. That consisted of offering him some walk-around money in bills, which Tembo refused, as well as the use of their car and of the servant girl for a companion, which he accepted.

I didn't think it necessary for our hosts to introduce Sunitha and me as national treasures, rather than anything more than accidental good Samaritans. But our hosts had made a big effort to show us a good time, and they brought us into their flowering gardens, patios and lovely home to introduce us to their admiring circle of friends. If nothing else, their well-intentioned efforts enabled Sunitha to relax enough to distract her from her cares. No doubt Tembo enjoyed the attention from the pretty maid, as we enjoyed the attention from so many wellwishers. But when the reception ended, it was time to return to the hotel.

"Mr. Cooper you make a perfect couple with Sunitha," Tembo said looking at both of us in the rearview mirror, as we sat in the back seat on our way to Cape Town, "even if you come from different places. I envy you."

I'm not sure whether Tembo was suggesting that we appeared to him happy or compatible and that we ought to be married. In any event, I didn't care to open the subject of my devotion to Sunitha to a three-way conversation. The rest of the way back Sunitha drew herself closer to me and ran her hand beneath my shirt, then onto my lap, timing it for when she didn't see Tembo's reflected eyes turned on us.

"You know how I feel about you," I reassured her.

"Don't you think Tembo should have the rest of the night off so we can be together alone?" she whispered as we approached the garage opposite the hotel. "Why don't you stop in that store to buy us something to celebrate our victory over the forces of darkness, Leon? If you'd send off Tembo, I'll be waiting for you alone in our room."

I responded to her request by tapping Tembo's shoulder, and announced our plan. In the liquor store I looked through the bottles of champagne, first as a vintner sizing up the competition, then as an ordinary man with a limited budget might. I felt buoyant that perhaps Sunitha and I had turned a corner, overcome some of our fears, and were able to make some tentative plans.

I arrived at the room, but no one was there. As I waited for Sunitha, on the TV I saw a report of shooting casualties at a mosque in Lansdowne, an incident that was part of the Cape Flats War. I clicked it off, refusing to hear more, not wishing thoughts of danger to overtake me again. I called down to the reception desk, but there was no word from her.

"Where have you been?"

"Finding my way back here," she answered haltingly and pulled herself close to me. She was shaking. "Now promise me no lights tonight! I'll be waiting for you."

She made love that night with a desperate intensity, which I believed was a sign she was using me to escape from something bad. Leon Cooper, lover and protector—probably one more role than I cared to handle. There beside her in the dark, listening to her deep breathing in the soundest part of her night's sleep, I hoped our separate desires for escape didn't constitute the foundation of our odd attraction to one another.

The next morning when she couldn't use the dark to hide herself from me, I saw bruises on her arms and cuts on her neck.

"Who did this! Where was Tembo? Why didn't he return with you?" I asked as she was dressing.

"Surely Tembo saved me! If it wasn't for him, I wouldn't be here. He damaged one thug badly, far worse than he received, and left his mate to carry him away. After it was all over, I insisted that Tembo get medical help, which, predictably, he refused to do, not wishing to answer any questions about the source of his injury."

"And why didn't you see a doctor as well?"

"Because I had no need of one, okay?"

"No, not okay! I shouldn't have left you two alone, and I'm not going to my office without you."

"You won't have to worry for long," she said as we were eating breakfast. "Tembo promised to send you a replacement for himself because he failed to protect me. Leon, I'm scared, and I don't want to be alone," she continued quietly. "We're going to be together for a long time, aren't we? But for now, for your sake, don't you think you'd be better off without me, just for a few weeks?"

Again, she had her foot out the door, mistakenly believing that she herself was the one who was attracting trouble, thinking she could best help me by leaving. Wrong! Even if that were true, I was now reluctant to let her out of my sight, even temporarily, and take the chance she might not ever return to me.

"Not again, Sunitha, no way! We can't be running away from our fears, or from each other. Starting this morning, I'm going to stay close to you and make sure you don't wander into another minefield."

But now that I'd made my position known, I realized her bruises and cuts may not have been bad enough to justify a visit to a doctor, but they were still obvious enough to attract attention at work, especially the bruise on her neck, which couldn't be hidden as easily as the ones on her arms. I was reluctant to discuss the details of our after hours life, so to avoid questions I set her up in a room off my office, where she worked on the phone and the computer. I remember shortly after the rescue incident how the men on the assembly line left their stations once they spotted me to shake my hand and greet me as a conquering hero because of the Camp's Bay rescue incident. Rather than feel any kind of pride though, I was concerned that my new fame might have been the cause of the latest reprisal against Tembo and Sunitha. Actually, I was relieved for distractions, such as when one of the foremen had a production problem for me to solve.

These were wine men, still not entirely comfortable with the brewing process. This particular Gazelle run was slightly off-taste, astringent. I'd been around Chandra enough to suspect that tannins had been released because the water temperature was set too high. I asked them to report back to me once they'd tested the defective batch for tannins.

Colin, from his off-site office, had overstepped his accountant's role and begun giving directives intended to introduce some ill-advised cost cutting measures, attempting to solve temporary shortages by shuffling workers between production, shipping, maintenance, and customer service! I managed to find and reverse some of Colin's unfortunate directives. I looked for Sunitha and found a note that she had gone to the cafe. On my walk from the plant to the cafe, I noticed a very slow-moving Oasis Security car, then another. I found her at a table with Hassan.

"Welcome back, Hassan!" I said, wondering what he wanted with her. "Evidently you're no longer on the run?"

"We're all on the run," Hassan said, "whether you believe it or not. Sunitha does though."

"Larabie, do you have anything to do with these Oasis guards here making the rounds?"

"Inviting them wasn't my idea, but Ted's, on the advice of his Botswana war mate Kruger, just in case there are reprisals here."

"On the run? More reprisals?"

"The worst part is there's no hiding from them anymore. Especially not for yourself, the rich Yankee businessman that screwed up their bomb at Camp's Bay, and that includes Sunitha. These days you two are even more unpopular with the black gangsters than I am."

Even if he was relaying the opinions of our tormentors and was dead on target, I didn't care to hear his opinion of Sunitha's and my precarious situation. I was more interested in whether it was Ted who sent him over as our third bodyguard, after Chandra and Tembo, since the break-in at the flat!

As that workday was ending, Sunitha seemed more

anxious. As a result, she told me she was afraid for us to return to the hotel, where Ozeer's men might be waiting for us. Her immediate plan was to return to the flat so Hassan could help her retrieve the important things she'd left behind—a plan intended to somehow take her bad karma away from me!

"Hassan, this is personal business," I said when Sunitha had stepped out to go to the bathroom. "I'm afraid you have overstepped your bounds."

"Our enemies don't know any bounds. If you weren't so important to my father, do you think he'd order us to keep you safe and sound by all means possible?"

He called Ted his father, rather than stepfather, but his exact relation to Ted wasn't as interesting as his new advisory role. Ted must have been taking my wellbeing seriously if he was so keen to put someone on continuous duty as my bodyguard. Even if assigning him to me was his father's idea, I didn't like him and didn't trust him enough to allow him to live in close quarters with me. I needed to meet with Ted to discuss security issues around Drakenstein and develop a plan using Oasis Security. Though I wanted to shake Hassan loose, he seemed to have no intention of leaving us alone.

There was nothing I could say right then to convince Sunitha that she was not the source of our bad fortune. It seemed odd that she was attaching such importance to the household things she was eager to leave behind after the vandals' raid a few weeks ago. Rather than argue with her, however, I agreed to return to the Rondebosch flat. She wanted to ride with Hassan in his Chateau van, but I prevailed upon her to stay with me in my car as I followed him. It became obvious though that Hassan was not heading towards Rondebosch, but if Sunitha knew where and why, she wasn't telling me.

We came to the edge of the township of Mitchell's Plain near sunset, and we stopped in front of a brick house set behind a waist high iron fence. From the front porch a burly coloured man with freckles came down the walkway.

"If you give me your keys, we'll keep that car safe," he said.

"This is no place for you to be driving a nice car tonight," Hassan explained as he directed me to pull into the empty garage. "Don't worry, can't you tell by his freckles that this man's Mongrel's brother? He's one of ours."

"I don't know what you're doing, Larabie, but whatever it is, I don't like it!"

"I had a feeling you shouldn't come with us, Leon!" Sunitha said. "Hassan, you must give him his car and escort him back."

"Forget it! I'm not leaving you with them, and I'm not turning back!" I insisted.

To protect Sunitha, I'd apparently committed myself to another fool's mission, traveling into a district whereby simply driving a newer car, I made myself an easy target. If Sunitha had deceived me by taking this roundabout journey with Hassan, still there was no way was I going to abandon her.

The next leg of our confusing trip ended at a familiar place, the shebeen where Tembo had brought me before, the one made of the two joined ocean shipping containers and housing the pool table. This time it wasn't a social visit, just a quick stop to allow a couple of new men to slip through the rear door into our van, and for a couple beside them into another van that followed our vehicle.

"Aren't you glad to see me?" the new man asked, and turned on the overhead light, revealing himself as Big Al Kosane. "I wanted to say goodbye to you in Bacini's, Mr. Cooper," he teased, "but you and your girl were in a hurry to leave us!"

What was the matter with him, laughing, making a joke of hauling out a time bomb! I couldn't avoid shaking the hand he offered me. I was growing uneasy with these tough men joining our caravan. I was reminded of the last time I was led into a wild ride with Hassan and his strong men.

I had a warning for Sunitha, so I moved with her to the centermost seats, away from both Hassan, Big Al, and his friend. "Can't you see they're taking us on another raid?" I whispered. "You've got to get out while you can. This is exactly what they did before, collecting their men before shooting it out at Maraville."

"Maraville?" she repeated, loud enough for Hassan to hear. "He promised we'd go to your flat after meeting up with his best friends.

"Yes, they are the best!" Hassan responded. "No need to worry, because tonight we will have better people than we did at Maraville, men who hit with velvet gloves."

Worry was precisely the effect his pledge had on me. By better people did he mean these followers were better troops, more efficient thugs than the ones in the skirmish at Maraville? Pressing close to me, she repeated her concern that if I stayed in South Africa much longer, I would surely die, or perhaps we would die together, as nearly happened to us in Bacini's. Incredibly, she admitted that the evening's journey with Hassan was her idea! When I pressed her, she confided her real purpose was to retrieve her Brahma one more time, which she still believed had the power to protect us, whether we were together or separated. Strangely, when we arrived at the entrance to my flat, he threw the car in reverse and quickly backed away out of sight.

"Those must be the men spying on you two, Hassan," Sunitha said, looking at me with vindication.

Now that we were out of their line of sight, Hassan conferred with the men in our four-vehicle caravan, who had followed us. He sent several of his followers on foot in opposite directions around the block, then drove three-quarters of the way around the block, stopping just in sight of the back of the target car. There, like a general at the rear of the line of battle, he watched his soldiers break into that blue car Sunitha had feared as our enemy's.

"I'm telling you, we don't want any part of this!" I shouted my position.

"Don't worry," Hassan said, "No one's going to recognize your face."

"You must drive us away from here right now! Do you understand?"

"No problem, my boys don't plan to hang around after we're done moving Sunitha's idol."

I questioned why the compound gate opened for three of our vehicles. They shouldn't have allowed us to pass. And why, after letting these cars pass, perhaps leading us into a trap? Why were two of the management's uniformed security guards leaving?

"What's going on here!"

"That's what we plan to find out, Mr. Cooper, one way or the other."

Before long the first of the vehicles emerged from the gate and came to a stop before us. Hassan leaned into the rear window with a flashlight to inspect the new passenger in the rear seat between two of Hassan's men, a man I was relieved I had never seen before. This captive unexpectedly grabbed Hassan's collar, who threw a punch to defend himself, but the handlers beside him pounded him until he wasn't moving. I had seen enough, but Hassan and his boys weren't done with their raid. When the second and third vehicles arrived with their captives, they were removed by Big Al and a couple of Hassan's boys, who shackled their arms behind them and hustled them to a van that appeared to be a taxi. More of Hassan's caravan friends jumped in after them to assist. The new convoy consisted of five vehicles now, including the one Sunitha said had been used to spy on us in our flat.

The only one of Hassan's men to remain with us was Big Al. "We were lucky we caught them by surprise," Big Al began explaining without my asking. "These Ozeer Boys are awful. We're fixing these three, so they won't be eating off your table any more, that's for sure."

"What do you mean lucky?" I asked. I couldn't take my eyes off an old scar on his arm.

"You didn't see any holes in them, did you?" Big Al asked. "Your man said use velvet gloves," he added, pointing to Hassan.

"Now that we cleared out the rats," Hassan said, "why don't we get your things before a new bunch comes back to nibble your cheese."

He warned me as Chandra and Ted and Tembo and Sunitha had, that I shouldn't live at Barclay Mews anymore, ever. For weeks Sunitha and I had been living day in the hotel with one bodyguard or another watching over us. Opening the door to my abandoned flat, I saw the vindication of their concerns and my own. My flat was not damaged, but destroyed—broken furniture, holes in the walls, most of our personal things gone! Amazingly, the brass Brahma remained, which Hassan and Big Al carefully padded with blankets to safely remove it.

"What if the men who had been watching and waiting for us had caught us alone, Leon?" Sunitha sobbed. "Can't you see our luck has run out?"

That incident did it! I had no desire to ever set foot in the flat again. We packed up our usable belongings and remove ourselves from the trap we'd evaded. I had to agree, we'd used up our last chance.

At the Inter-Continental, Hassan and Big Al spent the night with us to protect us from a possible next reprisal. Sunitha's plan was original was to move her Brahma over to Chandra's house the next morning, leaving it there in the meantime to bring him the good fortune Chandra and Aunt Giri deserved.

Once we were out of the depressing flat, we went for lunch at St. Elmo's Pizza, on the condition that Hassan sit at another table so Sunitha I could talk privately. The two of us agreed as long as I stayed in South Africa, there was no longer any place for us to hide. No matter what I'd accomplished, I realized I was too shaken to be productive anymore. I'd overstayed my welcome in a land where I'd always be a stranger. It was time to return to the States and take Sunitha with me, if that was what I still wanted to do. Whenever we'd discussed America, she seemed confident that she could adjust to any new position I might be able to find for her at the home office. We spoke of our commitment to one another, although we knew we would be tested in a country so different from South Africa. We even spoke of marriage, though we agreed our first concern was to relocate.

She wanted to know how long I was asking her to visit the States, and I told her as long as her visa permitted. When she asked if the visa was for the purpose of working for the Cooper Company or for me personally, I told her I doubted we could pay her until she first got a work permit.

She couldn't get a visa until she got a passport, which normally took weeks. I used what influence I had to fast track her application. We had it in hand days later, and we went to the American Consulate for a permit to work in the States. The consulate officer told her she'd need either a green immigration card or a marriage license to an American citizen.

"Which did you say you preferred?" she asked me with a mischievous smile, as if we hadn't been through that many times before.

She had her exit documents, so all that remained was to confirm the reservations for our airline tickets to New York. I could have used another week to tie up my affairs, but it didn't seem like a good idea for us to postpone our departure and remain near our enemies any longer than necessary. I had enough time to make the rounds to my key people to announce I was recalled to the home office in America. I explained to Chandra that South Africa wasn't big enough for Sunitha or me, not with gangsters tightening their net around us. Ted was up north on a safari victory trip, and I wouldn't be seeing him again. By cell phone I pointed out to Ted that I accomplished far more than required as the Chateau's consultant. He seemed pleased though that I acknowledged he'd been telling me my days in South Africa were numbered and cheerfully wished me luck, whatever that meant. All that remained was to arrange for our final trip to the airport.

Our plane was accelerating on the runway, lifting towards the clouds, when Sunitha's grip tightened on my arm. I had to remove her hand. "Do you care much for flying, or not?" I asked.

"This is my first time. I don't know yet. Do you think South Africa is very pretty?"

"Very pretty, the way the mountains rise from the sea. I'm going to miss it."

"Once we're in the clouds," she said looking upwards, "you must never again worry about dropping into this strange land of your darker dreams."

She was speaking loudly enough for others to hear. "I know how you feel," the passing flight attendant said, "Some people like you, Mr. Cooper, can get vertigo and don't know up from down. Then some like yourself, Sunitha, who are used to the ground and have never been in the air—they let their nerves get the better of them."

Even leaving the country wasn't enough to let us

escape our notoriety! She must have picked our infamous names off the passenger list. This stewardess had a dazzling smile and a close-shaved head and blue-black coloring. She was a beauty who I must have seen on my incoming flight two years ago, "Excuse me, but don't you work with Alicia? You're the one she introduced me to when Kruger at the Inter-Continental Hotel."

"Yes, I'm Napu. Alicia doesn't fly any more. She's moved onto better things, as I see you have, Sunitha. My congratulations."

"Leon, you seemed in some kind of trance speaking with her," Sunitha said, once Napu had served our drinks and moved on to the next passengers.

"I must have been mesmerized, focusing on that golden Maltese cross around her neck. A few centuries ago, if she were a man wearing one that big, she would have been a Christian Hospitaler crusader on the march against the Moslem infidels."

"You know more about history than you let on. Are you saying she may be on a crusade against me?"

A startling question, not one I wished to consider, yet completely on-target. "I'm saying you don't know this stewardess any better than I do, so forget about her, even if you believe she slighted you. We're starting a new life where she'll become no more than a distant memory from your former life."

My advice to Sunitha for self-control was easier said than done for her, seldom overlooking innocent comments she often took for slights. I would do my best to put the unpleasant events of the last several weeks out of my mind. Trying to put our preoccupations behind us, I began chatting about what Sunitha could expect in an American apartment, particularly the larger size closets and dishwashers and refrigerators.

"Is that what America is all about—bigger, better, and more of it?"

Her question had an edge to it, which was understandable, given all she'd been through with me lately, dodging invisible enemies. It occurred to me our decision to bring her away, not only from her family and friends, but from her country might not work!

"I hope it isn't all too much, too quick for me. What do you think?"

"I think I'll just have to run interference for the team."

"As in some sort of a game?"

I didn't care to explain the American game of football in case she was teasing me and knew about the sport already. Instead of speaking anymore, she occupied herself with a love comedy on the video screen, which made her smile. I read the thick *Cape Argus* Sunday edition, looking for reports of the Cape Flats War, but there was nothing, as if hostilities had been suspended that week.

We were in the rear of the plane, where the thrumming of the engines lulled me to sleep, bringing a dream of a propeller airplane. But this time I wasn't a paratrooper and this wasn't the B-29 from which I was being forced to jump. Instead, I wasn't a passenger, but the pilot of a single-engine mail plane from the 1920s, delivering sacks of mail. My engine sputtered and lost power, forcing me down in the desert. I was greeted by a boy, a prince.

In that dream I'd become very young and little, even

smaller than the little prince. I then removed the pilot's seat from the wreck and to sit on it, but my legs weren't long enough to touch the ground. The seat moved back and forth, and in my child's mind it felt to me like my mother trying to rock me to sleep. I resisted and opened my eyes. The woman beside me was not my mother, but Sunitha.

"You were speaking of a tree," she said," rubbing her hand against my arm. "Where were you?"

"Sitting beneath a boabab tree in a near-desert country. I was flying over it when my mail plane gave out."

"Thanks for sharing that," she said, kissing my cheek.

When I looked away to my right, I realized we weren't alone. I had inadvertently shared my dream with the stewardess Napu as well.

"A fantastic story," Napu said with an incredulous expression. She waited for further explanation, but I offered none. "Sorry to interrupt, but now that you're awake, I'll let Mr. Harold Cooper know. I'm surprised you didn't travel first-class like he does, unless, of course, he's your boss."

My brother was indeed on the same plane with me! He had arranged to visit South Africa without ever contacting me! For what purpose? If he was on this plane, he was going to explain himself to me.

"I sense your anger, Leon." Sunitha said, holding my arm so I couldn't follow Napu to where Harry was sitting.

Remembering Sunitha and I were a team now, I slowed down and waited for her to rearrange her hair in the washroom and for myself to cool down. Together Sunitha and I proceeded to the first-class section where

I looked in every seat, but no sign of Harry. A relief, I concluded, a case of some other Harold Cooper Napu has mistaken for my brother.

"Don't you care to see your brother?" Napu asked as we returned to our seats.

"Not really," I said.

"Great," she said undaunted, and led us to the front section, then up a few steps until we were in the upper level first-class lounge in those days that some airlines provided for their long haul routes.

I saw the back of Harry's head and recognized him by his familiar bald spot, though I'd never seen the gorgeous woman in black stretch pants on the swivel seat next to him.

"If you'll show me yours, I'll show you mine," I overheard Harry suggest to her before he saw me.

As they burst into booming laughter, Sunitha tried to leave before he could focus on us. I didn't care for his juvenile quip, no more than Sunitha did, but I'd come too far to retreat, now that I'd won the tough business assignment to which he'd challenged me in South Africa for the last couple of years.

"Hey, Leon, what the hell are you doing? Don't just stand there, do something!" Harry ordered and rose to his feet to give me one of his bone-crunching handshakes. "What are you looking at?" he asked me, his light gray eyes piercing into mine.

"Your safari outfit—no shortage of pockets," I said and reached into a pocket between his knee and his waist. "This pocket's big enough to house a puppy."

"Hey, don't play pocket billiards with me, Leon," he said removing my hand from his pocket, guffawing again. "I only play that game with Jane. Hey Jane, has my little brother introduced you to what's-her-name?"

"I'm Sunitha," she introduced herself.

We sat on either side of them, Sunitha next to Harry. The ruby pendant I bought yesterday to celebrate our escape and our new life together engaged his eyes. Looking away from the stone, he gazed at her long neck and her generous mouth, then at her catlike eyes.

"A nice piece," he said. He winked at me.

He lifted the pendant for his trademark connoisseur's inspection of things precious, the back of his hand resting below her neck. He clasped her hand, then dropped it as she arose out of his reach.

"Finally, I get to meet you, Mr. Harry. Leon has told me so much about you," she said.

"Nothing bad, I hope! Well, are you going to hang around, or else run away?" he asked, guiding Sunitha into her chair, after which he perched himself between us. To see me, he had to look past his female escort. "They won't let me take home any trophies from this safari to which invited. The only trophy I'll be taking from South Africa is this one," he said, pointing his thumb at his companion next to him. "Ted introduced me to Jane, and now I get to take her home. She's a lingerie model from Johannesburg. What's the story with this lady of yours anyway?"

"You always did things first class, Harry. You have a beautiful view from here," I said, looking out the window behind the minibar, avoiding his intrusive question, not wishing to risk embarrassing Sunitha in any way.

"Yes, this view is outstanding. That's why I like to travel first-class and sit high, Leon. And that's why I made sure you came up here before sunset, while we could still see wild Africa below us. I'm a little bit disappointed though. I don't see a savannah with gazelles, zebra, or wildebeest. It's a big wasteland down there, just like where you crashed and burned in your dream, according to the African stewardess who hunted you down for me."

"That's because it's the Sahara Desert!" Jane interjected. I was impressed with her full lips but suspected they had been puffed up with cosmetic filler.

"Since when did my dream become public information? Actually, it was a dream out of a book, Harry, from *The Little Prince*, though I realize you've never been much for reading outside of business."

"The stewardess says you were babbling about one of your mishaps, which you've had plenty of lately. Leon must have been telling his story to some imaginary friend," he said, trying to discredit me.

He whispered something to her, making her giggle. I could see from Sunitha's expression she didn't care for Harry, and was signaling with nods of her head for me to take her to our seats below. But for me this reunion with Harry had been too long coming. I thought it best to let her go back to her seat, and handed her a copy of *The Economist* to give her an idea of how the biggest and most dominant companies of the world ruled.

"Well, if I made as many enemies as you have, Leon, I'd have nightmares too, talking to boogiemen! Now, Sunie, how about doing me a favor and go visit with Jane, if you don't mind."

Harry again whispered to Jane, then led her and Sunitha to the stairway leading down to the first-class cabin. "Did you come up to the bridge to drink with me or insult me?" he asked me once we were back at the upper lounge, alone.

"I wasn't expecting to be traveling with you... and your companion," I said. He secured a couple of single-serving liquor bottles for us, but rather than join him, I took water.

"Well, does Jane look good to you, Leon, or what?"

"Don't worry, I've seen nothing. I respect your privacy, Harry."

"Really, don't you think she's a looker?"

"Depending on what you're looking for. So long as your wife is looking the other way!"

"No problem. I'm going to drop Jane off after we head to Florida Disney for a week. So, what are you going to do with your girlfriend in America after you're done showing her the sights?"

"Harry, I always thought the best kind of mind is one that minds its own business."

"That's a good one," he said with a grin, then slapped my back, "coming from my brother who we wondered if he'd lost his mind from battle fatigue. But I'm sure the old man will take that into consideration if you decide to bring her home."

I was not about to tell him my plan to find her a position at the home office, no more than about my plan to live under the same roof with her and to get her a green card. That is, if she could overcome her well-warranted depression and adapt to America. This conversation had taken an unpleasant turn, one I wanted to discontinue, but I never liked to leave his insults unchallenged.

"Now, Harry, how can you talk about me losing my

mind, when here you are bringing home guaranteed trouble, jeopardizing your marriage?"

My brother was looking into his glass, rather than at me. Though he richly deserved my challenges to his insults, I may have pushed him too far. "I didn't know you were so concerned about my household, Leon. Do you want to know what concerns me more than my immediate family?"

"Go ahead."

"Our extended family, whether we've been doing as much for our name as we could have."

"You've always been the family historian, but I don't suppose you've come halfway around the world to speak to me of our great-grandfather and founder of our company, Hiram Cooper."

"No, Leon, you have it wrong. Great-great-grandfather Winston taught Hiram everything he knew about making whiskey, just as I've tried to teach you everything I know, brother. Maybe you're giving credit to Hiram because he was the one who built our Elm Street house where we grew up. You never did get a handle on our history, did you?"

"Harry, did it ever occur to you that you prefer to look at the past rather than the future, which affects your ability to accurately see the present."

"Is that why you think you're seeing things so clearly? Because instead of having a drink with me, you're sipping on bottled water? You always had a thing about water, ever since Mother died."

"You still don't acknowledge she got her cancer from the contaminated water we all were drinking! Drink what you want, Harry! Live or die—suit yourself!"

"Face it, Leon, Mother took sick after she decided to walk out on the old man. So don't blame her sickness on Dad or St. Louis."

Harry regarded the old man in his capacity as CEO as his meal ticket, so naturally he couldn't afford to be critical of him in any way, no matter what the facts. Harry never acknowledged that if Dad hadn't taken up with that red-haired woman who did the catering at the Masons, our mother wouldn't have been ejected from our Elm Street home.

Since we were boys Harry and I have had personal differences. Inadvertently, I'd handed him the IPO debacle as a perfect excuse to discredit me, which he evidently was continuing to use as justification for undercutting me in the Gazelle project. During his unannounced stay in South Africa, even he had to see I succeeded in a dangerous assignment, despite insufficient support from him and the home office. If he was baiting me, it was most likely to avoid having to admit my recent successes.

"I'm surprised nobody from the home office showed up the entire time I've been here."

"Don't I recall that you volunteered for this project and didn't want anyone who didn't understand the natives to muck it up for you?"

He knew I would have had an easier time reassembling the Gazelle plant with men from the home plant, rather than having to rely on long-distance communication and local talent—and worse, leaving me short-funded for the project, and ultimately having to finesse a financing deal from DeVilliers.

"No, I don't recall saying that, no more than I recall

your explaining why you've popped in on me, unannounced on this plane."

"What else could I do under the circumstances after what I heard you've been up to, Leon, if you know what I mean?"

Of course, I didn't know what he meant because he didn't know himself. If he was trying to pick my brains, I was not going to accommodate him.

"I've been working seven days a week with little time for anything else."

"Leaving yourself no time to see the sights, the wildlife? No time for fun? That's not what my sources tell me."

What sources? Ted? Chandra? Or details from my telephone conversations he'd managed to extract from Bernice? If he thought by making up a story about me, that I'd fill in the details for him, he was going to be disappointed.

"And I suppose that's why you came here, Harry, to take a vacation and see the sights for yourself. Wasn't it you who thought there were lions roaming a few miles from Adderley Street?"

"Do you take me for a fool?" he asked, startling me, but not enough to pry an answer from me. "I know where the man-killers live in South Africa. I saw them along with Ted and his righthand man Otto Kruger. Those boys both handled themselves well under gunfire, so they'll do fine running the show, now that you've taken your curtain call."

"Then you made a deal with Kruger? What about his new wife Alicia—do you plan for her to take an active role outside of the one pub she's been running?"

"I know you have a personal interest in her. We'll see how she performs, just as we waited to see you perform under fire. Alicia's quite a creature, isn't she, pretty like my Jane? They produce some fine-looking blondes in South Africa, don't they? Do you know they named Kruger Park after Kruger? What's so funny?" he asked when he noticed my smile.

"What color were these lions anyway?"

"Tawny yellow. The strongest male with the biggest balls owned the harem until some upstart beat him and took over the operation. There's a lesson in nature."

"I don't remember you ever so reflective. What's come over you, Harry?"

"You know, back home I do my best thinking while bass fishing and on my working holidays. There's nothing like watching lions sleep and stalk and go in for the kill. I'm really an outdoors boy at heart."

"Then I take it you've enjoyed your vacation?"

"I would have preferred to get down to business in Cape Town a couple of days earlier. You know how I enjoy my work and how bored I get with long vacations."

"Am I to understand after a few days of safari in Kruger Park, you returned to Cape Town without contacting me?"

"There didn't seem to be much point, especially after your notifying the home office of your intention to quit, due to personal reasons."

"For your information, I'm relocating, not quitting. And my reasons aren't personal, so much as survival. I'm no longer safe there."

"You certainly made some enemies. You might have

thought of that before posting your photo in the news-paper. Me, I always try to go about my business dis-creetly. But when you inadvertently did the right thing in full public view, you now get more attention than you expect. Good job," he said, then shook my hand.

"You're too kind," I said ironically, astonished that he seemed to be praising me.

"Nonsense! We're brothers, and we're more alike than you care to admit. We both play hardball and play to win," he said, pulling from his pocket some papers with figures. On my lap he spread Gazelle's current quarter figures; on his lap, the business plan Ted and I had presented to Frederick DeVilliers for our loan. "That's why I must congratulate you on what you've done for us here in South Africa. Thanks to your efforts, Leon, I think we may hit that $100 million annual target you're projecting. Especially now that he's offered to use his influence to buy our products, promote and prominently display them.

"That's a nice offer he made to you, one he never made directly to me."

"Ah, you're feeling unappreciated. Well, I'm here to set it right with you, Leon. Congratulations on a job well done and on your good numbers."

"So, you're finally beginning to understand what I've been doing here for the last couple of years!"

"Seeing is believing, and I've seen fine results, despite the huge obstacles you've had to overcome. And I'm especially impressed with how you've been using DeVilliers to set the roof support timbers in our mine, so to speak, while we ride up to the surface in the elevator."

"What do you mean?"

"I mean in this country DeVilliers proved to be a better source of support for you, financial and otherwise, than we could have offered from St. Louis. In case you were wondering, that's why we hung back on extending financing, and waited for you to arrange it locally. Our thinking was that in the event that by some act of God or man—such as an uninsured typhoon or revolution or insoluble labor problems or an unreceptive market in which the roof were to collapse on our South African Chateau wine and beer operations—with other people's money on the line rather than just ours, we would have a better chance surviving with reduced financial damage. In other words, if worse came to worst in this country, we'd much rather deal with South African lawyers and courts than American ones. In any event, it's an undeniable achievement on your part—the distribution network you've launched and the new source of money you've secured.

"And I'll tell you off the record, we're planning to reward you with an expanded position once we debrief you in St. Louis! But first things first, it's never a good idea to keep a lady waiting. I'm going to retrieve them."

He paused briefly to comb his hair, preparing himself for the women, a man with more than a bit of vanity, a family trait, I had to admit.

Maybe he was appealing to my vanity, my desire to hear some words of praise from him and trying to smooth over the hard feelings between us since the IPO debacle. He was telling me the home office had been prudently waiting for me to find more money locally. The truth was more likely that they were spooked by how fast I built up the local Gazelle beer distribution network, which they had originally intended to be secondary to wine exports into the States.

If I were to give Harry the benefit of my doubts, then I'd have to accept his explanation that the board rejected my requests for further backing because they were afraid to overextend themselves after my losing so much credibility over the failed IPO. Now it appeared with the addition of other people's money, I'd redeemed myself to the company, judging from the promotion I was about to be offered. Perhaps that was the reason Harry went through all the trouble of placing himself on this plane to deliver good news with uncharacteristically kind words. If I'd regained some standing, he would want to be on good terms to use me as an ally, now that my exile was over. Or maybe my suspicions were misplaced, and in good faith he was trying to make a truce with me. I wish I knew the truth!

Harry returned to the lounge with Jane and Sunitha. Once he secured a fresh round of drinks, he fell quiet for the time being, looking out the window at the setting sun. "Did you ever notice night falls but never breaks, but day breaks but never falls?" he said. "Even if we're flying too high to see the earth, we have this glorious golden sunset now shifting into purples. I've always appreciated beautiful things. In the next life maybe I'll be an artist. I always liked to sketch and doodle, especially on long telephone calls."

I liked this more thoughtful side of him. He wished he could appreciate beauty before him, as he did Sunitha's ruby, though apparently not Sunitha herself.

"My son Bruce beat me in the talent department,

especially in visualizing and mixing oil paint colors, but I told him to forget about playing artist, except in his dreams. Instead of art school, I sent him to business school, and now he's not far from graduating and hopefully following in my footsteps."

That could mean he planned to bring my young nephew into Cooper, hoping to make him the number three man behind Father and himself! I wondered how much politicking he'd already done in the home office to pave the way for Bruce. Just one more reason to get to St. Louis without delay—so I could tell the true story of what I'd achieved in South Africa and reclaim my rightful place.

"Why don't you forget about me?" Jane spoke to my brother. "If you miss your family so damn much, why don't you go directly home to them? I can use my round trip ticket back home after I tour by myself, Harry." Then she turned to me: "This dream of smashing up your puddle jumper airplane—what was that all about?"

He couldn't have expected her mutiny, not in front of the rest of us. As much as he might have deserved it, I took no pleasure in his embarrassment. I had nothing to say, but she seemed to be waiting for my answer, nevertheless.

"Well, are you going to tell us anything more about this child prince hallucination of yours?" Harry implored.

"Okay, in the twenties Saint Exupery, the Frenchman who wrote *The Little Prince*, was flying over this Sahara Desert below, delivering the mail. He crashed and was never found. I dreamed I was the pilot who met the prince on the ground. That's all."

"Were you dreaming that because you felt you're something of a hero?" Jane asked.

"Well?" Harry pressed me again.

"No, I've just realized here and now, the dream was about you, my brother who was acting as both the pilot and my commander. You were the one who pushed me out of the door of the plane to drop me into a hostile landscape without any backup!"

That was it! Harry's hidden place in my being shoved out of the belly of the B-29 on a fool's mission, the nightmare I was finally leaving behind in Cape Town! I may have revealed too much, spoken without thinking. Now I'd speak only of the fairy tale, not about the fears I'd managed to overcome.

"You see, once he crash-landed the plane, the little boy prince was on the ground, waiting, just as you were waiting for me in this plane. He'd rather draw than speak, so they communicated with each other by words and by drawing pictures. He proved to be a more pleasant companion than the grown man, Harold Cooper, next to me." Harry rolled his eyes and didn't seem to want to hear any more, but I wasn't done. "The little prince grew so wealthy and powerful he was able to acquire all the stars in the sky!"

"That doesn't sound like a bad deal to me," Harry said in his own defense.

"The wealthy prince's problem was anxiety. He became so anxious about what he owned that he dedicated the rest of his life to counting his wealth, which included every one of the stars in the sky. This task so overwhelmed him that he was driven to drinking all day and all night."

"You talking about me, little brother?" He looked directly at me, perhaps because I'd rattled him, then dumped his schnapps into a plastic cup full of beer nuts.

"We have a lot of catching up to do, but this isn't the time," I said.

The focus had been shifted from my personal nightmare, but I wished to end the conflict for the time being. I hadn't wanted Sunitha to hear the differences between my brother and myself. When I nodded towards her, she took it as a signal for her to say something good about me.

"Leon, you didn't tell Harry everything you did at Camp's Bay to save those children in the pool," she said in my behalf.

"That's why you'll find we're so proud of him in St. Louis," Harry endorsed me, another sudden reversal.

"I don't care to talk about it anymore than Harry cares to talk business, coming back from his holiday with his Jane."

"Me, your commander, pilot, and co-pilot, all at the same time?" Harry asked. "That sounds impossible, like being in three places at once."

That last dream was a breakthrough, learning it was really Harry in my parachute dreams! Harry in the pilot's seat and alone with me in the Flying Fortress B-29. Either I couldn't hear him over the engines or don't want to when he ordered me in one of my troubling dreams to hook myself to the static line and jump. He set the controls on autopilot then walked back and pushed me out! In one of these final dreams, once I was out the door, this time I was not hanging cold and helpless from my canvas chute, but gliding with the enormous wings of a Pliocene bird, yet still a man.

"Sometimes we need a push, but if I pushed you too hard, Leon, then you're going to have to forgive me."

He made a gesture of peace. I nodded my head yes, not quite acceptance, but agreement for the time being, at least until I knew whether we really could be allies.

"God, what a wasteland! What kind of chance would a man have down there in the sand desert? I love to travel up here, if only for this high view." Harry said.

He was gazing below at the yellow sand of the dying day, as if he were the captain in command. By the map on the screen with the shifting airplane symbol, I saw we'd finally left the African desert. Unlike the open jaws flight that had brought me originally to South Africa, this was a direct flight. It became a cloudless night with a full moon, and I could see the reflected ocean below, the remaining barrier between us and my familiar country.